I0660337

SNAKE'S WHISPER

ORPHANS: BOOK TWO

© Christian Adrian Brown 2025

Snake's Whisper is a work of fiction. Names, characters, places, and incidents are products of the author's imagination or are used fictitiously. Any resemblance to actual events or locales or persons, living or dead, is entirely coincidental. No part of this book may be reproduced or transmitted in any form by any means, electronic or mechanical, including photocopying or recording, or by any information storage and retrieval system, except as may be expressly permitted in writing from the author/publisher.

Forsythia Press
Canada, ON
www.cabwrites.com

To my mother, who continues to inspire me from ethereal realms beyond our own. And as always: to my passionate readers and fans—strangers and friends who believe in me more than I believe in myself.

—Christian

Orphans Official Soundtrack on Spotify

"Rise Up" Music Video

www.cabwrites.com

FOREWORD (A RECAP)

Greetings, esteemed reader! The journey of literature is a vast and winding road, filled with countless characters and intricate plotlines that weave together to form the tapestry of our shared narratives. It's only human to lose track amidst such richness, especially when diving into the labyrinthine world of 'Orphans.' Fear not, for I have crafted a summary to illuminate the path behind us before we venture into the shadows again. Let us embark on this voyage of recollection together.

Raven's Cry begins with a young woman caught in a cataclysmic storm between reality and an otherworldly realm. Ana Windborn's body convulses violently, her mind held captive by the Dark Mother's cosmic grasp. A horrific landscape of alien celestial bodies flashes before her eyes, her name reverberating through the void. This painful encounter with the ancient force is not merely an affliction but a command: "Find the Wolf." Once she regains control, soaked in perspiration, Ana realizes this is no hallucination but a directive that will shape her destiny.

Malachi Linklater, bearing the weight of sorrow and duty, pays tribute to his Auntie Jewel at her funeral. The gathering is a testament to Jewel's impact as it brings together diverse mourners from different backgrounds—both rural and urban, Indigenous and non-Indigenous. As he stands before them all, Malachi grapples with his personal loss, amplified by the grim reality of life on the reservation where too many Indigenous women like Jewel meet violent ends far from home.

The story takes a sharp turn when Malachi is attacked at a bus stop by an abhorrent eldritch creature—part spider, part octopus. Its corrosive secretions reduce the bus stop to rubble while Malachi is paralyzed by fear. Just as doom seems imminent, Brock Stoneheart swoops in for the rescue. Malachi's dormant powers stir to life in this moment of peril, revealing their connection to an age-old force within him. As Brock consoles him post-attack, they both comprehend they've been swept up into something much larger than themselves.

Transitioning back in time by a couple of decades, we find another of Malachi's yet-to-be-known aunties, Mary, revealing a chilling narrative from the worn pages of her late Aunt Martha's diary. This scene unfolds under the flickering light of a campfire in Chapter Three, where she reads entries thought to be inscribed by H.P Lovecraft himself, describing his encounters with otherworldly entities beyond human understanding. The narrative unfurls to reveal the aunties' distressing history, including Jewel's chilling confrontation with a monstrous physician who robbed her of her womb—an atrocity that was disturbingly routine during those days. These unveiled truths weave together yesteryears and the present, hinting that Malachi's life is more than just about enduring—he is entwined in an immense cosmic riddle.

The narrative, recounted from a time long past, escalates in intensity as Grace discovers a chilling scene shrouded in the forest's depths. Four women lay lifeless, their bodies meticulously positioned in a ceremonial design with an infant at its heart. This baby is the subject of Lovecraft's prophetic texts—the child destined to be christened Malachi by his doting aunties. The aunties complete their pact in these supernatural events by covering up the murders and raising Malachi as their own—a cursed child bound for an apocalyptic destiny.

In Chapter Five, Malachi and Brock embark on a journey toward the southeastern region of the USA, spurred by obscure hints of an approaching apocalypse. As they traverse unfamiliar terrain, both men must confront their newly acquired abilities and significance in the unfolding cosmic events. Fate intertwines their paths, binding them through shared experiences and a growing realization that the threats they face are fragments of a colossal and ominous conflict. Their quest into the unknown deepens their bond, providing instances of brotherhood interspersed with moments of uncertainty.

Chapter Six shifts focus to Gabriel Mothmann, who is immersed in covert experiments involving an enigmatic artifact. Gabriel's fixation on harnessing the celestial powers of the Outer Gods becomes evident as he grapples with his fear of the artifact's potentially destructive capabilities. This chapter underscores his intricate personality, the friction between his human desires, and the extraterrestrial forces he yearns to dominate. Gabriel's escalating desperation to suppress these cosmic terrors suggests his crucial role in the imminent battle.

In Chapter Seven, Brock discloses details about his tormented past, revealing visions of wolves, rituals, and supernatural horrors that persistently plague him. As his powers intensify, he gains more insight into their ties with the forces menacing their world. The narrative reveals that he was once taken under the wing of a drifter, a solitary soul who found him when he was still a wild and perilous creature and schooled him in the ways of humanity. The mentor's name was Charlie, a moniker he lovingly bestowed upon his steel, constant companion and vehicle. Brock's internal struggle between his primal instincts and inner beast paves the way for his transformation—one expected to unveil his true essence and purpose.

In Chapter Eight, Malachi and Brock are swept into a shared, vivid dreamscape where they encounter Snake—a mysterious figure who forewarns them of looming dangers. Brock is no stranger to this spiritual guide; this very being initially beckoned him through nocturnal visions to seek out Malachi. This meeting in the dreamworld deepens their camaraderie while awakening something profound and unspoken within each of them. As they blink awake from this collective slumber, they find themselves surrounded by additional monstrous entities from an alternate realm—creatures they now identify as "Walkers," a term found in the ancient tome gifted to Malachi by Mary. With newly discovered and formidable powers pulsing through their veins, the young witches swiftly vanquish these threats, leaving them simultaneously baffled and invigorated by their newfound strength.

Chapter Nine unfolds with Ana, propelled by the enigmatic whispers of the Dark Mother across the vast expanse of the continent in search of her elusive "wolf." She finds herself standing on Canadian soil. In a fleeting moment of respite, she converses with her court-appointed psychiatrist, the affable yet sophisticated Dr. Marrow. He's a man whose charm is as captivating as his medical acumen. With their dialogue concluded, Ana embarks on her journey to locate a house that haunts her recent visions—a sight familiar to us readers as it is none other than Grace's abode. Upon reaching there, she finds herself in the warm embrace of the aunties—women who radiate acceptance and understanding towards her predicament from the first encounter. Fuelled by hope and determination, Ana yearns to master her emerging psychic prowess under their guidance. Her journey of self-discovery leads her to uncover cosmic truths that bind her destiny with the Dark

Mother, an entity of formidable power. This chapter also introduces a long-held secret kept by Grace: an obsidian shard linked to the Dark Mother's might. This artifact hums with a potent, unseen force threatening to destabilize their world. Grace's revelation of this secret causes a rift in her relationship with Mary, foreshadowing future conflicts.

Chapter Ten delves into the evolving relationship between Brock and Malachi as they grapple with understanding Malachi's uncanny abilities related to chance and destiny. As Malachi begins to accurately forecast the outcomes of hundreds of coin tosses, he is embroiled in a profound introspection regarding the reach and genesis of his newfound abilities. He wonders if he's been granted dominion over fortune itself or if he's somehow attuned to the very essence of universal pandemonium. Their bond strengthens during this exploration as allies and individuals tied together by fate and blossoming affection.

Chapter Eleven returns to focus on Ana's battle for mastery over her rapidly growing psychic abilities; she can sense Malachi's safety from great distances. As her powers evolve further, she inches closer to comprehending her role in the impending cosmic battle. In addition, when she meets with Grace and Cynthia, they confront the unsettling mystery surrounding Mary's disappearance. The tension escalates due to long-kept secrets now coming into light.

In Chapter Twelve, the narrative threads begin to intertwine as Steve's association with the enigmatic and intimidating figure of Mr. Leng intensifies. Steve becomes aware of the perilous forces he is dealing with, unknowingly becoming a pawn in a cosmic game that connects him to Malachi and Brock. This realization foreshadows more significant threats looming on the horizon.

Chapter Thirteen provides a brief respite for Brock and Malachi as they share a tranquil moment at a campground. However, their tranquility is abruptly interrupted by Snake's intrusion into their dream world. In this crucial encounter, Snake initiates a blood magic ritual, signifying their awakening to their intertwined destinies. The chapter concludes with Brock being driven into hiding, caught up in Leng's strategic manipulations.

The plot thickens in Chapter Fourteen as Octavia Mothmann enters the scene. As Gabriel's ambitious sister, she begins to conspire against him to invoke dark forces associated with Cthulhu. Her apocalyptic visions and personal aspirations set her on an inevitable clash with Gabriel, suggesting an impending family betrayal that threatens to tear apart the essence of their world.

In Chapter Fifteen, Ana's supernatural abilities continue to evolve. She encounters Elder Sue, an individual well-versed in the spiritual and mystical, who provides guidance on her burgeoning psychic powers. During this same period, she meets Lenny Clearwater, a bouncer whose strength and charm give a sense of security in an increasingly perilous world. The initial seeds of their relationship are sown here, hinting at future disputes and challenges.

Chapter Sixteen focuses on Brock and Malachi as they narrowly escape capture. Their bond is tested when Malachi is forced to face Brock's transformation into the Wolf, which is triggered by a rude man making an offending slight. Despite the escalating tensions and dangers, they find solace in each other's company, their connection deepening with each shared experience.

In Chapter Seventeen, we delve into Steve's uneasy alliance with Leng. As they hunt for Malachi and Brock, Steve begins questioning Leng's intentions as his manipulative tactics become increasingly evident. It becomes clear that Leng isn't what he seems; he hides a monstrous nature behind his facade—he is a corrupt Elder God serving as the vanguard for Outer Gods on Earth. Steve, not easily fooled or led astray, starts picking up on these concealed aspects of Leng's identity. With the impending threat of cosmic horrors growing ever closer, it becomes apparent that Steve will inevitably play a significant role in the unfolding conflict.

In the eighteenth chapter, Ana, Lenny, and the aunties face a series of unsettling portents. As they delve deeper into these mysteries, Ana's latent powers uncloak horrific revelations about Mary Blackwood. Ana's enigmatic role in the celestial war starts to crystallize as the looming threats in her vicinity grow more palpable.

In the nineteenth chapter, a tense exchange unfolds between Malachi and Brock as they delve into the latter's tumultuous history and his previous encounters with justice. The young men also discuss what to do with Brock's conspicuous and beloved vehicle. Simultaneously, Steve and Leng inch closer to pinpointing their whereabouts because of Brock's unique antique car. All the while, Gabriel amplifies the sense of impending danger with his machinations well underway.

The twentieth chapter marks a pivotal point in the narrative as Ana finds herself locked in direct combat with Mary Blackwood. In an unexpected twist, Mary declares her loyalty to Cthugha—an entity shrouded in darkness and power. The confrontation escalates into a nerve-racking scene where Lenny is ensnared within the confines of an illusory reality. Yet, Ana's formidable determination and emerging powers wrench him back from the brink of unconsciousness. This allows him just enough time to step in, providing Ana with the opportunity to pierce Mary with the fragment of the Dark Mother —an assault that successfully thwarts Mary. However, it probably doesn't end her life.

In Chapter Twenty-One, Brock and Malachi strategically abandon their traceable transport. Their journey leads them to cross paths with a retired soldier named Robert, who offers them fresh supplies and new identities, helping them evade detection. However, their path isn't clear for long—Octavia's influence has corrupted Gabriel's soldiers, causing them to launch an attack. The ensuing battle is intense and spectacular, with Brock and Malachi escaping by the skin of their teeth. As the fog of war clears, Octavia's secret allies, the Red Fates, momentarily appear to gather evidence that will ensure Gabriel's future destruction.

Chapter Twenty-Two reveals Ana at an altar linked to the cosmic entity Cthugha. In a shocking turn of events, Lenny is swallowed up by dark water that seems to originate from the altar itself. Thanks to the Dark Mother's magic, however, he doesn't remain lost —instead, he is reborn in a dramatic resurrection that signifies his deeper connection with the cosmic forces at play. It's plausible that the Dark Mother, a being intertwined with destiny and luck, has orchestrated this precise interference and the forging of a shadowy guardian to safeguard her servant, Ana.

Finally, in Chapter Twenty-Three, Brock and Malachi establish contact with Ana over the phone. This conversation cements their bond and confirms their roles in this cosmic struggle they are all embroiled in. As they brace themselves for the imminent battle and unknown terrors that await them, it becomes clear that the stakes have never been higher.

The climactic conclusion unveils the true nature of Steve's relationship with Leng. Throughout their peculiar bond, they have navigated conversations touching on identity, servitude, and loss. Despite Leng's tainted godlike consciousness, he begins to perceive potential in Steve—a mere mortal who reflects fragments of his divine persona. (A handful of cryptic remarks on the telephone from the enigmatic Gabriel Mothmann appear to have subtly steered their dialogues towards this course as well.)

During a chilling moment steeped in ominous empathy, Leng discloses his monstrous grandeur to Steve. Cornered by this revelation and driven by a desperate will to survive, Steve surrenders to Leng's manipulations and consents to an unthinkable act—he offers up his soul. In doing so, he chooses a twisted form of life over certain death.

The sinister magic of Leng invades him, irrevocably transforming him into an entity far removed from his human origins. This marks the genesis of a new contender in the cosmic war—a once principled police chief now turned operative in an otherworldly struggle.

As *Raven's Cry* winds down, we see Gabriel bathing in triumph, blind to the sinister undertows stirring unnoticed. From these murky depths slithers Calibos (Cal), the Snake and final Aspect, both ward and captive—for his own safeguarding—of Gabriel Mothmann. In their roles as father and adopted son, they relish an uncommon interlude of tranquility, a serene prelude to the looming tempest stirred by Cthulhu's restless slumber.

Glossary

329

PROLOGUE: ENEMY OF MY ENEMY

"Christian prayers are as meaningless as my regret," Leng retorted, his tone laced with an otherworldly chill.

How much time had passed? A handful of days, maybe more? Steve's grasp on reality was shattered, perhaps reconfigured by the parasites that had claimed his brain as their dwelling, weaving their alien filaments with unsettling precision. Sickness overwhelmed him whenever he dared to ponder their activities within his cranium. He had ceased looking at his reflection, too terrified to witness tiny shadows flitting beneath his skin as though it were merely a thin sheath of rubber. The spiderlings appeared to have tunneled deeper into his being recently, which should have alarmed him more than it did. But now, he found comfort in minor triumphs such as maintaining control over his hands or the prospect of emptying his bladder after enduring for what seemed like an eternity. These sensations felt remote and surreal now, much like most of his human discomforts. The capability to retain one's urine for such a prolonged period was a peculiarity he preferred not to dwell on.

As they journeyed through the verdant woods and undulating landscapes of South Dakota, Leng abruptly ceded complete bodily control back to Steve. The immobilizing hold that restrained him slackened with a tremulous exhalation.

"I require your vigilance," declared the Spider God. "I perceive an intersection of energies nearby, a pull on the ley lines. Evermore... I am intrigued by what ruse this crafty witch might be concocting..." Yet they did not explore Leng's intuitive suspicion or investigate who or what Evermore might be.

Nevertheless, Leng frequently murmured the term 'crafty witch' concerning Gabriel Mothmann: the deity's erstwhile comrade, boss, or even enemy—he surmised from Leng's various angry or puckered expressions when mentioning the man. While pondering these enigmas, Steve asked to pull over and relieve himself—his wish granted by the pondering God. However, when a jet-black stream gushed from him instead of urine, he turned towards the pines and offered up an urgent prayer to his ancestors.

Subsequently, cleansing his hands with a moist wipe as if he'd been laboring in an oil field all day, he resumed driving. As they progressed down the interstate, veering away from the supernatural force that Leng had sensed, the Spider God appeared immersed in even deeper contemplation, his visage etched with concern or maybe even fear. What could possibly instill fear in a deity? Steve mused and was disconcerted by the likelihood of discovering the answer.

Before long, the charming rural settlements gave way to rugged grasslands, evergreens, and stony landmarks that characterized Middle America. The police cruiser darted through the night, trailed by fog cascading off tree-laden bluffs like a spectral waterfall. In the distance, like behemoths cloaked in haze, the Black Hills of Dakota towered over sparse forests—their jagged white summits aspiring towards a star-speckled sky.

As breathtaking as these natural spectacles were, he knew they were insignificant compared to Earth's genuine enigmas. A man might conquer a mountain or even embark on an interstellar journey, but there were phenomena far surpassing such feats—one riding beside him now.

Later that night, Leng seemed to drift into slumber or meditation within his trench coat. With Leng's formidable energy dormant for now, Steve recollected with horror the moon-sized head festooned with ruby eyes and the incomprehensible dread of encountering such a gargantuan spider entity. He pondered how all that could be ensconced within a slender human form without visible signs of distension.

Back at the diner, Steve had sworn some form of fealty to Leng—though the particulars eluded him—it bore the weight of a servile vow. He'd consented to assist Leng in return for...something... The mere endeavor to dredge up his brush with such cosmic terror sent shivers skittering down his spine. The pact he had sealed was irrevocable, leaving him pondering his inevitable destiny.

Steve dialed the radio until it played jazz music from the 1940s, a genre—along with classical—that Leng appeared to tolerate or at least didn't deride as 'cacophonous simian screeching' as he did whenever pop or modern melodies were aired.

The alternating beams and shadows on the highway moved in rhythmic succession like ebony and ivory piano keys dancing to their own tune—hypnotic and harmonious. Steve's head began to droop. The landscape blurred, the car interior felt nebulous and undefined, his mind awash with a dizzying lucidity. The lights from an overtaking motorcycle streaked past in astral trails. It felt as though he wasn't earthbound but navigating celestial freeways between constellations until a small dark orb ballooned rapidly in size, and he plummeted through its atmosphere towards gleaming azure fissures on its surface.

Steve jolted awake from the phantom collision. Were they lodged in a crater? No, merely an ordinary highway, it seemed. His dreamlike vision had been so nuanced that it seemed more akin to a recollection than an illusion and hadn't disrupted his driving. The shroud of the night now appeared even more unfathomable, its obscurity intensified by a moistening cloak of precipitation and fog. The sensation of stolen time seemed to amplify the disconcerting unease accompanying their odyssey.

"Ah..." intoned Leng, his voice reverberating in the car's silence.

"Did I doze off?" Steve wondered aloud. "Was I dreaming?"

"That was not your dream."

Leng opted to remain enigmatic, leaving an eerie silence in his wake.

"So where's this joyride headed?" Steve asked, endeavoring to dispel the tension.

"To the setting sun we travel," Leng replied cryptically.

"And what about Malachi?"

"All paths converge at destiny's crossroads."

Steve snorted at the nebulous reply. "Yeah, Confucius says. Maybe you should pop another fortune cookie and see if it has a better GPS than you."

"Westward," Leng restated with frosty exactness.

"Great."

"If specificity is what you yearn for: California."

According to recent border patrol footage, the abrupt mention of the Golden State deviated significantly from Malachi and Brock's current route—southeast. The image of Leng on a sunny beach, donning a visor and fanny pack while slathering his pallid skin in sunscreen, nearly made Steve chuckle aloud.

"We do not pursue recreation or sun worship," Leng retorted tersely.

A shiver coursed down Steve's spine as he recalled that the deity inhabiting his body could perceive his thoughts. Any escape seemed hopeless—not that he'd seriously contemplated them before now. He realized there was no point in attempting to flee; he wouldn't get far.

"Indeed, flight would be ill-advised," concurred Leng, validating his apprehensions.

Steve scowled. "Can I at least have some privacy up here? If I'm stuck being your puppet, I deserve some respect."

Leng fixed him with a penetrating stare, eyes dark and otherworldly, and the hideous shadow that lurked within the God suddenly loomed over Steve like a black tidal wave. "Respect is not demanded; it is earned through worthiness. You are no thrall of mine—but if you persist in playing one, I will reprimand you accordingly."

Abruptly, the minuscule entities that had infiltrated Steve's skin surged with life, squirming and nipping. The agony was unbearable—vastly surpassing the time he'd trampled a fire-ant mound in his youth. It was akin to being ignited from within. He clung to the steering wheel as his body spasmed, saliva frothing from his mouth and eyes rolling back into their sockets. However, as swiftly as the torment erupted, it ceased.

Steve stomped on the brakes and slumped over the steering wheel, gasping for air while vehicles swerved around them.

"Why did you do that?" Steve managed to croak out between ragged breaths.

"A lesson in obedience," Leng responded coolly.

Despite his fury and terror, Steve refrained from arguing further. He veered off onto an embankment and released a tremulous sigh before amplifying the volume of a classical orchestra playing softly on the radio.

Leng seemed to appreciate this minor gesture of tranquility. "I do not yearn for mindless minions," he said, his tone gentler now. "The saga of your ancestors' downfall...I understand what it feels like to witness pride transform into despair. My tiniest offspring were once intelligent and beautiful—even these microscopic parasites within you are as complex as snowflakes and brighter than your most brilliant minds. My grand progeny and I presided over cities like radiant willow trees with psychic branches nurturing arcane secrets in our eternal gardens...But when I accepted Shub's proposition, I also accepted his relentless hunger, which proliferated amongst my children like a plague—"

A surge of distortion swept across the rainy windshield, morphing it into a glassy panorama through which Steve was subjected to a nightmarish tableau—a grotesque exhibition that bore no relation to Earth's natural history: three-dimensional figures from progressive stages of evolution stood motionless on a murky stage, like antiquities of a turn-of-the-century freak show. The initial display showcased the arachnid-sapiens: humanoid entities with bald heads encased in glossy alabaster skin and punctuated by four symmetrical sets of luminescent eyes. Muscular torsos melded with their centaur-like bodies, though their equine waists were supported by eight limbs rather than four, each curving like a violin's neck and sheathed in iridescent chitin.

In the subsequent still-life, the beings appeared gaunt, their multiple eyes now roving within waxy, fluid faces and proboscises jutting from their drooping maws. A malignant energy had ravaged their insides, distorting their ashen skins with pustules and ridges, twisting their spines, and making their robust appendages rubbery. The final evolutionary monstrosity—the arachnid-monstrum as para-anthropologists might label it—showcased a colossal tumor-like creature teeming with eyes and fleshy growths; its form prickly like an urchin due to twisted bones; its ribcage torn open by teeth; and maintaining eight limbs albeit haphazardly distributed across its bulk as an indication of some residual biological connection. The spark of Leng's memory or imagination was extinguished by a single pass of the windshield wipers.

"Christ," Steve exhaled.

"Christian prayers are as meaningless as my regret," Leng retorted, his tone laced with an otherworldly chill. "The Lengeth you've seen are grotesque caricatures of our former selves. We consume instead of conserve. We annihilate rather than safeguard. With our cacophonous mouths, thrashing tendrils, and bloated forms, we can never return to the halcyon days when we wove and hummed the threads of Celestine music, symphonies that mirrored eternal rhythms, melodies that bewitched celestial bodies. Once, we were cosmic poets and creators...Weavers of tales, myths, and ballads...Guardians of the grand, unending narrative."

A third psychic pulse ripped through the darkness like a veil lifting to reveal an expansive panorama before Steve's eyes. Like a celestial bird in flight, he soared past three suns too distant and icy to ever warm the shadowy undulating landscape beneath him where snowy sand cascaded over gleaming crystal plains and valleys. Far ahead, a distant star sparkled like a diamond on black velvet, drawing him towards it. What materialized in breathtaking detail was an intricately peaked city constructed from crystalline biomass, each structure teetering dangerously in its enormity yet held steadfast by transparent buttresses and filaments.

This towering city ascended like a crown—an envy of Babylon if conceived by alien theologians. Steve felt he was nearing a holy place where millions gathered in reverence; somewhere within this webbed metropolis dangled a pendulous deity both feared and revered who surveyed its subjects, realm, and all the void beyond with hundreds of omniscient eyes. Melodic hymns echoed from the city—strummed by wind across crystal strings played by the vibrations of millions scuttling across translucent bridges—their eight legs strumming at the city's harp. At the same time, their existence resonated across alien skies.

Steve's soaring consciousness reeled from such ecstasy. He gasped as he was abruptly yanked back into his body; the song on the radio had transitioned while raindrops morphed into drying dew on windows. Once again, he had driven automatically while his mind journeyed through another epoch and locale. Trees had receded from the highway, replaced by flat fields, dormant farms, barns, and mounds of machinery running alongside them.

"Your spirit appears to be slowly yielding to my essence," Leng stated, his words hanging ominously in the air. "Most men would vehemently resist such a profound intrusion on their soul, yet you appear rather compliant." Steve swallowed hard as fear twisted in his gut.

"Tlanex-Tli," Leng continued, each word tumbling from his lips like an arcane incantation. "That is the vision you have witnessed. The place of my birth... or perhaps our shared homeland now, I dare suggest. Magnificent, wouldn't you agree? My offspring and I were selected by the Outer Gods for our ability to assimilate energy and knowledge; therefore, our memories are endless and eternally preserved... Yet even my formidable intellect can become clouded under the influence of the Outer Gods' insanity. Until recently, my memory was an enigmatic fog. It appears I am regaining both lucidity and dignity."

A distant gaze claimed his eyes as he continued, "It began when the hymns of my world... echoed back to me through the phone line. Melodies that should never infiltrate this dimension or epoch. Gabriel had a hand in rousing me from this stupor, I believe. Whether this calls for scorn or gratitude remains unclear." He turned to Steve with an enigmatic smile, "You, too, possess a talent for dredging up my memories."

"But regrettably," he exhaled heavily, "the Tlanex-Tli you've observed will forever be just a memory... parched by Shub's insatiable thirst. She triumphed in that round of the Eternal Game."

"Shub?" Steve interjected.

"Shub-Niggurath—The Devouring Worm or Mother—an Outer God," Leng clarified.

"And this 'Eternal Game'? What's it about? Like chess? Checkers?" Steve asked, his casual tone masking his growing dread.

Leng's laughter was low and ominous. "Your naivety is rather charming. Yes, it could be compared to your mortal game of chess, but with four participants, kings who are cosmic horrors, and the victor is awarded the right to obliterate the board. Then a new board is chosen, and the cycle restarts." Leng sighed in a way that suggested an eternity of fatigue. "Even I—who have lived so long that mortality seems an alien concept—an Elder God—find myself humbled by these four heralds of chaos, beings from dimensions beyond time's boundaries. Their incursion into our reality remains an enigma; they infiltrated like whispered secrets in dreams—insidious suggestions indistinguishable from one's own subconscious thoughts—guiding you towards intrusive obsessions...madness. I withstood their malevolent influence, but not without falling prey to a form of insanity that has stolen my memories. There was another who might have survived, though she would be dust by now." Leng's face reflected a torment akin to agony. "Continue to mine more of my identity and direct my fury where it needs to go. I have grown tired of this chess match with the Lords of Chaos. It's time to overturn the board. We will shatter their game. But for such a task, we need power—a weapon."

Given his already formidable capabilities, *power* seemed an amusingly superfluous concept when applied to Leng. Steve tried to unravel the intent of this unhinged deity.

Steve looked at him. "So... we're going to California for what? To find this weapon?"

"Yes."

"Where is it?"

Leng hesitated, closing his eyes as if sensing something beyond Steve's comprehension. "I will know when we approach our goal. The artifact will resonate with me, as I am what repels it. I am certain."

"So we're on some kind of treasure hunt?" Steve asked.

"We are in search of the god-killing artifact of the Atlanteans," Leng replied.

"God-killing," Steve murmured quietly.

"Do not entertain any heroic fantasies," Leng warned. "Though the shadow of my demise may loom due to my defiance, it would not change your fate. Despite your status as a Godbeast, only an entity born of both mortal and Outer God blood—a lineage I lack—can wield such a weapon."

Steve scratched his head in confusion while Leng watched him with disappointment.

"You're a detective," he nudged Steve firmly. "Detect."

"Malachi or Brock?" Steve guessed.

"The enemy of my enemy is my ally," Leng stated cryptically before leaning back in his seat, engrossed in thoughts about future possibilities.

PART 1: DARK ALLIANCES

CHAPTER 1: ROADKILL

"Guard against such emotions, lest they devour you,"
Pythia cautioned solemnly.

In the southeastern reaches of Michigan, where rustic byways carved a path through the feral wilderness, a sable Hummer prowled with an air of predatory confidence. This audacious demeanor was mirrored in its driver, a robust figure with an arm casually dangling out the window to bask in the crisp embrace of the autumnal sun. He was an image conjured from the annals of 80's rock history, donned in a tattered tank top and crowned with a crimson baseball cap that sat atop a cascade of golden curls. While Malachi's buzzcut still bore the sharpness of its recent shearing, Brock's hair had rebounded into untamed Viking-esque locks as spontaneously as spring shoots pierce through winter's frost-laden earth. It became clear why he so meticulously maintained his beard and nails—nearly every evening pit stop dedicated to grooming rituals. A potent rejuvenating magic pulsed within Brock, imbuing him with an unrivaled vitality that had completely eradicated any vestiges of the mystical weapon that had scarred him during his altercation with the super soldier.

Malachi's thoughts meandered towards this arcane weapon now concealed beneath their luggage in the back seat. He remembered the odd sensation when he'd attempted to touch anything other than its handle—an unseen repulsion akin to forcing together two like poles of a magnet. He contemplated its creator and purpose.

Something bothering you? Brock queried, gaze locked on the road unfurling before them, lips static.

Nah, Malachi responded telepathically.

Alright, give me a shout if you feel like chatting.

Sure thing.

Brock flashed him a grin while Malachi observed the bucolic landscape and charming farmhouse rolling past them. Their telepathic communication flowed naturally now; no physical contact was necessary. The only instances they resorted to traditional speech were when they found themselves amongst ordinary people—which was rare—and only when it was crucial to refuel or rest. As far as they could discern, there were no current alerts for their apprehension—or at least none being broadcast on American soil—which meant less tension during these infrequent societal interactions and even allowed them to savor burgers like two ordinary pals.

The capaciousness of their vehicle permitted them to fold down the back seats, providing a makeshift bed that saved on accommodation costs and prolonged Brock's dwindling cash reserves. At night, they slept nestled together like contented pups. But despite the palpitation of their hearts and the electric thrill of their contact, their relationship remained platonic. Neither seemed prepared or inclined to cross this boundary. Love could wait until after Armageddon—if they survived it.

Malachi's thoughts shifted from their travels and simmering emotional entanglement to those ensnared in their conflict. Do you think Robert will be alright?

The retired vet who tangled with witches in 'Nam? Brock chuckled. He'll be fine. Heard from Ana lately?

Malachi retrieved his phone from the door pocket and skimmed through his messages. Just crossed the border, passing through Buffalo—the city is ugly as sin. Will text you ltr. No updates since then, but her check-in had only been earlier today. Reflecting over their exchanges, he realized he and Ana had become digital correspondents, exchanging jests and observations about their journeys several times a day since connecting post-junkyard showdown. They shared a similar cynicism and a resilient "still kicking" outlook on life, people, and situations in general.

Malachi, his spirits sagging under the weight of Ana's silence, dispatched a digital prod as an emoji before relegating his phone to the shadows of his pocket.

"She'll be fine," Brock assured him. "She's resilient as fuck."

"True enough," he conceded. "And Lenny's with her—that man is a beast."

"A bigger beast than me?" Brock interjected with a smirk, tugging at his lips.

"Well..."

Through the sepia-tinted lens of youthful infatuation, Malachi found himself wandering down memory lane to Lenny—the musclebound ex-convict with hair woven into intricate braids who was one of the first men he had ever felt a magnetic pull towards, though it took him some time to recognize these stirrings as adult longing rather than childish intrigue. He wondered if Ana harbored similar emotions for her current companion. However, when he cast a sidelong glance at Brock—the sun-dappled Viking beside him—Lenny's rough-hewn charm seemed lackluster compared to Brock's luminous allure.

"Maybe," replied Brock, his thoughts also drifting toward images of the brawny stranger—a raven of contemplation pecking incessantly at the recesses of his mind. "But he's not my type," he added with a piercing look.

He lifted his hand from the gear stick, letting it find its home on Malachi's knee. Together, they gazed out onto the horizon as it underwent a metamorphosis, the sun taking refuge behind an idyllic treeline and birds stitching their path across the canvas sky —heralding another day, another chapter in their journey, and another collection of treasured shared experiences.

***

Stirred from the abyss of sleep by the muted thud of Brock's dawn exertions, Malachi uncoiled in the rear seat of their motored beast, basking in a beam of sunlight like a satisfied feline before assuming an upright position on their makeshift cot. Despite winter's frosty caress on the vehicle's shell, he seldom sought shelter; Brock's body heat was a furnace that radiated warmth into the compartment. Malachi swiped away condensation from the window and strained to pierce through the circle of snow-kissed pines and beyond into the chilly, fog-draped wilderness for his companion. Discerning the golden smear cavorting among trees proved arduous for his groggy cognition until he spotted him momentarily within a whirlwind of snowflakes.

When Brock finally alighted, suspending his aerial antics momentarily, he performed a Herculean push-up that sent him skywards: clapping hands overhead, twisting mid-flight, clapping again before descending onto the unforgiving terra firma—an impressive feat in isolation but mind-boggling when threaded together into a shimmering figure eight. Before Malachi could digest this spectacle, Brock catapulted himself again with primate-like agility, vanishing from sight only to materialize as an ephemeral silhouette amongst tree branches. Memories of childhood web-slinger animations flooded Malachi's consciousness—Brock would leave Spidey choking on dust.

He studied his friend for some time longer, musing over the raw physical prowess of Brock's extraordinary abilities. Depleting one of their scarce remaining water bottles left in their hoard, he left to attend to nature's call. Upon returning to find Brock at the car—bare-chested and slick with perspiration—he exhaled audibly. Brock used his t-shirt to dry off while Malachi deftly ignored the peculiar scent—a bizarre blend akin to patchouli—that emanated from the man and lifted his gaze from Brock's sinewy chest up into his tempestuous stare. The lupine glint in Brock's eyes found its mirror in Malachi, who had materialized from the foggy forest like a moonlit fawn primed for the chase. His shorn scalp accentuated his chiseled features; the slender neck led to a lean silhouette framed against his hoodie; the green stare as natural as the enveloping woods; his lips, an enticing crimson slash that roused Brock's primal instincts.

"Wha...?" The veil of distraction lifted from Brock's features.

"I said: your power is off the charts," Malachi clarified, his words carving through the charged silence that often enveloped them during these intimate encounters. Their unspoken communication only amplified their longing, but articulating thoughts aloud provided a grounding effect. "But honestly," he pressed on, "is all this self-punishment necessary?"

"My whole life has been about pushing boundaries. I've been afraid to reveal my true self to you. That ends now."

After their confrontation with the super soldiers at the scrapyard, Brock had returned to his extraordinary exercise routine—a practice he insisted was a personal standard but had momentarily abandoned while acclimating to his new companion. Yet Malachi detected an undercurrent of urgency in Brock's dedication and suspected it wasn't solely about physical conditioning. "You certain that's all there is?" he ventured.

"We must be prepared," Brock responded, his face shadowed by unease. "I can't afford arrogance anymore. There are bastards out there who'd love seeing us in the ground."

Malachi closed the gap between them, perching on the edge of the trunk lid. "I can't fully read your mind—yet." He chuckled lightly before stating, "You need to unload—let me shoulder some of your burdens."

Brock cast aside his makeshift towel and joined Malachi on the trunk lid. "On top of worrying about being murdered, we're almost broke, too," he admitted.

Malachi had observed Brock mentally calculating meal expenses lately and choosing canned provisions they could warm over campfire flames instead of enjoying their typical fast-food binges during their travels. The grumbling echo from Brock's stomach last night after sharing a few tins of stew bore witness to their skimpy meals. Sustaining Brock's superhuman metabolism demanded substantial energy reserves, Malachi deduced.

"This damn hunger won't let up," Brock muttered, his stomach adding a low growl for emphasis.

Malachi saw a simple solution. "I could ask one of my aunties for some cash? With our fake IDs, we're still off the radar."

"I hate handouts," Brock grumbled.

"This isn't about your pride."

Malachi scrutinized the hardening contours of his friend's face. Brock was self-reliant, living by himself since boyhood, surviving on sheer determination and effort. If Malachi were less urban and more rugged, they might manage on wild game and fresh creek water. But in their current predicament, he was the weak link.

"Okay, perhaps it is about pride," conceded Malachi. "You're as stubborn as a mule. So am I."

"I should be capable of managing things—looking after both of us. I've been gearing up for our rendezvous since Charlie's murder. Ninety thousand doesn't go far nowadays."

"Hold on, ninety grand?" blurted out Malachi, then recalled Brock's preference for dealing strictly in hundred-dollar bills and realized the figure wasn't outrageous.

Brock's gaze drifted towards the emerging dawn. "Twenty thousand went straight into Robert's pocket...But that's a bargain considering what we gave him—we got a decent deal on the vehicle, too. Another sixty-something grand on fuel, food, travel, and accommodation getting me to you and then getting us around... You've noticed how much I eat and how lean our meals have become... We've cut corners by sleeping in the Hummer, though. No idea how much further we'll have to travel after reaching Rhode Island. Likely end up going around in circles till we hit Timbuktu or someplace equally absurd... We'll be broke by then, though. I eat like a horse, and you're an expensive date."

A blush crept up Malachi's cheeks at this revelation. "Sorry."

"You're worth every penny, Malachi. I wouldn't want to be anywhere else."

Brock stooped into the yawning trunk, his hands burrowing into his duffel bag in search of deodorant and a clean shirt. He changed swiftly, movements honed by necessity. Meanwhile, Malachi maneuvered around him to straighten the disarray of blankets at the rear before circumnavigating to the vehicle's passenger side. He leaned against the frosty metal exterior, extracting his phone from the pocket of his worn hoodie. His gaze fell on Ana's digital missive—an emoji of a pointing finger prodding a phone—her unique way of saying 'call me.' He promptly dialed her number, and she answered without delay.

"Lenny! Watch where you're going!" Ana's voice rang out unexpectedly. "Sorry, Lenny thinks he's in an F1 race."

"NASCAR, babe," Lenny's voice echoed in the background. "F1 doesn't use stock cars."

"I have no clue what that means," Ana admitted.

"Babe? You two sound like newlyweds straight outta Vegas," Malachi jested.

Ana's response was momentarily delayed before she retorted with a sharp bite: "That's not...Shut the fuck up. Anyway. Where are you guys?"

"We're heading east on the interstate. Roughly two states away from Rhode Island. Probably just over a week out. Your location?"

"Just breezed past Detroit."

Intriguing and lyrical, Malachi mused, the proximity yet distance of their paths was a paradox wrapped in an enigma. Their trajectories, though closely knit, still maintained an uncanny remoteness. "You sure you don't want us to wait up for you?"

"Nope, I feel like we all need to maintain momentum."

"You mean that kind of *feel*?"

"Yes."

"Understood," said Malachi, then added: "Oh, I hate to come off as a freeloader, but we might need some cash soon. Acquiring black market transport and IDs isn't inexpensive."

"Ha! For some silly reason, they're still depositing my paychecks," Ana chuckled lightly. "I suspect my benevolent doctor may have a hand in this...Anyway, Cynthia's unconscious in the backseat for now, but I'll discuss it with her once she surfaces, and we'll figure out something for ya."

"Thanks, appreciate it." An icy shiver pierced Malachi, the burdens of their duties and bygone confrontations cascading over him like a frigid wave crashing against his exposed flesh. "You guys doing okay otherwise?"

"We're breathing."

"That's your standard?"

"That's my standard."

Malachi allowed a grin to play on his lips. "Well, until our next chat, then?"

"Yeah—" Just as he was about to sever the call, Ana's urgent voice forestalled him. "Hey, hey, you still there?"

"Yeah."

"I nearly forgot. Had this peculiar dream."

"About?"

"A dead goat. White fur...massive horns...laid in a roadside ditch brimming with these gorgeous pink flowers. They were breathtaking but radiated an aura of danger...like roses and their thorns—but not roses. Bigger blooms, tropical-like. Further down the road—a highway—a wolf and a raven stood united, their gazes fixed on the cadaver. I had the impression they were wary of approaching it." Ana's voice trembled slightly with apprehension. "But then it shambled upright in a zombie-like manner, flinging flowers and blood indiscriminately...its throat had been cut, but that didn't seem to deter it much. It bellowed like a bear before lurching towards the wolf and raven...then I was jolted awake." Ana exhaled deeply." It felt important, though," she added.

"That kind of importance?"

"Absolutely."

"Thanks for the premonition."

"No biggie, stay safe."

"We will. You too."

The conversation with Ana terminated abruptly, and Malachi re-ascended into the confines of the automobile. Even under the relentless gusts from the Hummer's vents, and despite Brock's reassuring presence at his side, Ana's ominous utterances—her foreboding prophecy—instilled a bone-chilling dread within him. As they navigated back onto the main artery of asphalt, slicing through a landscape of frost-bitten scrubland, Malachi scrutinized every ditch and stretch of gravel flanking their path for any seemingly dead animals that demanded their utmost caution.

***

"Utterly ignored," the woman whispered. They embodied domestic harmony on the roadside, the man, woman, and their child, attired in ski jackets and bright scarves—designer sunglasses added a chic flair to the parent's visages. Indeed, their appearance was as flawless as an image torn from a high-end designer catalog. The backdrop to this scene was a frosty expanse tinged with the desperate air characteristic of stranded winter voyagers. Such picturesque appeal should have been impossible to ignore for even the most insensitive passerby—a slowing car or a window being rolled down—to question this family, their cherubic-looking child, and whatever misfortune had resulted in smoke spiraling from beneath their vehicle's lifted bonnet. At least someone could have checked on their condition. But no such incident occurred.

Instead, the Hummer drivers seemed to acknowledge them only to speed up and veer around them. As they watched the diminishing rear of the Hummer, their hopeful grins contorted into grimaces; all three scornfully glared at the departing vehicle until it became a mere glint against dawn's illumination.

The mother—possibly once a Slavic model—adjusted her ruby hairband and pivoted towards her attractive husband, who might also have retired from modeling; his azure eyes narrowed under his salt-and-pepper eyebrows as he gritted his teeth in resentment. Their fair-skinned child mirrored their expressions, but then something peculiar happened: her face aged swiftly as if wilting under harsh sunlight while her pigtails squirmed like snakes. This eerie transformation obliterated any trace of childhood innocence with otherworldly savagery.

"Our usual deceit won't work," uttered the child creature in an archaic language resembling Greek that only Hadrian might understand.

"They're on our tail," responded the father.

"We've got their plate number, at least," the mother said. "I'll reach out to Mrs. Mothmann."

The father nodded and approached the car's front to shut the valve he had tampered with earlier, quenching the smoke. As he engaged himself, the child-entity withdrew into the backseat, her face returning to its youthful plumpness as she caught her monstrous reflection in the car window. Simultaneously, their mother moved away from them, striding a gravel path as she tapped on her cell phone.

The call was promptly picked up; sounds of merriment echoed in the background— some sort of gathering or festivity. "I need to handle this," came a velvety voice from the other end. "Yes, yes, fifty million is fine. But I want that contract signed today. Excuse me."

A sequence of noises ensued—papers rustling, heels clicking resonating in a large area, and finally, a door shutting.

"Have you found them?" Mrs. Mothmann inquired.

"We indeed have," responded Pythia. "The Aspect of Earth brandishes his newfound power like a beacon—it will inevitably draw every entity that identifies such energy towards him sooner or later. I doubt he even understands his own actions."

"And?"

"Direct confrontation was not our course of action," Pythia conceded with a hint of reluctance. "Our aim was to make contact, collect tangible foci—strands of hair or flakes of skin—for our rites, but they simply sped past us—as if sensing the danger we presented."

"I see..."

Octavia maintained her composure better than her impetuous brother. Years of navigating the shark-infested waters of California's ruthless industries had sharpened her negotiation skills to a lethal point. She could entrap dreamers and visionaries in contracts that involved unspeakable acts, blackmail, murder, compromising sexual situations, blood magic, and ultimately eternal servitude to her and The Deep One. Such a game required strategic patience.

"You acted prudently," Octavia finally voiced out. "They are more formidable than I initially assumed, and following the Detroit fiasco, they must be on high alert. My brother's attempts at communication with the Aspects continue to confound me. Nevertheless, I've managed to successfully undermine his plan and pin the blame on Gabriel—his men, weapons, and blunder. So all is not lost unless he can trace the enchantments to you three."

Pythia dismissed this notion with a scoff. "Our magic is rooted in antiquity—we cast spells spoken only by Alexander himself—we even taught him some verses. No mortal witch could decipher our work."

A cruel smirk twisted Octavia's lips as she reveled in their malevolent deeds. The Red Fates' indifferent response to her desperate plea for assistance was still vivid in her mind's eye.

In an unhurried show of apathy, they had risen from their repose within her private sanctum, captivated by the charm of modern trinkets—telephones, VR headsets, and other modern toys—their curiosity ignited by the zeitgeist into which they'd been summoned.

They'd gathered, hands clasped tightly together as they whispered ancient incantations whose true power lay dormant until the cataclysmic release of psychic energy that radiated from them. The overwhelming power cast Octavia's study into a maelstrom of disorder, hurling her onto the frigid marble floor. Their psychic javelin shot through the celestial dome, targeting Gabriel's Spirit Walkers miles distant, subjugating them to their new sovereign: Octavia. A single incantation from these primordial Godbeasts rendered billions worth of technomagic useless, reconfiguring it according to her fancy. Yet, was this truly her desire or merely the will of these entities and the overlord they jointly served? Her conviction in her own significance had faltered amidst this grand display.

Indeed, MANN Inc.'s inner sanctum was rife with anxiety over Gabriel's unsanctioned and botched assassination attempt near Detroit. A meeting had been arranged for him to grovel before the Board later in the week, but his typical scorn for formalities would likely result in his absence. This would give Octavia free rein to sow seeds of discord.

What should have been Gabriel's moment of triumph devolved into a demonstration of incompetence with MANN's president at its epicenter. Hushed whispers suggesting he was following in the ill-fated steps of the late Mothmann patriarch circulated amongst those most inclined towards idle gossip.

"Mrs. Mothmann? Are you there?"

"Yes," she answered absently, "I was momentarily lost in schadenfreude."

"Guard against such emotions, lest they devour you," Pythia cautioned solemnly. "I've witnessed envy's destructive power, capable of toppling even the most formidable rulers. It seems discretion is a wise choice here. These two Aspects are embryonic entities, akin to butterflies still enclosed in their cocoons. They may be oblivious to the traces they scatter around, making them easily traceable." She paused momentarily. "There's a catch."

"And that would be?"

"Necromanteon, the insatiable devourer who once feasted on the very life essence of Salem's witches—bragging about her consumption of entire covens devoted to Cthugha— she is well-acquainted with the luminous aura that distinguishes the Golden One's followers and has arrived at an unsettling deduction. The recent ground-shaking surge of cosmic energy that pulsated through Detroit's veins implies that not one but two of our elusive quarry are teetering on the brink of a sacred, ritualistic convergence."

"In layman's terms?"

"They're *awakening*, possibly already awakened."

"What! But how? Without performing necessary rituals?"

"I can't say for sure. These Aspects are enigmas. We don't have any historical precedents to understand this situation. It complicates everything. Now you better understand our hesitation with direct engagement."

Unlike Gabriel, Octavia recognized her limitations and refrained from meddling in areas beyond her knowledge. On such matters, she deferred to those more versed—her trio of Grecian Godbeasts who were once steeped in sacrifices and revered as supreme demigods and oracles during humanity's golden era: Pythia, Trophonius, and Necromanteon. "What do you propose?" Octavia queried.

"I'll consult with my compatriots," Pythia replied wisely. "A divination seems necessary to measure our adversary's strength."

As if responding to some unseen signal, an old truck driven by a lonely old man rumbled over the crest of a hill towards them—a moth lured by their flame. It wasn't their intended target, but it would do for now. The Godbeasts sprang into readiness, bracing themselves for the impending task.

"I will reconnect once we have inspected the entrails, which have just arrived," Pythia stated cryptically before ending the call.

She flashed an incandescent smile and hurried off to join her comrades in flagging down their oblivious sacrifice.

CHAPTER 2: SEQUINS AND SORCERY

"Your sex disqualifies you," Evelyn retorted harshly. "The burden of motherhood is too heavy, as you know."

Octavia entered the stark, ultramodern conference chamber at the epicenter of MANN Inc.'s New York City fortress. Her ebony stilettos echoed a stern symphony against the mirror-like marble underfoot. Outside, a storm raged with unyielding ferocity, its chaotic energy casting sporadic bursts of lightning that bathed the expansive room in an eerie interplay of light and shadow. This spectral glow, both ethereal and alien, seeped incessantly through the towering window panes, enveloping the gathering of corporate witches in a shroud of icy luminescence that turned their meeting into an uncanny ritual. Despite the uproar reigning outside, it barely permeated within this solemn assembly. The chamber was steeped in potent magic and protective hexes so powerful they could withstand a nuclear catastrophe.

The three figures at the table were cloaked in shadow, appearing like grotesque masks in the semi-darkness—hinting at hidden strategies and enigmatic motives that emerged like waking nightmares as Octavia and Oliver, her aide-de-camp, approached.

As Octavia took her seat at the head of the elongated glass council table, she felt an oppressive weight of anticipation pressing upon her. Oliver faded into an obedient specter behind her—ready to act when called upon. The witches observed her with a blend of curiosity and suspicion glinting dangerously in their eyes. They all had inklings about why she had convened this gathering—having skimmed through the classified summary on Detroit's kill zone turned fatal for its executioners.

Seated to Octavia's right was Evelyn—the Mistress of Deceptions—with deep jade eyes that constantly changed color and intensity, reflecting her volatile temperament. She was a master manipulator capable of distorting reality with just a flicker of her delicate fingers. Her glossy silver hair framed features that seemed to waver and warp under the boardroom's peculiar illumination.

To Octavia's left was Lucian—the Enchanter—a towering figure as sleek, polished, and captivating as an obsidian panther clad in his Armani suit so luminous yet dark it seemed to absorb surrounding light. His eyes were abyssal pools hinting at infinite power and ancient wisdom. His voice, which she recalled as a mix of sweetness laced with venom, could weave spells that ensnared the mind and enchanted the senses.

Across them was Isadora—the Hemomancer—with her carmine lips curled into a ruthless grin that sent icy shivers down Octavia's spine. She wore an elegant black dress more suited for a sultry singer than a boardroom meeting, clinging to her figure like a shadow, accentuated only by ruby jewels adorning her neck and wrists. Isadora's realm was blood magic, harnessing the raw energies pulsating through veins and throbbing with life. With just a single droplet of crimson life force, she could command existence itself—a fact that made even the most hardened witches wary of crossing her path.

Octavia's gaze swept over her arcane companions at the council table, sensing the underlying tension permeating the atmosphere like a thick fog. Each was a formidable entity in their own right—their powers beyond mortal comprehension—and none took kindly to being questioned. However, Octavia was acutely aware that her brother's indiscretion warranted punishment. Gabriel threatened their delicate balance of power and risked invoking Cthulhu's wrath upon them all.

"Cousins," Octavia began, her voice steady and commanding, "The matter before us requires our attention."

"You behave as if you're in charge here," Lucian countered sharply, "and yet your brother—as usual—is nowhere to be found."

"I've reviewed his report," Isadora interjected with a sultry whisper. "It seems like an honest mistake. You could stand to be more lenient towards your brother. Such bitterness will age you quicker than sun exposure, dear cousin."

Isadora's perfect, porcelain skin was famed among them. This effect was achieved through blood baths of freshly killed innocents, a rejuvenating ritual inherited from her ancestor, Lady Bathory.

"I'll pass on your particular brand of skincare regimen, thank you," Octavia retorted crisply. "I wouldn't have convened this meeting—in person—without a valid reason."

"And what might that be?" Lucian prodded.

"A betrayal by my brother," Octavia disclosed.

Isadora rolled her eyes dramatically. "You've gathered us for another pointless pursuit."

"That's incorrect. Gabriel has misled us, and I plan to prove it."

Isadora impatiently drummed her glossy red nails on the glass tabletop as they awaited Octavia's evidence. With a quick snap of her fingers, Oliver extended his arm over her shoulder and handed Octavia a flash drive, which she slid into a concealed slot on the table. A whirlwind of digital symbols lit up the transparent oval surface before them while the room was suddenly filled with the static buzz of transmission—a recording. A deep, almost beast-like masculine voice reverberated: "We are closing in on targets. Records show this property is owned by a Robert Smith; civilian casualties are expected."

A sudden sizzle, a low whisper of static, and a reply emerged from the ether in an imperious, refined tone that they all instantly identified—Gabriel's: "No bloodshed. One witness is acceptable. Your task is negotiating a truce or subduing the targets—bringing them to Evermore unharmed."

After a pause came a reply: "We're killers and hunting dogs, not diplomats."

"Do as you're told; don't disappoint me."

The soldier seemed to waver, his mind teetering on the precipice of indecision. Yet, in the end, he succumbed to acquiescence: "Roger that, boss."

Their conversation dwindled into silence, the boardroom now resonating with an unspoken strain. Isadora's previously smug attitude had dissipated, her complexion appearing more ghostly than ever. Lucian was caught in his private musings. Evelyn, the eldest among them and cloaked in age-old wisdom, preserved her composure as she asked: "Where did you acquire this?"

"Field agents replicated one of the Spirit Walker's cerebral sims before Gabriel could correct his mistake," Octavia shot back.

"Agents?" Evelyn probed, her instincts on high alert for any hint of deception—a game at which she was master.

But Octavia harbored no intention of revealing her covert alliance with the Red Fates. "I have means and resources that are none of your concern. Gabriel has just shown us that we must always guard against treachery within our ranks. I do not meddle in your concealed secrets or reserves, dear cousin. Be thankful that I have decided to employ mine for our mutual advantage. The Deep One will not ignore such disloyalty."

Evelyn found validity in these words and leaned back in contemplation.

"But what does this signify, exactly?" Lucian pondered aloud. "It's simply evidence that he refrained from killing the Aspects. Maybe he had a different agenda: experimentation, torture?"

"We are not here to decode the whispers of the Deep One," Evelyn asserted firmly. "Our responsibility is to adhere to His commands, and His instructions have been clear on this subject: the Aspects must be eliminated as they present a risk to His—and by extension our—supremacy. We are bound by blood to Him; if His power diminishes from this world, so too may ours."

"What could Gabriel possibly be scheming?" Isadora erupted in exasperation.

"What does it matter?" Octavia dismissed coldly. "An inquiry will only grant this traitor more opportunities to weave falsehoods and slip away. He has demonstrated his ineptitude and is undeserving of guiding us into the era of His return."

Lucian, the only man at the table and potential heir to Evermore was hit by a sudden realization. "I have no interest in Gabriel's position."

"Good, because I do," Octavia stated bluntly. Her three cousins scoffed and gasped until they grasped her earnestness.

"Your sex disqualifies you," Evelyn retorted harshly. "The burden of motherhood is too heavy, as you know."

Every Mothmann woman, from the moment she first stepped into womanhood, was steeped in the chilling lore of their lineage. The brutal reality of childbirth and its lethal price tag was instilled deeply within them. To stave off such a fate, they were administered potent concoctions of progesterone—a few chose the extreme of having their wombs surgically or magically removed. Despite contraceptive precautions or vows of celibacy, some Mothmann women fell through the cracks or into temptation.

The family graveyard bore testimony to this tragic pattern. It held vast swathes dedicated solely to those women who dared to challenge destiny or foolishly pursued matters of the heart. Their ends were uniformly gruesome—consumed from within by a malignant offspring borne of witchcraft.

A macabre meadow littered with ornate tombstones stood as silent sentinels over their final resting places. Each stone carried an epitaph that ranged from somber to whimsical. They were stark reminders of grim Mother's Day sentiments: "Here rests Hermione, a brave mother who made the ultimate sacrifice" or "Here lies a cherished womb."

This last inscription, which belonged to her dearest Rebecca, particularly repulsed Octavia. It oozed morbidity and cold pragmatism. It encapsulated what women represented in the Mothmann lineage: mere vessels for birthing legitimate heirs.

"The hour has arrived to shatter convention," Octavia proclaimed, her voice echoing with the zeal of a doomsday harbinger. "The barrier securing our dormant Lord's prison has worn thin over the eons. With MANN Inc. and Evermore's full force under my control, I can unleash cataclysms, power outages, cyber onslaughts, and technomagical pandemics to generate the necromantic energy necessary to obliterate that seal once and for all. There will be no generations succeeding me. It concludes here. So, the question of heirs or succession is moot and void. You either stand with me amid our world's sunken wreckage, ruling over humanity's masses, or perish alongside my adversaries. I have comrades whose existence you cannot fathom, united by our obligation to our slumbering master. Do you possess such loyalty? Because among all our predecessors, you three have reaped the most benefits from serving the Deep One—unfathomable longevity, affluence, and comfort. The dream has expired; it's time to pay your dues as the nightmare draws near. Stand with me or announce your defection on this spot."

When silence filled the room so profoundly that one could hear a pin drop, they delivered their answer.

"Excellent," she resumed while casting an ominous glance from Evelyn to Lucian and then Isadora, "From your hands, I demand a triumvirate of illusions, a formidable geas, and an artifact steeped in blood to manifest the omnipotence of our Lord."

"For what purpose would you require such a potent artifact?" Isadora barely managed to murmur.

"To breach Evermore's defenses and claim my birthright," Octavia retorted, her voice resonating with righteousness. Illuminated by a flash of pale light, the three cowed witches acknowledged the new sole matriarch of the Mothmann clan.

***

Octavia rose from her throne-like seat, the grandeur of its leather construction dwarfing the other chairs surrounding the glossy oval table in the echoing boardroom—a pale echo of MANN Inc.'s formidable New York fortress. The return to Los Angeles was welcome, her realm where no impertinent kin or stormy sibling could challenge her reign. Here, she was the lifeblood and conductor of every social event, the puppeteer behind each business deal, an angel and devil perched on each celebrity's shoulder. She viewed her city as a divine tragicomedy of human existence: a landscape carved by Faustian bargains, power struggles, a high culture born from raw desires, blood-soaked sorcery, and her master's infinite cosmic malevolence.

Yet now, she reveled in a delicious realization that she stood on the precipice of ruling not only this city or their ancient bloodline but also Earth itself. As she drifted towards the glass wall, she cast her thoughts outwards—to what lay beyond—the world and its impending destiny. The Hollywood hills sparkled with unspoiled dreams once owned by starlets who traded their bodies and souls for fame. As dusk crept in and darkness spilled across the valley, leaving twinkling settlements—tiny ships lost on a darkened sea—she saw this scene as a foretaste of when the Deep One would rise to consume mankind.

In this dreamlike state, shadows rolled over the valley lights while ominous sounds disguised an underwater ruin echoing with grotesque gurgles and screams from human slaves tormented by merfolk—the symphony of suffering. Above this bleak submerged wreckage hung an indigo sky streaked with alien trails and constellations. Nothing earthly seemed to have survived when her reality clashed with the Deep One's dream world.

However, shaking herself free from this macabre vision, she acknowledged perhaps it was too fanciful; the Outer Gods had a reputation for annihilating civilizations they encountered despite promises made to their worshippers. They only favored entities similar to themselves: utterly self-centered and fueled by an unquenchable thirst for destruction. Yet, her Hollywood sojourn had shown her that humans could embody far greater monstrosities—men or women.

So she committed herself to becoming the most abhorrent, merciless creature on Earth—for survival was the ultimate prize. Still, the enduring promise to the faithful was that those chosen would rule over society's remnants and continue the worship of the Deep One through devoted sacrifices and tributes as recompense for the deep-seated insult Atlanteans had dealt Him. Her ancestors pledged ten thousand years of human suffering—that was the Mothmann's final term in their infernal contract.

She wondered if she'd tire after a hundred years or a thousand of overseeing slaves and conducting blood rituals. Still, then, she considered her sadistic delight in human torment and tyranny would likely reach unprecedented heights once freed from even society's loose chains. Indeed, a daunting new epoch beckoned, and soon she would step into it.

A viridian spark caught Octavia's attention on the window's reflective surface. The emerald pendant, an enigma of deceptive simplicity and profound magnetism, dangled from a timeworn gold chain encircling her neck. Its once vibrant luminescence was now subdued by centuries of relentless erosion. It throbbed in sync with her pulse—an eerie tether she could not sever. This pendant was the unsettling inheritance of the Deep One mirrored back at her, an artifact crafted by her dedicated forebears in the smoldering forge of arcane practices.

As her fingers curled around the talisman with a possessive clasp, reality around her smeared into obscurity. Visions swarmed like hornets—horrifying tableaus of indescribable dread and pandemonium: metropolises buckling under the oppressive might of titanic marine leviathans; heavens cloaked in darkness as winged nightmares eclipsed the sun; mankind prostrated before entities so repugnant they defied articulation. Each revelation outstripped its predecessor in terror, a procession of apocalyptic phantoms that left her gasping for breath.

The emerald was more than mere ornamentation—it served as Cthulhu's conduit, his pledge of cataclysmic resurgence etched into every gleaming facet.

Octavia's malevolent smirk, chillingly akin to a demon jester's countenance mirrored in crystalline panes, gradually lost its vibrancy as the sound of a door creaking open and then shut, reverberated behind her, succeeded by encroaching footfalls.

"Transaction completed, Mrs. Mothmann," announced Oliver, the crisp formality of his words laced with a faint echo of Spanish rhythm.

Octavia's lips curled into a grimacing frown, her voice dripping with disdain as she responded, "And what did that insufferable man demand in return this time?"

Oliver's response was curt and businesslike. "The usual trifecta: wealth, status, digital fame."

"Hmm."

He paused before adding, "Plus one more thing... children."

"How old?"

"Straight from the cradle."

"How utterly predictable." Octavia's laughter rang out like chimes in the air.

She turned to face Oliver fully, her gaze sweeping over him with a strange blend of annoyance and intrigue. There he stood, a compelling contradiction—disheveled yet captivating. His eyes were wide and green as unripe apples, magnified by the lenses of his gold-rimmed spectacles. His hair was an untamed wilderness atop his head, and stubble darkened his lean face. His slender frame was clothed in a rumpled T-shirt and khakis that suggested he had just awoken from some chaotic afternoon nap.

Yet beneath this outward appearance of eccentric disorganization was a refined gentleman whose charm could disarm even Hollywood's most hardened cynics without

Octavia's intervention. He bore an uncanny resemblance to Cary Grant—if one looked past his seemingly nervous exterior—revealing a strikingly handsome countenance hidden beneath layers of apparent disorder.

But it wasn't just Oliver's looks or charm that captivated Octavia; it was also his unwavering dedication to their work. Sleep seemed to be a luxury he seldom indulged in; instead, he fueled himself on caffeine and occasionally Adderall when fatigue threatened to claim him. In Octavia's experience, few could stomach or appreciate the darker aspects of their business; she had wiped countless minds—and existences—of those who couldn't cope.

Yet Oliver remained resolute, even after witnessing contracts signed in blood on ancient parchment—the grisly initiation ritual for every rising starlet. His steadfastness was a testament to their shared comprehension of the nefarious nature of their work.

Oliver's past painted a sinister portrait that justified his acceptance. The thorough background checks funded by the federal bureaus the Mothmanns owned revealed his journey from the grim underbelly of North Hollywood. Remarkably, he had managed to sever ties with the notorious Los Muertos family—a feat usually accomplished only post-mortem—and had risen from gang life into academia as an honor student studying media.

The indelible ink of a serpent's tail, coiled and slithering up to his chin, was the only physical testament to Oliver's brutal history. It was an unyielding memento of the blood he'd spilled and witnessed in a life he had since abandoned. Under Octavia's unwavering scrutiny, he extended a scroll towards her, its secrets bound by a strand of scarlet silk.

Her nimble fingers slipped the knot and unfurled the contract: an ancient parchment bristling with enigmatic symbols, stamped at its base with a man's signature beside a blood-red wax seal—a horned octopodal insignia signifying their lineage, the Mothmanns. As she studied the document, she discovered an erased line that confirmed Oliver had met and exceeded his contractual obligations.

"Two infants per year?" Her voice trembled as she echoed the terms.

"I managed to bargain him down from four," Oliver responded dryly, maintaining his professional demeanor despite the unsettling content of their conversation.

"That's... good," she said, her tone barely masking her shock.

Oliver found himself contemplating whether the flicker of trepidation on Octavia's face indicated some form of empathy. She had negotiated many grotesque deals with their clients before—never once flinching at their morbid demands. How many children? How often? Is disposal part of our duties? Each added stipulation led to increased costs and performance targets. She was undoubtedly a creature birthed from nightmares, an insatiable corporatist who casually approved the downfall of sex workers, migrant laborers, and innocent newborns yet to take their first steps in life. Why would two infants suddenly provoke such concern within her?

A realization crashed into him like a rogue wave—regret for all the horrors he'd willingly overlooked flooding over him in an auditory shudder—the echo of a name: Maria. He swiftly pushed this unwelcome emotion back into the shadows before it could catch Octavia's attention.

"Put away the contract," Octavia ordered her visibly perturbed aide.

"Sorry." Swiftly reclaiming and resealing the document, Oliver distanced himself from his mistress. "Can I get you anything to celebrate the occasion? A martini, perhaps? Double olives, as per your preference?"

"No," she declined. "I prefer to maintain a clear mind this evening."

"You've been keeping quite a few clear minds lately," he commented.

"I..."

Octavia brushed aside his remarks, her heel clicks echoing as she navigated the expanse of floor-to-ceiling windows. She discovered a hidden door camouflaged within the glass panels and emerged onto an elevated balcony that offered a panoramic view of her realm below. The murmurs of the city rose on the night air, almost decipherable as they merged with the desperate pleas for acknowledgment from those dwelling in her dominion. The shimmering allure of yearning... No wonder she had succumbed to the same temptations she'd made a career out of offering to others. Or were her dalliances more than mere carnal indulgence?

Oliver shadowed her without uttering a word, positioning himself within arm's reach as she delved into her contemplations. After a long pause, he dared to break the silence: "I trust our indiscretions haven't shaken your confidence in me."

Their indiscretions. Vivid flashes from their shared past assaulted Octavia's mind: Oliver's syrupy kisses and large hands exploring her body; his sweat blending with the intoxicating aroma of his exotic cologne; his lean body adorned with a light dusting of hair hinting at some wild beast beneath; an intricate canvas of skulls, serpents, and Latin phrases etched on his skin like an erotic spell; his impressive manhood—it always seemed to be the slender ones who were so generously gifted—pressing against her dew-kissed skin before claiming her.

She had relived that moment numerous times when alone with herself or certain accessories, each replay igniting a wave of heat within her core. Her father's singular life lesson echoed in her mind: Fuck your kin, fuck your enemies—before you destroy them—but never, under any circumstances, fuck the help. Yet she had defied this cardinal rule.

"I've already put it out of my mind," she retorted. "Don't mention it again."

"Understood."

"Besides, we have much to concentrate on. The final days are upon us, Oliver. We must start enforcing our agreements."

"I'll start making calls first thing tomorrow."

"Excellent. Our clientele must ensure the transition is seamless. Those who refuse to comply will have their agreements terminated—with a stress on termination. However, we can afford to leave President Mulvaney and our recent acquisitions undisturbed for a few weeks. Remind the others that their role is to pacify concerns and to orchestrate the subservient class. Cthulhu has been anticipating this banquet so intensely he'll want to savor it. For ten millennia or more. We'll require spokespersons and influencers who can manipulate and persuade their followers that the sky isn't falling—"

"Won't it be?"

"Yes. Quite literally, I expect."

"Understood."

In silence, they shared a tense anticipation of what lay ahead. Gazing somberly at the resplendent grandeur of this sinful lair, they were aware that its days were numbered.

"It's been an honor working with you," Oliver admitted. "I've seen things I never thought possible. You've made the evil in the world make sense."

"There's worse to come, Oliver. Horrors no one should ever witness. Be prepared."

The assistant, seasoned in the subtle shifts of his mistress's moods, had understood the unspoken signals that marked his dismissal. On the evening of their indiscretion,

Octavia hadn't needed to articulate a single syllable; he'd merely traced a nonchalant trail over her shoulder, donned his attire with hushed exactness, and disappeared. Tonight, his departing words lingered like spectral echoes long after he had evaporated into the ether. "I'll take my leave now. Goodnight."

In the ensuing silence, Octavia experienced an alien sensation welling up within her —a hollow ache that gnawed at her core. It was as if an unseen hand had plunged into her being and stirred up an appetite she couldn't comprehend. For a fleeting moment, she contemplated summoning him back.

But then she caught herself and trained her eyes on the boundless night stretching beyond her window. Her reflection confronted her—eerily solitary yet fiercely unyielding. She was no stranger to solitude; it was a condition decreed by lineage, a life-long sentence served in allegiance to nebulous powers.

Her hand instinctively gravitated towards her abdomen, her womb, an organ not destined for nurturing but for channeling arcane energy. The notion of terminating the pregnancy flickered in her mind like a rogue flame teetering on the brink of a wick's edge. With just an influx of eldritch power, before the parasitic fetus took root, she could extinguish it immediately.

Yet, as Octavia stood amidst shadows inching toward dawn's nascent light, she was reluctant to inflict such harm upon herself. A startling realization washed over her: she required this child more than she dared acknowledge—not driven by any maternal instinct but fueled by bitterness toward Gabriel.

The concept of nurturing this nascent being transformed from an act of motherhood into a tool for vengeance—she would birth and offer up any living thing on the altar of revenge if it meant bringing her brother to his knees. "Let the Deep One bear witness," she whispered, her voice echoing in the silence, "The Red Fates will have their due. I will see him undone."

CHAPTER 3: SECRETS

Entangled within shadowy undergrowth stood a monstrous form with elongated limbs crowned by luminescence atop its misshapen ovoid head—a damp, formless skull caught in an eternal scream.

"Sounds like the boys are doing well," Cynthia observed, her words elongating into a languid drawl as a yawn tugged at the corners of her mouth. She nestled further into the blanket draped over her like a protective shield—likely the handiwork of Lenny, ever mindful of others' comfort—while sleep's beguiling lullaby had held her captive. The muted exchange between Ana and Malachi was an unexpected alarm clock, rousing her from dreamland.

Her gaze drifted towards the sun-dappled fields outside, where winter's vestiges still clung stubbornly to the landscape. Her thoughts wandered to her adopted son and his current whereabouts. A momentary frown creased her forehead until she caught sight of herself swaddled in woolen comfort, resembling an age-old matriarch adorned in traditional attire. With a grumble of mild outrage, she shrugged off the blanket and straightened up. "He didn't want to say hi?"

Ana turned around in the passenger seat to face Cynthia, offering a look of sympathy and regret. "Sorry, he didn't."

Cynthia's voice was laden with yearning as she responded. "He'll have to forgive me someday."

Ana nodded in agreement before turning back to face forward. She started to nod from the hum of the tires.

Lenny's question sliced through the quiet: "Speaking of giving someone the cold shoulder, you ever gonna call your shrink? If it's anything like a parole officer, those aren't calls you want to ghost."

Marrow. Damn it all. Ana flicked on her phone and thumbed through his most recent text—dispatched after a barrage of unanswered calls: I don't know where you are or why you're avoiding me, but I've reported you missing. Please, at least let me know you're alive. Instead of soothing her psychiatrist's mounting anxieties, she'd kept her phone off to thwart any potential tracking attempts. Evidently, they were being hunted, and none knew by whom. Now, the device's sole functions were receiving messages and maintaining a line of communication with Malachi—not that there were any other individuals she held in significant regard anyway.

Furthermore, something about Marrow felt off; his excessive readiness to write prescriptions and his fatherly demeanor were tainted by uncomfortably personal recollections. He'd never understood that her visions weren't mere hallucinations, and it irked her deeply. What if she'd encountered people like Lenny, Sue, and Cynthia earlier? Regrettably, Brock and Malachi's status as persons of interest meant they couldn't just jet off to Rhode Island without setting off a few alarms in some surveillance system. She also couldn't be sure if the same lethal hitmen who tried to kill her friends were lying in wait, her picture at the ready, to kill her at an airport terminal. A road trip appeared inevitable for each group until they found strength in numbers at Rhode Island. Perhaps she had something to occupy herself with...

As the truck droned along the highway, the mesmeric rhythm of tires against tarmac nearly coaxed Cynthia back into sleep's welcoming arms. But Ana's soft utterances, strangely ominous as an incantation, snapped her back into consciousness. Ana was hunched over something in her lap, whispering under her breath. The uncanny sound of fingers grazing over a papery surface set Cynthia's nerves on edge and sent shivers down her spine. Unable to endure the disconcerting noise any longer, she asked: "What are you up to?"

"Doing a bit of light reading from Mary's grimoire," Ana quipped, her silver-blue eyes dancing with mischief.

Cynthia bolted upright, her sharp features creasing in alarm. "You think that's safe? Hell, is it even wise?"

Ana offered an indifferent shrug. "So far, so good." She continued, a hint of amusement playing on her lips. "Besides, Malachi got a wealth of knowledge from H.P.'s journal, which is essentially what these spellbooks are: a hodgepodge of introspections, bizarre convictions, and trials." She paused before adding with a wry grin, "It's eerily similar to my thesis draft—utterly captivating."

"Fine," Cynthia conceded reluctantly. "Just tread carefully with that thing—it's dangerous."

"There might be some healing properties hidden within," Ana countered.

"How do you mean?"

"Were you aware Mary was battling cancer?"

"No! When did this happen?" As Cynthia uttered the words, a torrent of memories rushed back—each one thick with the stench of tobacco and riddled with forewarnings about Mary's lethal addiction.

"From the old diary, enclosed in brackets," Ana recited. "Just returned from my doctor's check-up. She's dumbfounded—so am I. The malignant growth has shrunk so much that it's invisible on their high-tech devices. But I felt it...this ease of a weight that had been crushing my chest. Each invocation of Cthugha brought it—a brilliance...a warmth. The compassionate heat of a deity who genuinely cares and heals...Christianity and its deceitful God...The apathetic spirits I've worshipped, oblivious to the ceaseless suffering of my people...I am more than obligated to protect these teachings—I feel driven to fulfill the divine will of the only true God...Now I understand why the American could let go of his biases and ignorance—they're insignificant, immature concepts. He must've perceived the pull of a holy duty and had been blessed by its touch. What comes after surpasses any trivial human disputes or grievances...Next time that shadowy being visits me, whispering, I won't merely chant its name—that name which had the power to cleanse my body of disease—I'll cling to every word it utters. Fuck the Great Spirit. All hail Cthugha."

Cynthia felt an icy shiver snake down her spine at the mere mention of such a cryptic entity. A bonfire, radiating warm orange light and showers of luminous sparks, painted an uncanny aureole around Mary as she relayed the story of the American's journey through Ojibwe territory, her voice adopting the mystical rhythm of a guiding shaman leading the dying author. Whenever Cynthia found herself tangled in the threads of that memory, she was thrust back into that creeping unease—like some invisible creature from the neighboring forest was scrutinizing their Halloween bonfires. Had there been whispers on the wind? A hissing rustle carried on the breeze? Gradually, Cynthia started to consider that there may have indeed been such sounds.

Ana continued: "She's got a boatload of entries like this right at the start. She keeps rambling about some notebook she used—the 'old diary,' I presume."

"Does she reference this shadowy being more?" Cynthia interjected.

"Shadow?" Ana echoed, rifling through a flurry of pages with a derisive arch of her eyebrow. "Ah yes, she harps on about it countless times...Where was it...Bingo! She believes it first appeared when her aunt passed away; that's when H.P.'s damned book came into her possession—"

In an instant, Ana's reality warped and writhed; one moment, she was ensconced in the safety of a car, her fingers dancing over ancient parchment; the next, she found herself anchored in a shadow-drenched bedroom that pressed in on all sides. She gripped the fragile hand of an elderly woman who was cold and slowly greening like corroded copper, her gaping face hidden behind an oxygen mask. An age-old tome sprawled across the rumpled blue sheets of what appeared to be her deathbed. The book radiated an aura potent with destiny; it was unmistakably H.P.'s testament. It held within its timeworn pages the life story and final edict of a witch's existence. A geas—a compulsory curse—had ensnared hapless Mary from the moment her skin brushed against its accursed surface.

Ana's consciousness hovered outside young Mary's body—drawn into this bygone reality—her gaze trailed Mary's to a window where they beheld a grotesque silhouette against the opaque glass. Is it just my reflection, distorted by tears? Mary pondered as she turned back towards her lifeless aunt and newfound burden.

Yet Ana held knowledge beyond this perception. With Owl's superior, otherworldly vision, she scrutinized the shadow until it emerged like a grisly pupae from gelatinous murk, revealing a Christlike figure that seemed ripped from his crucifixion, embodying both brilliance and malevolence. Entangled within shadowy undergrowth stood a monstrous form with elongated limbs crowned by luminescence atop its misshapen ovoid head—a damp, formless skull caught in an eternal scream. As this being ascended, light and smoke billowed around it like flame suddenly fed oxygen; Ana could sense its voracious desire to traverse through realities—from its abyssal origin into Mary's mind—to incinerate her with its splendor. Yet, this was merely a sliver of the entity's consciousness, a mere whisper from a larger, more sinister intellect. As if an unseen behemoth lurked somewhere beyond her perception—above and yet encircling the Earth—invisible but omnipresent. It was as though she stood on the shore of an unfathomable sea, catching sight only of the monstrous shadow beneath its surface while the true horror remained hidden in its depths. This grotesque phantom was but a spectral emissary of that incomprehensible cosmic leviathan.

Desperate to escape this appalling vision, Ana's consciousness recoiled from the entity. Her retreat was like a linebacker smashing through glass props, yet this tormentor, this figment of Cthugha, manifested itself in every subsequent dream. As an ethereal observer, she watched Mary glance over her shoulder in a grocery store, almost sensing the resonating shriek of the entity as it beckoned to her from behind the frosted glass sliders where the ice cream was kept. It made another attempt to seize Mary's attention on a roadside, its quivering, rubbery hands reaching out towards her speeding car amidst a spectral field ablaze with illusory apocalyptic flames—the conflagration it yearned to unleash upon this world.

Mary could only see an empty field and a distorted shadow resembling a scarecrow, which filled her with such dread that she floored the accelerator, screeching tires echoing behind her. The entity tried relentlessly to establish contact in most mundane public settings—a doctor's office, a recreation center, even during private moments—no place was safe from its psychic intrusion. Even when she sought refuge in places teeming with others or when she sat paralyzed by fear beside her oblivious sleeping partner, there was no respite.

Despite possessing an iron will forged by surviving childhood terrors, Mary felt herself crumbling under relentless pressure. Soon, she would capitulate, sobbing and pleading for solitude from whatever lurked in the shadows of dead stars, incessantly clamoring for her attention. When that moment finally arrived—with broken eggs and spilled milk pooling around her feet as groceries tumbled out of dropped bags—the monstrous deity rose ominously from the hollows of a dimly lit T-Mart parking lot, setting the world aflame with a kaleidoscope of fire. As it consumed her, she let out an agonizing wail—

"Fuck! Fuck! Fuck!" With a start, Ana hurled the book as if it had burst into a pyre in her hands. It skittered off the dashboard, crumpling into an unceremonious heap wedged between her knees on the worn rubber mat. Like a seasoned rally racer navigating a treacherous mountain pass, Lenny steered their vehicle with unruffled precision through three lanes of frenzied traffic before bringing them to an abrupt standstill at the roadside.

"Gotta treat this thing like it's packed with dynamite," Ana muttered.

Lenny's voice remained steady as he asked, "What did you see?" His pulse may have been spiked by adrenaline, but his tone betrayed no hint.

"It... An apocalyptic sunrise... A god." Ana shook her head fiercely, trying to scatter the jumbled thoughts that threatened to engulf her. "Cthugha...I caught a glimpse of him or some part of him. But there's no way that was all there is to him. He's colossal. It might've just been an echo or some underling... Whatever." Her words poured out in a flood of confusion and dread.

"The instant Mary touched Lovecraft's accursed book, it tormented her. It wormed its way into her mind, warped her reality, reduced her sanity to ashes. I can't even guess how much of Mary remains inside her head." She paused for breath before continuing in a more solemn tone.

"Malachi thinks we're fated to be foot soldiers in Cthugha's war," she said quietly. "But he's no benevolent deity looking out for humanity. I'm now convinced he's pure evil."

***

"Planning on finishing that?" Lenny's gruff voice cut through Ana's fog of thoughts, his broad hand indicating her neglected meal. The once steaming fries and Salisbury steak had cooled to a lukewarm mess, the meat marinating in its own gravy.

"What? Oh..." Ana blinked, yanked back into reality by the symphony of the crowded diner. The high-pitched pleas of clumsy children vied for attention against the tired sighs of their beleaguered parents. Her pale hand gripped her fork with such force it trembled, the utensil resembling more a weapon than an eating tool; her other clung desperately to her phone. She was torn between wanting to lash out or summon aid—an internal struggle that amplified her unease. But a chilling realization settled in: no cavalry was coming.

One cosmic tyrant expected her to set this world aflame while another... well, deciphering the Dark Mother's intentions was like trying to read smoke signals in a storm. This cryptic entity had been her guide through danger thus far; she seemed the lesser devil in this armageddon chess game. Regardless of where fate tossed her or what role she was scripted for, peace didn't seem to be part of the narrative ahead. Conflict and death were inevitable co-stars, and she would share top billing with Malachi, Brock, and a yet-to-be-revealed fourth player.

"It's gonna be alright," Lenny comforted around a mouthful of potatoes as he claimed her abandoned plate with a hunger that rivaled mythical beasts—he had an appetite that belied even his formidable size.

"Lenny..." Ana's gaze snapped up at him again, resulting in an involuntary gasp and dropping both fork and phone onto the table with a clatter. Holy crap! His eyes were as black as tar pits! After days of deceptive normalcy, she'd almost forgotten about his transformation—blessing or curse—during the surreal ritual in Mary's clandestine shrine. He seemed blissfully unaware of his otherworldly appearance, continuing his meal unperturbed.

"Lenny...close your eyes," she urged in a whisper.

"Close my eyes?"

"Now!" she repeated with an insistent edge as their rotund, middle-aged waitress, a spitting image of Mrs. Claus minus the red suit, ambled over with a coffee pot and a cheery smile.

"More java, lovelies?" the waitress chirped.

"I'm good," Ana managed to reply. Lenny finished rubbing his eyes. Ana sighed in relief as he met the waitress's gaze with warm hazel eyes and that lopsided grin that always sent butterflies fluttering in her stomach.

"Allergies," he offered as an explanation. "Yeah, you can top me up too."

"You want some pie, handsome? Peach cobbler, county's best."

"That sounds killer. Yeah, sure."

Once the waitress, her hips swaying like a pendulum, retreated from their table, Lenny shifted his gaze to Ana. "What was all that about?"

Ana braced herself for the inevitable fallout. "Your eyes did this...this abyss thing. Like you were some deep-sea creature or something. And it's not the first time either."

"Nope, it isn't."

"Wait...what?"

A few days prior, at a roadside motel, he'd caught an unsettling reflection of himself in the foggy bathroom mirror while wrestling with unsolicited thoughts about Ana: his eyes transformed into those of a marine beast from uncharted depths. He'd spotted those same obsidian orbs replacing his own on more than one occasion while driving, each time flicking his gaze between a slumbering Ana and the rearview mirror—her celestial beauty warranting every bit of safeguarding he could muster. Yet each occurrence seemed to vanish with a firm rub or blink—as if wiping away these sinister imprints—for now.

"I didn't want to freak you out," he admitted, spearing the final piece of Salisbury steak and consuming it whole like a constrictor snake would its prey. "You've got enough on your plate."

Ana extended her hand across the scarred tabletop, placing it gently on his wrist. "But something's going on with you."

"Nothing I can't handle."

"Anything else I should be aware of?"

Lenny's chewing slowed as he mulled over her inquiry. The transformation within him was subtle and menacing, so gradual that it slipped beneath his internal radar. He found himself stronger, faster, sharper; his senses heightened to an almost feline level—or perhaps akin to an apex predator like a lion. Sleep had become elusive; instead, he spent nights wide awake behind heavy drapes—attuned to insects scurrying within the walls or eavesdropping on hushed conversations of other motel dwellers. And when he concentrated, he could tune into one captivating rhythm: Ana's heartbeat, as fragile and enchanting as butterfly wings dancing in a breeze. It seemed no sound was now beyond his auditory grasp. Nor were scents. People emitted a kaleidoscope of odors, more complex than mere perfumes—an onion-like pungency of desire, a metallic whiff of anxiety, an innocent floral aroma akin to fresh blossoms. Their waitress was one such innocent.

As a man who'd been submerged in some unholy baptismal pool and brought back from the brink of death, it made perverse sense that he hadn't returned unscathed. But it wasn't the worst thing that had happened to him. If these peculiar abilities enabled him to protect Ana and guide her through their hellish journey—any sacrifice would be worth it.

Ana snapped her fingers before Lenny's glazed eyes.

"I'm good... Better than good," he said after shaking off his reverie. "Whatever happened, it's like an upgrade."

"Upgrade? What the Hell are you talking about?"

"Every sensation is amplified," Lenny explained, his eyes catching the dim light of their surroundings as he emphasized 'amplified.' Ana felt a chill creep down her spine. At least those eyes hadn't morphed into an inky black again. She mentally thanked whatever cosmic entity might be listening for such small favors. "Should we seek medical help? Consult a doctor, maybe?"

Their shared laughter echoed in the room, bouncing off the walls as they acknowledged the ludicrousness of her suggestion. No medical professional listed under 'physicians' in the phonebook would have any expertise on this particular predicament—unless they happened to also be practitioners of voodoo.

"But seriously, what's gnawing at you?" he probed.

As if to underline his casual attitude, he tossed a handful of fries equivalent to a baseball into his mouth, swallowing them whole without so much as flinching. His appetite was like a bottomless pit. He set his fork aside and rested his enormous arms on the table, hands standing tall and open. Ana let her fingers glide over his; Lenny's calloused palm was as reassuring and steady as bedrock.

"I'm at a loss," confessed Ana, her voice more composed than before. "Every route seems like it leads directly into disaster."

"I can handle it," Lenny responded with a self-assured grin.

"You ever navigated through Hell? Because that appears to be our GPS destination."

"I signed up for this knowingly."

"Do you really understand? We're still clueless about what's happening to you."

"Ever heard that old Native proverb, Ana? One stick breaks easily, but bind them together? They become unbreakable. You're not alone in this journey. I'm entwined in your chaos now, too. Maybe that's why I got my upgrade: to help you."

Images of the Dark Mother's chilling initiation of her ally played in Ana's mind. He'd been anointed for the mission like a knight chosen for a holy—or perhaps unholy—quest. Lenny's theory seemed the most likely explanation in this realm of twisted logic.

"Didn't mean to piss on your Valentine's parade," Cynthia's voice sliced through their intimate bubble, her form materializing at the edge of their table. She'd been a silent specter for a few heartbeats, ignored by the pair lost in each other's eyes. "Just finished exorcising the last remnants of that hellish Chinese takeout from yesterday—I can't fathom how you youngsters stomach it. I feel sorry for whoever is cleaning the toilets today. Anyway, time to hit the pavement."

"Your dessert, darling," Mrs. Claus interjected, expertly sidestepping Cynthia with an air of practiced grace.

"We'll snag it on our way out, thanks," Lenny responded smoothly. "And could we settle up?"

"Absolutely!" The waitress' reply rang out cheerily.

A shroud of discomfort descended upon them, muting conversation as Mrs. Claus scurried back and forth from the kitchen, eventually reappearing with a bag and bill. Lenny settled the tab, his generous tip instantly winning him favor in her eyes. As they exited, she waved them off from the doorway. "Watch yourselves! Storm's brewing up west," she called after them.

"Thanks for the heads-up, but east is our compass point," Lenny tossed back nonchalantly.

Ana halted mid-stride at his words. The wind seemed to tug at her soul as she turned towards it, her gaze drawn into the flickering grey curtain shrouding the pines beyond. A turbulent storm was churning in the west; her scalp prickled with static as if she were caught within those brooding clouds. Abruptly, she was disembodied and catapulted into this electrified maelstrom like a feather caught in a hurricane—hurtling towards an awe-inspiring golden glow pulsating in the distance.

Ana let out a sharp gasp as reality yanked her consciousness back into place. Lenny was there to steady her, his firm grip grounding her. An unearthly voice echoed through her very marrow, making her shiver in response.

West...Weapon...Find...Hurry, it whispered with chilling resonance. The Dark Mother's command faded into silence. She glanced up at Lenny, whose eyes had deepened to a stormy sea hue. But that was the least of her worries.

"I need to get Malachi on the line," she said urgently. "We've got a change of plans."

***

A sudden tremor of awareness rippled through Leng, jerking him upright in his seat. His gaze was magnetically drawn to the stark pallor of the moon, a spectral disc hanging ominously over the jagged silhouette of distant escarpments. It was akin to being laid bare under its ghostly glow as if an unseen and colossal raptor circled high above him. He froze momentarily, a rabbit caught in the talons of fear, wary that this celestial predator might single him out. The peculiar sensation receded as quickly as it had come, and Leng's tense muscles relaxed once more.

Steve Longfeather shot a sidelong glance at his enigmatic companion. "Everything okay?" His voice was laced with casual concern.

"I felt a disturbance in the weave," Leng replied obliquely.

"That worldwide webby thing you spoke about?" Steve often found himself playing detective with Leng's cryptic tidbits of wisdom, given that his otherworldly master wasn't exactly generous with explaining how to navigate existence as a demi-god in a world teeming with magic and hyper-technology.

"It is not merely a 'webby thing,'" Leng corrected him gently but firmly. "It is an etheric matrix pulsating with magical energy your former species has yet to fully comprehend or perceive. Every creature and object contributes either consciousness or patterned energy into one vast collective—accessible only to those capable of interpreting such frequencies."

Steve's mind flashed back to his high school football days when he'd taken a blow so severe it had necessitated multiple head scans for potential brain damage. "So...like an EEG result? Charting brain activity?"

Leng's austere expression softened minutely with approval. "Indeed, Earth could be seen as a sentient organism, and these pulses are akin to neural oscillations within this expansive consciousness. Given my spider-like nature, I perceive in threads; thus, I see larger patterns as webs—or a single web in this instance. Something stirred within this web; it is not the first time I sensed such potency."

"The incident back in South Dakota?" Steve ventured, his tone cautious.

"No, although similar. All magic wielders, beasts, and Godbeasts carry a unique energy signature. The entity in South Dakota felt elusive yet alluring, threading its way through the web like a..."

Leng's voice trailed off as he searched for the correct analogy. Drawing from his knowledge of mythology, Steve offered a suggestion. "Like a snake?"

"Indeed," Leng nodded gravely. "Precisely so. But with an aura of magic so profound, it could only belong to one type of being."

"One of these Aspects?"

"Snake. The South Dakota Aspect must surely be Snake, given that Raven and Wolf have already emerged from the shadows, their powers having brushed against mine in a chilling dance of fate. Owl remains a mystery, her essence alien to my senses. Although, I sense it is a *she*. Wise and all-seeing—she will undoubtedly be the most formidable amongst them. I suspect it was her presence I just felt: a supreme witch and Godbeast casting an immense eye across the fabric of existence, evoking the sense of being scrutinized by an omnipresent observer."

Leng's gaze was locked onto the war map, its intricate details multiplying with each passing second. His boundless intellect wove a tapestry from countless threads of destiny, chance, and circumstance. Raven and Wolf had ventured eastward, their power flaring in sporadic bursts of blinding intensity. Though Leng and his kin had halted their chase, such displays could attract other unwelcome entities. Yet, for now, at least, the pair seemed capable enough to hold their own; he could reasonably anticipate their survival until he and Steve secured the Atlantean relic and formed their cataclysmic alliance.

Should they fall prematurely, however, another Aspect within South Dakota would also be proficient in wielding Atlantean magic. A fresh complication materialized—Owl, the fourth Aspect, had surfaced and seemed set on heading westward.

Was Owl shadowing them? Could she, too, have knowledge about the divine weapon? Leng found himself grappling with this unforeseen twist.

His manipulation of the Aspects relied heavily on his ability to sway them with promises of Atlantean magic: I am your ally; I am here to assist you in conquering your foes.

Even if all four Aspects survived the world-shattering fusion until the final confrontation, they would require either the relic or similar aid to exist within the disintegrating penumbra cast by Cthulhu during that apocalyptic clash.

And despite currently slumbering, once roused, the Deep One would sense Leng's betrayal—regardless of its success—and unmake him as well. The stakes were not merely high; they teetered on the precipice of apocalypse.

A tremor coursed through Leng's form, yanking him from his contemplations. He retrieved his phone from his jacket pocket only to scoff at Gabriel's name displayed on it before tossing it into the backseat.

"Is that your old boss?" Steve inquired.

Leng's gaze was frigid. "A petty witch with delusions of grandeur. I have encountered many such men or manlike entities: beings who dare to provoke the dormant horrors only to be swallowed by their audacity."

"But isn't that what we're trying to pull off?" Steve asked, a hint of jest lurking in his voice.

For once, Leng found himself without an answer.

CHAPTER 4: BLOOD SEX MAGIC

The pair of remaining Godbeasts, garbed in their spectral white attire, perched ominously atop the violent sea of crimson waves.

"What's your verdict on the family we left with their car troubles?" queried Malachi, his emerald eyes sparkling with curiosity. Brock paused, his gaze roving across the animated campground like a hawk surveying its territory. A woman, picturesque in her denim overalls and autumnal red coat, was nestled under a tree, engrossed in a book as if she were an ethereal entity from an Impressionist painting. Usually, such tranquility would appeal to him. But today, the raucous laughter of a father at a nearby picnic table made him recoil as if he'd just heard the crack of a gunshot.

A stout brick edifice stood not far off. Sounds of human activity echoed through the air, along with the nauseating blend of stale urine and urinal cakes that mingled with the greasy smoke wafting from a food truck parked nearby. The cacophony and odors felt amplified; every nerve ending in Brock felt raw and exposed.

Beyond the asphalt circle and parked cars loomed trees encrusted with winter frost, their dark shadows forming prison bars against their trunks. A feeling of entrapment washed over him; people's presence wasn't comforting but somewhat claustrophobic. Scanning about twenty faces bundled up against the cold, sipping hot cocoa contentedly, he eyed them warily, expecting their smiles to twist into grotesque masks revealing cannibalistic teeth.

Malachi's touch grounded him—his slender hand had found Brock's in an unspoken reassurance. "Hard to say," he finally replied to their earlier encounter with an eccentric family. "But I've had this uneasy sensation since we ran into them. Ana did give us a heads-up."

"Are you worried?"

"Far from it."

"Not even an iota?"

"Nope."

"I trust you've got our backs, too." Malachi's smile radiated a warmth that outshone everything around them, making even the sun seem lackluster.

They squeezed each other's hands before letting go. Their bond was still undefined, and they needed to stay alert, knowing that unseen forces were against them.

Brock excused himself, retreating to discard their refuse and cleanse their cutlery within a dimly lit lavatory, its walls adorned with moss-hued ceramic squares. The meager repast had left an empty grumbling in his stomach—a grim reminder of their dwindling canned food supply. He received quizzical looks from men, which could be attributed as much to his wild appearance—days' worth of unshaved stubble, sweat-stained t-shirt, and grumpy aura—as to his makeshift dishwashing. Malachi always looked impeccable, while Brock felt he was becoming more feral by the minute. After drying the dishes under a hand dryer, he sniffed his pits to see if he passed the smell test but garnered another baffled look from a man who hurriedly exited the restroom.

For Malachi's sake, despite their dwindling finances, he decided they'd take a break tonight. On his way back, he bought a couple of water bottles for the road. Malachi was wrapping up a phone call when he returned to the table.

"Got it," said Malachi. "Thanks again for keeping us in the loop. Stay safe out there...and pass my regards to Cynthia." He ended the call before pushing his luck any further.

"Trouble brewing?" asked Brock.

"Nah," Malachi responded nonchalantly, "just an alteration in our course. Ana's heading west."

"And why would she do that?"

"She believes there's something significant waiting for her." He mind-whispered: A weapon.

A weapon? What sort?

Something super powerful. That Dark Mother—the entity guiding her—gave her some vision or directive. She's following that now; we'll catch up when we can, but Rhode Island is where we need to be—don't think doomsday will wait around.

Brock, a man who had wrestled with the wild and emerged victorious more times than he could count, held trust as a precious commodity. His circle of confidence was small, reserved for Malachi, and recently expanded to include Ana. The idea of entrusting his life to an enigmatic entity, no matter how seemingly benevolent, was laughable to him. He'd danced on the razor's edge of mortality too often to be so naive. Except for Charlie...Charlie had been different. Once upon a time, Brock had willingly placed his existence in Charlie's calloused hands, knowing full well that trust was as brittle as human life itself.

Lately, memories of Charlie seemed to echo around him like phantoms in the dark. It felt like his old mentor was still with them on this treacherous journey, perhaps guiding them from beyond the veil, much like Ana's unseen guardian.

"Some good news coming our way," Malachi declared, his lanky form unfolding with an effortless grace as he rose from his seat. "Ana just transferred some funds into a new account I set up." The IDs Robert provided are solid gold, he shared through their mental link. "Tonight, we dine like royalty, wash off the stink of the road, and sleep on something other than car seats!"

Brock's response lacked Malachi's enthusiasm; he still felt the prickling sensation of being hunted even if their pursuers remained shadows at the edge of perception.

"Sounds good. Let's get moving," Brock said tersely before they retraced their steps back to their vehicle.

In no time, their Hummer rumbled down a gravel path that snaked through the dense woodland towards a strip of highway. As the sun surrendered to twilight's reign, a polished cobalt sedan gracefully glided into the parking lot. A couple of striking appearances and their child emerged, dressed as if they were about to grace the cover of a winter fashion magazine. Yet, despite their coordinated attire, an icy aloofness hung between them like a frost-laden breath in winter air. They moved independently of each other after casting dismissive looks upon those idling aimlessly nearby.

The father sauntered towards the men's restroom but refrained from using it, instead choosing to run his fingers along the rim of a forsaken sink. The mother drifted towards a food truck to order hot chocolates, her fingertips dancing on the counter in an intricate pattern as though she was deciphering hieroglyphics etched onto its surface. Their peculiar offspring scampered off towards an abandoned picnic table and clambered atop it with arms outstretched as if imitating Icarus preparing for flight—her tiny hands tracing over its weather-worn grain.

"N, come here," came her mother's urgent call. The child hopped down from her perch and dashed back, their unusual behavior observed by a woman engrossed in her novel beneath an oak tree's shade. Despite being bundled up in her coat, she felt a chill creep down her spine as she wondered if the suspenseful narrative she was engrossed in had begun to warp her perception of reality.

As this trio—Godbeasts hidden under mortal guises—lingered at the heart of this common rest area, unease rippled through the crowd. Like animals sensing an approaching storm, they began gathering their belongings and retreating hastily. Even the food truck shuttered its windows without sparing a glance at its cash register before speeding away from the scene.

In mere minutes, only these Godbeasts remained, savoring their hot chocolates beside their vehicle. "Quite delightful," Trophonius commented with a nod of approval. "I believe they've used authentic cocoa."

Necromanteon smacked her lips in contemplation. "I would prefer the tang of blood."

"You should savor it," Pythia counseled gently. "In no time at all, this mortal realm and all human accomplishments, whether trivial or grandiose, will crumble into nothingness." She paused before adding thoughtfully, "We just missed them."

"Indeed," Trophonius echoed solemnly.

"Indeed," Necromanteon concurred.

Pythia contemplated the energy humming between them—a potent residue of divine power that had been palpable during Trophonius's investigation. She and Necromanteon had felt remnants of other Aspects' power radiating from the food truck and picnic table —an indication that they were awakening to their powers almost entirely. The scarlet aura lingering around their pit stop and an intense sensation swelling within her chest hinted at a possible explanation: they were either lovers or deeply in love—a powerful catalyst but also a vulnerability.

"Did you sense their ardor?" she queried. "A flame as fierce as Prometheus's fire."

"Unresolved, like a bull's tension during rutting season," Trophonius responded. "Even Aphrodite might fail to quench such desire."

The mention of Aphrodite stirred within them a wistful nostalgia, an ache for their species' glorious past now entombed in the annals of history. Once, they were revered as the mighty Greek pantheon, now reduced to mere echoes shrouded by countless epochs of oblivion.

Their hearts throbbed with longing for that golden age when witches would sway under moonlit skies in communion with cosmic horrors or when innocent maidens were offered at their feet as vessels for unions beyond mortal comprehension. They reminisced about those days when they were puppeteers manipulating mankind's fate, reigning supreme amidst blood-drenched festivities and power struggles that shook the very foundations of existence.

As the trio of Godbeasts—Pythia, Trophonius, and Necromanteon—delved into the depths of their memories, a tumultuous sea of emotions stirred within them. Visions from epochs long past seeped into their consciousness—the opulence of Dionysian revelries where mortal worshippers drowned in rivers of wine and waves of ecstasy; the brutal clashes waged in Ares' honor where valiant warriors surrendered their lives to quench his unending desire for strife; or even the hushed murmurs that echoed within Athena's marble sanctuaries as scholars sought enlightenment from these perceived deities.

Their corporeal forms, tangible yet spectral, were often misconstrued. Humans, with their finite understanding of celestial workings, venerated them as true Gods. Yet, they bore a closer resemblance to the Nephilim from Christian lore—hybrid progeny birthed from the divine and earthly coupling. Much like countless pagan narratives interwoven into humanity's collective psyche, the truth about their origin was veiled by Judeo-Christian reinterpretations. The complex intricacies of their history remained cloaked in an enigma—warped shards of myth concealing an incomprehensible reality.

No matter how much they yearned for those halcyon days, they knew that Cthulhu would unleash an apocalyptic surge that would bar them from reclaiming their erstwhile glory. It appeared inevitable that Cthulhu would claim victory in this iteration of the Eternal Game—he commanded more pieces on his side.

As they ruminated over their faded youthfulness, the fervent tempest left in the wake of the Aspects sparked a concept in their minds—an idea potent enough to alter fate's course. Just as they had once incited bloody frenzies amongst their followers eons ago, this untamed energy could be harnessed as a weapon. They could conjure a haze of desire to easily delude and annihilate the Aspects.

United, they let out a communal sigh, a symphony of stress release. In unison, they emptied their drinks and discarded the barren vessels onto the soil with an air of closure. "A magnificent notion," Pythia proclaimed, her voice reverberating with the shared comprehension that flowed between them like splayed tarot cards—their path was chosen.

"A bacchanalian enchantment," Necromanteon suggested, her words tinged with an undercurrent of macabre pleasure.

"An epilogue steeped in sensual indulgence and decadence," chimed in Trophonius, notorious for directing the most blood-drenched, enduring orgies amongst them; grand spectacles that spanned months until the final depleted participant, smeared in bodily fluids and gore, exhaled their last breath.

"I envision no more dignified departure from this realm," Pythia agreed solemnly.

Their laughter echoed ominously as they re-ascended into their conveyance, minds scheming the ideal setting for their lethal trap.

***

Though seasoned by the allure of Canada's untamed vistas, the Appalachian Plains unfurled a virginal vitality before them. It was a sprawling tapestry of wilderness that seized their breath in its grandeur. Brock, his window cracked open, found his senses ensnared by the symphony of life thriving within this verdant cradle. His flaring nostrils and twitching ears bore testament to his keen awareness of every rustle and scent carried on the wind's whisper.

Often, he surrendered himself to the simple pleasure of earthy pine aroma, a soothing balm that eased their flight from unseen threats lurking in their wake. Of all the States they had crossed, this one whispered promises of sanctuary to his road-weary soul.

Then, like an oasis shimmering amidst desert dunes, the radiant sign for Grand Plains Hotel pierced through the endless greenery. Their SUV veered onto an on-ramp and spiraled up through manicured pines before merging into a line of vehicles clamoring for entrance into an already congested parking lot.

"Planning on becoming part of our little community?" The query came from a man who resembled an antiquated puppet draped in a uniform adorned with gold filigree over blood-red fabric. He peered out from his kiosk at Brock as they pulled up.

"Maybe just one night." Brock cast a sidelong glance at Malachi, who was practically glued to the passenger window, eyes wide with wonder at the sight of the imposing chateau-style fortress before them. Its skeletal wooden frame peeked out beneath stone layers while large windows garbed in crimson drapes observed them like vigilant guardians. The place looked plucked straight from some tech mogul's fever dream. "Or two," he added after a beat.

"You're in for quite an adventure," assured the attendant with an intriguing gleam in his age-weathered eyes.

Brock quirked an eyebrow, pondering if the man's words held a hidden warning. The attendant looked old enough to be a relic from the prohibition era, his mind possibly adrift in senility's foggy labyrinth. Surely, there was no veiled threat. "Great, thanks. What's the cost?"

"Fifteen dollars per night," the man replied with nonchalance. "They'll add it to your tab. Just need some ID."

The exchange went without a hitch; ID for a ticket—one Brock was told to display on his dash.

"Did you know they have an Olympic pool here?" Malachi suddenly piped up, pulling his gaze away from the window and waving his phone around—the hotel's Travelmania listing still displayed on its screen. His cheeks were flushed with excitement as he grinned at Brock. "And you're going to love this—all-you-can-eat buffet included!"

Brock couldn't help but chuckle at Malachi's infectious enthusiasm. Despite everything, there was still room for simple joys—like an unlimited buffet after days on the road.

A sudden thrill shot through Brock like the spark of a flint against steel. He responded by pressing the accelerator, propelling their vehicle forward. The gatehouse attendant, an awkwardly janky figure, descended from his perch with a wave goodbye, causing a ripple of annoyance among the queue of waiting drivers. To Brock, there was something oddly marionette-like about the man's movements, as if unseen strings guided him. Shaking off this curiosity, he refocused on finding a parking spot in the rapidly filling lot.

Amongst a hive of glossy black buses teeming with athletic youths and spry women sporting varsity jackets and sweaters, Brock deduced that some were likely sports teams en route to matches or tournaments. A stark contrast to this youthful exuberance was offered by navy-blue double-decker buses marked 'Vanlines Voyages,' disgorging groups of elderly Asian tourists who moved slowly under the weight of their luggage while enthusiastically capturing every mundane detail with their cameras. It hit Brock then— they had arrived in the throes of rush hour.

Brock managed to wedge their bulky vehicle between two almost comically small sportages before he and Malachi stepped out into a gentle snowfall. As someone attuned to nature's cycles, he felt winter's frosty touch finally claiming its reign. They fetched their bags from the back seat and hurried across the lot towards an imposing flagstone staircase leading up to revolving glass doors.

Stepping inside revealed an opulent lobby where brass trolleys navigated by valets in crimson uniforms zipped across polished marble floors. Hidden behind tall log pillars were cozy lounges featuring crackling fireplaces and plush couches—the faint scent of cigar smoke reaching Brock from these secluded corners.

The place was a stunning blend of rustic charm and dizzying luxury—blood-red carpets stretched out across the floor; stag heads, mounted birds, and even life-sized bear taxidermy decorated the walls, while numerous gold-framed landscapes provided a visual guide to Ohio's diverse ecosystems. It was clear that no effort or expense had been spared in pampering their transient guests.

A friendly receptionist beckoned them from behind an intricately carved wooden desk. Even the cash registers were cleverly disguised as antique models, hiding modern screens from the customer's view.

"This place is bloody brilliant," Malachi mused aloud.

"Looks like it'll bleed us dry," Brock countered.

Malachi rolled his eyes. "Travelmania rated it five stars."

Brock wasn't exactly fluent in the language of star ratings for accommodations, but he understood enough to know it meant a hefty price tag. Even with Ana's generous addition of cash to their joint account, he was wary about spending half of it on a few nights' stay.

"C'mon, don't be such a miser." Malachi nudged him forward. You only live once, right? And who knows how much time we've got left?

"Alright," Brock relented without much conviction. But Malachi remained undeterred; the promise of crisp linens and luxurious care stirred his cosmopolitan sensibilities.

As they moved towards the counter, they became magnets for attention. The whispered exchanges among clusters of cheerleaders and their obvious interest in him and Malachi made Brock uncomfortable under this almost invasive scrutiny. A potent scent wafted over him then—a mix as intoxicating as an alchemist's blend of rare Eastern spices—that teased at his senses and seeped into his awareness. It smelled both strangely familiar yet frustratingly elusive—like a word forgotten yet lingering on the tip of one's tongue. Each breath was like navigating through an ancient spice market under the watchful gaze of a crimson sun.

Echoing through the lobby, the world music's rhythmic pulse, a Grecian chant spun into a serene lullaby, wrapped around him like the comforting embrace of an old friend. Each note held its own narrative—a sorrowful dirge reverberating from the heart of ancient caves, a jubilant hymn riding on the back of Aegean winds, a soft murmur from moonlit olive groves. The melody lulled him into a trance, akin to the hypnotic dance of waves kissing the shore in an eternal waltz with time. His supernatural senses, however, failed to decipher this intoxicating aroma or dissect why the music was so unsettlingly captivating. This left him adrift in a sea of perplexing uncertainty, his mind teetering on the edge between fascination and apprehension.

"Brock," Malachi's voice echoed, "we need to settle our tab."

"Huh?" He hadn't realized he'd lost himself in thought.

"The lady was kind enough to accept my driver's license instead of credit card collateral. We still owe her for our stay."

A sense of uncanny familiarity washed over Brock as he took in their hostess: her sapphire eyes were enigmatic riddles; her cheeks bore aristocratic angularity; obsidian curls spilled from beneath her hat—the very image of timeless allure. His gaze hovered momentarily over the valley between her breasts where a golden chain cradled a heavy medallion or locket. Yet it was her voice—a sultry symphony that defied geographical placement—that jolted him out of his reverie as she announced: "Two nights in our honeymoon suite—"

"Wait... honeymoon what?" Brock interrupted, confusion threading through his tone.

She gestured around the room with dismissive elegance that spoke volumes about her refined sophistication. "We're rather fully booked at present," she explained with an air of strained patience. "You appeared out of nowhere without a reservation. But you're not obliged to stay...you could always try elsewhere..."

Brock's attention was drawn to the entrance, its sturdy frame trembling under the sudden assault of a storm that had swallowed the hotel with disturbing speed. The tempest seemed almost summoned by some malevolent entity. Valets struggled against the chaos, attempting to herd wobbly luggage carts and confused patrons into some semblance of order. Bum-bada-bum-bada-bum. Their frantic efforts mirrored the pulsing rhythm of the subdued symphony playing in the background.

A sharp pain stabbed through Brock's head. Was it exhaustion? During nocturnal hours, he usually pretended to sleep, his mind either gnawed by worry for Malachi or vigilantly watching over him during his restless slumber.

"It doesn't look like you'll be leaving anytime soon," commented their hostess, her name reduced to a single letter "P," embossed on a golden pin above her generous bosom.

"Brock," Malachi said, curtly, "can you handle the bill?"

"Sure thing," Brock responded, turning back towards their hostess. "How much are we talking here?"

"One thousand, two hundred and fifteen dollars, and eighty-eight cents."

"Holy hell," Brock exclaimed.

Malachi blushed at Brock's outburst, but before further embarrassment could ensue, Brock settled their dues promptly. Two keycards encased in luxurious gold-leaf paper slips were placed on the counter along with a brochure filled with images depicting opulent lifestyles—a clear bait for additional expenditure during their stay.

Room. Shower. Buffet. Room again—they would stick strictly to this frugal plan if they hoped to survive this place without entirely draining Ana's generous contribution.

"Mud wrap?" Malachi pondered, his eyes scanning the glossy pages of the brochure. Brock pivoted on his heel, eyeing the elevator's glowing call button.

"One moment, please," P cut in smoothly, her hand disappearing beneath the counter to retrieve an ornate clamshell walkie-talkie. A tall man emerged from some hidden corner of the lobby; his grim attractiveness was offset by an air of familiarity that made Brock's skin tingle with unease. The man's face was difficult to discern behind tinted glasses and a chauffeur's cap, leaving Brock unable to place him fully.

The stranger delicately balanced two crystal flutes filled with champagne on the counter—each topped with a single floating rose petal—and bowed before melting back into obscurity.

"Compliments of your suite," P offered nonchalantly. "Not implying anything about your sleeping arrangements, but it's part of our Honeymoon package."

Malachi claimed his glass without hesitation, picking out the rose petal to chew on before taking a hearty sip. He slid the second flute across to Brock, who eyed it warily.

"When in Rome," Malachi proposed with a smirk, clinking their glasses together.

P rolled her eyes at their exchange as she returned her attention to her monitor.

Brock sighed reluctantly and downed his champagne in one gulp—including swallowing the flower petal—setting down his empty glass just in time to catch sight of an odd scene: a petite figure in white strolling along the dimly lit corridor where elevators chimed. Bizarrely enough, she appeared to be trailed by a goat.

By the time he'd processed what he'd seen—or thought he saw—Malachi was already headed towards another set of elevators. When Brock looked back again, only Chinese tourists and admiring glances from women and envious men remained.

You should be jealous, he thought, his focus returning to Malachi. I'm with the most beautiful creature in the world.

Malachi caught the sentiment and responded with a knowing smirk. The background music swelled, harmonizing into a vibrant crescendo; the lights intensified, bathing everything in vivid colors; a searing heat kindled within Brock's core. He wondered if tonight might finally offer an opportunity to quench that relentless flame. With determination, he grasped Malachi's hand and led him towards the awaiting elevator.

Once the Aspects had vanished, Trophonius materialized again, his towering form casting an ominous shadow over Pythia. With a fluidity that spoke of centuries-old practice, Pythia extricated herself from the stiff confines of her role at the reception desk. She invited Trophonius to share the remaining drops of champagne—the bottle still untouched from her meticulous preparations for the Aspects' arrival. The clamor of pleas for lodging and other essentials was delegated to their human underlings as they dismissed the persistent throng.

"That proceeded with less resistance than I foresaw," he admitted in a voice that echoed with ancient authority.

"Their divine essence is still unrefined, lacking discernment," she retorted, her words laced with timeless wisdom. "The haunting melodies, fragrant incense, and enchantments that pervaded our sanctuaries are potent snares for any mortal—or Godbeast."

"I harbor no doubts about your capabilities, but will it be enough?" he queried as his hand traced a path down her spine in an intimate gesture.

"Pomegranate, celeriac, hemlock, and a hint of something extraordinary," Pythia responded cryptically. Her knowledge of age-old brews was unrivaled by any mortal or supernatural alchemist. From her stronghold in Delphi, she and her coven concocted potions reminiscent of Hellenic times: elixirs facilitating communion with spirits, mercury-infused draughts bestowing longevity, blood-frenzy brews transforming warriors into relentless berserkers even after their hearts had ceased beating.

Regrettably, these wonders had faded into obscurity. All her Pythia—women she had chosen for their extraordinary foresight and nurtured as if they were her own progeny—had either fallen during the Roman invasions or chosen death by drowning over violation and murder. Yet, she had survived this cataclysm and salvaged a fragment of celestial marvel: an ancient glass vial stained yellow with age, filled with a luminous crimson liquid.

As she touched her amulet, envisioning the tiny vessel concealed within, her mind wandered to the thought that this was all that remained of the mighty Aphrodite, the Godbeast of Love; that one day, she too might be reduced to nothing more than a smear of blood or a fleeting memory.

"What delightful sorrow," Trophonius murmured. He wrapped his arms around her from behind, their bodies swaying in sync. The oblivious human crowd failed to perceive them—mortal minds instinctively recoiling from acknowledging supernatural truths. But soon enough, these flesh-bound souls would be confronted with the awe-striking terror of the Godbeasts who once ruled over mankind's ancient civilizations. Their quaint haven would soon morph into an orgy of violence, desire and sorcery.

"Aphrodite's blood is the world's most potent aphrodisiac," Pythia mused aloud. "I remember how her Roman violators transformed into self-devouring cannibals after tasting it. I doubt my addition of hemlock will do more than sedate them; however, Aphrodite's blood should achieve our goal: intoxicate them and make them susceptible to the Feast. If they don't consume each other first, they'll embrace our blades and fangs as eagerly as sacrificial virgins on our altars. I've also poisoned the carafes in the café—I expect quite a spectacle come dinner time."

"Excellent," Trophonius responded with a predatory grin—a chilling display of gleaming white teeth and raw hunger.

***

Brock, his form quivering under a disquieting heat, fumbled with the lock. His body vibrated from head to toe, and the once steady rhythm of his predator's intuition became an erratic pulse. Despite his formidable tolerance for alcohol, he found himself mirroring the fleeting disorientation of drunkenness.

Once inside the opulent suite, he bolted towards the washroom, dousing his fevered face in icy water. As he met his own gaze in the mirror, a hollow echo of hunger staring back at him—a hunger he knew all too well—made him decide more cold water was necessary.

"I need a shower!" His voice ricocheted off the marble walls as Brock discarded his clothes hastily, catching sight of his own muscular reflection—a primal beast stirred by desire—and hurried into a lavish standing sauna large enough for several occupants—a thought he swiftly pushed aside.

Perched on a marble ledge while frigid droplets assaulted him from every direction, Brock's skin still smoldered beneath the icy barrage. The sensation was odd but not unfamiliar—it reminded him of being tempered steel undergoing its final refinement until he wrestled control over these base impulses under the relentless cascade.

Emerging from this meditative state, Brock saw himself anew: a weapon with duties that could not be forsaken. Drying off and slipping back into his pants, he scrutinized himself in the mirror—his wildness seemed somewhat tamed now.

Stepping out into an extravagant modern chamber, a golden trolley laden with spirits beckoned dangerous indulgences, as did an enormous bed adorned with plush pillows and ostentatious silks whispering promises of decadence. The storm outside swathed everything in its pristine whiteness; light spilled through panoramic windows, illuminating every corner of the room.

Like some predatory creature stalking its prey, Brock moved across plush carpeting that teased his bare feet like a lover's touch. His arousal surged with each step closer to Malachi, who stood, entranced by the storm. An almost magnetic force threatened to draw him into an embrace as Malachi's shoulders tensed in anticipation. But Brock, bound by duty and honor, resisted this potent gravitational pull. He clenched his fists and chose to stand beside his comrade—his friend, his battle-brother.

What is this consuming passion that threatens my self-control? And what is this peculiar sensation? Why does the strange melody from below seem to resonate through the floor and into my skull?

As Malachi turned towards him, locking him in a mesmerizing gaze of emerald flames, his lips glistening crimson as if freshly kissed by blood, all questions were silenced.

"Your chest," Malachi's voice echoed, his hand settling on the rhythmic fortress of muscle guarding the heart he'd claimed. The compulsion to touch him was a relentless prickle beneath his skin.

"We shouldn't—"

"Hush."

"Malachi, something's not right—"

"Silence."

A sudden feral strength surged from Malachi, gripping Brock by the shoulders and hurling him onto the plush carpet. He descended on Brock, one hand pinning him down while the other clawed at his shirt. Brock lay beneath him, playing defenseless, although he could have easily overpowered him.

Then, like a jarring climax in an orchestra of insanity, chilling chimes and chants slithered into earshot, coiling around his spine like a lascivious serpent. It squeezed blood into his thighs, groin, and head—each pulse a symphony of torment and delight.

All prior impressions of Malachi—their nebulous camaraderie and his promise of unwavering protection—dissipated into a haze of carnal desire. A primitive urge to devour him whole seized Brock's thoughts. He had once said: I could...eat...you...up. He now pondered on the flavor of Malachi's flesh and how it would respond to the forceful impact of his bite.

Blood. Sex. Penetration. Carnage. The demonic melody whispered lewd suggestions into his ears as Malachi squirmed above him—heaving heavily, saliva dripping from his mouth—appearing ready for any beastly game that played in Brock's mind.

Yet it was this brutal contrast—the thought of harming this being he loved—that dismantled the repugnant magic. He roared, "No!" His dormant strength stirred awake, grappling Malachi by his wrists and flipping him over. The demonic laughter from his possessed friend further eroded the spell.

His rejection of the magic ushered in a realization of the sickening lust that swirled within him. Brock staggered off Malachi—who continued to moan and touch himself— trying to reach the bathroom but instead crashed into the couch, heaving violently. What spewed out was a red liquid, shimmering like molten rubies.

The expulsion left him feeling better, sore and raw inside, but once more in control. Wiping his mouth clean, he stumbled back towards Malachi, pulling him upright before he could finish unbuttoning his pants.

"Fuck me...Eat me," he wailed in an obscene cry akin to a lascivious banshee.

A ferocious slap across the face from Brock echoed through Malachi, eliciting a low groan from his lips. The force of the blow momentarily stunned him into submission. Brock seized this opportunity and dragged Malachi towards the washroom with an iron grip. Without any gentleness, he clamped his hand on the back of Malachi's skull, tilting it over the sink.

Brock forced two fingers into Malachi's still babbling mouth in a violent demonstration of power. A beastly instinct took over Malachi as he bit down hard on Brock's fingers, aiming to sever them. But Brock's fingers were like tempered steel; they held their ground against Malachi's futile attempts.

Soon enough, a torrent of bile erupted from within Malachi, spewing into the basin like some abhorrent creature being expelled from its host. When the retching subsided, sobs started to wrack Malachi's body. Brock held him silently for a moment before pulling away—anger simmering beneath his calm exterior. He wiped off Malachi's face with a hand towel and looked at him with an affectionate gaze reserved only for him.

Malachi's breath hitched, his gaze drawn to the grotesque residue in the sink. A single, partially digested petal floated in the sludge, an unwelcome interloper in a sea of revulsion. "What just happened?" He managed to choke out.

"Dark sorcery... poison." Brock's response cut through the air, as crisp and unyielding as the man himself. Anger simmered beneath his words but didn't mar their clarity. "I think we've expelled it."

Brock's thoughts raced back to their recent encounter—the woman and possibly the man who had served them those cursed drinks. The recollection of three strangers and their blue vehicle clung to his memory, bitter and unshakable, as a sudden understanding washed over him. One detail emerged starkly from the rest—the woman's lips, consistent in every memory, even when winter attire had obscured her features during their first meeting; lips that were both enthralling yet foreboding, akin to the puzzling 'P.' It dawned on him then: the roadside trio were likely two of the same individuals who had handed them those ominous beverages at the hotel.

"We need to get the fuck out of here," Brock announced suddenly, his voice echoing with urgency. "We've walked straight into a trap laid by those three we crossed paths with earlier."

Malachi's gaze skated towards the exterior, where a snowstorm battered against the glass barriers. I could try to teleport us directly to our vehicle. His thought tapered off into ambiguity, his mind still clouded from the residual poison of that otherworldly venom. He was no Brock in wielding his abilities; his powers were more reflexive than deliberate—protective barriers erected in the face of peril. A stab at exact magic could terminate unpredictably and disastrously.

Brock, however, had another plan brewing.

No, he rumbled within Malachi's mind. The tables have turned now. They are the ones who should be running from us.

***

Barely pausing to shrug into their abandoned garments, they shouldered their bags; Brock with his weighty duffle and Malachi his snug carryall, harnessed like soldier's rucksacks with straps wrapped around each shoulder. They found themselves confronting the door, its frame awash in a malignant crimson radiance, underscored by an eerie orchestra of jingling tambourines and plaintive strings. The walls around this egress quivered like sentient membranes, barely veiling the nightmarish entities lurking just beyond their tiny haven. Another heartbeat spent under this grotesque distortion of reality might have seen them swallowed whole.

Brock, whose perception stretched beyond that of his companion's, harbored a handful of hypotheses about what the shadowy figures and nauseatingly moist sounds— the gasping wheezes and terrified screams echoing throughout the hotel—could imply: monsters, carnal acts, murder...and more perverse enchantments.

"What in God's name is out there?" Malachi demanded.

Brock clasped Malachi's hand in his own and tightened his grip reassuringly. "We sprint straight for the lobby and head for the car. Anything tries to stop us—I'll smash its face, and you can toss them aside with your magic."

"I'm not entirely certain it functions that way, but... okay," Malachi conceded with visible apprehension. Sensing Malachi's fear pulsating through their intertwined fingers, Brock squeezed again. When that didn't seem sufficient, he gently turned Malachi towards him. Overwhelmed by an instinct to protect, he wiped away a smear of blood or possibly tainted wine from his friend's cheek using a thumb moistened with saliva. His hand lingered on warm honey-hued skin as he found himself entranced by eyes as deep and captivating as a woodland horizon aglow with moonlight.

Brock was struck by how undeniably enchanting Malachi was, in body, mind, and soul—how absurd it felt to have denied or resisted this truth. He refused to accept that their narrative would conclude here, yet the accumulating evidence of deadly confrontations suggested otherwise. Just days prior, they had narrowly evaded death at the hands of super soldiers. Now, they were ensnared in a cosmic nightmare with unknown threats still prowling outside their door. The mastermind behind these assaults remained a mystery.

Brock often retreated into bravado because faith was all he possessed. But each violent surprise eroded his resolve. What if he perished without revealing to Malachi how deeply significant these shared experiences had been? He'd never felt—

"I think I love you, too," interrupted Malachi.

Brock's heart surged as he smiled, drawing Malachi into his protective hold. For a moment, they breathed heavily, the harsh reality of their predicament momentarily eclipsed by the warmth of their shared bond. Hell might have been hammering on their door, but within was a sanctuary of bliss. Their lips grazed each other's, and their hands found familiar places around their waists and backs until finally—after an eternity—they kissed.

Transitioning from the ethereal to the ordinary was a slow, hazy journey. Their bodies untwisted from the intricate tapestry of tongues, mouths, and limbs they had spun together. They found themselves sprawled on the carpet. The details of their descent from an upright stance were lost in the fog of shared passion, including Brock's gentle guiding of their entangled forms to the ground. Yet, they could vividly recall the tempestuous undercurrents that had swept through their consciousness, the sensation of moving within and alongside another soul.

Every now and then, a physical echo would intrude upon this spiritual ballet: a rough graze of stubble whispering tales of Malachi's lover's ruggedness or the scent of feathers and sage—nature in its most primal state—lifting Brock to euphoric heights. Their flesh-and-blood selves seemed almost inconsequential in this communion. It was an intimate act stripped of base carnality, a moment frozen in time where they reveled in each other's luminescence and danced with it.

However, reality took on a grotesque hue, shrouded in ominous shadows. Indeed, malevolent entities lurked nearby, soon to make their terrifying presence known.

Brock disentangled himself from his delicate partner and extended a helping hand to him. Their hearts pounded against one another as if threatening to surrender once more to an insatiable craving for unity.

"Damn," Brock managed to articulate, encapsulating their ineffable bliss.

Malachi grinned. "I think you're underselling it slightly."

"That's some dangerous territory we're treading."

"You got that right."

A bone-chilling howl echoed from one of the neighboring rooms; their joy receded but lingered as a warm ember nestled beneath their ribcages. Malachi made a silent vow never to let that spark fade away. He would resist anyone who dared attempt to snuff it out. Observing the hardening determination etched on Malachi's face, Brock, too, felt a tingling sensation spreading across his chest and scalp. This electric charge deepened his companion's eyes from a vibrant green to an abyssal black. It was not alarming; it was as if everything had fallen into place. The Raven he had journeyed with in the spirit realm had finally joined him for the hunt in this world.

In tandem, his own Wolf spirit, a formidable force he usually kept leashed, was needed now more than ever. Today, Brock unbarred the cage doors and let the beast surge. He surrendered to its primal power; fire ignited in his eyes, and a golden aura sparked around his torso, forming a radiant halo.

"I reckon we're ready," he announced, his voice more like a growl than human speech.

"We are," Malachi affirmed resoundingly.

Brock swung the portal wide, ushering them into an abyss painted in shades of blood and horror. Their arcane bond held them steady, unflinching in the face of the grisly distortion of reality that unfolded before them: walls shimmered with a sickening slickness, as thin as jellyfish skin and traced with black veins; disembodied whispers echoed from unseen horrors; discordant notes from a ghostly orchestra filled the air. The sight of a man half-engulfed by a creeping flesh-moss, suspended from sinewy tendrils, eyes bulging grotesquely from his partially devoured skull like some forgotten feast of an ancient Venus flytrap, failed to ignite fear within these stalwart Aspects. From his mouth spilled crimson blossoms in an intricate tangle that mirrored his own tortured existence. Similar floral displays hung from mounds or figures that might once have been human, sprouting from random doorways along this nightmarish hallway—forced open by swollen roots of the pink infestation smothering each entrance.

Malachi grimaced at the uncanny resemblance between this parasitic flora and the petal he'd previously coughed up. He envisioned amorous souls staggering into these rooms, tearing at clothing or sinking teeth into each other's flesh—as Brock had nearly done—and understood the depth of debauchery and terror they'd stepped into. Brock bit back any comment on the stench beneath the cloying perfume of flowers: a repugnant cocktail of overripe sweat, semen's acrid bite, and metallic blood—an ocean's worth. A fine mist of pollen danced in the air like fairy dust.

Brock quickly ripped off part of his shirt to fashion makeshift masks for him and Malachi. "Here," he grunted.

Malachi noticed something only because Brock pointed it out to him—a faintly glowing exit sign almost swallowed by all this bloody chaos. Brock's aura became their beacon through this Lovecraftian insanity, as they moved toward this possible escape. It was impossible not to steal glances into the quivering darkness of the open rooms. Through their shared senses, Malachi was subjected to visions of the depravity within: bodies entwined like thorny vines, writhing—some still caught in their death throes. One man, encased head to toe in crimson moss, stumbled from his bed and collapsed at their feet before dissolving into a frothing mound sprouting death blossoms. Unflinching, knowing there was no redemption for those lost to such corruption, they stepped around his remains and pushed forward.

In another room, two grotesque moss figures were backlit by harsh storm light as they engaged with each other's lifeless forms. Despite the music's escalating crescendos, an unshakeable sense that Death had staked its claim on every room in this hotel washed over them. Thus, they cautiously navigated this charnel house down the squelching tunnel, averting their eyes from further glimpses of horror until they reached a metal door mercifully untouched by crimson blight. Brock exerted his strength against the resistant door, and they stumbled onto an unsettlingly elastic platform. The surface beneath them wobbled precariously as if they stood atop a water-filled balloon. A deep groan echoed from the abyss below, sending tremors through the landing, further destabilizing their shaky balance.

"Bloody hell!" Brock steadied Malachi.

"I'm good," Malachi assured quickly. "Let's just get out."

You're just as badass as me, Brock mentally reminded him.

A surge of adrenaline coursed through Malachi's veins, and a startling revelation dawned upon him—I am more than just a spectator in this cosmic horror show. His awareness of Brock's heightened senses echoed within him, and with it came an unexpected dash of the man's unyielding courage. Brock's grip on his arm was firm yet gentle as they descended a winding staircase that seemed to have been sculpted by a madman—each step an unpredictable dance between solidity and illusion, slick with the residue of blood-hued tendrils too lethargic to ensnare them.

As he embraced his newfound identity—the ethereal raven spun from smoke and mystery—he felt an increase in agility that defied logic. His steps became feather-light, barely brushing against the tainted stairway, akin to walking on water but leaving behind shadows instead of divine luminescence.

Brock glanced sidelong at Malachi, who now felt as effortless to hold as a helium balloon. The sight of his lover's wings unfurling—majestic and natural—caused Brock to release his grip. Malachi took flight alongside him with an exhilarating rush, erratic yet precise like a falcon trained for the hunt.

They plunged headfirst into the gaping maw of malevolence that sought to consume them. But they were elusive prey—a golden wolf and an arcane raven—for the sea-anemone swarm of writhing tendrils or the moss-clad marionettes flung at them like undead soldiers rising from their graves.

Any crimson contagion that dared brush against their protective halos was instantly incinerated with a sizzling shriek. They left behind a trail ablaze with gold-and-black combustion before bursting through fragile doors at the stairwell's bottom.

Brock and I need to catch our breaths after that one, Malachi thought as they surveyed their new surroundings—an opulent foyer now obscured by demonic overgrowth. Red-mossed pillars stood as lone reminders of the room's former grandeur, while heaps that once might have been a reception desk lay forgotten.

The walls curved inward like snowdrifts under the weight of red corruption—a squirming mass akin to a snake pit—that sealed their exit within moments. However, three figures radiating an insidious melody and malevolent aura were more menacing than the threat of suffocation.

Surrounded by shambling moss-covered undead was a trio—a man, woman, and child—dressed in immaculate white togas. They danced and offered up their eerie chants to an unseen orchestra. Malachi recognized the sensuous woman and robust man—now stripped of their human disguises. The third Godbeast was unlike any they had seen before: her face shriveled like a voodoo talisman, her hair wild and undulating like Medusa's serpents.

In times past, Brock may have charged headlong into battle with these entities. But he had learned restraint from his previous encounters with such cosmic horrors. A dead animal—a goat perhaps?—lay on a glossy altar that emerged from the crimson sludge while the smallest Godbeast extracted its still-beating heart and crushed it.

Brock and I need to be careful here, Malachi warned internally as the full force of their enchanting melody rippled through the air, causing moss-covered creatures to halt mid-step before collapsing in reverence on their knees.

But when this spell struck Brock and Malachi, it evaporated against their radiant halos into red mist without inflicting them with perverse desire or hunger. Brock and Malachi loved each other—a love pure, noble, and young—and such love was not easily undone by even the darkest witchcraft.

With that realization, the three Red Fates ceased chanting, and the phantom music subsided to a low hum. Although the squirming surroundings slowed its festering, Brock sensed the latent danger of this tightening chamber.

"Our efforts bear no fruit," the ancient Godbeast confessed, discarding the pulpy remains of a goat's heart. Their ritualistic attempts had come to naught; the Aspects were not merely stirred but fully awakened in their arcane strength. Necromanteon unsheathed a sickle from her waistband, while Pythia and Trophonius brandished similar implements —relics from the dawn of mankind, wrought in Hephaestus' celestial smithy and imbued with power capable of wounding an eternal being.

"The only course left is to fell them," declared Pythia.

A scoff echoed across the cryptic chamber from Brock. Despite their archaic dialect— Latin or Greek, perhaps?—he seemed to comprehend their speech effortlessly.

"Should've taken us out when we were off our rockers," Brock retorted. "This won't be a cakewalk for you now."

"Why did you attempt to pit us against each other?" Malachi chimed in. He, too, deciphered their conversation without effort, his words echoing with a resonance akin to Brock's voice—as if he was borrowing more than just his friend's auditory senses. The fact they shared sensory experiences had ceased to surprise him.

"You're out of your depth," cautioned Pythia. "You're ensnared in a cosmic conflict far beyond your understanding—a war sparked before humanity learned to smelt bronze. We shaped your civilization, and now we must tear it down at our master's behest."

Malachi found her somber tone odd for such a blood-lusting creature and repeated his question: "But why?"

Pythia traced her finger thoughtfully along her sickle's blade as she replied, "Because destiny has deemed it so. All else has been mere spectacle—a divine farce indulged by my kind, tainted by the vile remnants of humanity. We've reigned as gods, yet the true deities will soon assert their dominion. Surrender is your only option. Would you consider that? Servitude to the Deep One? He's no benevolent god, oblivious to even the notion of mercy. At best, you can hope for a quick demise. Cthugha, however, will never rule Earth; his interactions with humans have weakened him. He is destined for defeat... and so are you."

"So we just lie down and die?" Brock retorted incredulously.

"That's a shit deal," Malachi added.

"Regrettably, it is the best offer available," Trophonius responded solemnly.

The Aspects replied in unison: "Fuck that."

Pythia shrugged nonchalantly at their defiance while Trophonius grimaced with deep displeasure. The hag-creature flashed a grotesque grin of decayed teeth. Sensing the end of their discourse, Brock and Malachi braced themselves for what came next: an abrupt metamorphosis that seemed to make the room fold inward as if seized by an unseen force. From every corner of this unholy sanctuary, moss-clad figures materialized: falling from the ceiling like raindrops, rising from the floor like demonic saplings, detaching themselves from pillars they had once been part of. In an instant, an army of crimson beings coalesced into an impenetrable phalanx standing between them and the Godbeasts.

Brock's mental command, "Go!" reverberated in his companion's mind like a thunderclap, and a tangible wave of terror surged forth. His thoughts were a whirlwind of worry for Malachi, the storm on the horizon threatening to consume them all. The moss-men swarmed together, intertwining into an organic barricade that pulsed with malevolent life. In a sudden, violent surge, they coalesced into a monstrous tidal wave of gnarled bodies that devoured its own in a grotesque display of self-cannibalism. A gargantuan limb, formed from writhing forms, lashed out at them.

Malachi vaulted into the air like a dark comet, his heart hammering for Brock's safety, but his mind honed on his own survival. He weaved through towering pillars with the uncanny agility of an otherworldly hummingbird, deftly evading sticky appendages and snaking vines that sought to trap him while also dodging airborne mossmen and debris cascading from above.

Perhaps an echo of Brock's latent awareness gifted him fleeting clarity amidst the chaos. He spotted an earthly figure—the hideous hag—brandishing her weapon with ominous intent before she launched herself towards him. Her movements held an unsettling elegance, reminiscent of a flying squirrel under demonic possession. In the pitch-black abyss of their battleground, Malachi's aerial grace was mirrored by the relentless pursuit of this crone.

Without warning, another monstrous tentacle—a macabre sculpture formed from entwined corpses—materialized before him with deadly intent. But Malachi was no ordinary bird or angel; he embodied speed beyond physical limitations as the living Manifestation of Flame—personified by and swift as subatomic particles and electrons igniting existence.

In defiance of physics' laws, he veered aside in an instant. The repugnant limb that had sought his life found a different victim: its trajectory altered to intercept the pursuing hag. Caught unawares, she collided with the horrific appendage instead of her intended prey. Like an avenging deity, it dragged her into the abyss from which it had sprung.

Her fate was swallowed by uncertainty as she vanished into a cataclysmic explosion of blood and gore. The impact was apocalyptic, causing even this alien limb to disintegrate upon contact with the Earth's surface. It dissolved into a crimson tidal wave that overwhelmed everything within its reach, transforming the ground beneath Malachi into a roiling sea of viscera and destruction.

As for the hag, there was no sign of her return from this bloody mire below him. But Malachi didn't pause to verify or refute her survival; he continued his flight above this grim spectacle. He raced back towards his soul-bound companion, who radiated like a beacon amidst chaos. There, bathed in sunlight, stood Brock—parting the sea of death blossoms with waves of golden energy he wielded like whips of light against the oncoming tide threatening to engulf him.

The pair of remaining Godbeasts, garbed in their spectral white attire, perched ominously atop the violent sea of crimson waves. They were a looming threat, too vast to comprehend. The room seemed to heave and buck with the roiling undulations of the blood-soaked tide while these malevolent beings reveled in the chaos. They rode the tempestuous waves with an unholy delight, their presence magnifying the terror that permeated every crevice of this volatile realm.

Malachi was acutely aware that they would lunge at Brock any second now, threatening to overwhelm him with their powerful assault or the relentless surge of the wave. As they ascended higher and darted between blazing chasms and viscous debris, Malachi propelled himself beyond any known limits—surpassing sound, light, or any earthly-defined speed. Once more, he transcended boundaries of velocity and luminescence, and molecular restrictions were rendered meaningless. In one heartbeat, he vanished; in another, he was shielding Brock with his wings in a protective hold—assuming for once the role of guardian angel to his friend.

In another fleeting moment—they hovered at a safe distance, watching as their pursuers—too engrossed in their momentum to halt—were swallowed by a vortex of damnation.

Brock clung onto Malachi's form as they hung suspended mid-air over what lay beneath them. The crimson sludge had thickened into a gelatinous mass, human forms sinking beneath its surface. They watched as bubbles erupted from below, but none produced a shrieking Godbeast—they didn't believe these immortal architects of horror would be extinguished by their own magic. Time was borrowed now, and escape from this deadly trap was paramount before it sprung back into lethal life.

"Holy hell," Brock exhaled shakily. "That was close...Too damn close...We need..." His words trailed off as a series of deafening explosions fractured the wall they'd been hovering near. The shockwave spun Malachi like a top, but he regained his balance just in time to see Brock's leg dip into the roiling sea of death blossoms beneath them—immediately singed by the eldritch acid.

Brock's tormented scream was all the motivation Malachi needed to bolt. Through the haze of smoke and dust, he spotted an exit—a gaping hole torn open in the building's side, spewing out a river of red. He shot through it without hesitation, carrying them both up into the frigid winter tempest.

Brock's bag slipped from his shoulder during their rapid ascent, but with an assurance that rivaled an archangel's, Malachi swooped down and snatched it from mid-air before touching down next to their SUV with feline grace.

Brock's body sagged against his companion, each breath he drew sounding like a gale in the eerie quiet. The frigid snow encasing his injured leg offered a numbing balm, dulling the sharp sting of an unknown injury—he couldn't decipher what had transpired, but he was sure of survival. As they observed their surroundings, Malachi's ethereal wings flickered and dissolved into the falling snowflakes, their luminescence fading into nothingness. Simultaneously, Brock felt his own supernatural strength ebbing away.

Together, they beheld the remnants of the once grand hotel—its form now grotesque and twisted, more resembling a weather-beaten tree stump than an architectural marvel. A blizzard raged around them, burying smaller vehicles under mounds of snow while peculiar pink petals floated down from above—a macabre parody of Japan's famed Sakura season. The sight was uncanny—malevolent even—and Malachi experienced a wave of relief as he perceived faint vibrations beneath his feet and watched as the monstrous structure began to implode.

A gaping chasm seared into the snowy landscape marked their escape route—an aperture rapidly sinking out of view. The entire situation defied logic—the appearance of such a colossal exit remained a mystery.

Brock cast wary glances across the desolate parking lot and into the ominous woods beyond, trying to discern if they were still being hunted. He sensed something—an entity perhaps—but its exact nature eluded him, and he dismissed any notion of further pursuit. "Let's not look a gift horse in the mouth," he murmured, echoing Charlie's old adage.

He extricated himself from Malachi's supportive grip and gritted his teeth against the pain that flared with every limping step he took toward their vehicle. With swift motions born out of urgency, he tossed their bags into the SUV's rear and took to the wheel, driving like a man possessed.

Hidden deep within the forest, nestled amidst snow-draped trees and towering mountains, their unseen savior carefully lowered his RPG and set it aside. His arms quivered from the recoil of firing the missile. Shielded by his military-grade parka and balaclava, he allowed himself a fleeting moment of satisfaction.

"Good to see you again, Brock," he murmured into the biting wind.

CHAPTER 5: THE SWEAT

Here stood fate's master builder, whom some associated with Lachesis—the divinity who severed life's threads.

"Greek blood witches?" Ana's voice sliced through the silence, sharp as a scalpel. "Damn it. I need a breather." Behind the plexiglass, an elderly woman, her form shrunken and hunched in a white apron and uniform eerily reminiscent of Malachi's tale, studied her with a curious gaze that suggested she was some sort of spectacle. Ignoring the old woman's scrutiny, Ana paid for their provisions—sandwiches, water, chips—and left Lenny to collect their purchases while she sought solace in the crisp outside air.

She moved cautiously over remnants of slushy snow that were winter's half-hearted attempt in this remote corner of woodland on Yellowstone's outskirts. Winter was imminent, but they would likely outrun it as they journeyed further west. She found respite under an awning beside a trash can overflowing with discarded cigarette butts. Although she had long since abandoned her smoking habit, the boys' harrowing encounter stirred up an old yearning to puff away her anxiety.

Her dream about a resurrected goat amidst an array of pink blossoms hadn't been symbolic but rather a cryptic prediction of Malachi's destiny. How foolish she'd been to think they were merely on some cross-country adventure; instead, they were humanity's last hope against complete annihilation—and one among them was missing. Suppressing the urge to return inside, purchase some smokes, and surrender to her nicotine cravings, she chewed anxiously on her nails.

"You still here?" he asked.

"Shit! Sorry," she responded hastily. "Lost in thought."

"I'm used to that," he chuckled softly. "Brock does it all the time."

"Well then," she urged him impatiently, "finish your story."

"That's pretty much it," he replied casually. "They kind of self-destructed under their own spell—drowned in that bloody mess—but I don't think they're dead. Something blasted a hole in the hotel wall, and I flew us out of there. We didn't stick around to see what happened to them."

"That whole hole thing is strange," Ana mused, halting her self-inflicted manicure, struck by a sudden realization. "Wait, you flew again?"

"Like a damn bird."

"More like an angel," murmured a nearby voice.

Brock's voice was an intoxicating mix of smoke and silk, warming Ana like the purring of a colossal wolf curled up next to her by a cozy hearth. His words were not merely spoken but sung; she could discern the undertones of passion and commitment. She recognized that sound—the sound of love. "You two are getting awfully close, huh?"

Malachi paused—she imagined him looking fondly at his companion before answering softly, "We are. I can't fathom tackling this journey without him. Or you, my long-distance confidante."

Ana allowed herself to smile as she observed a young mother showering her infant son with kisses from their parked truck's backseat; his laughter echoed through the air as he wriggled joyously in her arms. She surprised herself when she said sincerely: "Love is the one weapon we have that they don't—it's not something to be underestimated."

"I thought you were too skeptical for such sentiments," he teased.

"I am...I was...I don't know." She laughed lightly, brushing off his comment. "Anyway, I wish we knew who they were."

"So do I."

The relentless waltz of fate seemed to have an inexhaustible ensemble of dancers. They'd managed to identify Mary as a puppet in Cthugha's grand scheme and themselves as his oblivious foot soldiers. The revelation stirred a tempest in Ana's stomach, making her insides flip-flop each time she dwelled on it. Her understanding of Cthugha was far from comforting—claims that he was some sort of Prometheus figure were suspect at best, largely because she couldn't validate Mary's unhinged proclamations. Maybe Cthugha harbored intentions of scorching the world into a desolate expanse but lacked the necessary channel to spread his incendiary gospel worldwide. As for Malachi's assailants—in the junkyard and now in this nightmare-inducing hotel—their motives remained shrouded in mystery and riddles. She felt like a seer bereft of her prophetic mirror, condemned to behold unchangeable futures.

"I feel about as useful as a chocolate teapot," she admitted into the silence.

"Nah, don't beat yourself up," came Malachi's reply. "Think about it—if we'd played Good Samaritan for those three hitchhikers, we might be six feet under instead of having this heart-to-heart. You saved our asses."

"Yeah, maybe... But you could've just flown outta trouble like some comic book hero."

Malachi chuckled dryly. "It doesn't work like that—or didn't anyway. I'm getting the hang of this stuff, though. You will, too."

A hulking silhouette ambled towards their truck—it took Ana two blinks to recognize Lenny as he swung open the driver's door and settled inside, causing the vehicle to dip under his weight. It wasn't just her imagination playing tricks; he was genuinely expanding, and steroids were an unlikely explanation. Could it have been some arcane cosmic concoction? She mulled over Lenny's peculiar transformation and his casual acceptance of the mystic energy humming within him. Perhaps her fear was her own worst enemy, the dread of what she might glimpse or evolve into. But she couldn't keep shying away from hazardous knowledge—like Mary's grimoire—when it singed her. If she was truly the all-seeing Owl spirit, she should let her consciousness sail on the tides of time. That could be her version of flight.

A similar thought seemed to cross Malachi's mind as he said: "We're almost at Rhode Island, so we'll get some answers soon. But don't wait for us, Ana. You found my aunties, uncovered Mary's hidden lair, and saved Lenny by invoking a cosmic deity for crying out loud. You've used your powers to steer clear of danger more times than I can count. You're no wallflower."

"I'm going to dig up some answers for us," she declared resolutely.

"You sound like you mean business. Good on ya'. We'll catch up soon."

"Bet on it."

Ana climbed back into the car and was greeted by the squelchy, crunching sounds of Lenny annihilating a ham and cheese sandwich. His bottomless hunger never failed to tickle her funny bone as he tossed the wrapper in the bag and reached for another sandwich.

"Malachi, how's he holding up?" Cynthia's question hung like a smoke signal in the air.

Ana's gaze flickered to the rearview mirror, catching a glimpse of the backseat. "He stumbled into a hornet's nest," she replied with a shrug. "But he's dusted himself off."

Cynthia raised an eyebrow, her curiosity piqued. "What kind of hornet's nest?"

Ana shrugged again, her lips curving into a wry smile. "Still piecing that together. But I'm on it."

"And your strategy for tackling this mystery?" Cynthia prodded.

"Well..." Ana began slowly, drumming her slender fingers against the dash. "I've got this shiny little fragment that amps up my mojo, and Mary's grimoire filled to the brim with arcane tidbits." She smirked at the older woman through the rearview mirror. "Feels like I've got enough puzzle pieces to start making a bigger picture."

"To unearth the truth," Cynthia retorted sharply yet sagely, "you need to have a chat with the spirits."

From the driver's seat, Lenny chimed in between bites of his sandwich: "You need a sweat."

**

The desolate ribbon of asphalt wound its way through the stark, skeletal ranges and crevasses of Montana, echoing the yawning abyss of nothingness. The verdant paradise that had been their companion was replaced by harsh, unyielding plains—a jarring contrast to the lush beauty they'd grown accustomed to. Lenny twisted the dial on the heater, raising a shield against the wind's fury that lashed out at their vehicle without mercy. Their fellow travelers on this godforsaken road were sparse and dwindled further when their route veered towards Wind River Reservation.

As dusk swallowed up the horizon in one swift gulp, an uncanny sense of isolation gripped them. They were but phantoms journeying through a wasteland scarred by time and abandonment. This grim reality prompted Ana to cocoon herself in a blanket, seeking solace in sleep until they reached friendlier landscapes.

Waking up to the welcome light of dawn, her dreams were thankfully free from nightmares. Rubbing the sleep from her eyes, she took stock of her surroundings: outside, extensive golden plains spread under towering mountains whose jagged peaks mimicked teeth within a giant's jaw; inside the car, Lenny sat as immovable as granite with his gaze locked onto the barren highway stretching ahead.

Ana spotted Cynthia through the vanity mirror. The woman appeared drained, with dark circles marring her eyes like spilled ink. "Are you alright?" Ana asked.

Lenny knew he wasn't being spoken to—he felt invincible—but he'd picked up on Cynthia's skewed energy too—like an old piece of furniture left out in relentless rain until it started to rot slowly under a neglected porch.

"Heavy shit she's lugging around," Lenny grumbled, his words stripped of any attempt at sugarcoating.

"God dealt the Linklaters another crap hand," Cynthia admitted, her voice carrying the weight of an echo-laden sigh.

"You thinking about Mary?" Ana asked, with her usual introspection.

"Hell, it isn't just about the deception," Cynthia shot back, her eyes fixed on the vibrant tableau unfolding before them. "She played us like marionettes. You know she was my guide in practicing 'good medicine,' don't you?" She raised her hands, weathered and gnarled as if they were extensions of an ancient spell-weaver. "Makes me wonder if what she taught me was more akin to black magic."

Ana held her tongue, offering Cynthia the space to unfurl her thoughts further. After an extended hush, she cradled her hands back onto her lap.

"Grace wasn't our sole explorer. We'd venture into the wilderness together over weekends—hunting and collecting herbs—extracting age-old remedies from nature's heart as our ancestors did. Mary sparked my interest in healing—said I had a knack for it. Soon enough, people started seeking my help for their ailments—from birch-based elixirs for pain and inflammation to ointments for infections; potent brews that could ease the grip of addiction to sex or drugs; even potions that could loosen a secretive man's tongue —we were always steeped in magic, each harboring a bit within us—but it felt pure and benign then—I never suspected it was witchcraft."

"It's just power, Cynthia," Ana interjected. "Magic isn't inherently good or bad—it's all about how you wield it. I refuse to accept that I'm evil—or you—or Malachi, Brock, Lenny, or anyone else who's got the guts to stand with us."

"Could be you're onto something," Cynthia conceded with a nod of agreement. "I did manage to make a difference along the way... Despite our tribe being one of the wealthier ones around here, most folks don't have a rainy day fund for emergencies or medical care. So they turned to me...A healer. My sister Jewel—the one we lost—she was a nurse and would send patients my way if she thought I could help them more than the system that had stripped them of their self-respect or bodily rights."

"What do you mean by that?" Ana asked, her eyebrows knitting together in bewilderment.

"Sterilization was the unexpected parting gift many women received after routine visits," Lenny chimed in, sparing Cynthia from having to unearth her sister's horror story. "You go in for a simple tonsillectomy, and bam! Surprise hysterectomy courtesy of your friendly neighborhood doctor."

"Jesus," Ana gasped.

"God and his boy aren't lending an ear, I'm afraid," Cynthia snapped back with a sardonic smile. "But I'm not stuck in the past anymore. If we do that, there's nothing but heartache down the road. The bastard at Wanashee Hospital who played God with so many lives? Slipped away like a fox from a bloody henhouse, leaving behind carnage and sorrow. Probably changed his identity, but I'd wager he didn't shed his twisted mindset. He'll hit those high notes if our paths ever cross again."

A psychic assault gnawed at the base of Ana's skull, causing her to wince. She ventured a question, her voice slow and hesitant as if she dreaded the answer it might coax forth. "You met this guy? What was he like?"

Cynthia's reply came laced with a dry humor that belied the gravity of their discussion. "A real charmer," she said. "Like most sociopaths are. Dr. Moreaux—sounds straight out of a horror flick, right? But man, was he easy on the eyes and smooth-talking: sun-kissed skin, immaculate beard, muscular body, funny and kind... until we saw what lay beneath it all." Her words were as sharp and precise as a scalpel's edge. "He had this peculiar way of talking... almost an accent... something Eastern European maybe? He'd say his words were like music notes flowing from his vile mouth—'Cynthi-ahh.'"

"Long A? Sounds like Count Dracula to me," Lenny chimed in.

Ana shivered as an icy whisper echoed in her ear—Aah-naa—and then the name: Dr. Marrow...Dr. Moreaux. The similarity was chillingly surreal.

"Jewel and a bunch of his other victims hired a PI, and he scoured every hospital in Canada and twenty or more states, but the good doctor vanished into thin air. If he's still breathing," she spat out venomously, "I'd bet he's running some hellish back-alley abortion clinic somewhere."

Ana's thoughts whirled like leaves caught in a storm. Was Dr. Moreaux now operating under a different medical license somewhere else? The thought sent chills down her spine like she was slowly submerged in a bath of ice-cold dread. How much of her life had been manipulated behind the scenes?

The fog that had once clouded Ana's mind began to dissipate, revealing the intricate maze of her past. She was drawn back to an era when her existence was a cyclone of medical jargon and psychological evaluations. Each day brought with it a crippling dread, punctuated by inexplicable fits that would seize control of her body, only to give way to periods of disconcerting tranquility—deceptive lulls in the tempest that was her life.

Her mind journeyed further into the past, bypassing the countless hours spent on therapists' couches and under the scrutinizing gaze of doctors who saw her as nothing more than an enigmatic puzzle. One encounter emerged from the shadows among this blur: her initial meeting with Dr. Marrow.

She recalled the heavy antiseptic scent in the consultation room at the shelter where they first met—one among many she'd shuffled in and out of over time. The room was compact and devoid of personality; its austere white walls bore insipid motivational posters that did little to dispel its clinical aura. As she awaited his arrival, anxiety gripped her heart while she twisted her hands into knots.

When he finally entered, his appearance took her aback. Dr. Marrow was unlike any psychiatrist she had previously encountered—his smile held a crooked charm that served as a comforting lighthouse amidst an ocean of stern professionals she'd been subjected to until then. His eyes radiated a fatherly warmth, starkly contrasting with his sterile surroundings.

His affable demeanor offered solace rather than another frigid dissection of what made Ana 'damaged.' He extended something no man had dared—understanding without judgment, empathy without condescension.

He addressed her gently yet assertively, his voice slicing through the frosty air like a lifeline tossed towards someone drowning in despair. He didn't peddle immediate solutions or miraculous remedies but pledged patience and commitment—the very things Ana yearned for from those tasked with mending her fragmented psyche.

As she sat opposite him, the haunting echoes of her past struggles seemed to fade, supplanted by a flicker of hope. In this moment, Ana felt truly acknowledged—not as a victim or an anomaly, but as a human being worthy of compassion and respect. She had been assigned to Dr. Marrow because of his expertise in violent crime psychology. In defending herself against an abuser, she had shown a fierceness that necessitated his specialized understanding. His presence marked a turning point in her life, offering her a chance at healing amidst the chaos.

Dispelling the memory—the myth—anger bubbled up within her, hot and raw. She'd been nothing more than a pawn in his sick game. Who was he? *What* was he? It sounded as if his handsome countenance hadn't aged since Cynthia's recollection. A crucial piece to this apocalyptic jigsaw puzzle had been nestled in her hands all along. Inside, she wrestled with this revelation while choking back a deluge of tears.

Lenny's nose crinkled at the sudden shift in Ana's emotions that filled the SUV like an unseen storm cloud. He knew pieces of her secret but wasn't about to pry them out from her unwilling lips. Yet he couldn't shake off the suspicion that her sudden silence was linked to this Dr. Moreaux—a man who now topped his hit list.

***

Fort Washakie unfolded itself in a serene display of country living, its landscape punctuated by mobile homes huddled along the sinewy trails of the land. These clusters gradually transformed into charming neighborhoods of clapboard residences, their white picket fences immaculate and interspersed among iconic landmarks like a post office, town hall, and even a police station. Gleaming trucks nestled in driveways or glided past on the thoroughfares, their occupants scrutinizing through tinted windows at unfamiliar figures encroaching their haven. The friendly waves from many motorists or passersby added an aura of warmth to this portrait.

Ana sat quietly, her mind swirling with the revelation of Marrow's dual existence that had been unveiled just an hour ago—the illusion of simplicity proving as elusive as trapping reflections on glass.

Guided by Cynthia's instructions, Lenny steered them away from the main road and onto more peaceful side streets. Cynthia had allies here—cousins, she referred to them—a term Ana had decoded to mean potent bonds but not necessarily formed by blood ties. They were supposed to seek refuge with these cousins until the following day. Their arrival conveniently aligned with an upcoming weekend ceremony—a fortuitous coincidence for partaking in a spiritual sweat ritual.

Their destination was a quaint bungalow dressed in white siding. Delicate lace curtains peeked out from the windows, adorned with pots bursting with vibrant flowers. Lenny skillfully maneuvered their truck behind a minivan squeezed into a tight driveway.

As Ana and Cynthia disembarked from their vehicle, stretching away travel-induced stiffness, Lenny busied himself, retrieving their bags from the back. Cynthia ambled towards the entrance and rang the doorbell.

Ana took a moment to observe Lenny—their driver and guardian who never seemed to complain—immersed in the waning light of sunset, which draped him in shades of deep violet like some deity presiding over twilight and shadows.

"Like what you see?" he asked, his eyes shimmering with curiosity. Ana, her cheeks tinted a rosy hue, found herself at a loss for words or even the ability to breathe. The sudden clatter of a screen door slamming shut saved her from having to respond immediately. Both their heads pivoted towards the porch where Cynthia had disappeared.

Cynthia stood on a slab of weathered concrete, her arms wrapped around an elderly couple. Their bodies were lean and bent with age, a stark contrast to their lively company. Silver hair threaded with black crowned their heads, braided meticulously. The woman was draped in turquoise jewelry that danced in harmony with her eerily pale green eyes—eyes that settled on Ana and Lenny as they neared.

"I'm Anne," the woman introduced herself, nodding towards her partner. "And this is Bill here—just Bill though, he can't bear 'William.'"

"Damn straight," Bill affirmed.

Lenny's nostrils flared wide, his senses ensnared by the tantalizing aroma of searing meat wafting from within the house.

"We've got some steaks on," said Bill, noting Lenny's interest. "Not sure if we can quench your hunger entirely, but we'll give it our all."

"Good luck indeed," Cynthia interjected with a grin that stretched across her face.

They stepped into the comforting embrace of what could only be described as a grandparent's home—every inch steeped in love and nostalgia. The walls were decorated with photographs capturing moments of the couple's life together and their now-grown children echoing their parents' faded grace.

Bill guided them to a hidden gem behind the house: a raised deck in a fenced backyard. Electric lanterns punctuated the twilight while lawn chairs and a wicker couch offered respite from their journey's weariness. They sank into yellow Adirondack chairs and watched as stars began to speckle the serene mountainous horizon.

As Anne took drink orders, Ana requested something non-alcoholic. No one objected to it, and Lenny defused any lingering awkwardness by asking for the same—most Indigenous homes kept zero percent beer anyway. Soon enough, they enjoyed cold beers, seared steaks (rare for Lenny), and coleslaw and engaged in spirited conversation.

"I didn't realize how much I needed this," Ana admitted when she found herself alone with Lenny on the couch—the others had retreated inside to clean up. "I mean... I've never known peace, not really. But everything's been so intense lately. Even if we're not being chased, it feels like we're always rushing...like time is slipping away."

"Ever heard the story of Turtle Island?" Lenny asked.

"Nope."

"I'm not exactly a master storyteller, and there are countless versions depending on which tribe you ask, but here goes nothing. Once upon a time, Sky Mother—"

"Who's that?"

"The Primordial Mother, the weaver of existence—tribes call her by different names. When life first stirred on this world, it was cloaked in water, hidden behind clouds, and uninhabitable. The Mother was so consumed by loneliness and despair that she chose to lay herself down and die. But from her celestial remains sprouted a towering tree that eventually gave birth to animals, mankind, and spirits. As far as I know, solid ground was scarce back then—the world being mostly a vast ocean—so beasts and men were constantly at war over the few existing islands. As if that wasn't enough drama, two malevolent beings—Frog and Whale—claimed this world for themselves, turning tribes and creatures against each other in their feud—the seas soon turned blood-red. As the world was about to face a major disaster, the Sky Mother sent spiritual messengers to comfort her hurt and pained body," Lenny paused for effect before continuing with his tale.

"But she's dead, though, right?" Ana interrupted him with a smirk.

"Eternal spirits don't really 'die'; they indefinitely shift between our realm and the dream world." Lenny continued after shooting Ana a flustered look—he always felt so bad at telling stories. "Four mighty spirits emerged from the cardinal points—the north, south, east, and west—they stopped all the chaos..." His face crinkled into an expression of confusion; his eyebrows knitted together in thought. "Then there's something about these four gifting a turtle with sacred earth, which caused it to grow so huge that it could carry all living things on its back—it alleviated their mortal fear and ended the evil spirits' reign over them."

Ana listened intently to Lenny's tale—or warning? The malicious entities known as Frog and Whale intrigued her further; aquatic nightmares possibly related to Cthulhu and his monstrous kin? She drowned this new riddle with another swig of her ale before throwing out a sarcastic comment.

"You *are* terrible at storytelling," Ana laughed, her eyes twinkling with mischief.

Lenny's face remained stone-like. "The point is: I think all this has happened before—or something similar. Most indigenous people believe in cycles: birth to death, war to peace. The survivors of the last apocalypse are why we're here today. We'll survive this one too."

"Just like that, huh?"

"Does it need to be more complicated?"

As their beers clinked together in a toast, Ana found the non-alcoholic brew they shared becoming less and less unpalatable with each sip. Lenny's choice to match her drink was a quiet nod to his underlying affection—a consistent thread of care woven through their interactions. As he set his bottle down, the damp curve of his lips—lips that had whispered countless reassurances—beckoned her like a lighthouse piercing through an all-encompassing darkness.

The memory of his surrender to an alien deity for her sake was still fresh in her mind —a testament of faith and trust in her, even when confronted by the unknown. This act had kindled something within her, sparking a flame that threatened to engulf them. Yielding to an irresistible force, she leaned into him, pressing her lips against his. Lenny tensed briefly as though taken aback, causing Ana's heart to flutter uncertainly. Had she misread their playful exchanges? But then he responded with equal fervor, his jaw softening, their tongues entwining in an intimate dance.

With a fluidity born not of practice but desire, he set aside their bottles onto the porch and drew her onto him—a commanding presence she seamlessly melded into. The exploration of his rugged physique left her breathless with delight before pulling him closer for a deeper kiss—an expression of repressed yearning for a genuine connection she never thought could be satisfied.

While Ana was adventurous in her exploration, Lenny treated her with the gentleness reserved for a delicate bird; he had never known such an intricate woman who understood suffering yet managed to extract joy from life's harsh clutches. The sound of footsteps from within the house prompted him to gently lift Ana off him as they quickly tried to appear composed. Their abandoned bottles on the porch stood as mute witnesses to their stolen moment, one coming to rest at Cynthia's foot.

"Beds are ready," Cynthia declared, bending down to pick up the bottle.

"Goodnight," Lenny said as Ana rose swiftly, acutely conscious of his arousal hidden beneath a strategically positioned pillow. Choosing not to make him stand and reveal his predicament, she wished him goodnight and followed Cynthia inside. They maneuvered past a sleeping Bill and an awake Anne, who waved at her from a nearby recliner. Upstairs, in a room seemingly frozen in time, Ana surrendered to the seductive call of sleep.

The unexpected closeness with Lenny had awakened something within her, a longing she'd suppressed for so long. As sleep overtook her, memories of Lenny's rugged warmth washed over her like calming waves. Even without her psychic powers, she was certain that wherever Lenny spent his night—whether lying down or standing guard—he thought of her, too.

***

The tantalizing aroma of breakfast yanked Ana from the clutches of her slumber, her stomach voicing its loud complaint about being empty. She bolted through a rapid-fire shower before joining the others at the kitchen table, where she enthusiastically devoured a heaping plate of eggs, bacon, and bannock lavished with homemade jam. Her ravenous hunger, or maybe her interaction with Lenny last night, delighted him; his eyes sparkled as they observed her through half-closed lids. Anne and Bill, the sweetest elderly couple who radiated incessant warmth and kindness, decided against attending the Powwow due to his troublesome back. They bid their hosts farewell with heartfelt hugs and solid handshakes before cramming themselves back into the car and setting off towards the ceremony, hell-bent on making it before the grand entrance at nine am sharp.

Gray foothills concealed a lush horizon. For a while, Ana was seduced by the surrounding beauty as their vehicle snaked down a highway carved into the verdant valley. The biting chill was a stark reminder of winter's reign elsewhere as they rolled down windows and sipped gas station coffee procured on the town's edge. The majestic mountainous landscape interlaced with thriving trees offered an exhilarating testament to life's magnificence—elements that humbled yet emboldened mankind.

Feeling playful, Ana shattered the silence: "Once we've saved this godforsaken world or some shit like that, I'm done with concrete jungles and noise pollution. I want my own quiet cabin somewhere—Innsmont maybe—or even here. Doesn't matter where...it just needs to be mine."

"Just yours?" Lenny asked in his jaded yet gentle tone.

"Maybe I'll let someone else's name onto the deed," she shot back playfully.

Cynthia chuckled softly at their flirtatious banter.

Another half hour saw them ascend higher into rugged terrain requiring four-wheel drive for steeper inclines until finally leveling out into an arrow-straight path sandwiched between two limestone giants. They veered onto a less frequented, worn road flanked by a shimmering lake that danced with the purity of its water. Following another truck, they passed through two totem poles adorned with fetishes and into a dirt lot filled with parked vehicles. Most attendees had already abandoned their cars, crossing the wild lawn towards the soft hum of voices converging around white tents arranged in a distant circle. The rhythmic pulse of drum music and chanting washed over Ana as she exited the vehicle, overlaid by tantalizing scents of sweet bread reminiscent of doughnuts and smoky wood from fires cooking bannock, elk, or other traditional foods. She recalled some trivia about bannock not originating from Indigenous people but being adopted and redefined by them from another nationality. Every culture seemed to borrow elements from others; all human conflicts and conquests were merely petty squabbles beneath the looming threat of cosmic entities ready to crush them underfoot. Her pleasant morning suddenly soured.

"Everything okay?" Lenny's deep voice rumbled through the silence, his towering figure casting a protective shadow over Ana as she wrestled with her thoughts.

"Just dandy," she shot back. "Ready to sweat my ass off."

"It's 'partake in a sweat,'" Cynthia interjected, her tone soft yet firm as she handed Ana a weighty burlap sack. The unmistakable shape of Mary's grimoire pressed against its rough exterior. "You'll likely need this for your...channeling shenanigans. Leaving it in the car would be damn foolish."

Ana bit back any words of thanks—the grimoire held no charm for her—but accepted it nonetheless. As they navigated the barren expanse of the parking lot, late arrivals studied her with curiosity, only to retreat under Lenny's stern gaze. She supposed her porcelain complexion and feline-themed jumper made an odd sight among this crowd. Yet, as they skirted the fringes of the gathering, a young boy munching on twisted bread offered her an unassuming smile and shyly waved his snack in greeting. It struck her then that acceptance was not universal but dependent on one's isolation.

Rather than resist this unfamiliar tide, she likened herself to a salmon swimming upstream: surrendering to the rhythm and flow of music, becoming one with pulsating beats vibrating through air and earth. The master of ceremonies' voice boomed like celestial thunder across the crowd, silencing all chatter and signaling the start of Grand Entry.

Before she knew it, Lenny led them towards where drummers and singers called forth jingle-dress dancers with their timeless tunes. Sunlight broke through cloud cover above and danced upon shimmering garments worn by young men and women spinning and stomping in sync with ancestral melodies.

Cynthia disappeared during the ceremony, only to reappear as it concluded. Ana's disappointment in the musical lull was short-lived, as applause erupted in appreciation for the performers. Friends and family flooded the circle, and drumming continued to underscore joyous exchanges among attendees.

"I chewed the fat with Chief Brokentooth," Cynthia stated nonchalantly. "Bill and Anne gave him a ring yesterday; he's got a sweat sesh ready for you."

"Like, now?" Ana asked, her voice laced with disbelief.

"You got a tea party on your schedule?" Cynthia retorted.

Ana shook her head no, and once again, they plunged into the crowd, Lenny at the helm. He seemed to intuitively know their destination. Beyond tents and celebrations, they pushed through waist-high grass towards an out-of-place scene from past eras: a circle of tepees nestled among sparse trees. Modern intrusions like four-wheelers and rifle-toting men patrolling the field disrupted this temporal illusion but failed to dissuade Lenny and his small entourage.

As they arrived at the camp, the trio of weather-beaten elders, huddled around a flickering campfire, scrutinized them with eyes as ancient as time itself. The fire's embers glowed like molten jewels in a dragon's hoard. Mysterious chants floated in the air from within the tents, making Ana's skin prickle with anticipation and unease. One of the elders, an odd blend of tradition and modernity in her denim attire and tribal relics, gestured towards a tent with her clinking headdress, their invitation to enter.

They were greeted by a warm haze that hung heavy with sweet-smelling smoke. Furs lay scattered around glowing stones embedded in an earthen hearth. Following her spectral guides, who shed their clothes to their undergarments, Ana took her place opposite Cynthia, whose features were hidden in the dim light. Then Lenny stepped out from the shadows, his sturdy form silhouetted against firelight as he threw water onto heated stones. For a fleeting moment, she caught sight of his raw masculinity—bronze muscles highlighted by patches of dark hair—which left her throat dry and heart pounding.

Settling into his spot to complete their triad formation, Lenny's deep voice harmonized with distant chants outside. Without further thought, Ana placed her cosmic shard and Mary's grimoire before her. Cynthia's theory that these items were instruments for her arcane craft was becoming more believable. But what next? That was still a mystery.

"Relax," Cynthia instructed gruffly yet kindly, "Breathe deep. Let this heavy air pull you under its spell like an anchor sinking into the sea depths. Listen to our ancestral songs spun by our friend here so beautifully it'd make angels weep. Tune into those ancient stories first told when spirits danced among us mortal folk."

Sweat trickled down Ana's body, a sensation as intense and slick as Lenny's touch had been the night before; an inner flame ignited within her, burning brighter than a supernova. She wished she could push him out of her thoughts but found herself stealing glances at the singer nearby, reconstructing his allure from memory as if he were under a spotlight. With surprising bravery, she admitted to herself that she might be falling in love for the first time. A wave of heat washed over her, either intensified or sparked by the suffocating air.

"Picture what you want, Ana," came Cynthia's voice from behind the smoky veil. "Whatever you're hell-bent on protecting—hold onto that image in your mind and chase it wherever it takes you—here or there or beyond our realm. Time ain't no prison for you like it is for us mere mortals. You are Owl—all-knowing and everywhere at once. Fly over mountains and valleys, rivers and oceans; journey across the infinite expanse of time itself towards truth."

I want to protect Lenny...you...Malachi...everyone I've grown to care about...this world that I've only just begun to appreciate...and barely understand..., she thought fervently. I need to identify this threat and figure out how to neutralize it. I need to know my enemy.

Ana couldn't tell if she'd voiced any of those thoughts aloud; her mind was spinning like a whirlwind, and her body felt fluid and slippery as if intoxicated. She began chanting along with Lenny's melody, impossibly and precisely echoing his Ojibwe lyrics. Suddenly, Lenny stopped mid-song. "Ana?"

Ana had fallen forward onto the fragment and grimoire, gracefully as if she were a prima ballerina taking her final bow.

"She's already crossed over," Cynthia confirmed with a hint of awe.

***

Ana's eyes blinked open, the room around her flickering with the dance of shadows painted by firelight. Her head rested on a pillow as smooth as silk, bangles chiming softly against one another as she moved. She stretched out her body, waking from sleep with an alluring grace that could rival a siren emerging from the depths of a sailor's dream. From the tips of her toes to the crown of her head, she was alive with an energy that hummed beneath her skin, drawing in those who shared her bed like moths to a flame. Men bronzed by sunlight and women blessed with curvaceous figures lay intertwined in the sea of sheets surrounding her. Like disciples reaching for their deity, they sought Ana—their inspiration, their muse—as she slid across the opulent expanse of the bed and let her bare feet meet the warm stone floor of this ancient temple.

She navigated down the stairs, encircling the raised platform with fluid ease. Her attire was feather-light, crafted by Rhapso's priestesses—renowned artisans of textile work. A strip of ruby fabric draped over one bare shoulder, secured beneath her bodice before trailing behind her like a crimson comet streaking through twilight.

With poise and assurance, she meandered through a grand chamber graced with towering pillars and sweeping banners reflecting her ethereal beauty. The scent of frankincense wafted from swinging braziers; it did not suffocate but rather cleared away any remnants of drowsiness from her mind—expanding it until she became more than just flesh and bone but magic and stardust traversing paths both earthly and astral.

"I am this era's Eye," Ana mused, a captivating Greek voice echoing within her—a voice that brought lucidity to this surreal state. Who is this woman? This entity? she wondered while wrestling with another consciousness residing within her.

Her host was neither mortal nor burdened with mortal fears or sorrows. The borrowed memories flickering through Ana were not of human origin. One moment, she saw her host presiding over a hedonistic banquet from her dais: the hall distorted by bodies writhing down steps slick with blood—whether from humans or slaughtered goats mingled among the convulsing crowd remained uncertain.

Suddenly, Ana found herself observing men garbed in the regal splendor of gilded armor, their status unmistakable as that of sovereigns. One figure stood out, his back turned towards her. He was draped in a cloak of vibrant crimson and crowned with a laurel wreath—could he be an emperor?—submissively bowing before this enigmatic woman as she murmured arcane words to an eagerly listening scribe.

Something about this commanding figure stirred a sense of recognition within Ana, an echo of familiarity that resonated in the chambers of her memory. Yet, frustratingly, his form remained indistinct, veiled by some mystical interference or perhaps purposefully shielded from prying eyes. His image wavered and distorted as if viewed through cascading water, obscuring his identity from her psychic scrutiny.

Regardless, the vision shifted abruptly. The scene fragmented like shards of glass and reformed into another tableau. Now, she stood at the edge of a pool filled with shimmering water that glowed with otherworldly luminescence. She reached out tentatively, her slender fingers brushing its surface and igniting it with radiant light. Two other figures loomed behind her—psychic apparitions detached from their physical forms. Ana recognized these formidable beings as her host's siblings; together, they formed the supreme triad of past, present, and future seers. Their collective gaze left no secret or destiny concealed.

Jolted from her dream within a dream, Ana found herself—again haunting the strange prophetess—now standing on a precarious stone ledge, an ancient city of Byzantium-inspiration sprawling before her host. The landscape was a patchwork of majestic sandstone manors gradually giving way to modest hovels and bustling docks that bore the ceaseless onslaught of the inky sea. Her host's sister, the Oracle of Death, foresaw how this civilization would eventually succumb to war and nature's fury. Her temple would become a casualty of time, lost until humanity's archeologists stumbled upon it. Alexander's fleet sailing off into the turbid horizon would lose its luster along with his ambitions and much of humanity's splendor. The world was yet too fragmented for Outer Gods to exert their influence over mankind's emerging tribes—not until millennia later when social media and technomagic would ensnare humanity in a lethal trance.

"All we're doing is killing time till then," the woman muttered with an air of resignation, "Just playing Pettia with living pawns." Turning her spectral whisper towards Ana, she addressed the entity lurking as a shadow in her mind. "Curious little Sparrow, pecking away at my thoughts."

"What—how? You can hear me?" Ana blurted out.

"I am Pythia," she replied solemnly, "a Seer of the past and hidden secrets. I am not bound by temporal chains; I hear whispers from antiquity and can trace their echoes into the present. It is but natural that I perceive you—observe you." Her voice had an edge of regret as she continued, "Sadly, your secret delving into history's burnt remnants will bring you not peace but sorrow. For mankind's survival is a myth."

"The reason why you resist—and your fellow Aspects do too—escapes me—I guess it must be an inherent trait…the essence of Nature itself," she mused aloud. "The Green Mother must fight whatever threatens her, as futile as battling cancer gnawing at human flesh may be. But we are relentless—there is no remedy or cure for us. My master devours all. The Deep One will rise, battle his opposite, and floodwaters will erase any trace of civilization."

Despite the creature's chilling nature, Ana kept her fear at bay and continued the conversation. Intriguingly, the bond between psychic host and parasite seemed to be mutual; as they talked, Ana began to understand more about Pythia's past and even felt echoes of her emotions—like her regret.

"But you're not exactly like your master, are you?" Ana asked with a hint of defiance in her psychic voice.

"Not entirely," Pythia responded quietly, placing a hand over where her heart would be. "I carry his destructive and violent traits—the part that relishes beauty only to annihilate it. The other half of us Godbeasts retain our humanity." She paused momentarily before continuing, "We were created through a ritual using human components much like your own bloody inception. We are kin in a way: cosmic bastards, graced with the power of the Outer Gods but burdened by our human weaknesses."

"I have made peace with my servitude," she confessed with an air of resignation. "I have chosen my side—as you have inherited yours." Pythia's spectral voice softened as she added, "The ultimate fate remains unknown to me, but I suspect Cthugha's flame will be snuffed by Cthulhu's engulfing darkness."

"I empathize with your predicament," Pythia added thoughtfully after a pause. "But I also fault you your courage."

"So, we're caught in the crossfire of... gods from beyond?" Ana probed, attempting to use the entity's verbosity to her advantage.

"Outer Gods, child," snapped Pythia, like an angry schoolmarm. "The primeval epoch bore witness to their bitter strife; Hastur and Shub-Niggurath have been cast aside. The contest for Earth's dominion and eventual consumption now lies between Cthulhu and Cthugha. Earth shall either be submerged or incinerated—no other fate awaits. You and your comrades will share this obliteration, if not carry it out yourselves. You remain alarmingly unaware of the colossal scale of your foes, do you not?"

The entity turned towards Ana as though she were a spectral companion witnessing a primordial sunset at her side. A celestial abyss occupied Pythia's azure gaze, tendrils of smoke wafting from her sockets.

Ana was irresistibly drawn to the immeasurable depths that harbored this divine monstrosity—eternal currents surging towards remote futures. This was undeniably one of the Morai—the heart and essence of antiquity's prophetic triumvirate, enshrined in endless myths and cultures. It was said that she presided over every creature, human, or monument's ultimate moment. Here stood fate's master builder, whom some associated with Lachesis—the divinity who severed life's threads. Yet Ana understood that this legend had been warped into a sisterhood when a brother existed amidst Morai's ranks. Collectively, they embodied an unholy trinity of divine monstrosities, typically garbed in crimson attire or drenched in sanguine fluid that gave rise to such folklore. If any skepticism lingered regarding this entity being one of the trio who assailed Brock and Malachi, Ana harbored no misconceptions at this juncture. But was she a detached ally, adversary, or something ambiguously nestled between?

Pythia clicked her tongue disapprovingly. "Starving sparrow—peck, peck, peck. Why content yourself with morsels from my mind when you can feast at a banquet? Since you are desperate for answers, I shall oblige."

Before Ana could accept or reject Pythia's offer, the oracle's eyes blazed like twin supernovae in full bloom. Within their dazzling brilliance unfolding like a luminescent cephalopod, Ana's consciousness was captured, jerked, and flung into the temporal currents.

***

"Here," Mary Blackwood's voice was as solid and unyielding as stone, her sunglasses slipping down the bridge of her nose as she surveyed the parking lot. The tinted windows of the BMW shielded them from prying eyes as she pointed towards a nondescript spot. "Their presence lingers here."

Beside her, Dr. Marrow's icy gaze traced the same invisible path, his Mediterranean features etched with an ageless quality that hinted at centuries lived rather than mere decades. His beard, lush and soft like a mink's pelt, framed a mouth set into a regal frown. His Armani suit strained against his muscular physique as he unfolded himself from the car with an ease that belied his powerful form.

Ensuring no curious persons were about, he whispered an arcane word into the cool shade of their chosen tree. "Occultare." A hum filled the air like summer heat waves echoing through winter frost. The shadows beneath the leafy canopy deepened to an abyssal black before fading away along with their vehicle—only a faint shimmer remained where metal and glass had once been.

"Aren't you afraid Ana will recognize you?" Mary questioned, her brows furrowing behind her sunglasses.

Dr. Marrow responded with dry humor, curling his words like smoke. "I'm more concerned about your people's fondness for mischief and theft." Even as he uttered his words, a sly smile stretched across his face. He whispered a barely audible incantation—darkness twirled around him like silk ribbons in a weaver's hands before abruptly dispersing to disclose a rotund man with crooked teeth standing where Dr. Marrow had been—a grotesque caricature garbed in a t-shirt proclaiming, 'This is our land.'

"Better?" He queried, smug satisfaction dripping from every syllable.

Mary bit back a sour retort at his blatant racism. Stripped of her grimoire, Mary was compelled to lean on the arcane prowess of Marrow—a witch who, in his innate mastery, transcended her understanding and needed neither charms nor eldritch bargains to wield his craft. Their pact echoed the delicate equilibrium that defined all alliances within the Order of Midnight—a precarious ballet between beings yoked by mutual objectives yet cleaved by profound disparities of character or, in Marrow's case, social standing—for he fancied himself nothing less than royalty. In his lifetime, Lovecraft had been the glue binding these discordant renegades together. Yet he had passed into oblivion long before Mary inherited the mantle carried by her ancestors; she couldn't shake off the feeling that his secret society had lost its original essence with his departure.

Her rapport with Marrow—or Moreaux as she initially knew him—was destined for turbulence from its inception. She recognized him as a violator of women and a desecrator of her tribe's sanctity. Each meeting at the hospital required her to feign ignorance of both his sadistic tendencies and their shared ominous secret—an act more exhausting than any magic she'd ever performed.

As they navigated the parking lot, Mary grappled with specters from their tormented past. She stole glances at their distorted reflections mirrored in sleek car exteriors—the sight of herself morphed into an aged Indigenous woman garbed in a sweat-drenched jumpsuit by Marrow's enchantment stirred revulsion deep within her gut. It was a grotesque illusion as fitting for her turbulent emotions as it was adept at concealing their true identities.

They halted near a black half-ton truck, Dr. Marrow's hand waving subtly over its surface—his arcane power humming softly in the air around him. His face fell slightly as he turned back towards Mary—the absence of her grimoire confirmed without a word spoken.

"Ana's smart not to leave it lying around." Mary sighed. "Let's see if we can find them and my book at the ceremony."

"Carnival," he corrected with a smirk that held all the warmth of winter frost.

Mary shot him a stern look before they set off once more—the gravity of their mission leaving no room for his usual provocations. They were not only after Mary's grimoire but also a shard of the Dark Mother—a potent artifact whose presence could tilt the scales against them and the Golden One.

Yet as they neared the bustling gathering, Dr. Marrow disclosed another objective— one that sent icy tendrils of dread coiling around Mary's heart.

"Her protectors need to be dealt with," his voice was soft yet carried an edge sharper than any blade. "I want Ana alone and terrified." His grin widened into something monstrous—a predator baring its teeth at its prey. "Fear will make her pliable."

"I can make Cynthia back down," said Mary, her voice quivering.

"You called *me*, Mary," reproached her ally, his words biting through the tension. To underscore his intentions—merciless and bone-chilling in their starkness—he continued, "You don't dictate the form of my aid. We kill Cynthia and that other individual."

***

"Anabelle Windborn," Steve Longfeather's voice echoed in the confined space of their patrol vehicle, a tone of triumph lacing his words. They were parked amidst the languid afternoon, with the sun casting long shadows over the landscape. The gentle hills rolled away into the distance, their crests adorned with stoic evergreens that swayed in rhythm with the cool breeze.

Leng was perched against the hood of their car, his eerie form silhouetted by the open passenger door. His abyssal eyes seemed to observe the human activity around them —people flitting in and out of a bustling restaurant nearby, others forming orderly queues at gas pumps like sheep herded for shearing. It was always a challenge deciphering Leng's focus, whether he was mentally elsewhere or simply choosing to ignore someone. Steve gave him another moment before pressing on.

A sense of accomplishment washed over Steve as he reveled in his detective work. He found himself surprised at how effortlessly he had uncovered this information. Yet, it wasn't just ordinary police work anymore—something had fundamentally shifted within him these past few days. His mind no longer functioned in linear patterns but delved into broader, more conspiratorial realms where every path held a secret, and each person potentially wore a mask of deceit.

So when he'd called into the station recently to track movements around Malachi and heard gossip of Cynthia and Grace escorting an unfamiliar young white woman to Elder Sue—his instincts had kicked in immediately. This was an essential thread in their web of mysteries that needed unraveling. The fact that she'd abandoned her car at Cynthia's place only made things easier for him; legitimate plates tracing back to California—their very destination—couldn't be mere coincidence.

"There are no coincidences," Steve recalled Leng once muttering, "only fates yet unmanifested."

"Did you hear me?" He finally broke the silence, addressing his enigmatic companion. "I've identified the third Aspect. Thought that might be of interest."

Leng waved a dismissive hand, not tearing his gaze away from the human tableau unfolding before them. "Her name is irrelevant," he drawled, his voice as cold and detached as ever. "All threads in this cosmic web will ultimately converge."

Undeterred by Leng's indifference, Steve carried on with his findings. "She's left traces everywhere—authentic IDS, car registration details; everything checks out." His enthusiasm for police work remained undiminished by Leng's peculiar temperament. "I'm digging into her financials now; we should have a solid lead on her soon."

"Good work," Leng conceded grudgingly, a hint of genuine approval creeping into his voice.

Feeling unusually amicable toward his strange partner, Steve beamed at the rare praise. He wasn't ready to admit it yet—maybe it was just a twisted form of Stockholm syndrome—but he was growing oddly accustomed to this grotesque deity and the bizarre reality of their predicament.

"Shall we continue our hunt?" he asked, eager to get back on track.

Leng paused for a moment before replying in an ominously casual tone. "Before we proceed... perhaps we should grab something to eat?"

Steve's gaze sank to the crumpled bag of half-consumed doughnuts, remnants from their last pit stop. His teeth had grazed over their tasteless bodies while he communicated through the radio, finding them as insipid as cardboard despite having chosen an assortment. The memory of his last substantial meal was lost in the fog of time, and any notion that he could exist without sustenance was quickly debunked by a visceral pang that twisted his stomach into a symphony of growls at the mere thought of food.

"Your body craves nourishment," Leng intoned.

"I'm managing," Steve retorted.

"Your body craves nourishment," Leng reiterated, settling back into his seat with an air of disapproval etched onto his waxy visage. "And you must reconcile yourself with the nature of your impending feast."

With newfound clarity and intellect akin to a spider's intricate web, Steve understood Leng's actions—his exit from the vehicle and scrutiny of their surroundings. It wasn't out of mundane curiosity or a desire for observation; it was the predatory vigilance of a hunter eyeing the forest, anticipating the emergence of an injured or solitary deer from behind the foliage. Or perhaps even weighing up his chances against an entire herd. No matter how Steve tried to humanize this entity in his mind, he couldn't overlook its monstrous history. This being had extinguished countless societies, races, and realms, siphoning off their life essence until they were barren husks. That same monstrous appetite now resided within him—an insatiable hunger waiting to be unleashed.

Tossing aside the bag of unwanted doughnuts through the car window like discarded evidence at a crime scene, Steve spun the vehicle around with reckless abandon. He slammed his foot down on the accelerator. He tore onto the highway in a plume of smoke as if hoping to outrun the shadow of his impending fate.

CHAPTER 6: TO HELL AND BACK

The searing gusts, laden with grit, smothered their hoarse cries.

Malachi's body convulsed, his mind ensnared by the lingering specter of a blood-red maelstrom that clawed at his awareness. In this nightmarish sleep, he felt consumed by a tumultuous crimson ocean, unable to wrestle free. Brock's voice had resonated from a distance, an intangible lifeline before the liquid terror invaded his senses and suffocated him.

"Hey, hey!" Brock pierced the quietude, one hand firmly gripping the steering wheel while the other steadied his friend.

"I'm good. Just some messed-up nightmare," Malachi rasped out between gasps for air. "Didn't realize I'd passed out."

Despite Malachi's unsettling state, it hadn't crossed Brock's mind to wake him. The ghostly residue of ash and dried blood tarnished Malachi's striking features—harsh reminders of their recent flight from danger. Their hasty cleanup with bottled water had only achieved so much; they remained far from looking like ordinary twenty-somethings on a road trip. From what Brock had caught in the rearview mirror, he was no better off—his reflection bore an uncanny resemblance to an escapee fresh from a prison brawl.

Brock's hand found its way onto Malachi's thigh; their fingers wove together instinctively—a silent pact born of shared horror. This tactile connection was now familiar territory—an anchor in their tempestuous reality. Fortified by this touchstone, Malachi scrolled through his phone for any message from Ana—nothing yet—but realized he'd been unconscious for over seven hours.

"Don't you need a breather? I can take over the wheel for a bit," he suggested.

"No breather. I just want to keep going."

Their last 'breather' had nearly spelled doom for them both. After consulting an online map and powering off his phone again, Malachi took in the snow-kissed hills undulating alongside the highway—Rhode Island was a winter wonderland.

Soon, they found themselves navigating through a quaint, historic town that seemed to envelop the highway in a gentle hug. Victorian houses, their faces embellished with elaborate fretwork and ornate gables, stood like regal matrons welcoming fatigued wanderers. The air held a subtle hint of pine and aged timber concealed beneath a blanket of snow so soft and pristine it was astonishing not to see children frolicking in it.

A certain property caught their eye, its charm irresistible. A hand-painted sign swayed lazily in the breeze bearing the words 'Traveller's Respite'. The letters were worn and flaked but exuded an appealing charm. As they parked their vehicle, the gravel crunched ominously under the tires—a sound that reverberated hauntingly in the silence.

Still bearing the invisible scars of their last encounter, Brock and Malachi stepped out of their vehicle with trepidation. They approached the looming structure before them as if it were a haunted mansion from a gothic horror tale. Each creaking floorboard underfoot and rustle of wind through barren trees sent shivers down their spines.

The elderly woman who greeted them at the reception desk seemed to come alive at their disarrayed state and request for shelter and sustenance. Brock, his muscles taut like a drawn bowstring, kept watch in their ornate suite while Malachi sought solace in the steamy embrace of a hot shower. He left the door slightly ajar, just in case.

When he emerged from the bathroom, wrapped only in a towel, Brock's stern gaze held an unspoken understanding. The playful smirk on Malachi's face dissolved into seriousness; he dressed silently as Brock took his turn to wash away the grime—the door also slightly open.

"Not now," Brock stated quietly as they stood parallel to each other at the room's entrance, fingers interlaced, bathed in soft sunlight—cleansed and ready for whatever new horrors lay ahead.

"I understand."

"Nothing I want more, though."

"Same."

They allowed themselves a fleeting kiss that sparked an intense flame. It rapidly escalated into frantic touches and strained clothing before they tore away from each other and hurried downstairs.

In an eccentric parlor repurposed as a dining hall for four, they stole moments of respite over lunch before continuing on their quest. An English high tea was served—a feast of tiny sandwiches and sweet pastries—and they indulged while playfully mimicking British etiquette when the overly attentive hostess was not around.

Brock observed no other life stirring within the ancient house but ignored her excessive hospitality towards her only guests. He politely declined her invitation for them to extend their stay, a twinge of sympathy piercing him as the frail old woman bid them farewell from her porch. But an undercurrent about her—an almost tangible smell of decay—put him on edge. His senses were remarkably acute; secrets often unraveled themselves through whispers or unexpected wafts of scent, but these recent sensations felt more like forewarnings. From her scent alone, he knew she had only days left; she would pass away quietly, perhaps even peacefully, in sleep.

They said their goodbyes and hurried back to their vehicle.

"Everything okay?" Malachi asked, noticing Brock's rigid posture and slight tremble as he froze with his hand resting on the gear stick.

"Ever consider how ephemeral everything is?" Brock mused a melancholy grin playing on his lips that sent a jolt of both sorrow and exhilaration through Malachi's chest. He guided the vehicle around, pausing at the precipice of rejoining the highway's ceaseless flow, the rhythmic blink of his indicator light falling into an eerie quiet. "We're not far from the Newport ferry, that'll take us right to Providence. Sorry for getting spun around and taking us too far south." Brock's sole navigational error in their time together was forgivable given the hasty and perilous circumstances they'd fled—Malachi hadn't even noticed. "Once we're there, what's our next move? You mentioned some historic site."

"Correct," Malachi affirmed. "Our target is Lovecraft's former residence in Providence —an exhibit now brimming with relics from his life. We'll probably trip over whatever we need—I'm practically a four-leaf clover on two legs."

"That haunted hotel could've done with a sprinkle of your serendipity," Brock quipped, reminding Malachi of their recent misadventure and his inability to steer them clear.

"Everything happens for a reason," Malachi offered with a nonchalant shrug. Without speaking aloud, he added in their shared mental space: If we hadn't sprung that trap, would we have bared our souls or banished my self-doubts? Without those trials, I might still be earthbound.

Brock recalled the awe-inspiring sight of being cradled by a shadowy seraph—a memory filled with wonder and warmth.

"I never saw it from that perspective," he admitted aloud. "Let's see where your luck leads us next." His grin was infectious as he revved the engine and surged onto the highway.

Meanwhile, lurking half a mile behind in an ordinary diner parking lot, their pursuer lowered his binoculars from within an unremarkable gray Jeep and began tailing them again.

***

The ferry's journey to Providence provided a momentary haven for Brock and Malachi amidst the tumult of their lives. They leaned against their SUV, drinking in the scene of churning waves speckled with sunlight shards that stabbed through the celestial canopy overhead. A biting wind whipped around them; Brock stood unflinching against its frosty assault, while Malachi found solace by simply sidling closer. The rest of the passengers stayed cocooned within their vehicles, blissfully oblivious to any other beings sharing this voyage. An elusive fragrance occasionally wafted past Brock—was it hickory or maybe the comforting sulfurous hint of childhood bonfires with Charlie? Its origin eluded him, swiftly swallowed by the sharp cocktail of salt and seaweed that ruled the sea air. They stayed outside until the sky's mood darkened, clouds mutating into an ominous tableau, thunder heralding an imminent downpour.

Beneath the storm's melancholy veil, they disembarked onto a stretch ringed by a phalanx of trees cloaked in pearly mist. The sporadic snow patches peppering the horizon took on a deadly glint reminiscent of perilous ice-coated battlegrounds—winter here was still wrestling, a titan locked in combat with autumn's stubborn persistence. The foggy drizzle coating winter's highway necessitated Brock's high beams to cut through its density while the treacherous road seemed keen to rip apart their axles. His fingers tightened around the wheel with white-knuckled fervor as he repeatedly glanced at his mirrors.

Have I seen that gray Jeep before? He queried internally as they navigated a lengthy stretch of straight road.

Before he could confirm its familiarity, it slowed and disappeared from sight.

"Man," Malachi noted with dry wit, "you're strung tighter than a hipster's jeans."

"These roads are crap," Brock retorted, his grip on the steering wheel unconsciously shredding more threads from the already worn polyester cover. Malachi wondered if Brock even noticed this new nervous tick—his steering wheel would need replacement soon enough at this rate. Perhaps being on edge wasn't entirely unwarranted; they had skirted death after all, and he doubted H.P.'s grimoire had been left unprotected for their convenience. Why should anything be easy?

To distract himself from Brock's simmering tension, Malachi unlocked his phone. Ana's cryptic text message glowed on the screen: Gone for a sweat. Will find answers.

As he slipped his phone back into his pocket, Malachi gazed through the rain-speckled window into the relentless downpour. The storm gradually swallowed the landscape, shrouding everything in mystical swirls of white mist. The rhythmic patter of hail against the roof lulled him, causing his head to nod and shoulders to sag...

"Malachi..." A voice stirred him from his drowsiness.

***

Malachi found himself folded into a haphazard lotus position, bereft of support of the car and its upholstery. His sparsely clad legs and restless fingers grazed over dew-damp grass littered with brittle twigs. A voice had summoned him here, hadn't it? Brock's voice? But where was he? Encasing this modest glade were skeletal pines, their gaunt branches reaching out to the icy moon as if pleading for warmth. Their frost-touched needles caught the moonlight in a spectral dance that cast an eerie glow around him. Despite the chill in the air, a heavy cloak draped over his shoulders rustled like whispers in the wind, offering an unexpected cocoon of warmth. The fire crackling before him lent comforting heat to this strange scene.

He took in these alien surroundings with a quiet acceptance that hinted at their dreamlike nature. The absence of Brock didn't unsettle him; instead, an unknown figure occupied his place on the other side of the fire without triggering any alarm bells within Malachi's psyche. Across from him stood a stranger: indistinct and wavering like an apparition seen through misty eyes. Could one even say he was standing? Details were slippery and elusive to Malachi's gaze—except for two glimmering yellow orbs that bore into him like sunlit amber and a rich baritone voice that echoed across the clearing.

"Finally," Snake drawled lazily, "we get some privacy."

Malachi frowned at this unfamiliar entity. "Privacy? Do we know each other?" A memory teased at the edges of his consciousness but remained frustratingly out of reach.

"We've crossed paths before, Raven."

The dream seemed to mold itself under Malachi's will—a rare control seldom granted by nocturnal fantasies—prompting his defiant response. "I'd prefer you stick with Malachi. Not everyone gets to use my spirit name."

The stranger let out an annoyed hiss, then moved around the fire with a fluidity that was almost...serpentine. From a swirling mist emerged a figure that bore an uncanny resemblance to a mythical djinn: upper body sculpted and lean, while his lower half seemed to dissolve into a tail of smoke. His striking features were breathtaking, an exotic contrast to Brock's golden boy charm. Ebony locks framed a face carved from obsidian, lips curled in a perpetual scowl surrounded by stubble, and those hypnotic amber serpent eyes that gave him an otherworldly aura.

"I am Snake," he announced with an air of condescension. "We are kin."

"Snake?" Malachi's eyebrows shot up in surprise. "As in the missing Aspect?"

"Indeed."

Malachi's disbelief cleared away the lingering fog clouding his mind; he sprang up, feathers rustling on his cloak like startled birds. "How did you get here?"

"How could I not?" Snake replied with a smirk. "Brock was easy enough to locate in this dreamscape—his yearning for you shone like a lighthouse beacon. But you two have been reckless—every surge of your powers sends shockwaves through the ley lines, alerting every supernatural entity tuned into such frequencies. It's nothing short of miraculous that you're still alive—it gives me hope our struggle won't be in vain."

"Our struggle against...the Outer Gods?" Malachi ventured.

Snake's grin widened into something deceitfully charming—a clear warning sign he wasn't entirely trustworthy—"Two of them indeed—one bent on our annihilation and another vying for control." He paused dramatically before adding, "I can see your thoughts spiraling with questions—I know so much about us, about this cosmic war we've been drafted into—you poor, clueless soul! Father has bestowed upon me a wealth of knowledge while you remain so...mundane."

"Father? You have a father?" As far as Malachi knew, Aspects weren't created through traditional biology.

With an almost seductive grace, Snake moved around him, his steps as smooth and precise as the creature he was named after. He halted just behind Malachi, his voice a low murmur that sent a shiver down the latter's spine. "More accurately, you could call him my adoptive father," he said, his words brushing against Malachi's ear in a way that made him tense. "I've taken it upon myself to arrange for you to meet him soon—he's rather at a loss about how to proceed."

"Proceed with what?" Malachi asked, trying to keep his tone casual despite the uneasiness creeping up his spine.

"After that unfortunate event near Detroit," Snake replied nonchalantly.

Detroit? Was he referring to...? Malachi turned sharply towards Snake. "Wait, your adoptive dad—did he send those creeps to murder us?"

Snake chuckled lightly, his voice carrying an air of aristocratic amusement. "Creeps? You must mean his bio-templars...and murder? That wasn't the plan at all," he corrected smoothly. "Father simply wanted to bring you home. He dispatched his soldiers for your retrieval; we had no idea their loyalties had been bought."

"They tried to kill us!" Malachi shot back.

"And they failed while you prevailed," Snake countered dismissively. "The rules of this game are quite straightforward."

"We're not pawns on some chessboard!" Malachi retorted indignantly.

Snake's smirk cut through the darkness like a crescent moon slicing through the night sky. "Not exactly," he said cryptically. "We are an amalgamation of divine and beastly elements—a product of ancient rituals once only known by enlightened witches who served the Outer Gods in an era when Earth was still pristine and magic flowed freely. After the Great War, however, magic became scarce; creating semi-divine offspring required generations of power gathering. We are the modern manifestation of that archaic sorcery."

Malachi's mind was a whirlpool of confusion, but he barely had time to process Snake's words before the latter continued, his voice edged with urgency.

"I regret that I can't assist you in navigating this maze," he said quickly. "I must return to my sanctuary before the Godbeasts hunting you detect me. For it seems like the entities you thought were dead are still very much alive," Snake's ethereal voice echoed in the foggy clearing. "Just remember, you're not alone in this fight. My father's war isn't with you but with the horrific Lords of Chaos. He's shackled to Cthulhu just as tightly as your fate is intertwined with Cthugha, both of you unwilling slaves to hideous masters. I'm offering an olive branch and a word of caution: each time you or Brock tap into your abilities, it's like lighting a flare in pitch blackness, drawing all sorts of insatiable monstrosities towards your luminescence. Emulate the serpent: shrewd and elusive."

As Snake spoke, he began to dissolve into wisps of smoke that swirled around Malachi, enveloping him in a grey haze. Soon, only two glowing amber orbs remained floating mid-air, and his spectral voice began to echo. The eerie encounter was nearing its end.

"We'll cross paths again after Rhode Island," Snake promised.

"Hold on! How do you know our plans? Who exactly are you?" Malachi demanded as reality started creeping back in, replacing his dreamlike state with the physical sensation of his own body—his stiff limbs and steady breaths.

He feared he wouldn't get any more answers as his consciousness drifted away from this surreal realm. But one response managed to reach him through the dissipating fog of his dream.

"Cal," came the distant echo.

"Cal," Malachi repeated groggily as he woke up to a dreary morning, his head nestled on one of Brock's travel pillows. A hazy curtain veiled Rhode Island's scenic beauty, leaving only frost-dusted trees and mounds visible. Even though he was awake now, everything felt as dreamlike as his encounter with Cal.

Brock gave him an intrigued look. "You were mumbling in your sleep."

"I think I just met a potential ally... guy's shady as hell, though," Malachi admitted.

Pulling off to the side of the road, they started discussing this unexpected development.

***

A ripple of vexation coursed through Malachi, the raw edge in his movements betraying his turmoil as he flung his phone into the glove compartment. The door snapped shut with a vehemence that echoed his internal storm. He emerged from the SUV, each footfall on the frost-glazed asphalt crisp punctuation beneath the wan winter sun. Brock materialized at his side, their shared gaze canvassing a cityscape shrouded behind an intricate tapestry of snow-draped woodland. It had erupted amidst downtown edifices like a spectral forest plucked straight from a forsaken fable.

The park was peppered with peculiar stone monoliths, arching like inverted horseshoes, wide enough to encapsulate ambling lovers beneath their stony embrace along serpentine trails. Benches and pedestals adorned with plaques offered intriguing diversions for those intrepid souls who dared to infiltrate this arctic realm. In the remote distance, sequestered behind an austere wrought-iron barricade and gateway, loomed a stark silhouette against the icy arboreal canvas: H.P.'s mansion.

Brock's attention wavered back to Malachi, and he extended a hand to rest on his friend's shoulder. His soothing gesture evolved into a firm knead that coaxed some of Malachi's palpable tension to recede. Still no answer? he projected.

Yeah, came Malachi's mental admission, tinged with unease. I just hope everything's fine.

She's got grit, Brock reassured him quickly through their mental link. So does Cynthia. And Lenny? He sounds like he could stare down Armageddon itself.

You're probably right. A fleeting grin peeked out from under Malachi's worry as he lifted his hand to press it warmly onto Brock's in silent gratitude before they both fortified their expressions into resolute masks and plunged deeper into the park.

Brock found himself hyper-aware of even the most mundane elements within this environment. The crunch of footsteps on frosty grass sent icy tendrils down his spine; a dog's labored panting twisted into the guttural growl of a hellhound in his mind; even sunlight glittering off the snow pulsated with an eerie vibrancy. The acrid stench of urine, both human and animal, clawed at his nostrils in the frigid air while a trio of homeless men huddled around one of the park's placards heightened his unease.

You holding up okay? Malachi's teeth-chattering brought Brock back to reality.

I think so, came Malachi's distracted response, his attention clearly ensnared elsewhere. Their haphazardly-acquired winter coat from a ramshackle pitstop they made earlier seemed to waver in its duty against the biting cold. Just a bit nippy, I suppose.

Something feels...off, doesn't it?

Yeah.

The source of their unease was elusive, yet an unshakable vigilance clung to them as they approached the gateway into Lovecraft's realm. The contemplation of what lay hidden within the unassuming, box-like dwelling, a facade concealing the clandestine affairs of one of the world's most infamous witches, did nothing to quell their mounting sense of dread. They were sharply conscious that each footfall towards this abode marked a stride nearer to the brink of madness—a bone-deep premonition that echoed in their souls.

"Think we can handle this?" Brock ventured.

"Hell no," Malachi shot back, his face grimacing. "But so far, being scared shitless and winging it hasn't failed me."

As they trespassed onto the property, an uncanny sensation slithered up their legs like frosty fingers tracing lecherous routes over their bodies.

"Jesus Christ!" Brock exclaimed.

"What on earth was that?"

The house seemed to scrutinize them through its draped windows like four shadowy orbs, sizing them up with an unseen stare. The sensation ebbed as swiftly as it had surged, leaving them rattled but resolute. Had they just crossed some mystical barrier or boundary? If so, they had been deemed worthy enough to breach it.

A portly man sporting a baseball cap and winter jacket emerged from the front door, casting anxious glances around before stepping aside for them to enter. "Creepy place," he muttered as he passed by.

Brock couldn't help but silently concur: Likely more than he realizes.

Communicating telepathically seemed the only suitable option in this setting; seamlessly shifting to this form of dialogue felt natural here. Following a short path, they hoisted themselves onto a concrete step—an anomaly amidst the otherwise vintage charm of the building. The rest of the structure appeared preserved or meticulously maintained from its early 20th-century grandeur: chartreuse panels, glossy ebony shutters, and weathered ivory detailing. Barren shrubs ensnared the house, their branches brushing against the siding with an uncanny resonance akin to alien appendages. Brock braced for another mystical jolt—relieved when it didn't materialize—as he grasped the handle and ventured inside.

Within, a soothing warmth enveloped them in tandem with the aroma of aged books and polishes used on mahogany frames, railings, and steps that filled the narrow entrance hall. A corridor ran alongside the stairs leading to a kitchen. To their right was a study where faux gaslamp flames flickered across glass boxes encased behind crimson velvet ropes; these boxes held relics of H.P.'s life—Brock doubted they would discover a grimoire among these artifacts but deemed it worth investigating.

Across in the drawing room, a young introverted bookworm perched on a chair adorned with lion's feet glanced up from his book over his glasses at them.

"No tours today," he declared, sizing them up from head to toe. "If you want one, come back Monday through Saturday. Feel free to take a brochure, though."

Plastic containers overflowing with tourist pamphlets littered an antique Roger's radio near the entryway.

"If you've got any questions after snooping around," said the clerk, "I'll be here. Just remember not to touch anything—we've got cameras everywhere."

Brock greeted him with a curt nod, his attention momentarily distracted as Malachi delved into the stack of pamphlets. A slick brochure, emblazoned with an image of a monstrous cephalopod creature, snagged his interest. He carefully extracted the leaflet that chronicled the history of this peculiar house—where H.P. Lovecraft had crafted an uncanny narrative before his untimely end: "The Haunter in the Dark." In it, Lovecraft's fictitious protagonist, Robert Blake, was subjected to the capricious horrors of a spectral mansion—one that twisted and contorted through dimensions and realities until it fractured his sanity. Could there be truth woven into this outlandish tale? Malachi mused. After all, he understood that Lovecraft's arcane narratives were more allegorical than fantastical.

Lovecraft penned this tale about this location, he communicated silently to Brock. Given the house's nature—that it could manifest anywhere or anytime—it might be less about the physical structure and more about the spell or magical power source that moved the house around.

Like a battery? Brock's thoughts often gravitated towards automotive comparisons.

Possibly... Malachi reflected on Ana's remarkable account of an immense cavern beneath Mary's unassuming cottage—a descent so profound it felt akin to skirting Hell's precipice. She had painted a picture of a celestial cathedral with rifts opening onto star-studded abysses, a mystical font for unholy sacraments, an altar, and a wall festooned with levitating runes designed for giants—all invoked by a Book of Shadows—a power source? I think he was illustrating effects from his grimoire—a tool potent enough to open portals or distort reality, Malachi hypothesized. Given that this place is fortified by magic, I suspect it's here.

"There's plenty more house left," drawled the smug young man, watching their awe-struck expressions from the entrance.

Let's find that grimoire, Malachi suggested.

Their search commenced in the study, with its multitude of book-filled shelves—the most rational place to unearth a tome. The shelves were laden with works from Lovecraft's inspirations—Shakespeare, Dante, and Poe—each first edition radiating an aura of majesty. However, no tome resembling Ana's description of an ancient, leather-bound grimoire presented itself among these literary gems. Malachi had half-expected it to leap out at them.

They scrutinized each glass case diligently, their curiosity momentarily piqued by an unusual set: a spyglass and dream catcher Malachi recognized from a passage in Lovecraft's diary. Brock listened attentively for any telltale sounds of hidden passages—murmurs or whispers amid the silence—but found nothing. Disheartened, they pressed on.

In the drawing room, they maneuvered around the indifferent attendant like seasoned archaeologists. They examined the mantlepiece and scrutinized sepia-toned portraits of Lovecraft while Brock gently tapped on the walls. The attendant feigned ignorance even more dramatically as they cleared this section of suspicion and ascended to meticulously furnished bedrooms.

Their exploration yielded nothing remarkable except for a small freestanding portrait encased within a tarnished nickel frame in one guest room. The photo depicted a burly man in overalls and a cowboy hat with his arm slung around a frail-looking Lovecraft amidst lush woodlands.

"Dude resembles Charlie," Brock blurted suddenly.

"The lumberjack guy?"

"Yeah, dead ringer."

Sure he was seeing things, Brock leaned closer to inspect the grainy features, but even his preternatural sight couldn't discern more details than shadow and beard from blotchy pixels. Charlie had passed away years ago; he looked somewhere in his forties, though they'd only ever celebrated Brock's birthdays. This photo was steeped in age and the scent of talcum powder—it was clearly older than Charlie himself could have been.

A low hum alerted Brock to another camera in the room, its location betrayed by a soft whir from the top left corner. They returned to the ground floor and moved on to a narrow kitchen devoid of any magical texts in its barren pantry or drawers.

"No cutlery in there," the attendant snarled from the foyer.

"We're not thieves," Malachi retorted sharply.

"Sure," came the skeptical reply.

Just as the specter of defeat began to loom, Malachi's slender hand extended towards a door half-concealed in the kitchen's gloomy corner. A sign daring 'No Entry' hung like a challenge. Brock reached out, his hand closing around the handle; it was locked, but an icy tremor ran through him—a spectral whisper of magic. His senses had been honed razor-sharp since their brush with the triad of witches; he was hyper-vigilant, teetering on the edge of sensory overload. He detected another concealed camera, its unblinking eye lurking somewhere above them in the kitchen.

Something is beneath us, he silently relayed to Malachi via their private mental channel. But we're under surveillance.

Let's not earn ourselves another warrant.

Brock pivoted to regard Malachi, whose androgynous beauty was accentuated by soft winter light filtering through a solitary window—an ethereal tableau that momentarily entranced him. He could discern his heartbeat echoing in his ears, Malachi's gentle respiration and even the distant murmur of another window nudged by the outdoor breeze.

Basement window? he proposed after regaining his senses.

They retreated from the kitchen and returned to the drawing room with the young man. Malachi engaged him in strained pleasantries while Brock hunted for any electric hum indicative of security equipment. Finding none, he deduced that surveillance must be remotely operated. "Enjoy your day," he offered casually as they approached the exit.

"Whatever," came the dismissive reply from their nerdy guide.

"Well then, whatever yourself," fired back Brock with an unexpected vehemence that startled everyone else present. "The apocalypse is nigh, so maybe try being less obnoxious. Remove your nose from those dusty books and experience life—maybe make a friend or even try and get laid—before cosmic deities reduce everything to ash."

Grinning, they left the youth grappling with his existential dread and ventured outside. From the porch, Brock led them to the house's rear, ensuring no electronic eyes were prying before pausing beside an inconspicuous cluster of shrubs. He surveyed their surroundings and glanced over his shoulder towards the ominous forest before parting the bushes with an almost divine command. This swift, snapping motion exposed the concrete underbelly and a rectangular basement window.

Brock crouched down, his imposing frame keeping back the foliage as he examined the window frame with tactile interest. His ears strained for signs of life: nothing but scurrying rodents and weaving spiders echoed back. The abyss below seemed free of any obvious surveillance equipment, and his sharp gaze found no evidence of white plastic protrusions indicating a glass or threshold alarm system along the skeletal window frame. His preliminary scouting left him suffused with satisfaction.

Malachi noted Brock's intense focus—the deliberate precision of each action. "You're behaving like you've done this whole breaking-and-entering gig before."

"Being a part-time wanderer and full-time screw-up teaches you some tricks," retorted Brock, sarcasm lacing his words before giving way to solemnity again.

Brock's concentration was palpable as he gently pressed his palms against the glass, each minute fissure spreading beneath his fingertips a testament to his deliberate force. Malachi watched, captivated by fractures radiating across the pane like intricate frost patterns from Brock's touch—an artistry of destruction hinting at his uncanny control over matter. When the entire sheet of glass was reduced to a spiderweb of cracks yet held its form, Brock delicately tapped its edges, catching falling shards as they fluttered down onto his hands like the first snow.

In a heartbeat, he'd swept away all remnants of glass with those iron-strong hands, washing off any lingering shards in fresh snowfall. Task accomplished, he twisted his robust form through the opening into an unseen expanse beyond. Brock's hands emerged from within this gloom, and Malachi cautiously surrendered himself to be pulled inside.

They found themselves ensconced in a cold, damp space—two comrades huddled together with hearts pounding from their audacious intrusion like star-crossed rogues. You're bloody brilliant! Malachi exclaimed in their shared mental space. So are you, came Brock's straightforward reply.

Hand in hand, they ventured deeper into the basement—a hoarder's dream filled with sagging shelves and toppled cardboard boxes overflowing with obsolete documents. Scattered around were accordion folders and manila envelopes; loose papers lay forgotten under layers of dust.

As they moved further from the sliver of daylight that pierced above them, Malachi relied more on Brock's primal instincts to guide them through this labyrinthine mess. He clung tightly to Brock's hand so as not to trip over any discarded items strewn about, and he suppressed several sneezes from the spore-like effusion of must.

While it seemed reasonable that their sought-after grimoire lay beneath this mountain of paperwork, an inexplicable force led them past the chaos and toward a cleared section of the cellar. Here, a dim recess beckoned beyond shadowy stairs that ascended upwards.

"Do you see it?" Brock's whisper cut through the silence.

Malachi squinted into the darkness. "No."

"A door."

Beyond the stairs, against a cobblestone wall, was a rectangular indentation outlined by a faint silver luminescence. As Brock moved closer—brushing aside cobwebs—the reality that he was staring at some form of doorway or portal became undeniable. It baffled him that Malachi couldn't perceive it, even as he reached out to trace its shimmering outline with his fingers.

A peculiar energy pulsed through Brock as his fingers intuitively found crevices to grip onto. He wedged his hand into these stony pockets and tugged. The wall crumbled forward in a soft whoosh, dusting their boots in sandy debris. With this illusionary barrier dispelled Malachi peered into the same dark portal as his friend. A gentle breeze tugged at their clothes and swept bits of debris from their feet into its abyss.

"How did you do that?" Malachi marveled aloud.

"I... I don't know," Brock confessed honestly. "I'm experiencing things that don't seem rooted in this reality... or at least not our version. Whatever's happening, it's intensifying. Perhaps we'll stumble upon some answers further ahead."

"But where does it lead?"

Brock paused before responding with the same uncanny intuition he'd just described. "To the grimoire." He sniffed the air, catching scents of coal, sulfur, and something very burnt. "And a world on fire."

"A world on fire?"

"Let's find out."

With courage enough for both of them, Brock gave Malachi's hand a reassuring squeeze and stepped into the portal.

***

The sensation of being ripped apart and hurled through space was a paroxysm of pain so profound it manifested as a blinding burst of light, an internal shriek that their raw throats mirrored as they were violently expelled onto a desolate expanse. The searing gusts, laden with grit, smothered their hoarse cries. Brock, his instincts kicking in faster, staggered to his feet and extended a hand to Malachi. Their voices were stolen by the shock; they squinted through dry eyes at the hellish panorama they'd been deposited into. A fleeting examination of each other revealed bodies naked and singed like devils freshly summoned from volcanic depths.

A rift in reality loomed ominously behind them: a tarnished silver gash in the cosmos pulsating with an uncanny rhythm—a chilling memento of their possible escape route. Before them sprawled an alien terrain of crimson stone, brutally carved into jagged buttes and deadly chasms by some unseen malevolent force—an imminent journey that promised nothing less than danger.

The ruthless trio of suns—one casting ethereal pink rays, one radiating harsh canary yellow light, and one blazing with white-hot ferocity—ruthlessly seared their exposed skin. Monstrous bird-like apparitions, akin to prehistoric condors yet far more malevolent, soared menacingly over the desolate stretch. Even Brock's steeled gaze couldn't discern these spectral predators' true nature. Their metallic shrieks reverberated through the barren wasteland, sending tremors racing down their spines.

Beyond this immediate terror lurked additional nightmares: ominous tongues of flame flickered wickedly from numerous pits scattered across the landscape. Dense plumes of ash and ember swept across this infernal domain, knitting together to form a volatile fog that threatened to swallow everything in its path.

They found themselves precariously perched atop one of the taller buttes, momentarily safe from the encroaching tempest below. But safety was transient—the fiery maelstrom would soon rise to swallow them whole. The triple suns bore down with demonic persistence, seemingly intent on reducing them to charred husks amidst this nightmarish world.

Feels like we've crash-landed into Dante's vacation home, Malachi thought, even his mental voice raspy. I wonder if this is where he got his brochures. If this isn't Hell, it's a damn good imitation. Any idea where we're supposed to go?

Brock felt that same mystical tug that had yanked him through the portal; each pulse of his heart, every throb in his temples pointed him in one direction—forward and slightly left. We need to head that way, he thought back, though how they'd navigate this hellscape remained a mystery.

If you can point us in the right direction, I can get us there, Malachi replied confidently.

He stepped back and focused—determined to defy destiny—and with an eruption of smoky power and a flurry of black feathers, wings sprouted from silver tendrils of magic along his back. Summoning his power felt effortless and invigorating now that he'd recovered from the initial shock. If this realm was cursed with wild magic, its eldritch energies had also revitalized him. Without hesitation, he moved closer to Brock, guiding the other's hands around his waist. Hold on tight, he commanded.

Brock was propelled upwards, feeling light as a feather in Malachi's grip. They pierced the atmosphere like an arrow shot from a bow, creating a bubble of cool air around them that stood defiant against the raging inferno outside. It was an impressive display of Malachi's power.

As Brock realized the ease with which Malachi bore his weight, he found solace in their proximity. His eyes slid shut, and he began to navigate their course through a mental bond. This place seemed soaked with magic potent enough to let them share more than mere words or images—they could swap entire perspectives, like exchanging old Polaroid photos. And so it happened that Malachi, the Great Raven, surveyed the decaying landscape of Brimstone beneath him using Brock's borrowed strength and enhanced vision. He sent these images back to Brock, who plotted their path.

Malachi felt power pulsate within him, but he had enough sense not to mistake this for invincibility. He skillfully evaded the monstrous beasts that dominated the sky around them, adjusting his altitude when they tried to intercept him. Their speed outmatched these serpentine giants, and soon, they lost interest as the duo continued towards the blasted mountaintops where grotesque birds nested.

Amidst this hellish orchestra, a sound akin to steel being torn apart during a catastrophic train wreck emerged. The airborne leviathans slowly came into focus. Were they dragons? Demons? Prehistoric monsters from an unrecorded era? What name could truly define such an abhorrent hybrid—an entity boasting the robust form of a four-legged dinosaur with talons resembling monstrous fingers capable of clutching mountain peaks and wings stretching broader than the grandest of canyons?

Their bodies were encased in scales as dark and reflective as volcanic glass—and must be impervious given the climate. The obsidian talons jutting from their massive limbs looked strong enough to effortlessly snatch a city bus like a child's toy. Each scale seemed to absorb light, lending them an ethereal aura as captivating as it was sinister.

Their heads were adorned with horns and sharp spikes, like demonic crowns—a sign of their rule over this realm. These weren't mere ornaments; they were weapons, each one sharp enough to pierce steel or shatter stone. The horns spiraled toward the heavens like grotesque towers, casting long shadows over their faces and enhancing their formidable appearance.

But the wings—those were a sight to behold. They spread out on either side of these creatures, comparable in size to commercial aircraft at full span. Each feather overlapped the next meticulously—each one larger than a human—and glowed with iridescent colors when hit by light at the right angle.

These beasts weren't just hybrids—they were nightmares incarnate: part dinosaur, part dragon, part demon...and entirely terrifying. Yet despite their dreadful appearance, Brock conceded that there was a certain hideous allure about them.

What the fuck are those supposed to be? he demanded.

No clue. Lovecraft's diary didn't say anything about this stuff...Aside from that line about a journey into realms beyond death—maybe here...Maybe Ana can shed some light—she's devoured a ton of that lunatic's tales.

Was he batshit crazy? Or just woke?

Do you mean awake? Woke has a different connotation—

Is this me being socially retarded again?

Yup.

A seismic shockwave ripped through the smog-shrouded expanse. Brock's voice, as brassy and unyielding as a bugle call, sliced through the chaos. "Watch out!" The sky exploded in a spectacle of cosmic fireworks, a pulsating starburst of light shadowed by an advancing surge of darkness that bled from a radiant core shrouded in nebulous swirls.

With the nimble agility of an aerial acrobat, Malachi dipped and dived to avoid the gale-force winds that had sprung up without warning. Brock squinted upwards at the maelstrom, where two celestial titans clashed in a high-stakes game of territory control. Their conflict set their surroundings ablaze with a swirling inferno, painting bloody silhouettes across the heavenly tapestry. The raw power radiating from their collision made Brock wonder if such battles had once scorched this planet's crust.

Navigating this latest near-apocalypse—Malachi weaving deftly between towering thunderheads—they were serenaded by a chorus of sky kings worldwide, all reveling in the spectacle of combat from their lofty perches or mid-air pursuits.

Just when it seemed they'd cleared the war zone in the heavens, an earth-shattering roar tore through the atmosphere, causing Malachi to falter mid-flight and nearly catapult them into a churning dust storm. He swerved away at the last possible second. The battle above drew to a swift conclusion, with one victorious champion left triumphant.

No sooner had they dodged one catastrophe than another presented itself—a flaming meteorite zipped past his wings, setting their tips alight, which was thankfully snuffed out by his terrified dive for safety. The descending mass was, in actuality, the lifeless body of the beast who had been vanquished in the aerial dominion dispute overhead. The sheer insanity and ruinous nature of their clash were nothing short of breathtaking.

Unheeding his own introspective ponderings, Malachi marshaled the full might of his otherworldly power. He strained against the unyielding grip of gravity, wrenching them skyward from the pull towards the ominous ruby-red mushroom cloud—a grim monument to the fallen celestial monarch. Reality seemed to tremble on its axis. The monstrous cries of the sky kings gradually faded, leaving a manageable turbulence Malachi could navigate.

This place is bonkers, Malachi's thoughts echoed in Brock's mind, tinged with apprehension. Any idea when we can get out of here? We can't exactly chill in this mess.

Brock's forehead creased in concentration as he reached out to touch the ethereal threads of mystical energy that pulsed around them. The magic was near, tantalizingly so, like a half-remembered song just beyond recall. Down there, his mental voice was firm and confident. It's down there.

They cautiously spiraled lower as the heat intensified, and ash plumes continued to billow from the fallen sky king's final resting place miles away. A vortex of gusty winds—

courtesy of Malachi's magic—shielded them from the blistering heat and possibly radiation.

But how much time had passed since they'd arrived? What state were their clothes in? Were they physically present in this realm or merely projecting their consciousness across celestial planes? Questions swirled through Malachi's—and therefore Brock's—mind like a whirlwind. Still, he understood enough about this nightmare scenario to know that any damage sustained here would have real-world consequences.

Finally, amidst the endless desolation, a distinct shape began to take form, indicating that they were closing in on their destination.

Obsidian towers, like monstrous sentinels of a bygone era, punctured the smoky canvas overhead. Their looming presence encased a vast courtyard where an ancient temple stood as the heart, its decaying columns akin to rotten teeth in a titan's maw. The scattered remnants of these monoliths lay strewn about, discarded carelessly by the celestial giant that once possessed them.

With his instinctive grasp on structures and mechanisms, Brock quickly identified the corroded heaps of triangular metal around them: ships of alien design. But these behemoths surpassed even the largest frigates he'd seen in any human docks. His mind wrestled with the idea that these relics were once vehicles. He shuddered at the thought of what cosmic entities might have commanded such immense vessels.

The scale of everything was mind-boggling; it made New York City's skyline seem like a child's playset. The notion that this could be one structure among many within an alien cityscape nearly overwhelmed Brock. Yet signs were everywhere: crumbled lines suggesting streets or pathways, ash-covered mounds hinting at other grand structures now reduced to ruins.

Carrying Brock aloft, Malachi moved warily through this colossal graveyard of decayed grandeur. Their surroundings diminished them to mere specks amid the ruins, yet Brock's sharp eyes spotted a monstrous staircase crumbling into oblivion. Its steps spiraled down into a tunnel leading deeper into this foreign realm. Guiding Malachi towards it, they appeared as tiny insects navigating through skeletal remains of leviathans.

Malachi found himself entrapped by abyssal jaws of darkness—a portal as awe-inspiring and intimidating as the Gates of Hell. Drawn into its shadowy depths, echoes bounced off cavernous walls, whispering forgotten tales before he came to rest within its spectral womb veiled in omnipresent gloom.

The air tasted like charred earth and ancient decay, a metallic tang of rusted iron tracks lingering on his tongue. Terror gnawed at Malachi's soul for a brief, harrowing moment. Then Brock emerged from the shadows, his form glowing with a soft golden radiance that danced around him like an ethereal halo. It sliced through the murkiness, casting spectral shadows on rugged walls while lighting their path forward.

The sound of sand dripping and hissing echoed eerily in this subterranean world, punctuating the silence like a solemn heartbeat. Brock took Malachi's hand, leading them deeper into the underground expanse.

Fear had been their uninvited guest since they'd landed in this alien reality—yet now it seemed to ebb somewhat. The term 'alien' felt somehow inadequate as remnants of a civilization eerily similar to humanity began to emerge—though on a scale that suggested beings of colossal proportions.

Fragmented basins littered their path—the shattered remnants of pottery strewn across what might have once been a bustling promenade now filled with ash dunes reminiscent of desolate desert landscapes. Partially buried statues peeked out from under embankments: hooded figures with vaguely humanoid features carved from stone.

Brock's mystical torchlight flickered, casting an eerie glow on the enormous idol before them. Its figure was draped in ornate robes, and a cascade of stone hair tumbled from beneath its hood. The statue clutched a caduceus in its hand—the twin serpents coiled around the staff seemed locked in an endless battle. The features etched onto its face were disturbingly human-like, yet no earthly being could match its terrifying grandeur.

As they pushed deeper into the echoing cavern, their eyes were drawn to a vast metallic mural painted with gleaming hues. It depicted disjointed scenes—maybe recounting the fall of these ancient dwellers? They halted to examine it more closely, Brock's light growing brighter against the embossed figures.

Rows of worshipers stood before a blood-red sun emblazoned with an eye reminiscent of Egyptian mythology. Flames surrounded them, sending waves of runic energy emanating from the sun—each figure seemed to be wrapped in a fire similar to Brock's own elemental blaze. Behind this fiery tableau lurked the silhouette of a spiky dragon, dwarfing even the apocalyptic sunrise.

"Looks familiar?" Malachi's joke fell flat, swallowed by the eerie stillness. The connection between these pyre-clad men worshipping under an infernal sun and their recent encounters with dragon-like creatures was disconcerting.

Their journey took them through increasingly ravaged landscapes. Evidence of some catastrophic event littered their path—a once orderly subterranean kingdom now lay shattered and silent. Regardless of this chaos, Brock remained steadfast. He felt a gentle breeze stir his hair, hinting at hidden paths ahead.

Suddenly, their path ended abruptly—a massive wall of debris blocked their way forward. Yet Brock sensed something else—a slight draft hinted at a secret passage amidst the ruin.

With renewed determination, they ventured deeper into the stony bowels of the earth. The grandeur they'd left behind was replaced by an oppressive sense of confinement—a creeping dread that gnawed at their courage. Their journey became a labyrinthine struggle, contorting through narrow tunnels choked with rubble and balancing precariously over gaping chasms.

Suddenly, the ground beneath them shuddered—a quake, possibly another clash among the sky kings?—sending tremors throughout their surroundings. Brock reacted instantly, lifting Malachi and sprinting ahead of a dust storm that threatened to engulf them. He navigated through blinding fog and tumbling rocks with uncanny precision until they found solid ground once more.

Exhausted yet alive, he paused just outside the settling debris to catch his breath before acknowledging their predicament—the way back was now blocked by fallen rock.

"Damn, we're fucked," Malachi's voice echoed, a dirge in the cavernous dark.

"I'll get us out of here," Brock's words stood as a bastion of resolve, a beacon amidst the tumultuous sea of uncertainty. The thought of their existence dwindling into nothingness in this subterranean nightmare was laughable—not on his watch. With the keen focus of a predator tracking its prey, he charted their path through the ever-widening void, his mind instinctively mapping out unseen terrain from previously noted patterns. In the enveloping darkness, his senses honed to razor sharpness, so when luminescent footprints began to materialize on the untouched stone floor, his surprise barely flickered.

"Looks like we've got guests," Brock's voice echoed in stillness.

"Lovecraft?" Malachi pondered aloud.

But Brock remembered an important detail from their previous exploratory discussions. "Didn't Lovecraft die at home?"

"I believe you're correct."

"So, who else could've been traipsing around here?"

"Perhaps someone with glow-in-the-dark sneakers." Malachi, too, could see these radiant tracks. "Why are these footprints shining?"

"I... I don't know. But let's find out."

They had one route forward—a dive into the abyss of obscurity. They ventured onward, no longer blindly groping their way but drawn towards an escalating brilliance. The peculiar and crumbling realm, its cryptic symbols reminiscent of ancient Egyptian tombs, gave way to modern elements; gleaming metal shards peeked through where timeworn cobblestones once lay. Any civilization that had prospered here or any archaic traditions it held were stripped bare as mere cultural garnishes. Brock's light became obsolete as more and more of this underground world shed its stony exterior to reveal a long metallic corridor illuminated by small pulsating blue lights—a testament to some form of mechanical life. From ancient epochs to visions of the future, they'd transitioned in mere moments, surrounded by an inconceivable construct humming with the formidable technological might of this fallen empire.

The remains of its inhabitants were finally visible—colossal humanoids draped in rags, their height rivaling the titans from human lore, strewn along the widening corridor —desiccated shells trapped in a state of arrested decay, twisted by their own regressive desolation. Neither Brock nor Malachi uttered a word as they navigated this necropolis of giants, eerily peaceful save for the buzzing sound and faint tremors from the dead world far removed from this preserved sanctuary.

However, it seemed they weren't alone in their descent into this tranquil crypt; mystical footprints—reflecting under the blue glow suggestive of celestial travel—led towards a massive circular door at the corridor's end. Its entrance had once been secured by concentric circles of dark iron but now bore a gaping hole peeled back like tin foil by some insatiable psychic entity.

"Bloody hell," Brock grumbled under his breath, his muscles straining as he aided Malachi in navigating the jagged outcrops that littered their path. Their cautious steps echoed in the enigmatic chamber ahead, bathed in an ethereal glow. Their eyes, wide as chasms in their awe-struck faces, drank in the unsettling spectacle of the terrain beneath and above them. It was a landscape that seemed to breathe with a metallic life of its own, undulating in an uncanny rhythm. The alien topography converged into two imposing structures—one clawing up from the floor, the other descending from the ceiling like a monstrous appendage. They were designed with an eerie precision to serve as pinchers, poised menacingly to hold something of potent mysticism.

And there it floated between them: an object so ordinary yet imbued with a captivating darkness. It was a skull, ebony as midnight and scrawled over with arcane etchings that pulsed hypnotically with mystic energy. The sight was jarring, this human artifact suspended amidst such otherworldly surroundings.

"Is that...a skull?" Malachi's voice barely registered above a whisper as he grappled with the incongruity of it all. His words hung heavy in the air, echoing his struggle to reconcile this stark symbol of humanity within an alien montage.

"Seems so," Brock replied, matching Malachi's bafflement. Beyond this peculiar apparatus lay another gaping aperture—this one torn through the ceiling—through which a faint wind whistled, carrying tortured echoes from outside their sanctuary. At least they had an exit strategy from wherever they found themselves.

As they traversed the vast chamber, their gaze darted around for any sign of a book—an ancient tome was their coveted prize. Obsidian fragments scattered and gently orbiting around the hovering skull like cosmic wasps painted an otherworldly picture that Brock hesitated to disrupt, his skin tingling with unspoken caution. He strained to catch even a hint of aged parchment or sulfur—the scent he associated with an authentic grimoire—but came up empty-handed. The realization hit him like a punch; what they sought wasn't here...or perhaps...

Their quest seemingly ended in disappointment. They turned back towards the skull, which seemed to pulse with an uncanny awareness. As they approached its pedestal, an alien energy enveloped them, escalating into an itch under their skin that Brock struggled to place—it was eerily familiar yet elusive.

"You good?" Malachi checked on him.

"Yeah, you feelin' this weirdness too?"

"Like I've had one too many shots—only there's no DJ or disco lights," Malachi admitted with a hint of humor.

"Exactly."

"Feels like that thing's looking at us," Malachi said.

"It sure does."

"You think it's what we're looking for? The grimoire?"

Brock took a deep, almost meditative breath, picking up the scent of Myrrh mixed with human sweat. This skull was from Earth—the only deviation they'd encountered in this realm apart from themselves. A thought flickered in Brock's mind: could magic memories be contained within vessels other than books?

To put his theory to the test, he gently guided Malachi behind him and lunged towards the relic with a resolute swiftness. An unseen energy thrummed in the air around him, a presence as foreign and alive as an extraterrestrial organism. It seemed to reach out, insidious tendrils coiling around his stomach and squeezing tight until nausea swelled within him like a tidal wave. The shimmering phenomenon was akin to stardust frozen mid-dance—an arresting spectacle that fascinated him even as it filled him with revulsion.

As he ventured closer, the invisible barrier of repulsion thickened, growing stronger like an electromagnetic field resisting his approach. Yet, he pressed on, spurred by a stubborn determination stronger than any physical discomfort.

He stood tall before the astral claws holding captive the artifact—a relic whose mere existence seemed to warp and distort the reality around it. The air pulsed with its influence, pushing against his senses with tangible force. Yet despite this visceral rejection from his surroundings, he remained undeterred—his resolve unwavering in the face of this otherworldly resistance. Ignoring the strange repulsion, he extended a hand for the skull—anticipating a magical jolt—but was met only with the cold feel of bone under his fingers. Swiftly then, he retreated from the unsettling energy radiating off the shards.

"Guess we got it," Brock declared.

As Malachi scrutinized the cavernous surroundings, his mind was a reel of fantastical escapades and mythical adventures that he'd absorbed in countless movie marathons with his aunties. He braced himself for a sudden cave-in or an activation of some arcane trap. Yet, all remained still. The only disturbance was the soft sighing of the wind through a crevice above, casting ripples across this undisturbed sanctuary.

"Seems so," Malachi conceded. "So, how do we get out of this shithole?"

"You gotta fly, Malachi." Brock replied.

Brock enveloped Malachi in a protective embrace, one hand firmly pressed against his back while the other cradled the eerily cold skull—his fingers settling into its hollow sockets as if custom-made for them. Theirs was an intimate touch that sent shivers of anticipation coursing between them; Brock's raw strength and warmth stirred Malachi's senses into a wildfire that propelled him like rocket fuel. At this moment, magic felt as straightforward as surrendering to that intoxicating heat.

As Brock nuzzled into Malachi's neck, the faint prickle of stubble ignited a spark within him that blossomed into passion. They were lifted on shimmering threads that spun starlight into wings, thrusting them through a tunnel seemingly sculpted by molten earth. The genesis of such a passage would remain a mystery for another day; right now, they were drawn forward by the promise of open skies and liberation.

We're on the brink of escaping this hellish place... Brock reflected telepathically, unwavering faith guiding their route back to their world's entrance point. Their perilous odyssey across time and space had instilled in them an aura of invincibility—there wasn't any cosmic monstrosity or terrestrial obstacle they couldn't vanquish together.

Malachi, swift and precise as a silver-tipped arrow, darted through the jagged exit that led back to reality, cutting through the oppressive gloom with his ascent. Their grip on each other tightened, unmasking their hidden desires and yearning. In response to this unveiled vulnerability, the skull resonated its thoughts directly into their minds. Its voice was a static-laden transmission; it carried a pompous, eloquent tone with an unmistakably American accent—reminiscent of some overbearing headmaster from a prestigious institution.

Degenerates... What new hell is this? Eternities in limbo only to be claimed by hedonists. Damn, my never-ending existence...

Malachi's seamless navigation momentarily stumbled, surprise prying him and Brock apart as much as the tumultuous winds permitted. Their eyes met in shared bewilderment, but something familiar in this unseen entity's grandiose speech ignited recognition in Malachi's mind. "Lovecraft?" he suggested cautiously.

The response was chillingly affirmative, pulsating with an unseen menace.

Indeed, sodomites... Indeed.

CHAPTER 7: THROUGH A DARK MIRROR

The abandoned totem pole erupted in a deafening explosion as if struck by invisible lightning. The voice

of Dr. Marrow echoed around them, disembodied and hauntingly resonant. "The steel must endure violence to become a weapon," he intoned ominously.

Engulfed by the relentless surge of Pythia's magic, Ana was adrift in the tumultuous currents of time. It was a chaotic whirlpool of blinding radiance and cacophonous noise. It was akin to being trapped in a cinema where countless films played simultaneously at deafening volumes—a symphony of discord that relentlessly assaulted her senses. Yet, she had no physical form here to shield her from this maelstrom—no mouth to voice her protest with a scream, no limbs to fend off the relentless barrage of visions that assailed her psyche: infinite threads of human existence—births, deaths, acts of passion, triumphs, and failures, beauty intertwined with despair. Even without ears, she could discern a voice slicing through the pandemonium.

"Witness the dawn of mankind's accursed gift and Earth's inaugural battle against the Outer Gods," Pythia proclaimed with an ominous solemnity.

The quantum chaos stilled momentarily before spitting out Ana's spectral form onto an icy wasteland like unwanted residue. She spun once more in this alien landscape, but now with slightly less disorientation. She hovered on a tundra besieged by snowstorms and biting winds. As fluctuating silhouettes—herself and Pythia—they floated amidst drifting snow, surveying a desolate expanse of rolling arctic dunes merging into towering icebergs or mountains—it was difficult to distinguish—and seemed irrelevant in this realm sculpted entirely from frost. Despite the howling blizzard that should have drowned out any conversation, they existed within a bubble of tranquil silence.

"Where's the damn sun?" Ana demanded abruptly.

"Veiled by ash," Pythia replied tersely. "Two and a half million years ago, our world endured an enormous impact near Mexico's coast, which thrust it into an Ice Age."

"And how am I supposed to believe all this?"

"The future echoes the past; it rhymes with a rhythm that endlessly repeats. I behold the past, and I dance in that rhythm. Hence, I understand the future. There is no motive for me to deceive you with illusions."

Ana wrestled with this riddle and the puzzle of human existence in such a hostile environment. Just when she was about to voice her bewilderment, Pythia abruptly seized her spirit and flung it across vast distances, the desolate landscape blurring into an indistinguishable smear beneath her. Abruptly, she halted, suspended above a gleaming crater adorned with intricate crests of obsidian ice—a rippling desolation pattern stretching across a frozen ocean trapped under massive layers of solidified water. Was this where Cthulhu had landed? A powerful gravitational and arcane force still emanated from the point of impact, pulling the glass-like debris into an asteroid belt. The energy pulling at her spectral form was one of death and emptiness.

"Why would Cthulhu rekindle a war that ended eons ago?" Ana mused aloud. "How could life have sprung from this void? Where are all the people?"

"They dwell amongst us," Pythia responded cryptically. "Humans are much like cosmic vermin—crush one, and scores scatter. The Ice Age should have rendered them extinct, encased their world in a spell of frost, and starved whatever survived the Outer Gods' dread invocation."

"Invocation?" Ana echoed incredulously. "You're saying some witch did this? Who would have that kind of power? Who summoned an Outer God here?"

Pythia remained silent.

"Clueless, aren't you?" Ana's words danced in the air, a playful sneer curling on her spectral lips. "And I was under the impression that your knowledge had no bounds."

"Even our Earth," Pythia intoned, her voice a dirge of sorrow and loss, "a living entity in its own right, is not immune to the relentless march of time. It suffers from decay and decomposition. It grows forgetful and scarred by ceaseless violence. We are merely receptacles for the memories it manages to hold onto."

"So, Mother Earth has gone off her rocker?" Ana quipped.

"Perhaps," Pythia returned cryptically, a mysterious lilt in her voice.

"What's the catch? What are you not saying?" Ana demanded.

"There are moments swallowed by time's gaping maw," Pythia began enigmatically. "Entities that drift through our ages as unseen phantoms do—erasing chunks of existence without leaving behind any trace." Ana chewed on this revelation, mulling over how effortlessly Mary had slipped past her psychic defenses under Cthugha's divine shield. Could an entity or deity possess such formidable power as to erase entire epochs from memory? In a world where each sunrise ushered in new terrors or groundbreaking revelations about their universe, she thought: why not?

"The manner in which the Outer Gods descended upon us matters little," Pythia resumed her mystical monologue. "What they cannot bend to their will is destroyed. The most pliable or useful species become their pawns—warriors and spies in cosmic games. Those who resist them or lack utility are promptly erased."

"Humankind has shown tenacity unlike any other creature these cosmic travelers have encountered," Pythia admitted, a note of respect creeping into her voice. "Even on the precipice of extinction, they burrowed beneath their planet's barren crust and thrived —albeit with Cthugha's meddling."

"So, he's one of the good guys then?" Ana asked.

"Shake off your anthropocentric views," Pythia admonished. "Discard the notion that you can fathom an Outer God's desires. The worlds Cthugha blesses are as searing and fierce as this world is cold. Yet, the friction between Cthugha's fervor and Cthulhu's icy wrath has borne much for humanity. Come, bear witness."

Their spectral forms danced upon the gusts of time, tracing the echo of currents that once roared through the long-dead Atlantic. They climbed over ancient, ghostly peaks shrouded in mist before plummeting through pristine ice and permafrost layers to reach the comparatively warmer—yet still frost-kissed—realms beneath this world. Here, luminescent flora and mosses cast an uncanny radiance upon sprawling caverns; their hollow depths were adorned with verdant gardens of fungi and serene rivers teeming with fish that carved deeper waterways into existence. Along these peculiar shores, Ana bore witness to humanity's raw beginnings: small tribes of survivors who had sought sanctuary from the icy cataclysm above.

These clusters of grimy scavengers—more beast than man—adorned themselves in bone fragments or scraps of fur and hide, their bodies huddled together for warmth. They scoured the riverbanks for edible greenery while others speared fish with stone-tipped weapons. Yet they lacked fire's transformative touch to cook their catch, consuming it in its squirming state. Beyond crafting these primitive tools, they showed no desire or capacity for advanced creation. Their attire was limited to what they could salvage from the carcasses of beasts and reptiles sharing this less frigid underworld—a realm where predatory creatures often culled their numbers.

These early humans communicated through primal grunts or senseless cries as they bickered over food or mates, relieving themselves without regard for propriety. They were a pitiful lot devoid of feeling or direction beyond mere survival—a disgraceful mob forever confined to darkness.

After drifting through this bleak tableau of suffering—an indeterminate period as time seemed fluid here—Ana and her guide reached a labyrinthine network of tunnels leading to a lush subterranean basin. Fresh glacial streams meandered around islands crowned with towering fungi reaching skywards like wheat sheaves. Further ahead, multiple rivulets converged into a pool, vast and deep enough to be considered a lake, brimming with transparent fish and other life forms providing abundant sustenance.

Here, Ana glimpsed the earliest semblance of society. The cave dwellers indulged in feasting and mating on the granite beaches in relative peace, even staking claim to preferred stalagmites or crevices as their personal spaces—a nascent sign of territorial development—for none here had been compelled to wander in search of food for countless seasons.

Ana and Pythia drifted over this scattered primitive settlement like curious birds before coming to rest by the lake's edge. There, they hovered over a lone Cro-Magnon man casually crunching dried weeds while gazing out at the water. His attire—pelts stitched together with twine, tusks, and fangs—attested his victories over many horrors of this underworld, none of which dared encroach upon this peculiar sanctuary.

"Those who came before us named him Ignis," Pythia's voice resounded, an ethereal echo that filled the cavernous void. The phantoms of early man in this place remained deaf to her words. "In their limited understanding, they reduced him to a mythic figure, a mere footnote in their grand narrative of history, rather than recognizing his tangible existence. He was the first to tame flame in the heart of the Ice Age, not through intellect but via divine intervention. His enlightenment was a gift from Cthugha—the Golden One. Watch."

At her command, Ignis felt an unanticipated wind surge across the water toward him. It bore a dry heat that prickled against his moistened grey skin—a sensation foreign and bewildering to his primitive senses. His instincts flared; he reached for his food supplies, prepared to flee at any moment. Yet this new sensation posed no threat; warmth enveloped him like a comforting shroud, and he surrendered himself to its embrace.

The unseen zephyr whispered cryptic syllables into his ear, which he echoed without comprehension. His peculiar actions attracted the attention of nearby cave dwellers and mushroom gatherers, who were drawn towards the spectacle unfolding before them. A crowd slowly congregated around Ignis as they reveled in the warm aura emanating from his body.

Suddenly seized by an inexplicable urge, Ignis bent down and picked up two glistening stones from beneath his feet. He struck them together with a fervor akin to a zealot partaking in holy rituals.

A spark ignited.

Light burst forth from stones that should have been damp in this desolate frozen wasteland; weeds at Ignis' feet caught fire rapidly. He stared at them with wide-eyed awe until the flames nipped at his toes, causing him to retreat hastily with a primal growl of confusion.

His fellow subhumans huddled around the newborn flame, their faces etched with caution. Yet as time passed and no harm befell them, their apprehension subsided, and they inched closer, their fingers reaching for the sparks as if they were ethereal creatures to be ensnared.

However, Ignis experienced more than mere curiosity. The whispering wind had imbued him with knowledge, including a word to commemorate this miraculous event.

"Fii-goor," he voiced the unfamiliar sounds. (Fire.)

His voice echoed through the cavern like an incantation, drawing others towards the source of light and warmth. This was the birth of mankind's first tribe—the Burning Tribe —bearers of humanity's first word and miracle.

"The burning bush mentioned in Christian lore is but a misinterpreted tale from primitive pagan culture," Pythia mused. "Similarly, 'the flood' is an allegory for a world consumed by ice, and Noah is but a reflection of Ignis."

As she spoke these words, the scene before them began to fade until all that remained was Pythia and Ana amidst an expanse of silver mist.

"Behold the genesis, the birthplace of strife among the Outer Gods on Earth," Pythia's voice resonated with an ancient authority.

"That flame?" Ana interjected, her tone a cocktail of millennial skepticism and raw curiosity. The fire she had seen was more than just a celestial spectacle—it was the primordial spark that set ablaze the countless lives of humanity—a strange gift or perhaps an eerie act of kindness from Cthugha, one of the Outer Gods.

"Cthugha's intervention," Pythia proclaimed.

"I'm still lost here," Ana confessed, frustration weaving into her voice.

"You see beyond what you understand—for we are kindred spirits," declared Pythia, her ethereal visage warping into something akin to a ghostly smirk. "The wind is whimsical and unfettered by any constraints—scarcely anything escapes our sight. We embody that force, the offspring of Hastur, the Everlasting Gale. You should heed Hastur's decree; he has already surrendered this realm to Cthulhu. Forsake your loyalty to the Golden One and join our ranks. Persuade your comrades to turn their backs on their master, and we might survive this round in the Eternal Game."

"I ain't anyone's puppet," Ana shot back defiantly.

"Impudent child!" Pythia chastised, her voice reverberating with timeless outrage. "Your world dangles on the precipice of annihilation. Witness the fate you rush towards— behold another paradise promised by the Golden One—"

The world exploded into life under Pythia's booming proclamation, her words like a spark in the dry tinder of the ethereal dreamworld. Reality buckled and burned, replaced by a horizon that glowed with nuclear intensity. A sky-dome writhed with monstrous specters of pure darkness—dragons, their forms etched from brimstone and charcoal, their hearts aflame with an ageless fury. Among them, even larger entities that defied comprehension swirled and danced like storm clouds.

With a gasp, Ana pulled herself from her stupor to survey the landscape below. It was a wasteland of fragmented stone punctuated by buttes that pierced the sky like cathedral spires. Molten rivers flowed through this tortured terrain, pooling in fiery orange lakes while geysers hissed out plumes of lava in mournful dirges for a world lost to devastation.

Ana and Pythia hovered amongst the clouds as she took in the ash-filled emptiness. The only signs of life were these furious creatures soaring nearby.

In solemn whispers that echoed through the void, Pythia began to weave a tale for Ana: "This was once home to those who worshipped Cthugha as divine. They were masters of theology and technocracy; their fervor for engineering mirrored religious devotion. Their innovative minds sparked by the Golden One into obsessions that toyed with atomic ambitions."

"What happened?" Ana's voice was small against the vastness around them, filled with defeat.

"The influence of Cthugha convinced them they could overcome death," Pythia responded quietly.

In response to Ana's arcane vision, titanic beings materialized before them—beings whose colossal sizes dwarfed human proportions. Cloaked in flowing azure garments that reflected an ocean's depth, they were enigmatic spectacles of scientific curiosity.

Their beauty was otherworldly; it defied terrestrial standards set by mortal beings. Their faces were elongated and symmetrical, high cheekbones catching ethereal light like prisms. Eyes as vast and mysterious as nebulae stared from beneath brows as solid and unyielding as granite cliffs. Hair flowed like rivulets of molten silver down their backs, shimmering with every subtle movement. They possessed an alien elegance, blending strength and grace—an exquisite paradox that left one both awed and fearful.

Their judgment was clouded by an irresistible divine potency radiating from them like a beacon at night. The genesis of this heavenly strength was never scrutinized; its conceivable limits remained untouched. Their conceit sketched a tableau of transcendence—an ascent to deathless echelons where they would align themselves with Cthugha.

A chill slithered down Ana's spine at Pythia's next revelation: they had accomplished their lofty objective but not in any manner decipherable to conscious entities like her. She watched as they drained more of the planet's vitality in their ceaseless quest until one day, they simply vanished—dissipated into oblivion.

Her vision warped again, revealing the environmental catastrophe caused by their doomed elevation. Those who had either chosen or were coerced to refrain from participating in the experiment were abandoned on a dying planet. Their giant bodies were left to wither like great trees, and their emaciated fingers were used to etch their errors onto stone tablets and metal reliefs in decayed temples before meeting their demise.

The last premonition was perhaps the most eerie: only monstrous airborne creatures prevailed now—once elegant beings resembling Chinese dragons but distorted beyond recognition due to Cthugha's insatiable greed and the residual effects of unchecked magic.

Pythia drew her psychic tendrils back, providing a respite from the torrent of temporal visions. Ana's return to the present was punctuated by a gasp that cut through the silence like a blade. The pause ended, and Pythia's voice resumed its haunting cadence. "Acheron Prime...a barren graveyard of what was once a thriving Acherai civilization. A universe eternally hushed, bereft of the peculiar marvel these entities embodied. Their staggering might fell short. Their resolute intellects proved insufficient. Overpowered by the Outer Gods, their helplessness remained unknown to them—until the bitter end. This is your inevitable fate as well, Ana."

Ana's voice emerged as a stubborn growl against the bleak prophecy, "I'm not built for surrender; it's just not in me."

"The outcome is preordained," Pythia declared, her tone as somber as an empty cathedral. "Cthulhu or Cthugha—water or fire—it matters little which prevails. Their disciples are legion, and they dwell in your midst."

The tranquility that had briefly cradled Ana's mind was abruptly shattered. Her consciousness was once again ensnared by a torrent of vivid visions—a malevolent psychic maelstrom that swallowed her whole, plunging her into the inky depths of a time long forgotten.

***

Within the timeless void, Ana became a spectral observer of Pythia's prophecy taking form. Many frantic tableaus unveiled themselves, one fading into the next, as though all of time were a misty shore through which she could walk, scenes revealing themselves in order of escalating horror and importance.

In its zenith, Babylon was a majestic monument to human aspiration and celestial intervention. The city sprawled under the cobalt dome of the sky like an intricate golden mosaic crafted by divine hands. Its lofty ziggurat, central to the city's vastness, punctured the heavens, its sun-dappled stone exterior glistening in the unyielding desert heat. Hammurabi, its sovereign lord, bore his crown with unwavering dignity and adamantine resolve.

Beneath this splendorous facade lurked a growing malevolence. Sinister seers slithered through the palace's labyrinthine corridors like eels in murky depths, whispering enigmatic prophecies into Hammurabi's ear under the pretense of divine guidance. Their words were sweetened with promises of dominion and eternity but tinged with treacherous undertones that gnawed at Hammurabi's sanity like starved leeches. The prophets spoke in riddles about cosmic horrors beyond mortal understanding—entities that lived in watery abysses and communicated through nauseating slurps and gurgles. They painted eerie images of grotesque orgies unfolding in fetid pools, where slippery creatures writhed in unholy ecstasy. These descriptions filled the air with an almost palpable fish-like stench that seemed to seep from unseen cracks in reality itself.

Seduced by these whispered visions, Hammurabi authorized dreadful rites to summon and commune with the grotesque deities. Hammurabi's obsession blinded him to all else; the city's magnificence buckled as if shouldering an unbearable burden, while its people were left to languish in ruin. Those wise to evil, fled their doom, though far more fools remained. The ziggurat's stone passageways, once proud and mute, now trembled with frantic prayers from priests whose earlier confidence had turned to desperation. They beseeched the heavens, their voices cracking as an unseen force tightened its grip, threatening to tear their world apart from the inside out. Babylon began its quiet descent, not through the clamor of war or the cries of conquest, but through the sinister unraveling of whispered deceits and the creeping chill of absolute madness.

Soon, Babylon's magnificence faded like desert sand caught in a relentless gale. The landscape withered over generations, temples decaying like dead tree stumps, roads consumed by an encroaching, soggy rot—a peculiar blight for a sun-baked realm. No one knew where the people had gone, though swampy pools teemed with formless, moaning creatures that bore only the faintest resemblance to humanity. They were primordial, amoeba-like eels—grotesque precursors to flesh and bone, as if time itself had reversed

108 of 331

and left them stranded. A meaty, slithering coil wore a tarnished golden crown, its blubbery form a pitiful echo of lost grandeur. In time, the memory of this place dissolved into obscurity, and the truth lay buried, too hideous for any to recall or seek.

The veil of the Shores of Time enfolded Ana again, only to tear apart and expose an epoch marked by feudal order. In this era, warlords had found a temporary truce, solidifying their territories and allowing culture to bloom anew. Within the revered confines of their academy, Confucius and Laozi engaged in heated debates.

Suddenly, a figure emerged from the shadows—a woman swathed entirely in crimson. Her speech was tinged with an ancient accent that echoed strangely familiar in Ana's ears. This red-garbed enigma offered the sages cryptic insights through cards spread out before them, bones cast like dice upon a table, and prophetic tiles rattling within her cup.

Despite their wisdom and usual skepticism towards such mystical practices, both sages were ensnared by the woman's enigmatic allure—a sensuality that penetrated even their hardened shells of scholarly indifference. She remained with them for many moons as the academy gradually shifted its focus from academic pursuits to esoteric explorations and eventually into forbidden supernatural realms.

An eerie whispering began to fill the corridors of the institution. Students were seen wandering aimlessly before disappearing into the academy's shadowy corners, drawn by an inexplicable aquatic muttering that echoed through stone walls. The hallowed halls of learning soon became breeding grounds for unspeakable insanity rather than temples of wisdom.

In time, Shen Zhu descended upon the mountain monastery with his troops like divine retribution personified. Fire danced across wooden structures while screams pierced through smoke-filled air as he cleansed every inch of corruption from the sacred mountaintop.

Legend whispers that even today, one can hear ghostly echoes of bickering sages within those scorched hallways while a spectral figure draped in red chuckles at their eternal discord.

Inevitably, the lineage of Zhu was destined to intertwine once more with the chaotic threads of the cosmos. This time, however, the Deep One was hell-bent on retribution for his earlier schemes being so rudely disrupted—his memory was an abhorrent abyss that spanned eons. As Ana's next vision unfolded, shrouded in a veil of mist rolling in from the sea, she arrived as an unseen observer in an ancient court. There knelt a man whose presence emanated raw power and fierce determination: Genghis Khan. His muscular frame was draped in elaborate Eastern garb, his body a network of hardened muscle and sinew encased in patchwork armor.

His face, once a testament to unyielding resolve, now bore the pallor of dread. The depth of fear etched into his eyes seemed to grow deeper with each passing moment as he clutched at a grotesque talisman that hung around his neck—a shriveled appendage that bore an uncanny resemblance to a monkey's paw.

Genghis had hoped this artifact would be a wellspring of good fortune for his expanding campaign, but its true nature was far more insidious. Unbeknownst to him, it wasn't the paw of any primate; it was the desiccated claw of merfolk royalty—an ominous gift from an enigmatic Eastern trader whose features blurred and shifted like sand beneath waves in Genghis' increasingly fragmented memory.

The once indomitable spirit within Genghis began to tremble under this oppressive influence. His noble dream to unite continents twisted into a dark thirst for tyrannical dominance. Visions danced before his eyes—cities aflame, chains binding countless souls, rivers flowing red with blood—and the artifact whispered promises of power and conquest into his ear.

And as Ana watched this transformation unfold from her spectral vantage point, she could see how deep the poison seeped into Genghis' psyche. His thoughts became mired in paranoia and bloodlust; he began ordering executions on mere suspicion, levying harsh punishments for trivial offenses—his reign of terror spreading like wildfire.

The artifact, the merfolk claw, seemed alive in these moments. Its shriveled fingers tightened around Genghis' thumb with a parasitic hunger, further corroding his sanity. As Ana watched the once-great ruler succumb to this obscene corruption, she realized that she was witnessing not just the fall of a man but the birth of a cursed legend.

Regardless of their nobility, wisdom, or strength, none could resist the Outer Gods' corrupting influence. Pythia, her spirit invisibly lurking within these nightmarish visions, affirmed humanity's doom with each unveiled truth.

In a bevy of visions, drowning her in a rushing tide, Ana traversed further annals of time, witnessing the rise and fall of civilizations. She observed as pyramids, once glorious and gold, decayed into skeletal remnants—a testament to an era long past. Shadowy figures whispered beguiling untruths into Pharaoh Ramesses' ear as he dreamt within his royal chamber of eternal life beyond mortal reach.

She saw these minions of Cthulhu around Stonehenge, their rubbery, tentacled silhouettes dancing under a blood-red moon, casting shadows that spanned centuries. Their influence was insidious and far-reaching—in every palace, temple, council, and senate. Like spiders spinning a deadly web, they ensnared humanity with delicate threads laced with tantalizing promises of power and immortality.

Even the pious Joan of Arc was not immune to their deceptive charm; misled by prophecies that crumbled to dust, her righteous path twisted into a tragic end.

The Cultists moved through history as architects, orchestrating humanity's downfall from behind the scenes.

The malignant plan was as transparent as it was horrific: to infiltrate and corrupt, to steer mankind towards its own annihilation. They were the masterminds of despair, gradually wearing away humanity's free will until nothing remained but obedience.

In the throes of her psychic revelation, Ana felt a chill creep into her soul—a ponderous entity that whispered of her inescapable torment. "What you've seen is but history," Pythia's voice echoed ominously. "Now behold the demise your kind races towards." New images blazed through Ana's mind, each more intense and disquieting than the last. She saw towering office complexes, their glass facades gleaming like drenched gravestones, swarming with stern-faced businesspeople.

Within these fortresses of deceit, a hive of alien technology hummed—machinery whirring, holographic screens flickering, and mechanisms so intricate they seemed plucked from extraterrestrial vessels yet bore an unsettling human touch. There were hovering metallic spheres controlled by subcutaneous palm chips and chairs where women in sparking cybernetic garments sat while serpentine tubes squirmed before piercing their bodies with chilling accuracy—technology she had never thought possible in her time.

Men and women clad in dark suits moved rhythmically like marionettes on invisible strings, supervising these experiments. Their fingers danced over a maze of ominous controls, checking screens and adjusting dials—their every action precise and calculated. These devices weren't mere tools; they were sinister conduits constructed to manipulate reality on an unimaginable scale.

They spewed a relentless torrent of expertly spun falsehoods—half-truths, fabrications, propaganda—all crafted to breed chaos and bewilderment. Other monstrous screens throbbed with unspeakable erotic imagery that could have been torn from Satan's secret trove.

Every message emitted from these mechanical abominations was as seductive as a lullaby, coaxing mankind deeper into blissful ignorance. Humanity had become entranced by the hypnotic glow of screens, unaware of puppeteers lurking within hidden shadows.

The cultists of yore had traded cryptic prophecies and cursed amulets for digital codes and subliminal signals. They'd insinuated themselves into society's fabric under a fresh guise—technology. Their mystical symbols supplanted by binary sequences pulsating with an otherworldly energy akin to magic. The esoteric knowledge of forgotten times had been craftily repackaged into a technological doctrine—a silent oppression that held humanity in its relentless grip.

Pythia's prophecy echoed ominously. Mankind had already capitulated in this unspoken war, surrendering its consciousness and spirit to the icy allure of machinery and digital seductions. It was already dead—its souls, at least, with bodies to follow.

When the onslaught of her visions finally receded, Ana was marooned in a hellish landscape she knew all too well: the charred remnants of Acheron Prime, with Pythia's silent phantom hovering beside her. Through the scalding air, the chilling truth gnawed at her consciousness: Earth was destined for the same fate as Acheron. Most of what she had accepted as reality was merely an elaborate deception—a cosmic pantomime orchestrated by otherworldly masters.

"I... I can't take it anymore," Ana stammered, her words fractured by gasps. The notion of humanity's impending doom was not the pinnacle of her mental breakdown; instead, it was the grotesque apparition that materialized from the nebulous sky. A titan as vast and lethal as a comet set aflame, its reptilian form screeching through the atmosphere towards them, served as the final unraveling stitch in her tapestry of sanity. Its maw—a yawning abyss lined with jagged teeth like stalactites ready to consume her—plunged her into a frenzy of terror. She let out a scream—an unadulterated symphony of fear reverberating through the annals of time—her spectral hands raised in vain against the inevitable cataclysm.

"You've reached your limit," Pythia's voice resonated around them, laced with an unexpected gentleness.

The Hellscape undulated around them like ripples on a disturbed pond before they plunged through a temporal vortex—the monster's deafening wail vibrating through her essence as they emerged into an altered reality. Once again, Ana floated beside Pythia's original form—her shadow self adjacent to the majestic figure surveying the awe-inspiring panorama of Ancient Greece sparkling beneath her temple. Pythia seemed comforted by her corporeal form and stretched towards the firmament with arms clinking with ornate bangles. After indulging in this feline stretch, she turned to Ana's spectral self with an imploring gaze.

"Do you understand now, Ana? We are combatants at opposite ends of a conflict where triumph is elusive for both."

"Why drag me through all this if you're only after my surrender?"

"To make you realize why resistance is futile."

"Bullshit."

Pain warped Pythia's striking features at Ana's retort. Despite their connection being initiated by Pythia tapping into Ana's consciousness, it was not one-sided for another potent psychic entity. Through this link, Ana discerned a faint longing and a warmer sentiment—hope?—submerged beneath layers of icy disdain. Perhaps Pythia had unveiled humanity's and her own dishonorable history because somewhere deep within her, a fragment believed those memories were worth preserving.

"So you're not exactly eager to throw in the towel on this round of the Eternal Game," Ana suggested.

Pythia quickly responded. "The yearnings of my heart carry little significance. I am shackled by invisible chains, as soon you will be. Your time is evaporating faster than you perceive."

Ana raised an eyebrow. "Is that some kind of threat?"

"Merely a caution," Pythia's enigmatic smile faded into an expression of worry. "There is one who seeks to drain the lifeblood of your comrades." She paused momentarily, spreading her fingers as if absorbing the scent of spectral incense. A sharp inhalation followed by a violent shake of her head marked the impact of her psychic revelation. "An entity... shrouded in sacrilegious power—one of the devourers and distorters of time I have warned you about. Stir yourself or risk being too late to divert or condemn the impending doom. Wake up!"

The ancient oracle's face contorted into something resembling terror at what she had divined. She clapped her hands together urgently; their sound echoed like a thunderclap through the ether. At Pythia's command, Ancient Greece convulsed and spiraled into a whirlwind of chaos; darkness yielded to color, silence supplanted by sound, and breath filled the void.

With a jolt, Ana woke from the dream realm.

***

Ana's first anchor back into the world was the rugged allure of Lenny's face hovering over her. His sweat, a peculiarly soothing mix of musk and antiperspirant, splashed onto her as he studied her with an expression of bemusement—as if she were comfortably tucked in bed rather than sprawled across his lap. Relief washed over his features as her eyes flickered open. It took a moment for Ana to grasp their situation; she was cradled in Lenny's lap amidst a jumble of garments. Her thoughts were thick and sluggish, akin to an old woman grappling with forgotten memories; her body quivered, drenched in perspiration, and utterly spent. A tongue as dry as aged leather lay heavy in her mouth, and she struggled to produce enough saliva to form words.

What on earth had transpired? A maelstrom of crucial recollections lurked at the fringes of her awareness, poised like a predator ready to strike. She almost recoiled from unearthing these memories—the mere prospect sent her heart pounding and throat constricting with dread.

Sensing her desperate need for hydration, Lenny presented her with a plastic water bottle. She eagerly gulped down the liquid until he gently pulled it away before she could overindulge. "Steady now," he warned, "you've been out cold."

The encircling darkness seemed to respect only them, leaving them untouched by its cloak. Twisting slightly, Ana noticed a camping lantern casting a warm crimson glow around the tent—a haunting echo of sunsets over forgotten ruins.

Suddenly, it hit—her memory came crashing back! The staggering truths she'd unearthed slammed into her all at once; no gradual exposure or repression could have braced her for this avalanche of revelations. A seizure clamped down on her—an automatic reaction to process the extraordinary—but that didn't stem the tide from surging further.

With swift agility, Lenny slid from beneath her, tilted her head back, and wedged something into her mouth to bite down on. His steady, resonant presence was the lifeline she clung to as his calming voice guided her back, one gasping breath at a time, into reality. But with clarity came a surge of terror and the chilling words of the Oracle of Delphi's parting prophecy.

Lenny withdrew his hand from her mouth—it had been caught between her teeth, 'the wedge,' yet miraculously bore no marks—allowing her to speak again.

"Lenny," Ana's words fractured the silence, her voice a tremulous whisper, "we're in deep shit. There's something... I don't know what it is, but it's coming." His hand found hers, grounding her; his gaze held hers captive. The glint of danger turned his eyes into dark obsidian mirrors—a sight that strangely anchored Ana rather than sent her spiraling.

"We'll handle it," he stated with a quiet certainty that belied the chaos around them. "Now tell me everything."

Ana's thoughts swirled like a cyclone, a maelstrom where reality and delusion danced dangerously close. She chose to reveal the most immediate menace first. "So my spirit guide—Pythia? Yeah, the Oracle of Delphi herself—straight out of some ancient myth... She says we need to wake up because there's something here that wants us dead. Some monstrous entity that consumes time—another absurd addition to my collection of insane realities." Her words hung heavy like an impending storm as she realized their number had dwindled by one. "Where's Cynthia?"

"She needed some air." Lenny's expression darkened further; shadows played hide-and-seek within the crevices framing his intense gaze, pulsating ominously like veins under the moonlight. "That was some time ago, though. You should get dressed."

Lenny grappled with his clothing as if they were new adversaries overnight. Once he'd managed to pull on his pants and boots, he battled with his shirt before tearing it in frustration and tossing it aside with a growl akin to thunder rolling in the distance.

Ana barely noticed Lenny's odd behavior as she navigated her chaotic routine of dressing up and gathering her belongings—most notably Mary's book that gave her a strange prickle of warning—amidst impending doom. It wasn't until he turned towards her—his aura bristling like an agitated bear—that she realized how drastically things had changed.

Lenny was no longer just a man. The darkness from his eyes had spread across his face in an intricate network of black lines and cryptic symbols. They resembled primitive scripts but were far more complex—an arcane testament to power etched onto his muscular form.

"Your... your body," she stammered, pointing at the transformation.

Lenny glanced at his newly tattooed forearms and hands, now adorned with dark nails—which seemed normal. He shrugged nonchalantly, "Let's go find Cynthia."

"But what if someone sees you?"

"They won't."

His declaration was as unshakeable as Ana's conviction in her visions. As she clung to Mary's grimoire and the Dark Mother's fragment, Lenny—growing impatient with their snail-like progress—lifted her up, and they were off. The mode of their movement was elusive to Ana; it felt like she was caught in a dance with this stone sentinel, her hand on his waist, head resting against his shoulder. Their surroundings swirled into a dizzying blur: one moment, they were within the confines of the tepee, then under the celestial blanket of a starlit sky near an erratic campfire, then amidst deserted vendor tents at this unholy hour. She thought she glimpsed tendrils of obscurity clinging to Lenny—as if he were spun from the fabric of night itself.

Their peculiar promenade concluded under the watchful gaze of a totem pole on the fringe of a spirited bonfire teeming with rowdy merrymakers. Lenny set her down, and they broke apart. On this night rife with marvels, seeing smoky wisps trailing off him like ink seeping from his tattoos barely registered surprise in Ana anymore. He stood half-consumed by darkness—a man simultaneously there and not there—a spectral figure tethered to the shadow cast by the totem pole as though he had surfaced from its deepest abyss—shadow-stepped.

"What kind of magic is that?" Ana challenged, her eyebrows knitting together in perplexity.

Lenny shrugged dismissively. "Seems like just stepping through a doorway."

The lively crowd around them remained blissfully unaware of their existence as if they were rendered invisible courtesy of Lenny's mystical aura. It was as if he had enshrouded them within his own personal sphere of enchantment. Ana tried to lock eyes with a nearby bystander, but he remained unresponsive, too captivated by his beer and the chatter with his fellow revelers to pay them any mind.

"Look, there's Cynthia," Lenny declared, extending a spectral hand towards her.

Cynthia was seated on one of the logs encircling the firepit, a bottle of beer cradled between her thighs. Her face glowed with satisfaction as she reveled in the joyous chaos around her: rhythmic drumbeats intertwining with guttural harmonies, an impromptu guitarist plucking Santana's tunes without disrupting the overall musical harmony, children darting about past their bedtime, and participants from all corners of Turtle Island partaking in an ancient ritual amidst urban modernity.

"She's safe." Ana exhaled a sigh of relief.

Lenny muttered something indecipherable under his breath—a low grumble akin to a disgruntled gorilla—yet even this failed to rouse any reaction from the oblivious crowd.

"I'm going to—"

"Hold on." Lenny gripped her arm abruptly as she tried to step out of his shadowy haven. His senses were keen and unerring like those of a bloodhound. He had sifted through the potent human odors mingling with the smoky, hickory, and sulfuric aroma from the fire until he detected Cynthia's unique scent. But another scent had piqued his interest—a sharper one tinged with undertones of parchment and an air of mystery. It was an unmistakable scent he knew all too well—the oily, repulsive residue often left on the book clutched tightly in Ana's grasp was that of a witch.

"Mary's arrived," Lenny murmured, his voice a mere rustle in the wind.

Ana clung to him, her fingers digging into his arm. "She's after her spellbook, right?"

"Possibly. Or maybe she's just here to cause shit. But we've got a surprise for her." Lenny was a being carved from conflict—his initiation into the world of arcane shadows and amethyst-tinted necromancy had transformed him into an entity pulsating with an odd yet potent life force. He wouldn't allow Mary to touch Ana with even one gnarled finger. His determination to protect her was a blazing beacon within him, restrained only by the self-control that prevented him from charging blindly into the chaos and flinging bodies aside until he discovered which mask Mary was hiding behind this time.

He knew she was concealed—hidden beneath some spell or illusion that defied his senses. Given enough time, he was confident he could detect her unique essence. But time was forever their adversary, never their friend.

Perhaps Ana could assist; she wasn't some frail damsel but a formidable seeress. "Can you see her? She's cloaked herself in some sort of magic."

"I can try." Ana scanned the crowd, but everyone seemed like regular people to her gaze. Like a child reaching for a comfort toy only to withdraw at the last moment, she almost grasped the Dark Mother's fragment before stopping herself. She needed to stop relying on crutches and aids.

Get your shit together—you're a goddamn time-leaping mind witch! Let's end this nightmare now.

Then she recalled something the Oracle of Delphi had revealed during their supernatural journey: The wind is whimsical and unfettered by any constraints—scarcely anything escapes our sight.

"I am the wind," she repeated softly like a mantra.

Monster-Lenny didn't interrupt her but observed silently as Ana's magic started to swell with each repetition until they were surrounded by a spectral vortex that caused their hair and clothes to ripple. She was more than the wind, he believed. She was the storm itself. As Ana's confidence soared and she demanded to see the truth, her righteous omnipotence clashed with the deceptive magic cast by their enemies.

Crackle! Swoosh! Bang!

The sky exploded into a whirlwind of dark clouds that obscured the moon. The calm weather morphed into a torrential downpour punctuated by thunderclaps that sounded like doomsday drums. The sudden deluge extinguished the campfire and sent onlookers scurrying for shelter like spooked deer. But it wasn't just water—it was a mystical solvent imbued with Ana's will that separated lies from truth, including the shadowy disguise hiding Lenny—his black mist evaporated, his dark tendrils falling onto him like strands of wet hair.

Those slow to find shelter were jolted into action when they saw the colossal half-naked man crouched behind a glowing witch. Their screams were drowned out by the thunder as they ran for safety. But not everyone fled—Cynthia detected something unnatural about this storm and noticed Ana nearby, looking like an avenging Valkyrie, with the shadowy half-man behind her. Two more figures remained across from the extinguished fire pit: an old hag and another man resembling some Indigenous trailer park royalty.

Ana's mind rebelled against the unfolding reality. This can't be true, she silently protested. But the tempestuous sky seemed to echo her turmoil as it unleashed a deluge upon them, washing away their magical disguises like watercolor paintings caught in a storm. The truth stood stark and glaring amidst the chaos, momentarily muting the storm's fury.

"Dr...Marrow?" Ana stammered, her voice barely audible over the rain's incessant drumming.

Cynthia's gasp of disbelief cut through the torrential downpour. "Mary...and Dr. Moreaux?" The individual Ana identified as Marrow was the very same surgeon whose malevolent practices had once reigned at the hospital where her sister was employed. This man had been responsible for the removal of Jewel's womb and the desecration of countless other women. Cynthia's utterances lingered heavily in the atmosphere, her expression locked in astonishment and confusion upon recognizing this sadistic figure who had stepped straight out of her darkest dreams and a friend who had betrayed her trust—the doctor seemingly untouched by time's passage.

Amid this watery pandemonium stood Dr. Marrow, grinning with malevolence—once a seemingly benign figure, now revealed as an insidious predator with a thousand faces. His lavish suit clung wetly to his form, enhancing rather than concealing his monstrous allure. Beside him stood Mary, her face a mirror image of the storm overhead—dark and brewing with ominous intent.

Lenny recoiled instinctively from the ancient stench that wafted off Marrow—an odor akin to graveyards left untouched for centuries. The man's devilishly handsome features were now grotesque under scrutiny—seductive yet hiding an insatiable hunger for souls.

"Cynthia! Get your ass over here!" Lenny barked, his voice echoing with primal warning across the field.

Dr. Marrow turned his gaze on Ana, his lips curling into a malicious grin that made her blood run cold. "I didn't anticipate you breaking my enchantment—my magic should be beyond your comprehension," he mused aloud. "A naughty and clever girl indeed."

Ana felt her connection to nature wane as her storm dwindled to a drizzle, but its energy still pulsed within her, both exhilarating and terrifying. She could sense Marrow's malevolent intentions creeping towards her like tendrils of shadow.

His guise as a caring doctor now seemed, in retrospect, a farcical masquerade that hid an entity far more sinister and inhuman. Visions flashed before her eyes—surgical lights illuminating gruesome scenes of body horror; hands garbed in antiquated attire choking the life out of a woman on cobblestones; the victims' struggles fading into nothingness as their lives were extinguished by this ancient monstrosity.

"Just who are you?" Ana demanded, her voice sharp with accusation.

"I am but a humble physician...a sculptor of flesh and bone," he replied with an air of faux modesty.

"And what are you?"

"You'd best hope you never find out," he retorted, his voice tinged with regret.

Thunder rumbled ominously overhead, setting the stage for the violent confrontation between these godlike entities.

"Dispose of Cynthia," Marrow commanded dismissively. "The Aspect and her Godbeast belong to me."

With a swift motion, Mary extracted a firearm from the depths of her rain-drenched jacket, aiming it with grim determination at Cynthia across the sodden field. "I bear this burden with a heavy heart," she uttered, each word soaked in remorse. A thunderous echo rang out as two shots were fired.

Cynthia's foot caught on a stone, sending her sprawling to the ground—an unexpected reprieve from death as at least one bullet whizzed through the space she'd just vacated. The stray shot found its mark in the totem pole adjacent to Ana's, splintering it and scattering wooden shrapnel into the air.

Ana made to run but was held firmly in place by Lenny's iron grip around her waist. His every instinct screamed at him to evade the danger, his body morphing into a wave of shadowy energy that surged forward like an obsidian tsunami before crashing into the earth and reemerging elsewhere.

The abandoned totem pole erupted in a deafening explosion as if struck by invisible lightning. The voice of Dr. Marrow echoed around them, disembodied and hauntingly resonant. "The steel must endure violence to become a weapon," he intoned ominously. "Survive long enough, and you will comprehend why this world is so unforgiving, and you too will become its villain."

"Psycho bullshit," Ana muttered under her breath, her world descending into chaos around her. She spun around frantically, gasping for air and trying desperately to make sense of their new surroundings amidst the swirling cloud of destruction they'd narrowly escaped.

Her heart sank as she spotted the fire pit now several hundred meters away—far from Cynthia, who was left alone either to fight or perish. But before despair could fully set in, Lenny seemed to read her thoughts and understand what she wanted.

A comforting darkness enveloped Ana, disorienting her momentarily before equilibrium returned. They found themselves kneeling near the fire pit once again. Lenny released his hold on Ana, who immediately scrambled towards Cynthia.

A gunshot shattered the silence.

"Hand over the book, and she may yet live," Mary's voice echoed across the field.

"Yeah, right, and I'm a unicorn," Ana muttered. Her psychic senses were ablaze with warnings of fatal danger—not just for Cynthia but for Lenny, who was already advancing towards Mary with a predatory stride. "Lenny!" she cried out in warning.

Her mental command yanked him back just in time to avoid a telekinetic energy blade that cleaved into the ground, causing an eruption of dirt and debris.

Where was Marrow? As Lenny rose, he saw only Mary closing in on Ana. Marrow had slipped away once again, hidden by illusion. As this realization dawned upon him, another alarm in his mind forced him to dodge aside—an acrobatic cartwheel saving him from being impaled by soil shrapnel as Marrow carved another explosive telekinetic line through the earth.

Lenny sought refuge within his shadows, liquefying his flesh into flowing darkness, and dove—Boom!

The explosive force catapulted him from the epicenter, violently dislodging his form from the very fabric of the earth. Once intertwined with the molecular structure of the soil and stone, his physical being was now torn asunder and hurled into a chaotic spiral through the air. In this disoriented whirl, his corporeal form coalesced again, reassembling back into solid matter from a state of dissolution. Lurching onward in his frenzied pursuit of a target, he let loose a primal roar from the depths of his being as torment flared within him. The rough-hewn pellets of earth lodged in his skin, some even embedded agonizingly in his forehead, incited a deluge of blood and obsidian ooze that blurred his sight.

Meanwhile, as Mary's looming silhouette began to ominously encroach on her hiding spot, Ana was running out of options. Should she fling the cherished book she clung to into the abyss and make a desperate dash with her friend across the barren wasteland, hoping against hope not to be cut down? Once Mary repossessed her precious grimoire, Cynthia would surely be met with a bullet. And Lenny—his monstrous outcry echoing around them—appeared destined for a similarly bleak fate. As Cynthia clutched onto her, desperation seeping from every pore like sweat, Ana tapped into that pervasive dread.

She plunged deep within herself, harnessing every iota of torment, wrath, and indignation that had ever scarred her soul—every unwanted touch she'd endured, every lie that had tainted her innocence—and focused it all on Marrow: an apt recipient for such loathing given his proximity and potential involvement in much of her life's upheaval.

Through the blood-smeared lens of Lenny's vision, the rain suddenly shifted its path. It cast an illuminating glow on the silhouette of a figure—a man seemingly constructed from glass and illusion—sauntering towards him with hands weaving patterns through air shimmering with magical fractals.

"Die!" bellowed the shadow beast.

Lenny morphed into an ebony wave crashing onto terra firma; he rolled along its crust in a thunderous trench before erupting forth before Marrow, who twisted away like paper artistry at the last possible moment. Unfazed, the shadow beast struck again, nearly trapping the witch amidst a barrage of rocks and soil. But Marrow proved agile and eerily prescient; Lenny's asphalt fury and pounding fists merely grazed a portion of the elusive witch as he vanished several yards back. Yet now Marrow was gasping for breath, wincing while clutching his side—his illusionary disguise torn to shreds. More importantly, he had been forced to confront his own vulnerability.

"Fall back!" Marrow commanded in a hoarse whisper that cracked from pain. "Fall back!"

Mary's growl echoed through the night as she retreated.

Against the tidal wave of primal rage and murderous intent, Lenny's instinctive concern for Ana triumphed over his desire to give chase. In an instant, he was standing by the log—shirtless and formidable—looking down at the two women.

"You good?" His voice was gruff but laced with concern.

"Yeah," Ana replied with bravado as she embraced him.

"Yeah," Cynthia echoed as she struggled to her feet, only to immediately falter; her face twisted in pain. Startled, she touched her abdomen and stared at her hand, now slick with crimson. The scent of fresh blood made Lenny's nostrils flare—a wound deep enough to reach vital organs. "Except for this."

Cynthia's eyes rolled back into her head as she fell into unconsciousness.

CHAPTER 8: THE LONGEST JUMP

*Goodness and kindness are merely linguistic
adornments that differentiate our primal urges from*

our brutish existence—mating, consuming, excreting.
Humans are nothing more than cattle in this world,
with few shepherds and four chaotic deities dividing
our herd for their obscure desires.

In the shadow-swathed cellar beneath Lovecraft's tourist trap, Malachi and Brock materialized from a pulsating concrete wall. Their anguished cries reverberated around them as they were reconstructed molecule by molecule. A silent plea was issued to the cosmos that the kitschy attraction had closed for the day, and its cantankerous young custodian retired to his dwelling. They crumpled onto their discarded clothing, forgotten remnants of a reality they'd left behind before venturing into that accursed realm from which they'd narrowly escaped. That their belongings had not been transported along with their flesh seemed an inconsequential mercy in minds that swirled with unanswered questions.

What was that barren wasteland? Malachi pondered in silence, an inexplicable sense of importance clinging to his thoughts about their recent ordeal. Perhaps answers lay within Lovecraft's spirit, dormant inside the obsidian skull they set upon a shelf while dressing under moonlight. The entity had been silent since its venomous tirade, labeling them sinners, yet an intellectual aura seemed to radiate from its hollow eyes.

"It feels like it's watching us," Malachi voiced softly.

"Yeah."

"Do you think it could really be him?"

"Why couldn't it be?"

"He's been dead for decades."

"Do you think that matters?"

Malachi didn't usually contemplate the concept of immortality, but their encounters with cosmic beings had forcibly broadened his perspective on life and death. Lost in thought, he lingered in his jeans until Brock helped him into his shirt and jacket with a brotherly pat on the shoulder.

"We accomplished our mission," Brock said nonchalantly.

A skull serving as a spellbook? It made some warped sense to Malachi; a spirit confined within an object might possess knowledge akin to a witch's grimoire. "We certainly acquired something—more than we bargained for," he replied wryly.

"That's good enough for me." Brock's infectious smile lit up his dirt-streaked face. "Let's leave this place and call Ana. I've lost all sense of time."

"Hopefully, it's only been one day."

"Let's hope so."

Despite Brock's confusion about the correlation between interdimensional travel and time, he had a nagging suspicion that their absence hadn't been long enough for the conflict of the Outer Gods to have reached its conclusion during their hellish journey. Eager to verify, Brock darted to the window, scooped up the skull, then tossed it onto the snow outside before clambering through the opening. He offered a firm hand to Malachi, who used it as leverage to hoist himself out.

Once back in chilly reality, Malachi felt less anxious about their cosmic escapade. The casual manner in which Brock handled such a potent artifact further eased his concern. They'd traversed dimensions together—there was nothing they couldn't tackle. Leaving Lovecraft's abode behind with swift strides, they vaulted over the fence; Brock cleared it in a single bound.

Within the serene confines of the park, Brock's hand found Malachi's in a gesture as natural as breathing. "Is this okay?" He asked, his voice a rare mix of vulnerability and strength.

Malachi's response was a silent shake of his head, his emerald eyes mirroring Brock's shyness. A queer romantic tableau that I find distasteful to observe. Restrain your tactile enthusiasm upon my personage; Lovecraft's disembodied voice echoed in their minds like distant thunder.

Brock raised the spectral skull to eye level, his blue gaze piercing its hollow sockets. "This jabbering... It only starts when we touch you, right?"

Your powers of observation are commendable for one more inclined towards brute force than cerebral pursuits, Lovecraft retorted. Yes, indeed, Aspect. The phenomenon is triggered by psychometric energy. You interpret my essence—me—through your cognition —

"Enough," Brock interrupted with an unceremonious drop of the skull into the snow. His rebellious act drew a chuckle from Malachi before he retrieved the discarded oracle while still holding onto Malachi's hand. Lovecraft's verbose commentary resumed instantly.

Such appalling manners! Were you raised by wild animals or overindulgent women?

"A hillbilly from Arizona," Brock shot back as they resumed their walk through the moonlit parkland. "Let me be clear: We'll ask questions and expect straightforward answers without sarcasm or interference from you or anyone else. Times have changed since your days among the living; who I hold hands with or kiss is not your concern."

You insolent oaf! You clearly don't comprehend to whom you direct your impudent remarks! I refuse to—

"Shut it, or I'll toss you in a trash bin where you can talk with rats for all eternity," Brock warned.

The threat quieted Lovecraft's spectral rambling, and they continued their stroll under the watchful eye of the swollen moon, the city's distant hum adding an ethereal soundtrack to their journey. Once back at the SUV, Brock fired up the engine and cranked up the heat, banishing the vehicle's icy chill. He retrieved his duffel bag from the trunk, gently tucking Lovecraft into a nest of clothing with a slight opening in the zipper—some inexplicable instinct compelling him to let the skull 'breathe.' They needed to coax information out of this spirit; a dash of diplomacy couldn't hurt.

As he settled behind the wheel, he detected a change in Malachi's scent—a whiff of fear replacing his usual sage-like aroma. "Malachi?" he queried.

Malachi's phone clattered onto his lap. "Ana left a message... while we were..." A sob ripped through him like paper shredding.

Brock hurriedly unbuckled his seatbelt and leaned over to comfort him, whispering in their minds as Malachi's sobs drowned out any spoken words.

What happened? Talk to me.

Cynthia's been shot. They're rushing her to the hospital.

Brock only needed an inkling of where to go. He revved up the engine and sped out of the parking lot without another word. Whether they could reach Cynthia in time for meaningful help or even final farewells was uncertain. But amidst this grim reality looming like an executioner's axe over them, Brock remained silent as Malachi frantically dialed and texted their unresponsive friend.

***

The Beaumont motel, a hulking behemoth of cold concrete and unyielding steel, crouched on the serrated brink of Narragansett Bay. A craggy stone staircase descended into the maw of the Atlantic's frothing tumult, stirred into an untamed frenzy by relentless snow flurries. The specters of the Grand Plains were now shadows in their wake, but Malachi found little comfort within their suite's art deco grandeur. He paced like a caged animal before the panoramic glass doors that offered a front-row view of the storm's tempestuous ballet.

Malachi's emotions echoed the churning turmoil outside. He had unleashed a barrage of texts and voicemails upon Ana's phone with an intensity bordering on romantic desperation, only to be met with the icy detachment of an automated response. Was she wounded? Beyond reach? Or worse... His mind teetered on a precipice, overlooking grim possibilities regarding Ana, Lenny, and Cynthia.

Lovecraft's leering skull—a morbidly whimsical kitchen decoration—seemed to taunt him from atop its perch on the flawless countertop. Its polished stare needled his skin every time he dared meet its gaze.

Brock eventually emerged from a steamy shower. Traces of soot stubbornly clung under his nails while a faint sulfurous aroma stuck to his skin. He guided Malachi towards the mist-filled room before confiscating his cell phone and vowing to monitor it for any incoming calls.

Malachi showered hastily, donned his rumpled clothes, and darted out only to find Brock sagged onto a couch, elbows bearing heavily upon his knees. The sight was disheartening yet oddly comforting—they would not face whatever ill tidings may come alone.

As they watched snow whirling violently outside and heard windows shivering ominously in response, they were yanked from their reverie by the sudden chirp of the phone. Malachi fumbled with the device before managing to activate the speaker.

"H-hello," Malachi's voice shook slightly over the line.

Ana's reply was a languid "Hey," followed by a silence that had Malachi metaphorically strapping in for turbulence. "Got your texts. Not much signal in the ICU."

"Intensive care?" The words slipped out of Malachi's mouth, barely louder than an exhale.

"Surgery's done. Now she's... comatose is what they're calling it." Ana's tone was matter-of-fact as she corrected herself. "Bullet nicked a lung, lots of internal bleeding."

"Do you think..." Malachi trailed off, apprehensive about the answer to his unfinished question. As a seer, Ana might have answers others didn't.

Her response cut through the tension like a scalpel: "The odds don't look good."

A sob clawed its way up Malachi's throat, but he choked it back down, drawing comfort from Brock's silent support.

When it was clear that Malachi wouldn't speak again soon, Brock jumped into the conversation. "Ana?"

"Brock?"

"Yeah. What happened?"

"Mary." Ana's answer was succinct and damning.

A low growl rumbled from Brock's chest at Mary's name.

"And my ex-therapist," she added casually, contradicting the weight of her revelation.

"What?" Brock blurted out, thrown off by this new piece of information.

"He's part of Mary's cult…playing some messed-up version of chess, they call 'the Eternal Game.' They're followers of Cthugha…Order of Midnight nutjobs…just like Lovecraft."

Both men turned simultaneously to stare at the skull—the puppet master directing this horror show from their suite. What if they just smashed that cursed thing? Sensing Brock's violent intentions, Malachi reached out, his hand resting on Brock's clenched fist —a silent plea for restraint. Maybe Lovecraft himself could spill some details about these cultists.

"Hey, you guys still there?" Ana's voice crackled through the speaker.

"Brock's thinking about going Hulk on Lovecraft," Malachi shot back.

"Hold up. Lovecraft? Can we backtrack?"

"Yeah."

Ana's voice dissolved into silence as Malachi withdrew the phone to his ear, their surreal sojourn through a dragon-infested underworld still reverberating in his mind. He relayed their journey with words that sparkled like the dragons' flaming scales. Ana volleyed back her own saga of an encounter with the Oracle of Delphi and a dizzying trip across the fabric of space-time—a glimpse into the same cursed realm he had unwillingly witnessed first-hand. With practiced ease, they distilled these grandiose experiences into wry one-liners and crisp narratives—an essential distraction from Cynthia's dire diagnosis. Serendipitously, they had seen the same fiery world, albeit through different perspectives, a place to which Ana could ascribe a name: Acheron Prime.

Brock's fingers closed around the skull mid-conversation, trembling with a palpable fury that surged through his veins like raw voltage. "Your buddies or whatever they are hurt our friend—she's lying in a hospital bed now, fighting for her life. I thought you needed us. Why would they do that?" he demanded.

You assume I possess omnipresence akin to the Crimson Fates, observing all past and present events through mystical waters. The identity of this friend remains unknown to me. Unless she is an Aspect like you, her fate bears no consequence. She is a pawn on a cosmic chessboard manipulated by those unspeakable Lords of Chaos.

"She's a good person, kind-hearted. She didn't deserve this."

Goodness and kindness are merely linguistic adornments that differentiate our primal urges from our brutish existence—mating, consuming, excreting. Humans are nothing more than cattle in this world, with few shepherds and four chaotic deities dividing our herd for their obscure desires.

"We're not cattle or pawns."

Indeed, you and your paramour stand apart from the rest. You were chosen as warriors and leaders. Once you grasp your immutable destiny, you will accept your fated role, and humanity's suffering will become mere distant echoes from a slaughterhouse.

Brock turned the skull in his hands, pondering how easily he could reduce the brittle artifact to dust.

I surmise your attempts at destruction would prove futile, Wolf. The ancient incantations that have reduced me to this state are beyond your comprehension. Have today's youth lost all reverence for their elders? You should seek my guidance for wisdom and enlightenment; I can mentor you through the trials on your path to becoming supreme warriors of the Golden One—I can lead you towards achieving transcendence: Your awakening?

Lovecraft's mental voice spiked in surprise as his psychic tendrils probed deeper into Brock's psyche, scrutinizing his marrow and soul. Whatever fleeting examination occurred, the result seemed to unsettle the disembodied entity. *Impossible. How? How did you...? You've already awakened.*

Brock couldn't fully grasp what this 'awakening' entailed, but he had shared blood, vows, and fervent kisses, intertwined minds, and hearts with the softly murmuring man behind him. That had to mean something. He felt reborn into a world of camaraderie, power, and joy amidst their relentless battle against sorrow. Perhaps Lovecraft's cryptic wisdom was merely a poisonous gift they were better off rejecting. Ana seemed to be doing fine deciphering their mission and adversaries on her own; they'd even connected with the fourth Aspect. Why did they need this verbose deceased blowhard who was part of the same vile cult as Mary?

"You're as useful as a paper umbrella," Brock retorted, his words as blunt and tone bitter. "We're already knee-deep in supernatural bullshit. I reckon Malachi will be on my side soon enough." With the skull securely gripped, he navigated behind the counter, yanking open cabinet doors until an integrated trash bin sprung into view. All the while, Malachi was too engrossed in deciphering his and Ana's bombshell revelations to pay any mind to Brock's odd behavior.

"Later," Brock tossed over his shoulder, an air of nonchalance hanging onto his farewell.

Do not act so hastily! I can prove beneficial!

"Oh yeah? Enlighten me." Brock held Lovecraft above a neglected mound of crumpled tissues and discarded snack wrappers.

Is the mortal woman you wish to aid still tethered to this realm?

"Cynthia's her name. She's critical but kicking," Brock replied tersely.

Ah, then there lies a chance to mend the delicate thread of life she clings onto—much like all pitiful souls teetering on the precipice of existence and oblivion. You possess the power to prevent her from crossing that threshold.

"You shitting me?"

Consider what you hold within your grasp: a soul trapped in purgatory. Death is neither absolute nor insurmountable. You are one of the Aspects embodying the four cosmic elements, the earth being your dominion—the solid, unyielding bedrock of creation itself. Each Aspect mirrors the magnificence of the Outer Gods themselves. Your...erm, associate Malachi embodies fire—the element that can mold, reshape, or ignite new possibilities. Chaos dances within its flames: magic potent enough to warp and shatter fate and reality. I can instruct you and him on harnessing these powers—they could potentially save the mortal woman.

"And how exactly would that work?" Brock demanded, his patience wearing thin.

Lovecraft fell into a contemplative silence, its psychic energy stretching out to fill every corner of the room. Brock could feel this magic seeping into everything like a deadly gas—an unseen peril that filled their space with an invisible dread. Oblivious to this supernatural event unfolding around them, Malachi continued his engrossed conversation with Ana while spectral shadows swirled and danced—a dark figure looming over Malachi before it abruptly vanished—leaving no trace of its mystical presence in their vicinity.

After the momentary pause, Lovecraft resumed his discourse.

I have gravely underestimated the Aspects' innate ability to unite. It appears you have encountered Owl as well.

"Ana? You mean Ana?" Brock queried.

Precisely. And Snake?

"We've crossed paths in dreams," Brock admitted reluctantly.

Remarkable. All four Aspects are nearly united. Two awakened. This grand experiment has exceeded all expectations.

"We're not playing lab rat to your mad scientist," Brock's voice rumbled, the earthy undertone echoing his frustration.

Ah, a misunderstanding indeed. Is Snake within reach?

"Not happening. He's off the grid and far from us."

Understood. We shall proceed with what we have... As the Aspect of Earth, you're the anchor for your comrades. Ana will function as a conduit and gateway to our comatose mortal's—

"Cynthia," Brock interjected, his voice hard as granite, "Her name's Cynthia. Get it right."

To Cynthia's soul, then. It is upon Malachi to alter her fate and summon her spirit back. Time is of the essence—death is as inexorable as taxes—it waits for no one. Inform your friends, and I shall direct you through this process—you'll need to gather for this séance.

A heavy weight settled in Brock's chest at Lovecraft's words, "That's impossible. She's almost on the West Coast, and we're still in Rhode Island."

Don't embody a dull pebble now, Brock. You and Malachi leaped across galaxies in seconds—to realms unseen by even mankind's most sophisticated scopes—unless humanity has mastered space during my absence. Comparatively, hopping from one American coast to another should be child's play.

Brock turned towards Malachi, his piercing stormy eyes wide with awe despite having experienced such power before, "Can he really do that?"

Indeed! Owl manipulates time while Raven navigates space and realities; you rule physical worlds with sheer strength—soon, water will temper and balance out these elements into an unyielding force of nature. Upon awakening fully, you can draw on each other's magic to some extent. I believe it was Malachi's powers—his ability to traverse dimensions—that you tapped into when you found me; were you physically close during this translocation? No need for explicit details.

Brock thought back—he had been holding Malachi's hand then. "Yeah."

Eureka! Together, you four can conquer any challenge—and three should suffice to resurrect the nearly departed. Now, let me illustrate my work's wonders.

Brock ambled towards Malachi, a perplexed furrow in his brow. His attempts at explanation only seemed to twist his face into an even tighter knot of confusion while Malachi looked on, equally puzzled. Brock sighed and gently pried the phone from Malachi's grip, replacing it with the skull. Theories and explanations flooded Malachi's mind like a surge of knowledge from an esteemed yet pompous professor; he absorbed every word.

Meanwhile, Brock found himself fielding Ana's volley of questions about their situation. So Malachi was getting instructions on teleporting them all to Mount Sinai hospital in Montana? Ana took it all in her stride, impressing Brock as much as she did Malachi.

"You're one cool chick," he declared.

"Tell me something I don't know," she quipped back.

Malachi rose from the couch. "Alrighty then. Can you put Ana back on speakerphone, Handsome?"

Brock tapped the icon.

"Pet names?" Ana teased.

A blush tinged Malachi's cheeks. "Lovecraft says you need to find somewhere private —like a garage or storeroom."

The symphony of Ana's movement, threading through the hushed conversations and syncopated beeps of a hospital corridor, filled their ears. "Alright, I've left ICU... hang on." The reverberating clatter of her boots against metal stairs and the creaking swing of doors punctuated her progress until she finally declared, "I'm in the parking lot—tucked away where no one else is loitering."

During this time, both men had slipped into their shoes and stationed themselves by the entranceway as if ready to embark on a journey—not through any physical gateway but via a mystical portal Malachi was about to conjure. Following Lovecraft's guidance, he asked Ana to paint a verbal picture of her environment. He constructed an image in his mind: Ana, petite and pixie-like in her comically long cat sweater draped over punk attire, scuffing her worn black Doc Martens against the pavement. The abandoned paper bag, spent fry sleeve, scattered paper cups and cigarette butts—the oil smears and crude graffiti marking the concrete wall—all these details were stitched into Malachi's mental tapestry of Ana's location.

Now, kindle your longing as you would for your paramour. Ignite it and stretch out towards her. Do not ponder—simply act.

With Brock's hand clasped firmly in his own and the skull nestled against his chest, Malachi surrendered himself to Lovecraft's commands and a mesmeric trance. His hand found the door handle to their suite. As he twisted it open, they were swallowed by an otherworldly blaze—it felt like stepping through heaven's gates themselves. The flames swathed them in warmth akin to Brock's enveloping embrace—a surprisingly tender yet potent sensation.

Fear did not graze Malachi as their corporeal forms dissolved into particles and catapulted from New Hampshire to Montana. When the luminescence ebbed away, the door creaked open onto a vacant hallway, unveiling a room where two sets of footprints were seared into the carpet.

***

As if a supernova had chosen to detonate before her, Ana shielded herself from the spiraling maelstrom of sparks and blinding radiance. A piercing shriek tore through the air, causing her to wince at the unexpected sensory onslaught. She dug in her heels, bracing against the almost gravitational pull drawing debris toward a focal point of arcane energy. Through splayed fingers, she caught sight of two figures stretching out into tall, looming shapes. She sought refuge behind a nearby concrete pillar, daring to peek out once the tumult subsided—papers fluttering down like snowflakes and cups rolling aimlessly across the vacant parking lot.

Two men emerged from the shadows, their bodies hunched as if they'd just completed an arduous marathon. The larger figure helped his companion rise. "Brock," Ana whispered to herself. His build flawlessly matched Malachi's affectionate description: arms that could rival those of a professional footballer, lean yet robust legs, and a face that seemed destined for glossy magazine covers. Malachi himself was even more handsome than his photos suggested; his allure held an otherworldly quality—an unexpected delight she hadn't anticipated. Yet his attractive features were contorted with discomfort; he barely stood upright before lurching towards a wall, where he promptly lost his lunch onto the concrete floor below. Brock quickly moved to him, offering soothing pats on his back as Malachi continued retching.

"Is he okay?" Ana asked anxiously.

Brock turned around and handed Ana a black object Malachi had inadvertently knocked against the wall during his malady. "Hold this," he said nonchalantly, "I think it's just magic travel sickness."

Malachi grumbled something indecipherable before retching once more.

Consumed by worry for her friend, Ana hardly noticed the cold, smooth artifact in her hands. Not until it communicated with her—a chilling sensation that felt like a murderer's blade slowly dragging down her spine. Hello, Aspect.

"Holy shit!" Ana yelped, dropping the object in surprise. Brock's reflexes kicked in, catching Lovecraft before colliding with the ground.

"You're quick on your feet," Ana remarked.

Brock grinned at her—his teeth stark white against his beard. "That's Lovecraft; be careful with him," he warned as he returned the relic to her custody. "He's not fragile, but he can be a real dick."

As Brock returned to assist Malachi, Ana cradled the skull-like artifact cautiously and sighed in relief when it remained silent. After what felt like an eternity, Malachi's sickness subsided, and he turned away from the wall—trembling slightly as he leaned on Brock for support. Ana retrieved Lenny's handkerchief from her pocket and offered it to Malachi, who gratefully accepted it to clean his mouth before carefully folding it and returning it to her with a weak smile.

"Hey," he greeted softly. "Nice to finally meet you."

For a moment, Ana hesitated before wrapping him in a hug; Brock enveloped all three of them in a warm embrace. He radiated an intoxicating mix of sweat mingled with herbs and pine—a scent oddly stirring hunger within her. Malachi, too, smelled of herbs, but his scent carried sweet undertones of sage that masked any lingering odor of vomit.

"You guys smell fucking fantastic," she mumbled.

Brock didn't verbalize his thoughts on Ana's strange aroma, a concoction of myrrh and blood, strangely similar to the dark perfume of the crimson witches hunting them: the signature scent of an oracle. Instead, they basked in this bizarre shared understanding, each taking in the other's presence. As they clung to one another in a peaceful yet exhilarating silence, Lovecraft, connected to them through their physical contact, redirected their focus back to their task. Time is a luxury we cannot afford, Aspects. We must press on.

"Let's go," Ana said with determination.

They split into pairs: Ana with her spectral companion and Malachi accompanying Brock. But Brock was a natural leader; he needed no direction from Ana as they crossed the parking lot and entered the building. He distinguished Cynthia's familiar scent amid the overpowering reek of human despair that hung heavy in the sterile white corridors they navigated. No quantity of bleach could scrub these halls clean from the lingering stench of urine, vomit, and decay left by countless individuals who had fallen victim to disease or injury. The conviction that Cynthia would not join such ranks spurred Brock onward with unyielding resolve. Despite his limited acquaintance with her, he acknowledged her significance to Malachi and even Ana, given their common experiences and her palpable grief. In the impending gloom ahead, every glimmer of hope was invaluable; Cynthia was one such ray.

The hospital was thinly staffed at this late hour; only a few nurses wandered its halls like ghosts, eyeing the unusual trio with eyes as black as coal dust. Swiftly hiding Lovecraft under her sweater before his peculiar skull attracted unwanted scrutiny, Ana trailed behind their leader past an empty reception desk overlooking a modest waiting area where an enormous man sat awkwardly in a tiny chair—his bulging muscles threatening to rupture his black t-shirt—looking as misplaced as a sumo wrestler perched on a Barbie stool. Brock stiffened, identifying the danger in the man's predatory gaze. However, as the man's eyes landed on Ana and then Malachi, his intimidating demeanor melted like ice under a summer sun.

"Little Raven," Lenny boomed, rising to his feet. "How in the hell did you... How are you even here?"

"Long story." Malachi shook Lenny's hand and was pulled into a bear hug, followed by a robust pat on his back; Brock received an identical greeting. Once released, Malachi glanced around at the 'authorized visitors only' sign taped over heavy swing doors and the unmanned desk where one would presumably get 'authorized.' "So what's the protocol here?"

Scratching his head in confusion, Lenny remembered seeing the night nurse rush off earlier with an upset stomach. He gestured towards her half-eaten burrito left behind on her desk, which bore a sour waft to him—the mayonnaise or some other creamy ingredient had started to turn rancid.

"Nurse took off," he said. "Quite some time ago, actually. She looked sick. I think that burrito is to blame."

Fate smiles upon your journey, Ana. The Raven's fortune bends destiny to its keeper's will. This instant is ripe for your grasp, Lovecraft communicated wordlessly to his charge.

Ana decoded the telepathic message. "Lovecraft says we're good to go."

Lenny was under no illusions about their visit being just a social call. They weren't here to gather around Cynthia's bed, exchanging get-well-soon pleasantries. "You guys do your thing. I'll play security if any uninvited guests show up."

Could this be another instance of dumb luck? Malachi mused, his brows furrowed in contemplation, as Brock led the way to the double doors, flanked by him and Ana. They glanced through the plastic windows, their eyes darting around for any signs of nurses or security personnel. Seeing none, they seized the moment and slipped inside.

The unsettling hush within was only sporadically interrupted by the soft mechanical sighs that echoed the precarious state of patients scattered throughout the ward. Every now and then, a solitary visitor would acknowledge them with a melancholy smile—an unspoken bond formed between those keeping vigil in this somber place.

Brock was on Cynthia's trail like a seasoned tracker. They had to quickly detour into an empty room once when an orderly pushing a cleaning cart ambled past, but thanks to Brock's heightened senses, they were prepared. Besides that minor setback, their journey was smooth sailing until they reached another deserted nursing station—another eerie side effect of Malachi's presence, maybe?

Here, machines that held life in balance played out their own symphony of electronic beeps and wheezes while death hung in the air like a faintly acrid perfume that made Brock's stomach churn. Cynthia's condition had been downplayed—whether due to blind optimism or misplaced confidence was unclear—but one whiff told Brock all he needed to know: this wasn't just any ward; it was where hope came to die.

Brock made a beeline for the door from which emanated Cynthia's sickly sweet scent. He closed it swiftly behind him before drawing the curtains and flicking on the dim fluorescent light. Malachi dashed to his auntie's side, overcome with grief, tears streaming down his face, while Ana hung back slightly, taken aback by Cynthia's ghostly pallor and frailty—she seemed more machine than a woman now.

The woman seemed to have deteriorated even further in the hour since she'd last seen Cynthia. Shadows clung to the corners of the room like death's minions waiting for their cue. Just like Brock, Ana's supernatural instincts were sounding alarm bells: death was growing impatient.

"We need to get a move on." Ana pulled out Lovecraft from underneath her sweater and positioned herself next to Malachi, with Brock taking up the opposite side. Malachi's grip tightened on his auntie's hand, a desperate clasp of hope. Ana positioned Lovecraft over Cynthia's abdomen, her fingers curled around the spectral author to maintain their link. "Alright, make yourself useful," she urged.

Implore them to lay their hands upon me.

"Guys, put your hands on our chatty friend here," Ana relayed. Malachi and Brock complied: Malachi's hand layered over Brock's, which rested atop Ana's. A wave of energy surged through them like plunging their hands into an icy mountain stream. Their fingers instinctively interlaced as they experienced the startling sensation, a gentle force tugging at their arms that seemed to bind them together at this moment.

Well done, you've managed to draw a circle of power. Lovecraft's voice resonated within their minds, now interconnected. Think of this as your intro to the world of foci, Aspects. Or maybe it's lesson number two if we're counting the portal you used to retrieve my remains—courtesy of two formidable witches.

Brock's mind flickered back to when he and Malachi had reached for the unseen doorway in Lovecraft's basement. In that electrifying instant, they'd tapped into each other's magic—and it wasn't their first rodeo either. It happened when they locked horns with those red witches, battled the super soldiers, and even during their initial face-off with those inter-dimensional spiders.

The Lengeth! I must say I'm impressed you slipped through their web so easily in your fledgling forms, Lovecraft continued, privy to Brock's thoughts. But you've got the hang of it now, lad. You and your...beau have linked your matrices countless times and become resonances for each other. One stone thrown into a pond creates a ripple, but two can make a small wave... Three of you reinforcing and amplifying one another can whip up a veritable storm of magic. The dimensional door you took to Acheron was just an amplifier for your powers—a conductor hurling your atoms across space-time. And that cursed trinket Ana carries? That's a resonator, too, albeit only useful for an oracle and not very practical right now.

"What cursed trinket?" Ana interjected.

The fragment of magic handed over by a nosy Elder God, Lovecraft responded mentally. I sense its presence on you.

"Acheron?" Brock posited. He vaguely remembered something mentioned about the topic back in the hotel room, but he hadn't really been paying attention. "Isn't that where we ended up? Where we found you?"

Yes indeed—a realm blessed by Cthugha himself, came Lovecraft's reply. But let's put a pin in that for now. Focus on the task at hand... Without the gate that transported you to that realm, I'll serve as your foci, and your destination will be this woman's purgatory. I am neither alive nor dead but suspended in a vessel of undeath—this necromantic energy will be ideal for a resurrection. Your friend is teetering on the brink of salvation... Channel your wills into me now.

By this point in their journey, none of the three Aspects needed further guidance on summoning their magic—born from condensed and harnessed emotion. They stilled their minds until the rhythmic beeping of nearby machines receded into background noise. Their breathing and heartbeats slowed to such a crawl that they felt like they were drifting off into sleep. Then, together, they slipped into communal slumber; drawing one unified breath from whose lungs was anyone's guess, they ascended into a new state of consciousness.

The trio found themselves in a surreal realm, their bodies transmuted into ethereal wisps. They circled Cynthia, who now hovered in the air like a celestial being, her medical attire replaced with pristine white linens. In this otherworldly dimension, she was an incandescent figure stripped of physical details, reduced to the pure essence of her soul. Their eyes widened as they watched energy pulsate through her form. Still, something was wrong: Cynthia's radiant aura sputtered and sparked erratically while fragments of her soul crumbled into gold-dusted motes.

"Cynthia! Can you hear me?" Malachi's voice reverberated through the spectral void. The luminous figure that once embodied his auntie remained silent, continuing to disintegrate into a constellation of glowing dust. He reached out for her, his hand passing through the dwindling light of her existence like smoke wafting through his fingers. Her essence scattered further when he withdrew his hand in despair.

Brock and Ana materialized beside him, their spectral forms glimmering in the supernatural gloom. Their faces mirrored helpless bewilderment; without Lovecraft's psychic guidance, they could not understand how to halt Cynthia's rapid dissolution.

Their efforts to rouse her had been fruitless. Physical contact was impossible; their hands simply phased through her like wind through leaves. What else could they do?

"Well, well... isn't this a fine mess," a familiar male voice drawled from the shadows.

A figure emerged from the nebulous darkness—Cal's presence as sharp and biting as sea salt and desert sand.

"Snake," Brock grumbled, instinctively recognizing Cal's serpentine aura.

"Cal," Malachi acknowledged with a grimace.

"I did promise we would connect after your New Hampshire gig." Cal shrugged nonchalantly.

"The fourth Aspect!" Ana exclaimed, "Are you psychic too?"

"In the midst of my trance, I sensed an allure... irresistible." Cal's voice was as cold as a winter moon. "Your arrival, impeccably timed or perhaps predestined. The fusion of energy I perceived set the ethereal realm ablaze, akin to a celestial bacchanal—it demanded attention."

"Oh shit! We need to be careful about that." Malachi muttered to himself.

"Indeed," Cal agreed with a smirk. "Now, what are you trying to accomplish here?"

"She's dying," Malachi stated bluntly.

"And?" Cal raised an eyebrow provocatively.

"We need to save her."

"You can't just force life back into the dead. But you can remind them why they might want to stick around in this travesty we call existence," Cal suggested with a sly grin.

"There's more to life than suffering," Brock countered, "There's joy, love..."

Cal vanished and reappeared behind them, his voice whispering across their minds. "Those are fleeting distractions from the inevitable descent into chaos."

Brock growled in frustration, "Are you here to help or piss us off? We don't have time for your cryptic crap."

"I'm here to help," Cal chuckled, extending his psychic influence toward Malachi and Ana. Like obedient pets on a leash, they followed him as he positioned them around Cynthia—Ana at her head, Malachi by her side, Brock where he was, and himself at her feet.

"Four points, four directions," Cal stated smugly. "Now that we're all set up like a proper coven, ask your question, Malachi. And make sure it comes from the heart."

The moment they aligned, a low hum of energy sparked to life, an ethereal dance of raw power swirling in gusty currents between the quartet. When Malachi shattered the silence, his voice boomed like a sonic boom. The Raven pleaded, "Cynthia, can you hear me? Please come back to us."

Her spectral form pulsed with otherworldly luminescence. "Malachi? Is that you? It's pitch black. I can't see anything. I'm exhausted... let me close my eyes for a bit, and we'll talk later."

"No! There is no later. You're dying."

"I know, my little Raven."

"What?"

"My life's been one hell of a rough ride. Now I just want some peace."

"But there's so much left unsaid! We haven't sorted things out yet. This can't be goodbye."

"Life doesn't always deliver what we want on demand."

"And what about Mary? You gonna let her get away with this?"

"I can't bear grudges against her. She's been ensnared by her own demons and bad medicine."

Was this how it ended? Forgiveness for her murderer and a somber farewell? Malachi bristled at this conclusion. As he scrambled for more objections, Cynthia's decay accelerated as if the effort of manifesting her consciousness drained whatever was left of her life force. Time was slipping through their fingers.

Cal intervened, his voice authoritatively echoing, "If we cannot coax you back with promises of light, perhaps the potent cocktail of revenge will do the trick."

"I don't want vengeance on Mary," came Cynthia's fading retort.

Cal's divine laughter echoed in their minds as he continued in his lofty tone, "I am the element that binds—quelling fire, pacifying turbulent earth, taming tempestuous wind—with our spiritual tether. I perceive how intertwined all our destinies have become. And while I cannot discern a face, I know one adversary whose path intersects with ours. A man...Cloaked in potent magic, elusive as an assassin's shadow on frosted glass. A ruthless and terrifying witch...One who has wronged someone you hold dear...Robbed her of something precious...Flesh...Sacred, life-giving flesh. A child? No... Meat and meaning. A womb?"

As his words hung in the air tentatively, Ana, their resident seer, tapped into the four corners and glimpsed within the ether the visage that eluded Cal—a face bearing a chilling resemblance to Marrow, snarling and soaked in blood.

"Jewel," Cynthia gasped out. "My sister. Dr. Moreaux."

"Yes...yes...So you've crossed paths with her violator before, and those amongst us will encounter him again, perhaps even you—if you choose to remain tethered to this mortal realm. Wouldn't you agree, Ana?"

Ana's response was unyielding, her psychic senses screaming: some or all of them would see Marrow once more: "Yes."

"There's your motivation then—the noblest form of revenge—vengeance on behalf of another. Is that enough?"

Cynthia's phantom offered no response, but her disintegration slowed and halted altogether, shimmering fragments suspended around her like stardust.

"Job's done," Cal announced as he stepped back from the power circle. The four cardinal points they'd held collapsed like a house of cards, their magnetic pull vanishing into thin air. "What happens to your friend now is up to her will to hold on to life. I must fade out before we accidentally summon something from the deep dark. You lot... you still have much to learn about this cosmic game if we're going to win it. Evermore is waiting for your arrival for training."

"Evermore?" Ana asked, curiosity creasing her spectral forehead.

"My father's old family home," Cal explained with an air of superiority that bordered on snobbery. "You've earned an invitation, which I strongly recommend accepting. Your list of enemies far outweighs that of friends."

"Hold on a minute," interjected Ana, a memory sparking in her mind like a match in the dark. "Isn't your dad that nutcase who tried to kill you, Malachi?"

"Well... not exactly," Malachi replied with a shrug. "Sorry, didn't clarify that during our last chat."

"And why should we trust him?" Ana shot back.

"I am Aspect number four." His tone was laced with amusement at their ignorance. "Do you really think what you've been through so far was hard? If so, you have no idea how deep into terror and death this fight against the Outer Gods will take you. These entities only understand one thing: power. Either wield it or be crushed by it. Comparatively speaking, you all are stumbling infants barely managing survival—it's astounding any of you are still breathing."

Ana, Brock, and Malachi were left speechless. Indeed, they had barely survived each terrifying encounter with the Outer God's forces. It would be a welcome change to have the upper hand against their enemies for once. Maybe Evermore held the key to their success.

"South Dakota," Cal declared, his voice echoing with finality. "Now that our souls have touched, I can guide you towards me. Bring the weapon you seek. Your first task should be securing the Atlantean artifact. Do that, and you might stand a chance against what's coming."

"Why don't you come with us?" Malachi proposed.

"The world outside these walls is not my sanctuary," Cal replied, regret coloring his tone. "And it's not wise for us to keep this cosmic connection open any longer."

South Dakota... Ana pondered, pieces of a mental puzzle clicking into place. Even amidst all the arcane trickery and deception, she'd felt Cal's presence weeks ago when they passed through the state. Regrettably, her opportunity to interrogate their intriguing guest had run out. Cynthia's form trembled, sending ripples through the unseen realm, making the dreamworld shudder and fracturing like glass under pressure. It exploded in a blinding light before disintegrating into shredded wisps that engulfed them with overwhelming whiteness.

As the fog of uncertainty dissipated, the world around her crystallized into distinct shapes and hues. Underneath her fingertips, she could feel the icy touch of the onyx skull resting against a chest that no longer resonated with death's ominous toll. The woman beneath it had danced away from the precipice of non-existence. This reality didn't escape anyone present, but it echoed most profoundly within Brock, who discovered himself synced to a rhythm of a steady heartbeat and lungs purged of lethal congestion. Cynthia had steered clear of danger; she'd chosen life over death.

"She's gonna make it." Brock pulled Malachi into a bear hug, planting a tender kiss atop his head. Flooding with relief and sudden weariness, Malachi sagged against his companion.

Ana scooped up Lovecraft and nestled him under her sweater. They'd been damn lucky to avoid being caught so far. "We should haul ass back to the waiting room before we get busted," she suggested an impish lilt in her voice. "There are some heavy-duty things we need to hash out. You might wanna ring up Grace too—I haven't managed that yet, and Cynthia won't be joining us." Her smirk was all sharp angles as she added, "Looks like you guys are stuck with me for good—no running off back to New Hampshire for either one of you! Now that everyone's here let's dig up some ancient mojo and give these Outer Gods something to sweat about."

With Ana's audacious grin and unshakeable confidence illuminating their path forward, Brock allowed himself to toy with the idea that their seemingly impossible mission might be achievable after all.

CHAPTER 9: TRIBE

The space around them pulsed with an alluring promise, their bodies yearning for the uncharted realms of each other.

"Grace is on her way." Malachi's voice broke the silence, his attention drifting from the cold, neglected fries in front of him to the phone he'd just slipped back into his pocket. The low hum of conversation around the table—a back-and-forth between Brock, Lenny, and Ana—stuttered to a halt. The cafeteria was an island of desolation in the sea of midnight, its vast emptiness punctuated only by a lone man hunched over a corner table, a waitress refilling salt shakers near pies displayed at the bar, and the gentle clatter of pots from a line cook in the kitchen beyond. It felt like their own private fortress.

"She seemed glad to hear your voice," Brock observed casually.

"We've called it even," Malachi replied. "Things are more messed up than I could've ever dreamed. Even my aunties' intentions. They did what they thought was right back then." He grimaced as if tasting something unpleasant. "But Mary... that witch can take a one-way ticket to hell. At least Grace knows she needs to keep tabs on her."

Ana shot him an incredulous look from across the table. "You really think she'd go back?"

"Nah, she wants her book." Lenny patted the oversized purse he carried for Ana like some emasculated husband—Ana had enough on her plate; he could manage this minor task. "She'll have to get through me first."

A ripple of anger stirred within Lenny, his eyes darkening ominously.

"Lenny, your eyes," Ana chided gently.

"Again?" Lenny rubbed his face as though trying to ease away an encroaching headache. When he looked up again, his gaze had returned to its usual warm hazelnut hue.

"This is so freakishly normal," Malachi commented dryly.

Their laughter filled the room, a burst of warmth in the cold cafeteria.

"It's really great to finally meet you guys," Ana said once their laughter had subsided. "In person, I mean. Weirdly enough, I feel like I've known you forever."

"We're kind of related," Malachi added.

"Dude, don't say that," Brock interjected with a grimace.

"Not in an incest way!"

Their laughter echoed again, earning them a disapproving glance from the solitary diner.

"Like a tribe," Malachi continued. "We're different members of the same tribe."

"You too, Lenny." Ana nudged her companion. "You're just as much of a weirdo as we are."

"Yeah," he agreed nonchalantly.

"Aren't you curious about...what you are?" asked Malachi.

Lenny shrugged. "Nah. I'll find out eventually. I know why I am the way I am: to keep her safe."

Ana blushed, and Brock offered an approving nod to the big man.

"So where exactly are we headed?" asked Malachi.

"California," replied Ana, leaning in close. "Maybe you can just, you know, teleport us there?"

The thought of another disintegration and atomic reassembly made Malachi's stomach churn; it had been worse than his leap to Acheron and left him feeling drained and weak as if he'd run a marathon on an empty stomach.

Lovecraft, who had been silently listening in on their conversation, began to stir within Ana's mind. His presence felt like a relentless pulse against her consciousness, an intrusive entity intruding where it wasn't invited. Ana, translocating multiple subjects repeatedly is ill-advised. Without a suitable anchor—like the Acheron gate designed to stabilize matter during the transition—such actions can strain both the initiator and those subjected to it. Memory loss, cognitive impairment, and even physical disintegration are potential risks. We should count ourselves fortunate that Malachi emerged whole and mentally unscathed from such careless tampering with reality.

"Great! Next time, maybe give him the safety briefing before you play god." Ana retorted, her hand instinctively rubbing at the spot beneath her sweater where Lovecraft's essence resided. Her companions didn't need any introduction; they knew all too well who she was addressing.

I merely observe and theorize while you experiment, dear girl. I am but a skull filled with the remnants of the magic that brought me back into existence. My hypothesis was that I could bridge the gap between spiritual and physical planes, and I succeeded. But acting as a conduit for Malachi's potent powers differs from being an anchor for more advanced magic.

"Advanced magic?" Ana raised an eyebrow curiously.

Magic powerful enough to warp reality itself, Lovecraft responded telepathically. The very might of the Outer Gods themselves manifests through such abilities that you and your fellow Aspects have already shown an aptitude for: spatial manipulation, gravity control, and temporal navigation. With practice and patience, you may master these or other unknown powers. Until then, we learn through trial and error—such is the path of audacious intellect!

Ana mulled over his words before breaking the silence that had settled over her stunned companions. "No more teleportation," she announced abruptly. "And definitely no messing around with it unless absolutely necessary, or, we figure out more of the science behind how you do what you do. That kind of magic can backfire."

"Backfire, how?" Malachi asked, his tone laced with concern.

"Backfire, as in you could end up looking like a chew toy for a pitbull on the other side."

"Holy hell," Malachi muttered, "Would've been great to know that!"

Brock mentally scolded himself for putting any faith in the eccentric author.

Given Malachi's unique abilities, I was fairly confident success wouldn't result in disfigurement, offered Lovecraft.

"Shut it," Ana snapped.

"What?" Malachi looked taken aback.

"Not you," she clarified dismissively. "Teleporting won't get us to California, so we're driving. When's Grace getting here?"

"She's on the next flight out," replied Malachi. "Should be here by the afternoon."

They huddled over their table, plotting their journey; Lenny and Brock were more interested in splitting leftovers than discussing travel plans. Thus, on a map spread between them, Ana and Malachi traced a week-long route to California's border. Once done, they powered off their phones—paranoia dictating caution against potential followers. With full stomachs and a plan in place, they all felt a sense of accomplishment.

If I may interject, Lovecraft began again.

Ana ignored him.

Ana?

Ana requested her purse from Lenny, her fingers recoiling as they brushed against the human-like leather of Mary's grimoire tucked inside. She moved to settle their tab, doing her best to tune out Lovecraft's relentless mental chatter while she waited for the elderly waitress to process their bill. Yet, no matter how hard she tried, her irritation seemed palpable in the taut lines of her face or perhaps in the twitchy rhythm of her movements as Lovecraft continued his psychic pestering.

"You alright, dear?" asked the waitress with a note of concern.

"Just cramps," Ana responded with a smooth lie that rolled off her tongue all too easily.

The waitress gave a sympathetic nod. "Don't miss those."

"Thanks. Keep the change."

She turned away from the counter and quickly detoured to the restroom before rejoining her friends. In there, she placed Lovecraft on the changing table with his eye sockets turned away until she was done. The tiny fib she'd told weighed heavier on her conscience than it should have. Maybe it was time she stopped lying to herself— pretending everything was hunky-dory when there had been no sign of a period since this doomsday rollercoaster ride began.

Was it stress? She knew she wasn't pregnant, and discussing feminine issues with a group of men wasn't exactly appealing, even if they were good men who cared about her and were part of her tribe rather than strangers. Lost in thought, she stared blankly at dripping hands over the sink before snapping back to reality and drying them off quickly.

The moment she picked up Lovecraft again, he resumed his telepathic prattling.

If you wouldn't mind, a question? Lovecraft ventured.

"I mean, I've got a shit-ton of issues right now but go ahead."

A mental sigh echoed in her head. I presume that's some kind of slang akin to the linguistic vomit you and Malachi seem fond of. Would you be so gracious as to confirm the current date and year?

Ana rolled her eyes before glancing at her phone. She relayed the information.

Ah, indeed. Not to rain on your parade, but considering celestial alignment, leap years, and planetary shifts... Your little band has approximately two to three months.

"Until what?" she asked.

Until the four Aspects must awaken, master their deep arts, and confront the Deep One, a prophecy etched in time by the seers of Atlantis.

"The fuck?" Ana blurted out.

The Seers of Atlantis were carefully chosen Delphic maidens...

"No! What was that crap about us having two to three months?"

Ah yes. That 'crap,' my dear girl, pertains to nothing less than Armageddon's clock. Did you think this was all for naught? That you were created without purpose? You and your companions are weapons forged for an ancient war. Your illusion of being carefree pals on a mission to save some insignificant human woman—regardless of any sentimental attachment—is a charming fantasy I've allowed you to entertain. Whatever you hope to achieve in the West, may Hermes guide your path because time is slipping away.

With Lovecraft's chilling revelation ringing in her ears, Ana sprinted back towards the table.

***

Winding through Idaho's rugged terrain, the labyrinth of ancient highways cut a serpentine path through fields that bristled with coarse vegetation and valleys painted in military hues. The stark beauty of this landscape seemed to breed hardy souls, as evidenced by the robust locals they encountered during their sporadic pit stops. These rural denizens were practical, industrious people who worked their land with a stoicism that was both admirable and humbling.

Each new day saw the four companions pressing on, their resolve matching the relentless determination of these tillers. As Ana spun tales of an impending apocalypse, sleep became a luxury none dared to indulge in; urgency had cast its shadow over their journey. Yet, despite this relentless pace, Malachi and Ana—more human than god—succumbed intermittently to sleep's sweet oblivion. Waking to find miles disappearing into the rearview mirror, they marveled at Lenny and Brock's unyielding stamina.

Lenny and Brock seemed more godlike and impervious to fatigue. They alternated driving duties without pause or complaint, fuelling their endurance with gargantuan meals that would make a weight-loss coach faint. On the road, they maintained a vigilant silence broken only by sporadic radio updates, eyes locked on the asphalt ribbon unfurling ahead while side mirrors reflected a world left behind.

Lovecraft—their spectral passenger—remained silent unless spoken to directly. He seemed content to exist within his thoughts, an enigma wrapped in ethereal tranquility whose psychic touch brushed against them like unseen cobwebs.

Time lost all meaning as they drove on, tension-laden currents carrying them across America's heartland. Yet amidst this existential threat, moments of youthful exuberance shone like beacons in the gloom.

One such moment occurred when Ana began rhythmically tapping spoons together—an impromptu concert from the backseat that filled their vehicle with the soulful echoes of a seasoned blues singer.

Lenny's voice cut through the music, his question reflected in the rearview mirror. "Where'd you swipe those?"

"Appropriations," Ana retorted, her rhythm unbroken.

Malachi chimed in with his usual wit. "I gave her permission for us."

Lenny's brow furrowed in the mirror, bemusement dancing in his eyes. "Hold up. Appropriations for what? You ain't Native American."

"I appropriated them," she shot back, her spoon-slapping continuing unabated.

Malachi couldn't resist a quip. "The problem with kleptomaniacs is they always take things literally."

The car shuddered, echoing the laughter that bounced within. Malachi and Ana's quick-fire quips and references to obscure movie trivia entertained their less pop-culture-savvy companions. Their banter filled the airwaves better than any radio show could. As twilight painted the sky with hues of violet, a peculiar sight caught Brock's eye—a lone sycamore tree atop a hillock, its gnarled branches reaching out like spectral fingers from a sea of waist-high grasses. They took a detour down the dusty path to this arboreal sentinel.

Under its shade, they savored sandwiches and salads procured from a roadside stand —Idaho was generous with its bounty. A collective sigh escaped them as they gazed upon terracotta fields dissolving into a fiery horizon that bathed distant mountains in gold—an image worthy of an artist's canvas. In that moment, thoughts of beauty, life, and things worth protecting filled their minds.

While they ate, Ana noticed Brock and Malachi sharing quiet smiles as they brushed crumbs off each other or offered bites from their food—a silent testament to their bond. When she glanced at Lenny to see his reaction to this display of camaraderie, his intense gaze suggested he might harbor similar feelings toward her.

As darkness began to creep in and they resumed their journey, it felt like an apt metaphor for their lives—moving forward even when shrouded by uncertainty.

Crossing state lines meant motel rooms with questionable hygiene but surprisingly good water pressure. Shower rotations were followed by swift departures, leaving behind baffled clerks who had been asked for excessive towels. Rest stops were taken as needed. Ana proved surprisingly adaptable without sacrificing her femininity amidst the testosterone-charged atmosphere.

During the multi-day trek toward California, their shared fellowship became a beacon against the encroaching dread of cosmic annihilation. If oblivion was on the horizon, then these fleeting moments of camaraderie were all that mattered—each one a precious gem to be treasured.

On the final night, they sought refuge in a rustic cottage advertised on a highway billboard. A grateful elderly proprietor welcomed the off-season business. They settled in quickly, stoking a fire and wrapping themselves in blankets. Malachi and Brock found comfort on the couch while Ana and Lenny sat hand-in-hand on adjacent chairs, their bond echoing an old married couple's familiarity yet tinged with the uncertainty of newly discovered feelings.

Lenny had not pressed Ana for more than she was willing to give; his past experiences had taught him patience. They would navigate this new terrain at their own pace.

When Brock rose to prepare another round of hot cocoa—a comforting indulgence despite California's lack of snow—Malachi began exploring closets.

"Damn, a guitar!" Malachi's voice echoed as he pulled out the cobwebbed instrument. Having snooped around his room back on the reserve, Ana remembered his aspirations of becoming a professional musician and was sure he was talented despite never having heard him play before. She nudged him encouragingly, eager to hear what melodies he could coax from the strings.

Malachi's fingers danced over his guitar strings with a surgeon's precision, each note he plucked resonating in the air like golden orbs. The melody that filled the room was more than just music; it was an echo of his soul, a captivating magic that stirred something deep within Ana. She sat upright, her gaze fixed on Malachi, entranced by the haunting melody.

Lenny watched from his seat, leaning forward as if drawn by the music. Brock stood frozen in the kitchen doorway, mugs of hot cocoa held captive in his hands until Malachi's playing ceased, and he remembered his task—distributing drinks.

"Damn," Brock muttered, admiration tinging his voice. "I'd forgotten how good you are."

"I second that," Ana added with a grin.

Lenny simply nodded. "Think you can handle requests?"

"Why not?" came Malachi's casual response.

As they surrendered to the enchanting allure of the witching hour, their laughter echoed through the cottage alongside singing and applause. The firelight shrank back into corners while shadows grew bolder and more daring. The bassy snores of two exhausted

Godbeasts vibrated through the walls: Lenny slumped over in his chair while Brock's head had found a new resting place on Malachi's lap.

Ana and Malachi exchanged knowing smiles over their now lukewarm drinks amidst this bearish symphony, both wide awake despite the late hour.

"Who would've thought they needed sleep too?" Malachi remarked dryly.

"Guess so." Ana sighed wistfully. "Despite all this cosmic horror shit happening around us... I feel lucky."

"Me too."

"Lenny... he's something else."

"I get what you mean."

Malachi glanced at Brock, who was lost in dreams whispered from his crimson lips. He could sense a chase unfolding in Brock's dream—the wilderness flashing before him as if it were his own imagination. Their connection deepened each day, merging thoughts, sensations, and emotions. It was an intimacy that should've scared him but didn't.

"Do you think we'll make it?" Ana asked.

After all they'd faced—legendary witches, super-soldiers, space-spiders and the uncertainties of dimensional travel—Malachi chuckled darkly. "We've come this far. Taking down some space Gods seems like child's play."

Ana snorted with laughter. "Outer Gods, actually. We need to know our lingo to win this war."

Her concerns echoed his own—their goals were murky at best. Despite his cryptic silence during transportation, the prospect of consulting Lovecraft remained tempting.

"We can just ask Lovecraft in the morning," she suggested.

"Why wait?"

"I guess...Maybe everyone should be involved?"

"Nah." Malachi carefully slipped from under Brock and tucked a couch pillow under him. He stirred but didn't wake up. "Neither of us can sleep anyway, so we might as well make the most of it."

Extricating herself from Lenny's iron grip was no small feat for Ana. Yet, with patience, she managed to free herself without waking him. His protective instinct warmed her heart; even in slumber, he sought to protect her.

"Ready to roll?" Malachi's whisper cut through the silence.

Ana tiptoed towards him, standing by the fire and eyeing the duffle bag where Lovecraft resided like a serial killer's keepsake. She reached for Malachi's hand and then bent down to pick up the skull—creating a psychic link that allowed Malachi to hear Lovecraft without physically handling him. A surge of energy passed between them, and their pompous passenger wasted no time speaking up.

Dearest and brightest Aspects, he said.

"So, we're the head of the pack now?" Ana shot back.

Lovecraft's response came as a gentle ripple in their minds, a laugh devoid of sound yet filled with meaning. A matter of personal preference. I've always found the dance of intellect more engaging than brutish showmanship. The intricacies and enigmas of consciousness have long been my favored playground.

Malachi cut in before Lovecraft could further wax lyrical about his preferences. "We need answers," he stated bluntly, his voice carrying an edge that mirrored his impatience.

I shall strive to shed light where shadows linger.

Ana stiffened slightly at Lovecraft's eagerness—her past experiences had taught her to be wary of men who were overly forthcoming with assistance. "Why are you so keen?"

I offered my aid and guidance. Lovecraft paused momentarily as if contemplating how much truth they were ready to handle, he continued: Time has allowed me ample opportunity for self-reflection; my mind is like a maze shrouded in fog, haunted by unfamiliar specters. Doubt has started to seep into my certainty, but doubt often paves the way for understanding; thus, I embrace this predicament willingly.

He abruptly switched gears, leaving his existential crisis behind. But enough about me! You didn't come here for that! I must apologize for intruding on your discussions and speculating about your fates. My century-old plan, left in the care of various misfits over time, may have unintentionally tipped the scales of destiny off-balance...

Ana's mind was seized by an image—the twisted grin that Marrow often wore when he thought no one was looking. "Misfits? You mean Marrow?"

That wasn't his name when our paths crossed.

"And what was it then?" Malachi asked curiously.

Bone. Dr. Bone.

"Not one for subtlety, was he?" Ana remarked dryly. "How did you two meet?"

The answer to that question eluded Lovecraft; his memory of their encounter was fragmented and hazy—like a mirror shattered into countless pieces. After a moment, he confessed: The specifics of our meeting evade me, as does the mystery of my transformation.

"You don't remember how you died?" Malachi blurted out incredulously.

I do not.

"Marrow probably had something to do with it," Ana suggested, her skin prickling at the psychic remnants of savagery she'd picked up from her former doctor. Her naivety in failing to see Marrow for what he truly was made her feel betrayed by her instincts.

You cannot blame yourself for your innocence, Lovecraft soothed. Nor shall I berate myself for mine. Dr. Bone is the embodiment of sociopathy—he has refined his sickness into precision and meticulousness...

"I'm lost," Malachi admitted with a sigh.

My current predicament remains a mystery to me as well...Either my soul is trapped due to some arcane mishap, or I am under the curse of a more powerful witch—of which there are many—including Dr. Bone."

"Marrow," Ana interjected. She darted a brief look towards Brock and Lenny, still lost in the depths of sleep. "Just to lay it out there, Malachi... your Auntie Cynthia wasn't a stranger to Marrow either. Except she knew him by another name: Moreaux."

Malachi paused for a heartbeat, his intellect quickly piecing together the implications. A wave of cold, righteous fury surged within him, distorting his usually charming features into a grimace reminiscent of a grotesque gargoyle statue at the whispered name—Moreaux. An appellation murmured in hushed tones between his Aunties during their late-night confabulations when Jewel was still among them as if uttering it could conjure up some nightmarish specter.

Ana noted the transformation in Malachi's expression and said, "I can see you're familiar with that name." "Let's refocus here... How did you meet him, Lovecraft? Did he teach you magic?"

Once more, Lovecraft found himself wandering the twisted hallways of his mind palace, peering into the ghostly reflections within the mirrors and straining to decode the hissing echoes of his past. The reverberations were as elusive as wisps of fog, never fully forming into discernible words or phrases. He recalled a room bathed in rich mahogany, with an entity whose sleek appearance was deceptively human-like, donning the guise of a physician. A question had been asked—its gravity lingering in the air like an imminent tempest.

Abruptly, reality fractured around him. The mirrored labyrinth shattered into fragments of wall and floating shards of reflective glass. Amidst this glimmering chaos, Lovecraft caught glimpses of fragmented truths: first, he was on a sled slicing through snow beneath towering pines; then he was somewhere entirely different—his sight trembling as he spat up bloodied pieces of his own innards akin to a tuberculosis patient; finally, he found himself sprawled on the floor of a smoky longhouse filled with scantily clad natives while Marrow—his body embellished with bloody red runes akin to those of an Aztec priest—led them in some blasphemous chorus. When the memory palace collapsed back into reality, it left him more perplexed than enlightened.

Lovecraft sighed inwardly. My dear girl, that answer remains cloaked in obscurity. Perhaps my memories will resurface with time. I can tell you about the man himself, though—oddly enough, I seem to retain quite a bit about him.

"That's weird as fuck," Ana replied. "But hey, could be useful... Spill."

Lovecraft resumed: Whether he is officially schooled in medicine or not is immaterial —I assure you there isn't another witch more proficient in human anatomy than your former shrink. The riddles of flesh have always been his obsession and realm—the rituals needed to conjure four beings from the void necessitated aligning with such a volatile, albeit enviable, character. In many ways, Marrow was the puppeteer behind the birth of the Aspects—the magic couldn't have been actualized without him.

The word 'birth' made Ana shudder. The sight of four women in a trance-like state, ripping out their own guts in a frenzy of insanity, was not something she ever wished to witness—yet it was the memory that haunted her from her visions when pursuing Mary. Marrow had directed that gruesome spectacle? Disgusting but not entirely surprising.

Ignorance is far from blissful, Ana; Lovecraft intoned mentally. It is better to confront this harsh reality now. Be aware that among all those sanctified for the creation of the four, he was selected to oversee the Rite of Wind. Your father...in as much as these terms still apply.

Ana blanched and trembled slightly but managed to ask, "So, who is he?"

I recall asking Charles to investigate—he had quite a knack for detective work. He dug up numerous aliases, old addresses, and legends.

"Legends?" Malachi chimed in with an incredulous tone.

Lovecraft commenced his spectral verse: In London, where the mists do curse, deeper than Hades' dire thirst, Jack's agile, Jack is swift; eludes before the cartmen lift. Another courtesan's life he'll sieve, into the Thames she'll naught but cleave. From sternum to end, a bloody tear, skin shimmering like an oriental sear. A fragment or two forever lost; under moonlight, maidens should accost: Heed the twilight when shadows swell, in London where the nightmares dwell.

A sudden revelation from Lovecraft set their minds spinning. Jack... London... Mutilated women... Prostitutes... Ana's eyes widened, her lips parting in a silent gasp.

Oh, so you've heard of that moniker, Lovecraft's voice resonated within their minds, a smug undercurrent to his telepathic tone. I was taken aback myself when Charles unveiled it—nearly choked on my tea, I did! But this Marrow has worn many masks throughout history. One incarnation matches the description and abilities of Aleister Crowley—the infamous witch—likely an alias itself. He may even descend from the rulers of Ancient Rome.

Lovecraft paused for effect, allowing the weight of his words to settle before continuing. Ancient tales whisper of a man like him dabbling in fleshcraft. Tales that stretch back to Rome and even Atlantis. Yet I suspect Marrow's roots reach deeper into the arcane past—I dare say he might have been an emperor himself, continually reinventing his persona over millennia.

Malachi couldn't help but interject, incredulity lacing his words. "But that would make him thousands of years old!"

Brock grunted from the couch at Malachi's outburst; even unconscious, he seemed to share his friend's distress.

Lovecraft responded with an ethereal shake of his head. Pledging oneself to Cthugha or another Outer God comes with many gifts—one being extended or seemingly infinite life span. He paused again before adding wryly: Though I admit my theory linking Alexander the Great and our subject is mostly conjecture based on patterns and subtle speech nuances.

He continued with a hint of fascination creeping into his otherwise pompous tone: His accent was particularly intriguing—a blend of aristocratic sophistication and regal bearing. It reminded me of a nobleman, a king, or even an emperor. The most cryptic historical manuscripts hint at a particular lisp or tendency to trill 'a's and 'r's.

Lovecraft's voice hardened slightly as he drove his point home: Jack the Ripper's actions upon the British public mirrored the sacrificial rituals of Atlantean witches crafting their flesh golems. These ancient spells have been lost to time, their last records burned during the Crusades by those who mistook them for demonic texts. Only someone knowledgeable of or from that era could understand how to animate lifeless flesh.

The silence that followed was heavy with the implications of Lovecraft's words. Malachi exchanged a glance with Ana, both young faces etched with uncertainty and fear as they grappled with this new information about their enemy.

In a sudden rush, Ana was pulled into the clandestine whispers of time itself. The voices were as tantalizing as ancient sirens, their call irresistible. Her surroundings shifted from the cabin's familiar confines to that of an unseen spectator in a vast, dank cellar shrouded in heavy scarlet fog—a chilling mist that reeked of violence. Chains clinked ominously in the distance, muffled groans filled the air, and a revolting stench permeated everything—it was decay at its most potent. All her senses were under siege, challenging her resolve to remain anchored in this gruesome tableau.

At the heart of it all knelt a man whose allure was heavenly and hellish—his muscular form on full display. He exuded both repulsion and majesty—a figure who could easily be mistaken for demonic royalty. Fresh blood adorned his skin while his colorless eyes rolled back into his skull; he chanted incantations in an unfamiliar language while his hands twitched erratically—the unmistakable signs of necromancy.

Before him sprawled an appalling heap: severed body parts akin to those found on a butcher's slab, organs, limbs, and torsos swarming with flies and reeking of rot. As he rose to his feet, an unholy energy stirred within this mound—it began piecing itself together with ghostly threads shimmering silver under the weak light until it stood erect—an abhorrent beast emitting bestial groans.

Its rib cage vibrated with such force that it mimicked a dragon's roar—that was what jerked Ana out of her vision. Tied by an invisible psychic tether, she and Malachi recoiled from the skull they'd been touching—they cried out, tumbling backward onto the floor.

The abrupt intrusion of reality yanked Brock and Lenny from the depths of their dreams, their awakening as disoriented and gruff as bears jolted by the echo of gunfire. With instincts honed by danger, both men surged to their feet, hands instinctively reaching for the familiar weight of their protective duties before they distanced themselves from the flickering menace of the fireplace. As they struggled to shake off their stupor, they held onto Ana and Malachi—offering what solace they could in the face of this horrifying ordeal.

Roused from his slumber by a psychic jolt, an echo of his friend's terror, Brock struggled to make sense of the chaos surrounding him. His gaze landed on a skull tossed carelessly to the floor—likely the epicenter of this pandemonium. Its hollow eye sockets seemed to leer at him with a wicked grin that sent chills down his spine. In the pit of his gut, he was certain that Lovecraft had orchestrated this madness—the vestige of a nightmare still tormenting Malachi.

"What in the world?" Lenny blurted out.

"I saw something... we saw something awful," Ana admitted, her voice shaky.

"You were messing with him, weren't you?" Brock accused, his tone terse yet concerned.

"Yeah," confessed Malachi sheepishly. "My bad. I don't think it was Lovecraft's fault, though. We were trying to figure out how everything ties together: Mary, Cthugha... Marrow—he's at the center of this weird conspiracy. And Lovecraft, well, he probably knows almost everything we need to understand. Or so we thought, but his memory is foggy. I thought it would be smart to question him. Sorry."

"No, you're right," Brock conceded. "We've been taking it easy and dodging responsibility. This ain't a vacation—we're trying to stop the end of the world." With resolve hardening his features, he pulled Malachi along and picked up the skull from where it lay near the fire. He gestured towards the others. "Let's all listen to what he has to say."

Ana and Lenny followed suit and joined them by laying their hands on the artifact.

Playtime is over, then? Lovecraft's voice echoed within their minds.

Brock barked, "What's Marrow's master plan? And why are you playing for his side? What are we missing here?"

You're almost there, Lovecraft teased. The shards of reality are scattered around you like puzzle pieces waiting to be put together. Consider me your guide in this endeavor. I was once a scholar and a witch from the Order of Midnight—an ominous title for the impending dusk of humanity. My role was to welcome the Aspects: the champions chosen by Cthugha—knights of Earth infused with—but uncorrupted by—Outer God blood. Given my current spectral state, I'd bet my last penny that Mary took up my mantle and brought forth the Aspect of Fire. Sequana, a shamaness hailing from South America, was responsible for summoning Water—her lineage carried on her mission after her passing. Creating four flawless supernatural beings is no small feat—it requires an elaborate ritual that unfolds slowly across ages. Marrow would have overseen Air's creation; there's no reason he would miss such an event. My protégé Charles—an Irish lad brimming with wild magic—was selected as the final witch to nurture the Aspect of Earth.

"Charles..." Brock murmured, his voice thick with curiosity, "What was he like?"

Charles? A gem among men if ever there was one! Before him, I wrote tales about magic and miracles without ever witnessing one myself. Maybe somewhere along his Irish bloodline, he got cursed by some fairy king or queen. I could never confirm this since fairies are beyond my spectrum of belief! If they exist, they're hidden away where not even the Outer Gods or their minions can reach them. It feels like I should know how he came upon his power... Yet again, my memory fails me... No matter, every now and then, humans surface with a volatile strain of magic that behaves erratically—we call this 'wild magic'—and that's all you need to grasp here. Wild magic often shows up in firestarters, werewolves, individuals who crave human blood—

"Vampires," Lenny interjected.

Noxiophilic Sanguinis, to be exact. There's a lineage of witches whose surname escapes my addled mind who are particularly vulnerable to this condition. Nonetheless, it's an authentic arcane condition, surprisingly manageable and hardly deserving of the hysteria it stirs up. Charles' affliction was less extreme but incredibly rare. He was an *architect*...Lovecraft lingered on the word as if tasting a fine wine. A natural-born creator. He had a knack for fixing things—radios, cars, all sorts of gadgets—and this talent even extended to his own body, aging at a pace that would make a snail seem speedy in comparison. He's as tough as nails—immune to bullets, blades, or even crushing forces—

Without warning, Ana was enveloped in an alien reality, her surroundings morphing into the tattered confines of a dilapidated canvas tent. In its gloomy interior, she stood vigil beside the cot of a man who, by all accounts of nature and time, should have been dust and echoes. His skull bore the grotesque disfigurement of an object subjected to a savage game of football—bruised and battered yet stubbornly resilient.

His speech came in halting fragments, each word painstakingly etched out like the last breaths of a dying ember. Across from him sat Lovecraft—the enigmatic author still tethered to the mortal realm during this spectral encounter—his hand clasped tightly around that of the man's. His whispers were hushed incantations that danced on the precipice between comfort and despair.

The figure sprawled on the cot was barely more than a living cadaver—a shell clinging to life with grim determination. This must be Charles.

Ah, you've managed to dust off a relic of my past, psychic magpie that you are, Lovecraft mused. I'm much obliged, Ana. That memory was cloaked in fog, but it's as clear as day now. We found ourselves caught up in an Appalachian landslide, and over several days, I observed his head slowly regain its shape like some macabre balloon—utterly riveting! So you see, a robust, enduring creature like him would be the perfect vessel to foster the Aspect of Earth.

Brock felt an icy jolt of recognition at the image of the rugged pioneer from Lovecraft's side table—the powerful build, sleeves rolled up to reveal brawny arms and suspenders—it was eerily similar to Charlie's peculiarities... That strange faint accent of his, faded English...Or Irish...No freakin' way...

Lovecraft, sensing Brock's conflict, validated the Aspect's worst fears: Charles, or, *Charlie*, indeed crafted you. If you wish to regard him as your father, be my guest... Of all Cthugha's chosen ones, though, Charlie was the most modest—a Watson to my Holmes. We were inseparable...the dearest of friends. That much is crystal clear in my mind. We set out on a mission to change the course of history and succeeded in many ways. We protected the innocent from damnation. We shouldered humanity's sins and struck deals with a Lord of Chaos to spawn monstrous offspring capable of battling what ordinary folks—or even witches—couldn't. Cthugha will be our deliverance.

"Cthugha?" Ana scoffed sarcastically. "Acheron is no paradise."

Cthugha's passion, akin to any fire, necessitates careful control. Would you leave your hearth unattended? The denizens of Acheron sealed their own doom with their arrogance. It wasn't Cthugha who led them astray but their insatiable thirst for his eternal flame's power. Or would you instead submit to Cthulhu? The Deep One would continue his icy rule from the last Ice Age and encase civilization in frost. It was the Golden One who emerged as humanity's last hope during what should have been our swan song. You'll grasp this in time. You must.

It's unfortunate that your caretakers failed to properly introduce you to your roles and responsibilities. This solitary journey wasn't meant for you. We were supposed to let you grow and flourish while still educating you on your destiny. It seems many of your guardians have either neglected or forsaken their duties.

"Well, Charles, Charlie, whatever his name was, is dead," Brock declared bluntly.

Lovecraft's retort echoed in their minds, a haughty dismissal. His demise is improbable. And irrelevant since I am here now, prepared to guide you under the luminescence of the Golden One.

Lenny snapped back, his voice rough as gravel. "That's a load of crap," he snarled, his grip on the skull tightening until it trembled ominously. "You've not given us a single straight answer about why I'm even here or what I am. Either you're clueless or too damn scared to dig deeper. Even Marrow looked like he'd seen a ghost when I showed up. So your 'my way or the highway' spiel? It ain't flying with me. We'll figure out our own path."

The clash between Cthulhu and Cthugha is inevitable and necessitates a choice from each of you, Lovecraft intoned, his words resonating with an air of self-importance. I offer to you and humanity the possibility that ensures our existence for another century or perhaps perpetuity, constructing vessels and empires to traverse the cosmos indefinitely if we harness the power of the Golden One wisely. Consider your response carefully, Brute or Brute's comrades. Your decision reverberates beyond yourselves—it shapes the fate of all mankind—present and future.

"I need some air." Ana abruptly stormed out of the cabin without another word, letting the door slam shut behind her with a resounding thud.

Lenny released the skull before following Ana outside into the night.

Malachi exchanged a worried glance with Brock—both men were visibly rattled by Lovecraft's revelations and their escalating fears. They gingerly returned the skull to its resting place before gravitating back toward the warmth of the fire.

Brock broke their silence first with an uncertain, "So...?"

Malachi responded with a wry grin. "We're royally screwed."

They leaned on each other, the weight of their newfound responsibilities pressing heavily on their shoulders.

***

The night sky was a jeweler's dream, stars strewn like precious gems against the velvet black. A frosty breeze flirted with the bare-boned trees, challenging the resilience of a smattering of cabins that seemed to have strayed from a Brothers Grimm tale. Ana lingered on the porch, her thoughts swirling like a tempestuous sea, each wave crashing painfully against her skull. Behind her, Lenny's arms wrapped around her like a comforting blanket, his solid build providing an anchor amidst the storm.

"Why me?" she lamented.

"You've always been one-of-a-kind," he whispered into her ear with a fondness that made her heart flutter.

"I wish I were ordinary," she shot back with a hint of sharpness.

"That's bull-crap."

"Maybe," she conceded. "But knowing too much can be worse than ignorance. My worries used to be about scoring my next high or not screwing up my life with bad decisions. Now? One wrong step and humanity is toast. Given my history with decision making... how am I supposed to get this right?"

Lenny didn't respond immediately but moved gently with her instead, swaying like an old oak tree in the summer breeze. His presence was more soothing than any bottle ever was—something she found herself no longer craving or needing.

"I've spent most of my life wandering aimlessly," Lenny admitted, his voice rough yet soft as worn leather. "I did time with real-life nightmares; learned pretty fast I wasn't cut out for alpha dog status. You adapt though—with survival as your end game—I swapped bad habits for workouts, focused on honing body and mind until I became a weapon myself—a cold, unfeeling machine that can't feel pain or emotions."

"When I got out," he continued after a pause, "I viewed women like they were storefront dummies. My cousin tried to play matchmaker, but I couldn't care less. But then..." His heartbeat echoed against her back, the rhythm quickening. "Then I saw you."

Ana swiveled around to face him; their eyes met under the star-lit expanse. Guided by an unspoken force, she reached for Lenny's head, and he—comprehending her silent request—lowered it down and to the side while she unraveled his raven locks, letting them cascade over his broad shoulders like a river of midnight.

The space around them pulsed with an alluring promise, their bodies yearning for the uncharted realms of each other. With a bold sweep of her hand, Ana tugged at his shirt, her movements echoing the fervid desire that engulfed her. Lenny reciprocated her haste, discarding the cloth barrier as though it was ablaze. Her fingers traced paths over his skin, a terrain of raw strength and compelling allure. His muscular physique was a symbol of masculine potency and a fortress providing her refuge; it quelled any lingering uncertainties about her longing—no, necessity—for this man.

Lenny's broad hands ignited a path over her breasts, shoulders, neck, and face before pulling her into an ardent kiss that tasted of smoky brandy and the velvety cocoa they'd indulged in earlier. He kissed her with such force and persistence that it stole the air from her lungs and suspended her in that breathless ecstasy from which they both emerged, gasping.

"We can stop," Lenny offered.

"No," Ana responded without hesitation. "Don't stop."

With a guttural murmur that echoed through the night like an ancient amorous incantation, Lenny lifted Ana effortlessly—her legs instinctively coiling around his waist—and carried her deeper into the forest's shadowy embrace.

***

"What in the world was that?" Malachi's words tumbled out, his body recoiling at the harsh growl that punctured the quiet. Yet Brock held him fast, enveloping him like a spider ensnaring its prey, pulling him deeper into their shared warmth on the well-worn sofa.

"That was Lenny," Brock's voice resonated with a hint of amusement as he caught Malachi's startled gaze. The distant sounds of bodies moving outside danced in their ears. "I reckon Ana has him well in hand."

Malachi blinked, comprehension dawning like a hesitant sunrise across his delicate features. "Oh."

"Indeed."

"So, we're alone then? For tonight?"

"Seems so."

The silence that fell between them was filled only by the crackling fire in the hearth and the rhythmic thrumming of two hearts beating in sync. Cocooned within Brock's heat and the flickering glow from the fireplace, Malachi felt both intoxicated and hyper-aware; every breath they shared seemed to stoke a flame within him.

Their bodies were entwined so closely that he could no longer discern where he ended, and Brock began; his consciousness blurred amidst their entangled forms. It was only by tracing Brock's calloused fingertips skimming over his torso that he recognized those wandering hands seeking to unlock his belt.

As anticipation fluttered within him like a trapped bird, Malachi rose, with Brock shadowing behind like a protective guardian spirit. Their shirts were discarded carelessly —his own falling atop Lovecraft—as they moved together in a dance as old as time.

Brock's desire surged forth like a ravenous beast emerging from hibernation, pressing fervent kisses along Malachi's bronzed skin—his nape, neck, and ears—each one sparking electricity beneath his flesh. As he leaned into this rugged embrace, he felt Brock's hands venture to his jeans, deftly unbuttoning them and tugging at the seams in a haste that spoke of barely restrained passion. Yet, even as Brock's hunger threatened to consume him, he reined it back, remembering his vow to remain a gentleman.

Don't stop—Malachi sent the silent plea through their mental bond—Ana had it right. The world is crumbling around us, and I've no patience to wait.

Malachi rose, the last vestiges of his clothing falling away like autumn leaves in a provocative dance. Brock's breath hitched as he took in the sight before him: Malachi, an alluring silhouette cast in the wavering glow of firelight, his sinewy physique a breathtaking tableau of copper-hued beauty. As Brock drank in the sight with awed silence, Malachi reveled in this precious moment—a dream spun into a tangible reality that was more than mere physical desire. It was a crescendo of companionship, longing, and redemption that had found its origin on a tempest-tossed highway when Brock had played his savior.

A silent confession passed between them—I love you so much—echoing loud and clear without words to muffle its intensity.

Are we ready? The question hung between them, unspoken yet clearly understood. Like the previous utterance, they weren't sure who initiated it; their thoughts were so entwined that it felt as if they'd both voiced it simultaneously—a testament to their deep connection.

Rising from his seated position, Brock hastily shrugged off his remaining attire before reclaiming his calm demeanor. They stood opposite each other, bodies magnetized by shared warmth escalating to its zenith amidst shared sighs of anticipation. The lines blurred as they kissed and touched; whose lips met whose or whose hands explored which body became irrelevant as they fused together in an almost mystical union.

In this transcendent exchange, Malachi felt as if he embodied Brock's muscular strength while Brock seemed to adopt Malachi's slender gracefulness. Two entities yet one; their physical forms dissolved into a sea of sensations while their minds acted as channels for ecstasy—whispering fervent promises and drawing each other closer until they were hopelessly tangled in an intimate knot.

As one being, they sank onto the bearskin rug—their bodies forming an intertwined figure eight—a tangible symbol of infinity. They whispered declarations of love and unity into the ether, their voices joining the symphony of passion that echoed around them—I love you. I am you. You are me. We are love. Their urgent murmurs transformed into a rhythmic chant, affirming their eternal bond and intertwined fate.

***

Lenny's grip on Ana was a flame, a fiery urgency pulling them from the cabin's shelter into the waiting woods. In a whirlwind of motion, her sweater and bra were shed under his adept touch, his hands steering them through the dense undergrowth without faltering, pressing fervent kisses to her skin. The night air was an icy caress against their bare flesh, a stark counterpoint to the blazing ardor kindling between them. Moonlight filtered through the foliage above, casting an ethereal glow that danced over their bodies as they emerged into a clearing—a verdant canvas spread beneath them. A field of wild lilies undulated in rhythm with their quickened heartbeats.

Lenny let go of Ana and divested himself of his pants, watching as she stripped off her remaining clothes and moved towards him—pliant and untamed—as if she were a spirit born from this very wilderness. He drew her close, and she straddled him amidst the fragrant lilies—their bodies fusing together in an intimate ballet under nature's watchful gaze. Each caress sparked flames hotter than dragonfire; every gasp echoed with raw yearning. Their passion transcended into something sacred—something celestial—as if each shared kiss was a journey into uncharted territories.

Whispers carried vows on the breeze while their kisses mapped unexplored landscapes on each other's bodies. Lenny found himself entranced in a rhythm as old as time itself—the way Ana moved against him ignited within him a primal hunger he never knew existed until this moment.

Her touch was wildfire; her kisses were molten desire cascading over his senses and consuming him entirely. It was a pleasure so intense it blurred into pain before blossoming back into ecstasy—a testament to the profound healing power that such intimacy could cultivate.

As dawn began to break, they reluctantly disentangled themselves and embarked on their journey back to the cabin. The memory of their incandescent encounter still vivid and potent in their minds, almost tempting them to abandon their friends to return once more to the enchanting site of their lovemaking.

As they retraced their steps back to the porch, they began gathering their garments, which had been hastily shed and neglected in the fervor of their earlier exit. Lenny picked up his discarded shirt as Ana's fingers traced over her sweater's fabric. They dressed under the rising sun's scrutiny, a silent understanding passing between them—an unspoken secret that made their smiles all the more significant. The primal intimacy they had shared was raw and potent, a memory etched into their souls for eternity.

149 of 331

Lenny wasn't alone in his journey of sensory indulgence and ecstasy, he discovered, as the musk of human exertion snuck under the door. It looked like they'd all been swept up in similar urges and desperations. He pushed open the door to unveil a scene of disarray: furniture capsized, seating displaced, bathroom door hanging askew, shower curtain torn down with damp footprints wandering towards two entangled men sleeping on the rug.

Despite having no romantic interest in men himself, Lenny was entranced by the complex spectacle before him. The intricacy of their intertwined forms was something he'd never seen before. Ana's voice fell away into silence for a moment, too. Then she wrinkled her nose and quipped, "Smells like a frat house post-rush week."

Brock stirred from his stupor at her comment, propping himself up on an elbow and nudging Malachi awake while inadvertently flashing Ana as he did so. "Guys! Seriously? What in the name of Amsterdam went down here?"

What hadn't happened? Malachi pondered, sore from kisses and scratches, marked by their wild exploration of every Kama Sutra position and several others he was sure they'd invented during last night's spellbound passion. Their feverish cycle ended abruptly as dawn approached, thrusting them back into stark reality with brutal clarity.

After a shower, they'd collapsed onto the floor in exhaustion. While Malachi had never experimented with hard substances like crack or cocaine, he felt certain that coming down from this intoxicating high—two minds lost in carnal ecstasy—was worse than any drug withdrawal. Brock's longing gaze suggested that he shared this yearning for more.

"For fuck's sake," Ana suddenly exclaimed, tossing a crocheted blanket onto her friends from an overturned couch before marching off to deal with the toppled shower rod and curtain in the bathroom. Once she'd restored a semblance of order, she slammed the door shut.

Meanwhile, Lenny set about righting the couch and tables in the room before knocking on the bathroom door and waiting for Ana's permission to enter. "Just need a quick splash. No funny business. Be decent when we come out," he said as he slipped in.

Brock doubted Lenny would keep his promise of restraint, considering what he'd overheard last night. They'd seemed nearly as supernaturally charged as he and Malachi. Maybe Ana and Lenny, who hadn't yet exchanged blood or mystical vows, had more self-control than he did. But how long before they—both Godbeasts, with Ana being a powerful seer—breached that mental barrier, too? His mind drifted from the incubus beneath his hands back to reality.

Despite last night's surreal events, a cryptic and deadly destiny loomed. They needed to get dressed and ready—he had a future with Malachi to protect, one now imbued with even greater sanctity and wonder.

"Last night was... a trip," Brock mumbled, his words lost in the abyss of the unsaid. "But it was also kind of a wild ride. We can't lose our heads like that again."

"I get it," Malachi replied, standing up and letting the quilt fall from him like petals from a cherry blossom tree in an ancient ukiyo-e print. Brock, always playing the stoic guardian, suppressed his instinct to shield such exquisite fragility. As they dressed, their fervor cooled into the smoldering ember of affection they had nurtured throughout their shared journey. Once fully garbed, they sat close on the couch, hands woven together with an innocence reminiscent of teenage lovers exchanging tokens of commitment.

"Feeling peckish?" asked Brock, his stomach protesting like a grizzly awoken prematurely from its winter slumber.

"Nope, but you're clearly famished."

With a swift kiss on Malachi's forehead, Brock dashed to the kitchen and began scavenging through their dwindling provisions to assemble sandwiches. Always mindful of others' needs before his own, he prepared extra for Lenny and Ana and handed one to Malachi, who accepted it with apathy and began consuming it robotically. The sustenance filled him but felt as insubstantial as dust trapped in an empty vacuum cleaner bag—nourishing yet devoid of fulfillment.

"Well, ain't this a picture," Ana quipped sarcastically as she emerged from the bathroom wreathed in steamy tendrils. "Nice to see some modesty on you two lovebirds."

"Whatever, fellow slut," retorted Malachi.

Her cheeks bloomed pink, and she sank quietly into an armchair. Lenny followed her out next, bare-chested and shimmering damply like a bodybuilder preening for adulation under stage lights. His stature seemed more formidable than ever, muscles pronounced yet sleekly defined in a way that made Malachi shudder with vague discomfort. He hadn't seen Lenny bare-chested since some summer gathering before his imprisonment when they swam in the lake. Back then, Lenny had been an innocent youth, far from the hardened survivor and imposing figure he was now.

Lenny pulled on a fresh black shirt, slipped on a pair of sunglasses—Ana's solution to his demonic-eyes issue—and picked up their bags along with Lovecraft, the author's carrier, and Ana's purse. He looked like something ripped straight from an action film poster.

"Alright, lads," Lenny announced nonchalantly, "Time to hit the asphalt. California's waiting—miles to go before we sleep."

Neither he nor their other driver rested, though. As Malachi stepped out of the cabin into the sunlight, still feeling an unnameable hunger gnawing at him, he couldn't shake off the foreboding sensation that soon they would be veering away from all familiar human routines.

***

A sickly sweet scent of coppery decay hung heavy in the air, a macabre testament to the life abruptly snuffed out. A crimson ribbon of lifeblood shimmered in the feeble glow of the apartment's single flickering bulb, winding its way from the entrance to the kitchen island. Atop this altar of domesticity lay sprawled the unfortunate caretaker, his curiosity rewarded with a brutal end at the hands of diabolical phantoms. His throat lay open in a grisly smile while his eyes, glassy and devoid of life, stared into oblivion like an abandoned spawn of Cthulhu.

In this tomb-like silence, his murderers methodically scoured through remnants left behind by those who had once called this place home. They sifted through discarded detritus with an almost scholarly interest, their gazes piercing every shadowed corner and probing every hidden nook. Yet their search bore no fruit; despite psychic imprints clinging to mundane objects like spectral cobwebs in a long-forgotten manor, none ignited visions within these godbeasts on their relentless pursuit. Another trail turned frigid as The Aspects continued their elusive dance.

Pythia delicately replaced a grubby towel onto its unkempt pile as if it were an artifact from a bygone era. Trophonius withdrew from examining the doorframe while Necromanteon emerged from her closet investigation like some primordial bogeyman birthed from darkness itself. They congregated behind a worn leather couch strewn with hastily discarded male attire.

"Their essence grows fainter; they continue to slip through our fingers," Necromanteon growled, her voice laced with venomous resentment stemming from her previous confrontation with The Aspects—a clash that had left her nursing wounds inflicted by their terrifying witchery.

Trophonius stroked his beard thoughtfully. "Their psychic residue lingers, potent yet increasingly elusive—as if they've become aware of our pursuit and adapted accordingly. Their earthly conveyance lies abandoned; we can no longer rely on such pedestrian human strategies. Peculiarly, sisters, all traces of them vanish here: at this very threshold."

"They've employed a portal," Pythia deduced. "A flaming gateway conjured by the one named Malachi. His power burns bright like a nascent sun... They've sought refuge in milder climes. I sense the cacophony of seagulls and the soothing murmur of coastal breezes. The eastern or western seaboard, perhaps. Yet their paths remain shrouded; as you've observed, they seem to have learned the peril of flaunting their powers imprudently. It's plausible that Ana or another force is obscuring their tracks from us."

Necromanteon's face contorted into a snarl, momentarily transforming her angelic countenance into something monstrous and ancient. "I believed you had swayed her? Convinced her of the folly of siding with Cthugha? She was destined to prostrate herself before mighty Cthulhu and beg for his mercy. Unless your diplomatic maneuverings have failed us, Pythia? Would it not have been more prudent to obliterate them while we still held the reins of fate? Now our destiny teeters precariously—perhaps our ashes will soon be scattered."

"Necromanteon," Pythia's voice wafted, a murmur laden with foreboding. "The Aspects... their essence is wild, untamed, a tempest of chaos."

The divine herald of mortality and the annals of time merely responded with a dismissive snort. "And that is precisely why they must be shepherded back to their eternal slumber."

"But—"

"Silence your objections, Pythia." Necromanteon's words were as icy as the crypt's kiss. "These godbeasts are apostates. It's oblivion they have earned."

"Beloved sisters," Trophonius interposed gently, ensnaring each by hand in a gesture of unity and solace. "We must not forget that throughout the countless epochs of mankind, we have always placed our preservation at the pinnacle; we bow neither to Outer Gods nor to terror itself. We have been exalted across ages, worshipped as the ageless deities of the Celts, and hailed as Nabu, Hutena, and Hutellura by tribes from Africa's heartland. In every era and corner of human existence, one truth remains immutable—our veneration. We are humanity's warp and weft. Regardless of who asserts dominion over Earth—if any—we shall persist. When monarchs crumble, pawns rise to command. I harbor growing doubts that even these so-called Lords of Chaos fully comprehend the tumultuous game board before them. The threads of destiny appear worn thin and ripe for re-spinning. Who then will emerge from this war's smoldering ruins? The Deep One? The Aspects?"

"Us," Necromanteon intoned solemnly.

"We shall," echoed Pythia.

"Indeed, sisters," concurred Trophonius, his voice imbued with a deep sense of unity. "For we are the true sovereigns and guardians of this terrestrial orb. So then, what path should we tread? What will best serve our interests in this ephemeral juncture?"

"Do you suggest insurrection?" Pythia probed.

"I suggest that we remain open to whatever opportunities may unfurl before us," Trophonius retorted with deliberate ambiguity.

"Hmm…" Necromanteon's visage folded into a scowl. "Yet we must relay some insight to that Mothmann harpy."

"But what?" Pythia implored, her lips parting in anticipation of an answer.

Lured by the tempest's mounting symphony outside, Pythia drifted towards the window; its violent shudder was a siren's call to her senses. The other oracles shadowed her as if bound by some ancient ritualistic dance—silent as wraiths and immobile as effigies. Standing shoulder-to-shoulder, their hands pressed against the glass like ethereal reflections ensnared in a dream—their faces etched with perplexity or dread—they recognized they were entangled in destiny's capricious grasp. The thrashing sea transformed into their prophetic basin—a boundless canvas cloaked in unfathomable riddles. Their gaze pierced the looming veil of cotton puff clouds and jet-black waves that masked Luna's luminescence—eerie as a slumbering sea monster's stare. Together, they drilled into this monstrous eye until it twisted into a portal, their consciousnesses voyaging through its depths.

The obsidian darkness split apart like the silken drapes within a Maharaja's lavish sanctuary, and they found themselves adrift in an otherworldly haven, beholding a luminous figure of ambiguous sex—devoid of distinguishing features, yet her femininity was instinctively discernible. She floated amidst four shadowy forms—the cardinal points on an invisible compass: north, south, east, and west—the four directions—the Four Aspects.

Without revealing their ghostly attendance, they watched the Aspects guide the woman back into reality's harsh clutches. Most captivating was the murmuring conductor of this ritual—an entity whose resonance felt alien even to these Godbeasts who'd borne witness to epochs spanning from dinosaurs to Christ. Indeed, it was Snake unveiling himself that had been the beacon across the chasm that enticed them here.

His power was staggering—potentially eclipsing his kin—for he was creation's keystone, inheritor of the Deep One's magic: water. South Dakota, whispered the Snake—who they now recognized as Cal—come when you wield the weapon you seek…South Dakota? A weapon? How generous destiny had been with its gifts.

After watching the Aspects weave their strategies and bid farewell—all blissfully unaware of their spectral spectators—the three oracles lingered within this dreamlike realm, plotting. What could this weapon be? Only the Aspects were feared by the Deep One himself.

The Atlanteans and their technomagical wonders were extinct—their lineage hunted to oblivion, their kingdom devoured by Cthulhu's final spiteful sigh: a seismic tidal wave that shredded continents and drowned half of Earth's surface under relentless surges.

"What could this instrument of power be?" Pythia mused aloud. Nothing could wound the Deep One except for the cosmic enchantments of Alexander. Yet, even the Witch Emperor, like all Atlanteans, had vanished from the earthly realm. His legendary talismans plunged into the abyssal depths of the sea, concealed from human reach. But not from a non-human grasp...

In a flash of celestial brilliance, they saw a floating, rotating ring of purest gold radiating with inner light. A simple yet awe-striking trinket once adorning the finger of perhaps the only human—or was he?—to have faced an Outer God using arcane spells and inhuman courage.

"The Serillian," they intoned in unison.

A whirlwind of prescience drew them back to the world's primal era, when the wound from the war with Cthulhu lay open and festering. The seabed, raw with tectonic tears, quivered as if under the breath of a thousand-year sigh. Waterlogged ruins whispered of a titanic past, where Earth had once shrugged off its celestial invaders in a violent spasm of survival. Slowly, the planet knitted itself together, each silted scar a memory of the Godswar's tyranny. Above, the ocean wore a mourning cloak, its surface roiling with the ghosts of battles past.

Humanity shattered into savage, mewling fragments, their minds and bodies broken by trauma, reduced to rutting in mud and gnawing bones while memories of glory rotted in their skulls. The golden spires and godlike technomagics of Atlantis—civilization's blazing apex—lay pulverized beneath miles of churning water, devoured by the apocalyptic maelstrom that erupted from Cthulhu's dying, hate-filled convulsions.

The Deep One's dominion waned, but under the saline shroud of Poseidon's realm, stubborn merfolk clung fiercely to their slipping crown. In the heart of their aquatic empire, a relic lay buried, cocooned in legend and the sea's secretive embrace. Skeins of destiny unraveled as the three godbeasts—Pythia, Trophonius, and Necromanteon—pierced the depths with their spectral sight. They watched, unseen, as scales shimmered and ichthyic fingers breached the brackish crypt, plucking a luminous prize from its sepulchral keep. A simple band of gold, yet its brilliance outshone the abyss, a ring that once girded the hand of Alexander. A relic that held humanity's last, defiant promise: the Serillian.

Their collective gaze followed its journey through realms of unfathomable darkness and sun-dappled shallows alike—a floating ribcage of coral, an armory of obsidian and eel skin, an altar of luminescent bones—all kingdoms far from its birthplace in the ocean's depths. For eons, the artifact shifted from one set of webbed claws to another, each minion too covetous to destroy it, too fearful to wear it. At last, through spectral sight, they observed in awe as Cthulhu's servants tore open an astral gateway on a stony beach. Great cephalopods hauled forth a gelatinous, smouldering embryo from beyond—a celestial beast, bound in chains and magic. In a brutal ceremony, the ground soaked red, they forged a witch's trap from the living flesh of this subjugated goddess. Her agonized web of sinew and bone twisted into an immortal cage, and she became the unwilling guardian for her most hated enemy's Achilles heel: the Serillian. Both weapon and warden were neatly dispatched. Vengeance and humiliation were Cthulhu's twin pleasures.

The three seers shifted focus, watching as an ancient cavern loomed—a crustacean fortress, white limestone armor laced with spectral niches that cradled elusive apparitions. Monstrosities, echoes of the Deep One's most unfathomable horrors, stood sentinel, and worse horrors still. But deep within, shadows unstirred by these guardians, another presence loomed—a giant among giants, its influence sprawling like the web of some cosmic arachnid. Spider-like in its secrecy, the entity hovered at the edge of their vast, gloom-laden wisdom. Threads of its mystery wove through every crevice, tangled into the very stone. It was there and not there, visible yet hidden—a spectral spider lurking where their sight could scarcely reach.

This was the eternal prison of the Serillian and its captor, a place where time stood still, their fates sealed forever. The echoes of the ring's grandeur would thunder through the ages, a distorted truth, reverberating in folklore and legend, woven into tales by bards and seers alike. It was a golden treasure of unimaginable power, capable of granting the deepest desires or unleashing the most dreadful curses. Yet, there it would remain, an immovable force, irresistibly drawing the Aspects toward it like moths to a deadly flame.

Amidst their shared foresight, even Necromanteon found a smile creeping onto her lips—not birthed from delight but from fascination at how destiny seemed to weave its complex tapestry so seamlessly around this sacred relic's journey. With their divinations complete, their vision evaporated, and they returned to their physical forms within an apartment awash in moonlight.

"Thou seemest pleased, sister," Pythia noted.

"I had deemed us in a deadlock," Necromanteon replied. "Yet it appears our quarry—and its aims—hath shown itself."

"So they seek Alexander's talisman," Trophonius deduced. "But can they command it?"

"They are offspring of ancient magic; hence, it is feasible," Pythia conjectured. "These children never cease to amaze us."

"What path shall we tread?" Necromanteon questioned.

"Shall we venture towards the West Coast or South Dakota?" Trophonius queried.

Pythia discerned the most prudent course of action. "South Dakota. We hunt down Snake and await tidings of the Aspects' triumph—or downfall."

"It seems fortune graces us with a smile," Trophonius remarked.

"Indeed, it does," agreed Necromanteon.

With renewed determination and gratitude, they set off to see if they could rouse a serpent from his hideaway.

CHAPTER 10: FEAST OF THE GODS

The vision of the colossal pit, spewing debris and squalor, mangled safety barriers, swallowed park

benches—save for one left standing as if for their viewing pleasure—jolted them from their frenzied euphoria.

With a relentless grip on the wheel, Brock and Lenny had been burning rubber for nearly twenty-four hours, pausing only briefly to refuel their bodies and beastly vehicle. Finally, they pulled into Daddy John's, a bustling roadside café and gas station. A stone's throw away from the petrol hub was a charming red building with a lacy white rooftop that seemed stolen from a Kinkade canvas. Inside, patrons flowed in organized chaos; queues formed and dissolved as people devoured their meals before returning to their vehicles or settling at outdoor tables.

Malachi staked out a table while the others ventured inside to order. Soon enough, under the gentle caress of unseasonably warm winds, bathed in pastel blue sky hues and embraced by sunlight, they found themselves savoring some of the tastiest fast food they'd ever had: a seafood feast of fresh shrimp, shellfish, and cod paired with homemade curly fries and crisp salads.

Despite being a spread that should have left them stuffed—especially Brock and Lenny with their hearty appetites—seafood remnants smeared with ketchup lay scattered across their trays like victims of some horrific war. Ana couldn't help but draw grim parallels to one of Dr. Marrow's bloodbaths.

"Not hungry," Brock grunted.

"Same," echoed Lenny.

Surprised glances were exchanged while Malachi and Ana nibbled at popcorn shrimp and salads, leaving most of the feast untouched. A silent exchange occurred between Malachi and Brock—something Ana had recognized from their intense eye contact and subtle lip movements. The air vibrated as if an invisible radio hummed somewhere nearby; she knew she could tune in if she wanted but decided against it.

Lenny forced down another mouthful of food, his face resembling someone eating dirt rather than seafood. A gloom descended over the table that not even the splendid weather could lift.

"Are you guys almost done?" A haughty city dweller with horn-rimmed glasses and an air of pretension interrupted them, a woman—presumably his girlfriend or wife, Lenny surmised from their intermingled odors—hovering behind him.

"Do we look like we're almost done?" Lenny shot back, his voice harsher than he intended.

"No!" The man raised his hands defensively. "Sorry, I didn't mean to intrude."

"Well, you did. So beat it."

Lenny's unexpected hostility sent the couple scurrying away while nearby diners hastily packed up their half-eaten meals and deserted their tables.

"Lenny?" Ana asked softly, concern edging her voice.

"Can't eat another bite," Malachi announced, his face contorted in disgust as he spat the unpalatable mush into a napkin and tossed it into an empty fry basket. The array of food strewn across the table held little appeal for the rest of them either, their shared dissatisfaction hanging heavy in the air. Their makeshift sustenance of corn chips, peanuts, and coffee—a stopgap solution at best—now seemed to mirror their dwindling desire for food. Their crankiness was undoubtedly a prelude to a decline in performance and potential health risks, particularly for Brock and Lenny, whose robust physiques required a steady influx of energy.

Ana found herself baffled by this sudden change in their eating habits—it was non-existent back at the cabin where they'd embarked on hormone-fueled adventures without needing to replenish. Her mind wandered back to those intimate moments with Lenny—the feel of him inside her, the sense of completeness. She grappled with an elusive thought that remained tantalizingly out of reach.

Once they had cleared up their leftovers, they returned to their vehicle and resumed their journey enveloped in silence. As they navigated through the afternoon on a battered highway, stomachs protesting loudly against starvation, even Malachi and Brock refrained from their usual telepathic exchanges.

Despite her hunger—or perhaps because of it—Ana found specific steamy memories stubbornly clinging to her consciousness. Through sun-streaked glass, she replayed scenes with Lenny like private cinematic vignettes—his coarse fingertips tracing patterns on her skin, his gentle tongue exploring her until she cried out.

"What's up?" Malachi asked.

"N-nothing!" she blurted hastily as if caught red-handed by a stern nun during confession hour. "Just dozed off."

"Sure you did," Malachi retorted skeptically.

The car descended once again into its morose silence, but Ana was no longer plagued by hunger. She had a nagging feeling that she'd missed something crucial, which gnawed at her. Her gaze flitted between the disgruntled faces and Lovecraft, nestled snugly in a bag between her and Malachi. The skull seemed to be grinning.

Curiosity piqued, she lifted him up. A gentle current filled her as their psychic connection sparked.

Greetings, dear girl.

It's afternoon now.

Ah, I am but blind and can only perceive the rudimentary shift from day to night. But that's not why you sought me out, is it?

No. Something strange has happened since we left the cabin.

The debauched den of Gomorrah you four so generously christened? Thankfully, my blindness spares me from witnessing your lascivious contortions. My hearing, too, is limited unless I am handled directly...

Wait, are you some kind of parasite?

How uncouth! No, dear maiden. I merely enhance my perceptions through a living conduit. Some minor psychic impressions are shared between the host and the ghost, though... Ah, yes, the matter of sustenance. I'm surprised this evolution took as long as it did, given how close you four have become and how much of your humanity you've already discarded.

The skull in Ana's hands shuddered with each revelation it shared, each new piece of information stirring up a fresh wave of tumultuous confusion.

Lovecraft's continued. You're sharper than most, child. Don't play pretend at ignorance now. You've never been human, not truly—rather a blend of divine and mortal —or beast, as you're labeled in the celestial taxonomy. A Godbeast, nearly fully awakened without the usual ceremonial pomp we'd typically employ to stir such magic—

an extraordinary and monumental achievement. Therefore, I deduce that the accelerated transformation of your fellow Aspects and Godbeast Lenny—drawing cyclically from each other's mutating energy—has led to an unexpected but logical result: maturity. In simple terms—you're all awakened or so near that final threshold is irrelevant.

Ana's mind spun around this revelation, tinged with confusion. I keep hearing the term 'awakened,' but what does it mean?

The latent power within you has been stirred awake. You are now the 'awakened' dragon—the terror of Gods and mortals alike. The ancients used Nephilim as a theological assignment for beings like you, entities possessing abilities far exceeding those of humans while simultaneously threatening the Gods due to their dominion over reality and the cosmic dream. Your intimate sacraments—the emotional bonds and scandalous exchange of potent bodily fluids—have solidified your covenant with power even more so than the blood and arcane rituals I'd conceived could have done. And in response to your unasked question about why food no longer satiates you? It is because you no longer feed on food—you feast on soul essence.

"I'm... I'm a soul eater?" Ana stammered.

"Ana?" Malachi queried, snapping out from his hunger-induced daze when he noticed Ana hunched over Lovecraft's spirit like she was divining cryptic prophecies from tea leaves.

Lenny glanced back through the rearview mirror, concern furrowing his brow. "You okay, Ana?"

"Just having a little chat, guys. I'm fine," she reassured them.

Malachi shot her a pointed look. "Remember what happened last time we chatted with Lovecraft. Be careful."

Ana shivered at the memory. "I remember...and I will."

Ready to continue? Lovecraft's voice echoed in her mind again. As for your evolved physiology...Emotions are the essence of humanity. Without emotions, man would be no different from a complex network of cells—beautiful as a star but equally lifeless. However, you're unique even among Godbeasts—with your ability to extract thoughts from others or exist in another moment. You can sustain yourself through others' lingering auras or concentrated recollections.

"So we feed off emotions?"

Passion is amongst the most potent.

Ana grinned. "So we need to get laid more often?"

Good grief, no! Desire isn't limited to the bedroom—despite your generation's tendency to boil all delights down to base physical gratification. One can lose oneself in the awe-striking wonder of witnessing a child's birth, being moved by a masterful symphony, scaling a mountain with nothing but one's own determination, or observing a brutal gladiatorial contest. As Godbeasts, only the crème de la crème of life's artistry and creation will sate you—not fast food (chickens don't have fingers!), crisps and other such junk you've been stuffing yourselves with—they won't quell any divine hunger. You've been trying to feed lions with salad—you need grand and dangerous adventures on which to gorge. Lovecraft paused, his voice continuing in a wary, foreboding rhythm. Keep in mind that while your primal indulgences might satiate you momentarily, I challenge you to seek nourishment beyond the realms of lust, violence, or other base instincts. Godbeasts can devolve into unhinged monstrosities, swallowed whole by their own fixations. This narrow focus is an ongoing inner conflict, for your perception isn't timid like humans but sharp—and sometimes arrogant—like a cosmic entity.

"Thanks."

You're quite welcome, young lady.

Ana gingerly tucked her supernatural guide back into his bag—Lovecraft was becoming increasingly useful each day. She pondered their discussion about Godbeasts, awakenings, and the risks of immortal hubris and obsession with destructive behaviors. Last night, she and Lenny had made love until dawn revealed them in all their naked vulnerability—a sight that sparked a touch of sanity and embarrassment. But they'd nearly continued, and she knew Malachi and Brock's cravings were just as insatiable. There had to be healthier ways for her friends to sustain themselves—continuous sex wasn't a lifestyle any of them wanted, nor one that would aid their mission. She mentally revisited Lovecraft's examples of divine sustenance—there were no expectant mothers or symphonies at hand. They were encircled by the rugged allure of Yosemite—a mosaic of scrublands, rocky outcrops, and the lower elevations of gray, dusty mountains—but climbing those foothills seemed too formidable a task for her and Malachi...But Lovecraft's final example: gladiatorial combat...The two masculine figures in the front seats caught her eye as an idea began to form.

"Lenny, find a spot to pull over," she suggested. "Somewhere secluded when you see it."

The gnawing pit in his stomach was a constant companion, but he responded to her with an indifferent grunt. The gentle undulations of the landscape morphed into towering cliffs as they maneuvered their vehicle through a narrow canyon, its shadows swallowing them whole. As they emerged on the other side, gravel mounds topped with yellow and green foliage tufts came into view—resembling closely shaved heads of devout monks. A subtle path branched off to their right, and Lenny followed it, guiding them between these monastic formations, skirting a tranquil lake, and ascending into the mountain's heart. Their journey was solitary; no other vehicles dared tread this path.

Suddenly, an abandoned viewpoint materialized, equipped with coin-operated telescopes and weather-worn benches cloaked in black paint. Lenny guided their vehicle into the vacant lot and parked it. They stepped out onto the gravel-littered ground, shuffling towards the guardrails and viewing towers while most of their bodies screamed for sustenance.

As Ana exited the car, she clung to Lovecraft, his silent yet potent insights filling her mind with curiosity. When she joined her friends at the precipice overlooking a lush abyss below, the fresh air and beautiful vista momentarily sated their hunger.

"Okay," Ana started confidently. "Everybody listen up. Lovecraft has some fascinating intel—"

"And here we go," Malachi interjected with a smirk.

"I've figured out why you guys are starving while I'm not."

Immediately, all eyes turned towards her; Lenny and Brock looked particularly ravenous. "I'm not exactly a doctor—"

Metascientist would be more apt given your current predicament, Lovecraft interjected telepathically.

"Alright... Metascientist," Ana continued, unfazed by her newfound ability to bridge minds and conversations. "What I'm saying is we're not fully human anymore. We're half-human, half-god. And the divine part of us seems to be overriding our humanity. We feel things more intensely; we must control our emotions because they can consume us. You guys must have noticed changes in your bodies and moods, too, right?"

Brock's mind flashed back to a homophobic trucker he'd almost pulverized at the start of his journey with Malachi. Lenny, too, had similar violent thoughts while Malachi pondered more physical transformations.

"When was the last time any of you took a dump?" Malachi asked suddenly.

Lenny scratched his head while Brock furrowed his brows; neither could remember. Ana hadn't felt the urge to pee since her rendezvous with Cal, and her period was off its usual clockwork schedule.

"Well, that's one change," said Malachi, surveying their silent faces.

"Since we're on the topic, my periods have been irregular," Ana added awkwardly.

"You're not...?" Lenny asked, turning pale.

"No way," Ana shook her head dismissively.

"But if you were—"

"It would be weird."

"But possibly good?"

"Maybe?"

The words hung in the air as they stood frozen, contemplating this unexpected possibility with twitching smiles on their faces.

"So nobody is peeing or pooping, and you're missing periods?" Brock clarified incredulously.

"Yeah," Ana said, snapping back to the present. "But that's not the crux of it, though I gotta admit it's kinda cool how we're all in this together, getting used to the weirdness. Lovecraft mentioned something about normal food not being enough for us—"

You may still partake in earthly delights for their own sake, he reminded.

"—but we can still snack and sip on whatever we fancy, just for kicks," she went on. "No clue where it ends up..."

Spiritual effluvium. Dissipated into ethereal streams that energize the ley lines of our world. Your waste is nothing less than magical. How splendidly grandiose. You are magnificent, gassy, self-sustaining fertilizers for the etheric realm.

Ana glossed over Lovecraft's pompous elaboration. "So, what we need now is emotions. A whole lot of them. Like what went down... umm... back at the cabin."

Brock's eyes narrowed suspiciously as he seemed ready to spring at Malachi.

"But we can't just be messing around all day—that's not adulting or logical," Ana interjected, pointing at him sternly. "Acts of stunning beauty or experiences that pluck at our heartstrings should do the trick and are way easier to come by than sexy times. I think we all agree that intimacy is pretty... intense."

This was an epic understatement, considering their recent night-long psychedelic trip through spiritual and physical bliss. Brock straightened up, and his knight-in-shining-armor resolve sparked anew. His previous worries about letting his guard down with Malachi after their deep connection felt oddly prophetic now. His divine passion could end their beautiful story or even trigger Armageddon if he didn't tread carefully. "What's your game plan?" he asked.

"Well, assuming no one's nearby—"

"We're miles from civilization," Brock cut in.

"Not a soul," Lenny agreed.

"Shouldn't we be careful with our powers?" Malachi proposed cautiously.

"If Ana has a plan to curb this damn hunger, it's worth giving it a shot," Brock snapped back before adding remorsefully, "Sorry—that was out of line."

"We'll get it done fast," Lenny assured. "Whatever this thing is, we're doing."

Both men seemed on edge, eager for an adventure, which was exactly what Ana had planned.

"How 'bout a brawl?" Ana said, finally revealing her hand. "A wrestling match or something? Lovecraft mentioned gladiatorial games—both spectating and participating. We'll watch while you guys throw down."

"Isn't that kinda risky?" Malachi asked hesitantly.

"I dunno, let's find out," said Ana with a devilish smirk.

With a gentle pull, Ana guided Malachi to the safety of a nearby bench. She cradled Lovecraft in her arms, her eyes gleaming with anticipation for the imminent spectacle. Brock and Lenny responded to her suggestion with a tangible eagerness, their competitive spirit flaring up like two ancient titans readying for battle.

They distanced themselves from each other, their bodies hunched and tensed like coiled springs. The gravel beneath their feet scraped and shifted as they dug in their heels, preparing for the clash ahead. Dust spiraled into the air around them, creating a swirling vortex that hinted at the brewing storm of power about to be unleashed.

Malachi squinted upwards at the sky, now shrouded by ominous clouds, while gusty winds whipped around them. He huddled closer to Ana but didn't voice his apprehension; it was clear that something beyond human comprehension was about to unfold before him. The men standing mere yards away were no longer just Brock and Lenny—they had transformed into ethereal beings of immense power.

Brock was bathed in a soft golden glow that seemed to radiate from within him, while Lenny was enveloped by an aura of shadowy mists. They continued to distance themselves from each other, their opposing forms radiating tension so intense that the air hummed with electricity.

As Ana watched these celestial warriors prepare for combat, she recognized them as cosmic entities bound by unseen forces. Brock embodied the essence of earth—solidity and magnetism—and Lenny mirrored this on another plane altogether.

Visions flooded her mind's eye: a crystal world ravaged by shadowy geysers and collapsing chasms filled with powdery earth—a realm constantly reshaping itself under relentless tectonic forces—an inhospitable landscape plagued by metallic dust storms—a monstrous creature feasting amidst chaos—a world devoid of life, yet kept in perpetual motion by an unholy force.

She remembered tales of Acheron, Cthugha's fiery realm inhabited by hellish dragons, and suspected another Outer God's involvement: Shub-Niggurath, the Devouring Worm. This must be one of her realms—a world corrupted by her influence.

Snapping back to reality, Ana began to understand Lenny's powers and his connection to that darkly twisted world. Her lover was more than just a man—he was an avatar from an alien planet, a fellow wielder of earth-based magic shaped by the Dark Mother herself—or so she believed.

Brock was indeed his brother in arms. She smirked at the thought just as the ground beneath them began to tremble violently. And then it came—the deafening roar of their clash that echoed through the air like a resounding boom!

Brock and Lenny, like Kronos and Zeus, collided with a force that sent a gritty shockwave rippling through the air. Ana and Malachi stood transfixed, their eyes wide, as the primal dance of combat unfolded before them. The intoxicating scent of dust and sweat filled the air, and each man's raw power was palpable; every punch thrown, every grapple engaged, was a testament to their strength.

Brock's hand was ensnared within Lenny's larger grip, their bulging muscles straining against the fabric of their jeans in a tense battle for supremacy. Words lost to rage and exertion were spat between clenched teeth as their energies clashed—brilliant streams of light entwined with shadowy tendrils.

With an eruption of darkness, Lenny emerged victorious from this struggle. Hefting Brock by his hands as if he were no heavier than a rag doll, he hurled him with a divine might. Like a comet streaking across the sky, Brock soared over treetops and crashed into a copse on the far side of the road in an explosion of leaves and debris.

Ana and Malachi's cheers echoed through the night air like Roman emperors drunk on gladiatorial spectacle. It may have seemed cruel or heartless to an outsider, but they knew Brock would rise again. Lenny's triumphant roar echoed around them just as a speck of light appeared from within the tree line. A golden phoenix erupted from its hiding place among the trees, homing in on its target with unerring precision before colliding with Lenny in an incandescent display.

The pair spiraled into a maelstrom of gold and black energy before crashing through guardrails over a cliff edge. Ana abandoned Lovecraft on her bench seat and sprinted alongside Malachi to peer down at the smoking trail cut through verdant foliage towards where their friends had disappeared.

Ana's words were swallowed by a sudden eruption of earth and wind that sent them diving for cover. It was only after they'd hit the ground that they realized—the mass had sailed over their heads, landing with enough force to knock them off their feet.

Their hearts pounded more from exhilaration than fear; this was just another spectacle in their world of godlike beings. Lenny emerged from a crater near the road, his form dusted with dirt and fragments of rock. His body was enveloped in shadowy tendrils that meticulously flicked debris away like an octopus grooming itself.

The parking lot was a battlefield of destruction, but miraculously, their car remained untouched. The aftermath lingered; telescopes lay upturned, posts were uprooted, and a cloud of gravel swirled at the center of the lot. In an instant, every piece of debris was drawn towards Lenny by an invisible magnetic force, swirling around him before being shaped into what appeared to be a hollow lens by his tentacle-like apparitions.

Ana stumbled back to her bench seat beside Malachi, snatching Lovecraft's skull from the edge just as it threatened to fall. A shield! Lovecraft exclaimed in awe, mirroring Ana's sense of wonderment at this display of raw power.

In the space between one heartbeat and the next, a mystical barrier materialized before them, its jagged edges shimmering in hues of crumbling earth. It was an ethereal creation of the Godbeast cloaked in shadow and soil, vast beyond physical comprehension. This was not a tool to be held in one's hand but a mental fortress built to withstand the storm of divine fury about to be unleashed upon them. And indeed, with a deafening roar, such celestial wrath came crashing down.

Behind him, Malachi felt Brock spring into action. His leaps were godlike strides that spanned miles with each bound as if he wore Hermes' fabled golden footwear. In three such leaps, Brock rejoined their viewpoint.

A tremor of ecstasy seized Malachi then—a sensation akin only to the intoxicating fulfillment he found within his lover's embrace. He watched as Brock hovered above their makeshift shield, fists clenched and braced for impact as sparks flew and magic crackled from this clash of titanic forces. It was reminiscent of Thor locked in combat with a giant ripped straight from Norse sagas. Yet, even such grandiose analogies fell short of capturing the awe-inspiring spectacle unfolding before them—the genesis of their very own pantheon.

"We are Gods," Malachi breathed out in wonder.

"Yes," came his lover's agreement.

With an earth-shattering boom that echoed across the landscape, the shield crumbled into oblivion while, around its vortex-like demise, the Godbeasts' battle resumed with renewed ferocity. Lenny conjured tendrils of solidified darkness and filth that erupted either from his back or the trembling earth beneath him—resembling nothing less than some humanoid kraken's appendages—but Brock met these with luminescent golden counterattacks as they danced amidst cascading debris.

At one point, though, Lenny managed to ensnare Brock within an enormous tendril rooted in muck, coiling around him from feet to neck and leaving only his furious face exposed—much like a wild python's prey. With tentacles sprouting from his back, poised for the killing blow, Lenny seemed to have gained the upper hand. But attempting to predict the outcomes of divine conflicts was akin to playing dice with fate. Brock refused to yield, and with a roar that shook the very earth beneath them, he ignited into a golden supernova of raw energy that vaporized his bindings and bathed the plateau in blinding light, forcing Ana and Malachi back against their seats as if they were spectators caught in a nuclear blast.

When the hum subsided, and brightness faded, two shirtless men clad only in ragged shorts stood within a hollow. Their SUV had not survived Brock's final onslaught unscathed and skidded down the debris towards them. Both Godbeasts rushed towards it, effortlessly lifting it back onto stable ground as if it were no more than a child's toy wagon rather than a half-ton metallic behemoth.

"Car," Brock warned from his position on the embankment.

The vision of the colossal pit, spewing debris and squalor, mangled safety barriers, swallowed park benches—save for one left standing as if for their viewing pleasure—jolted them from their frenzied euphoria. They bore no shame but moved with a newfound wariness as they congregated near their transport, brushing away vestiges of their skirmish in a ludicrous mimicry of normality. A family station wagon trundled past them; its inhabitants—a quintet appearing to be a family unit—stared wide-eyed at the unimaginable devastation and the duo of barely garbed men who seemed to have clawed their way out from the underworld's depths. The father's agitation surged, and he accelerated abruptly whilst his wife screamed incoherently behind the glass.

"I wouldn't have stopped either," Ana observed with a hint of sarcasm.

"Understatement of the year," Malachi shot back.

"I feel full," Brock confessed.

"Same here," Lenny concurred while clapping his comrade on the shoulder. They growled at each other before dissolving into laughter—their joviality reverberating across vast distances to reach the motorists fleeing in horror.

CHAPTER 11: HER NAME

Connected to all of his offspring—from giant brood mother to broodling—he felt their fear too when the skies transformed from frosty white to an eerie purple when reality tore open with a deafening

screech when Shub Niggurath's grotesque wail shook the world with thunderous might.

The doorknob groaned under Steve's iron grip, the metal crumpling like a soda can under his strength. A shudder of fear and anticipation held him in its icy clutch, his hand frozen on the cusp of turning the handle. Instead, he pressed his other palm against the cool door, feeling a faint throb vibrating through his sturdy shoes, echoing from floor to metal and into his skin.

"You don't have to do this," Steve whispered in the silence.

But you must, countered the cosmic entity nestled within his skull, sovereign over countless microorganisms scuttling across his bones. They buzzed with threats should he defy them. Yet their dominion over him had waned; they were now subjects to him rather than masters. He then understood that any hunger-driven action would be born solely from his desire. His last meal—a week-old doughnut—had been as appetizing as sawdust on his tongue. He yearned for something warm and richly flavored—a libation not found in any liquor store.

His mouth filled with saliva as alien mandibles slipped out from behind human teeth, causing him to halt in revulsion at the grotesque metamorphosis seizing him. Casting a glance towards Leng's skeletal figure lurking behind him—the Spider God clad in outdated detective garb—he received only an approving nod.

Summoning courage, Steve crushed the handle and burst into the room with predatory grace.

A woman applying lipstick before her mirror caught sight of nothing more than an elusive shadow before darkness swallowed her vision. Steve's mandibles sank into her neck like a beast's feral bite. Within moments, venom left her paralyzed while she foamed at her mouth without making a sound. As both lover and murderer, he tore away her clothes with brutal force until only tatters remained. He squeezed her like an overripe fruit and drained her of their shared passion.

Unaware, his hands left ghostly trails on her skin, which shriveled and dried like prunes under the sun. The constriction heightened as she shrank in size, their shared ecstasy culminating in a macabre dance while the hot scarlet liquid flowed between them like a hallowed sacrament.

Ultimately, all that was left was a withered husk—no larger than a Christmas ornament swathed in white cotton—falling amongst the wreckage of clothes and jewelry. Steve leaned over the sink, black bile and saliva splattering into the porcelain basin. As his flexible jaw retracted its mandibles, he confronted an undeniable reflection of his monstrous form. He touched his face with morbid curiosity, torn between horror and fascination.

"Feeding can be more...elegant," Leng's voice echoed from where he stood against the doorframe, "but first, you must learn to control your hunger."

A chilling numbness gripped Steve, the stark evidence of his monstrous transformation reflected in the gruesome tableau he had created. Methodically, he cleaned the sink, the icy water unable to wash away a stubborn shadow of black ichor that clung to his shirt. The stain was relentless, indelible as the truth of what he had become.

With a detached stoicism belying his inner turmoil, he gathered up the desiccated husk and discarded belongings, consigning them to oblivion within a garbage can. The lid closed with an echoing thud over the spectral remains—a grim testament to his descent from man into a monster.

"Her wallet," Leng directed languidly toward a neighboring stall.

A sharp jolt pierced Steve's triad of hearts—one nestled comfortably in its human home within his chest while two aberrant pulses throbbed from alien locations: one rooted at his skull's base and another lurking lower on his left side. He pondered if more would sprout within him as time passed.

Bending with an unnatural twist of his neck, Steve collected the woman's wallet and saw scattered IDs littering the tiles. "Crystia, Jane, Janet, Lucy…." He murmured under his breath. "What is this?"

"You may have forsaken your humanity, but not your honor," Leng replied with an antiquated cadence that echoed centuries of existence. "You can reconcile your new form with your old virtues, Steve. This woman—a thousand names for a thousand lies—was no saint; she was a parasite thriving on Medicaid fraud, leaving poverty and death in her wake. You've pruned her from society's tree and saved her potential victims. You're welcome."

Steve found himself at a loss for words before Leng's revelation.

Lost in a foggy labyrinth of half-realized dreams and realities too harsh to face fully, Steve gathered the counterfeit IDs and discarded them among the woman's lifeless remains. The silence around them was palpable; no human ears were near enough to catch their conversation.

Exiting the restroom, they crossed an almost empty parking lot towards their car. A woman emerged from the gas station's entrance as they climbed into their vehicle; she bore a haunting resemblance to his recent victim, her dark hair identical. She called out for someone named Lucy. Steve considered claiming her too, but hesitated. The risk of exposure didn't unsettle him—he had transcended such mortal concerns—though they had dallied here long enough.

Guiding their vehicle through the inky canvas of the night, Steve allowed the harmonious strains of a classical symphony to seep into the silence—an appreciation he'd cultivated alongside his master. From time to time, they would both find themselves bobbing subtly to an orchestral crescendo that resonated with them. With the arrival of dawn, its stark white light felt like an abrupt interruption, bringing winds that swept across the dales and compelled trees to bend in unison.

Suddenly, a ripple of unease coursed through him—his brood of spiderlings squirming restlessly within—a disconcerting sensation he'd grudgingly learned to tolerate. Promptly bringing their car to a halt on the interstate embankment, scattering gravel in its wake, he and his master sprung out onto one side together, gazes transfixed beyond the trees towards mountains bathed in golden sunlight.

Beyond those granite sentinels pulsed energy more radiant than any Californian sun; it vibrated with raw might that rumbled and convulsed the earth beneath while dispatching tremors skyward, disrupting unseen energy fields encircling the planet. Threads of pure energy danced across mountain tops like spectral tongues tasting starlight. This awe-inspiring spectacle expanded until it mirrored a second sunrise, casting iridescent hues across the landscape. But no mortal beings paused their metallic steeds to marvel at this display alongside Godbeast and deity, for none were blessed with sight capable of perceiving such magnificence.

"Ana is not alone anymore," Leng's voice broke through cryptically.

"I reckon you're right," Steve said quietly.

Having tapped into Tecumtek's server network, Steve had been monitoring Ana's financial maneuvers—particularly her personal savings account, which mysteriously continued to top up despite her absence of steady income. Evidently, this influx of wealth had been sanctioned and commanded by her government-appointed psychiatrist, a generosity Steve found himself unable to comprehend. Regardless, between Leng's supernatural prescience, his legion of psychic creatures traversing the global web, and Ana's careless digital imprints, she was as effortless to track as a wounded deer leaving a trail of crimson on pristine snow.

Recent phone logs indicated that she and Malachi were at the coastal ends of the country. Leng corroborated this division of Aspects by tracing residual magic signatures left by potent Godbeasts. However, they'd lost track of Malachi and Brock days ago, and no subsequent flares of wild magic were detected. But now, Steve had a lead: they were with Ana and possibly their final comrade.

For several moments, divine pyrotechnics pirouetted across the heavens before gradually receding back into ordinary daylight. "That power felt like it originated from awakened beings," said Steve. "True Gods, akin to you."

"And you as well, my spider-son," Leng responded his tone a slow and deliberate symphony of menace. "They appear to have overlooked the requisite rituals to harness their potential."

Steve, having learned to interpret the subtle shifts in his master's demeanor as a seasoned mariner reads the sea's changing moods, noticed a flicker of unease cross Leng's face. "What's bothering you?" he ventured.

"I had presumed them more pliable...more open to our influence," Leng admitted reluctantly. "Divine dispositions are not easily tamed—if they refuse our alliance, we must deem them foes."

Steve bit back his initial response, still unaccustomed to sharing his thoughts openly. Yet ever since he'd committed the cardinal sin of taking another's life, he sensed an altered dynamic between them. By shedding the last remnants of his human morality, he'd demonstrated unwavering loyalty to Leng—their bond now transcended mere servitude: Lengeth and hybrid, deity and beast—predators perched atop this celestial food chain.

After several minutes of contemplation, Steve finally broke the silence. "I believe I can persuade Malachi to join us. We all seek liberation from the Outer Gods' grasp. I can reach him—not as a man fearing loss of humanity but as a Lengeth with wisdom coursing through me."

Leng mulled over Steve's words while tuning into the incessant whispers of creatures beneath his skin that echoed agreement before weighing up the potential outcomes of this new strategy.

"Very well then, my spider-son," Leng conceded at length. "We must promptly make our presence known—if they persist in brandishing their power so recklessly, they may soon require our aid against the 'mer.'"

"And what exactly are these 'mer,' Master?" Steve queried.

"To those versed in European folklore, they are known as mermaids, sirens, or selkies," Leng elucidated with a hint of arrogance. "But those privy to arcane knowledge recognize them as abominations twisted by Cthulhu's will. The Aspects will attract them like moths to a flame...and I fear their thoughtless display of power might rouse an entire legion of horrors bred for Cthulhu's conquest."

***

Night's shroud fell, their path drawing them towards an unremarkable motel, a hunting ground for Steve Longfeather. With a casual wave of his hand, Leng spun an ethereal veil of fog that enveloped the motel, hiding it from the inquisitive gaze of passing motorists on the highway. Cocooned within this spectral mist, only his honed senses took note of Steve's selected target: a repugnant individual evading justice whose repulsive acts ranged from drug trafficking to multiple murders. The muffled screams of dread issuing from this criminal were music to Leng's ears; they confirmed the law of nature—the strong feasting on the weak—a tune that had reverberated throughout his cosmic invasions until reaching Earth.

Amid an eerie calmness, Leng was entangled in a web of self-reflection. His thoughts meandered through time and space, brushing against the lives of his progeny—those birthed in unfathomable epochs past and those freshly introduced to existence. A tremor coursed down his spine as he extended his awareness towards his swarm—their presence at reality's fringes echoing back like a nightmare's discordant symphony.

The sound was reminiscent of countless voices gnawing at sanity's boundaries—an incessant hum akin to maggots writhing in putrid flesh, their minuscule mandibles clattering in eager consumption. The image was so graphic and nauseatingly precise that he withdrew from it with an involuntary shudder. He severed the psychic link abruptly with a mere thought.

His encounters with them had become increasingly infrequent and strained over time. Their company shifted from comforting or stimulating to something he sought to escape—a bitter aftertaste lingering long after their departure. Instead, he found refuge in Steve's company—an oasis amidst a desert of alienation.

The Lengeth—the primitive minds spawned from him—were grotesque distortions when juxtaposed with their creator's towering intellect. They were warped parodies of what their race once was—enlightened beings now mere echoes of their past splendor. It felt as if they were taunting him with their crude imitation—a cruel joke played on an interstellar scale.

With each passing moment, Leng felt more alienated from these monstrosities he had brought into existence. His insights had propelled him beyond any conceivable boundary—he wielded control over matter itself; atoms obeyed his whims as he wove complex patterns across the tapestry of existence. He was no longer merely Leng—he had evolved into something far superior: an entity brimming with infinite knowledge. Yet every towering being sprouted from humble roots, and the climb to magnificence extracted its price. The excruciating clarity he was being thrust into no longer provided sanctuary from the torment of his own missteps. He whispered consolation to himself—you couldn't have known—though his heart echoed back a hollow ring of deceit.

Leng was drawn back through the sands of time toward his darkest memory. The landscape of Tlanex-Tli unfolded in his mind's theater, revealing infinite vistas of crystal valleys and quartz forests. Its cities sparkled like clusters of diamonds under the celestial dome. Yet, he was forced to witness the gradual decay of that magnificence, a once vibrant tapestry now scarred by frostbite, torn apart by brutal winds, and consumed by snow-crowned mountains. His people were thrust into an environmental apocalypse, unlike anything they had encountered in their psychic voyages across limitless galaxies and myriad planets.

What was unfolding? Not only his world but others to which his species cast their minds were caught in the grip of violent terraforming. Before this alien energy's onslaught, celestial bodies didn't crumble, combust, flood, or decay within mere decades —they aged with grace like wise elders. Suns dimmed but didn't extinguish; planets transitioned silently into silver epochs spanning millennia before evolving into grand husks teeming with parasitic life for eternities untold.

Leng and his brethren found themselves floundering amidst these monstrous anomalies, unable to comprehend how such aberrations could wreak havoc on a world perched precariously on the edge of its prime. They remained unaware that these phenomena sweeping Tlanex-Tli were not random elemental spasms but immense malevolent consciousnesses far beyond their superior cognizance exerting malignant growth.

Then came another wave—a more ferocious ice age—that drowned all save for Tlanex-Tli's loftiest fortifications. Ravenous tempests of frost stripped their world to its skeletal core, leaving only dull bastions fortified against the icy onslaught. Yet, these attacks from the Deep One were misinterpreted as mere chaotic weather patterns.

However, as their world teetered on the brink of a chilling finale, Leng's moment of revelation arrived—his folly—his belief that he had discovered a counteracting force capable of restoring their world to its former arid glory.

As a colossal entity, Leng existed in a sleep-like state. In this state, an idea took root and spread like an insidious weed—it seemed such an elegant solution to counter his world's waterification. However, these thoughts were not his own; they were whispers from chattering entities pressing their eager tentacles against reality's thin veil—the Lords of Chaos seeking entry—which they found through him as a conduit.

Leng's fervent pursuit to harness and control this energy served as ritual and necromantic sacrifice, empowering Shub-Niggurath's ravenous manifestation in his world. He remembered the terror that seized him and his offspring as they performed the ritual to dry their world, united in a mental coven, their power channeling into the sky in celestial beams like lighthouses piercing the night. Connected to all of his offspring—from giant brood mother to broodling—he felt their fear too when the skies transformed from frosty white to an eerie purple when reality tore open with a deafening screech when Shub Niggurath's grotesque wail shook the world with thunderous might.

In the aftermath of their ritual, the truth dawned on them like a chilling frostbite— they had beckoned forth an entity, a revelation that arrived with the merciless sting of regret. Through Leng, the Devouring Worm infiltrated Tlanex-Tli and granted his desire: a world of aridity and sand, but in such excess that it drained his realm to lifelessness. His people's thirst mirrored his own—an insatiable vampiric yearning—morphing them into brutal conquerors.

As he looked upon the subsequent generations of Lengeth, he saw no remnants of their humble beginnings. Each lineage was more grotesque and primitive than its predecessor—spawned by gnawing brood mothers who had devolved from sages to factories churning out dull-witted offspring.

His wisest daughter stood alone in resistance. She perceived the alien forces behind their environmental catastrophes and cautioned him about Shub-Niggurath's designs. Yet now, she was nothing more than a husk amidst the skeletal remains of their rotting world —a destiny he imposed for her audacity. He confronted his monstrous past—and ongoing existence—with a sorrowful clarity as he surveyed the desolate landscape that once brimmed with potential.

Gabriel's peculiar song echoed in his mind again, its melodies intricate and profound, reminiscent of tunes his people had lost the ability to play. She had been his most musical child, an appreciator of universal beauty, songs, and artistry. Perhaps her funeral hymn resonated within him—a perpetual reminder of his sins.

"Quezecoptyl," Leng voiced softly, each syllable trembling with deep emotion.

"Father?" The word reverberated around them in the still parking lot.

Jolted from his mental maze, Leng jerked back like a vampire confronted by a crucifix brandished by a man of true faith. An unusual tear traced a path down his waxy cheek, an anomaly swiftly wiped away by Steve—who had appeared as if he'd been dining with the gore-drenched Count Orlok himself.

"We're done here," Steve announced, his voice nonchalant despite their situation. He wisely refrained from questioning the lone tear that had slipped from his master's eye but couldn't resist adding: "Appreciate your generosity. That should hold me over for a while."

Leng scrutinized him before replying in his antiquated dialect, "Indeed, you seem hale and hearty." Shaking away the melancholy remnants, he continued, "The time has come to test your newfound abilities. We have traveled at a mortal's pace; now, we shall move as gods do. Join me on the world web."

Extending a hand towards what seemed like empty air, Leng conjured silken threads from nothingness. They swirled and twined around their limbs like marionette cords controlled by invisible puppeteers. Under this eerie tapestry spun by cosmic looms, Steve relinquished any lingering traces of his earthly existence and allowed himself to be spun into the arcane expanse of creation.

CHAPTER 12: ATLANTIS

Hovering above an altar slick with gore was a talisman—a simple ring crafted from white gold that could have adorned the hand of Atlantean nobility.

Ana could feel the irresistible pull of a hidden force, as if some cosmic magnet tugged at her psyche, growing stronger with each passing moment. It drew them—the Aspects—relentlessly towards an unseen point somewhere off the western coastline.

Their journey led them through landscapes that were beautiful in their own right: lush and green vineyards, their grapes gleaming like amethysts under the sun's watchful gaze; miniature cities that softened California's rugged terrain into a cultivated panorama, promising limitless adventures to any who dared to explore. Yet they moved through these contemporary wonders without pause or appreciation, stopping only for fuel for their mechanical beast.

The clash between Brock and Lenny at the amphitheater nestled within the mountain's cradle served as a banquet, more nourishing than any conventional repast—akin to indulging in a lavish spread until satiety gave way to surfeit. Her comrades appeared sated, their appetites for corporeal and ethereal sustenance momentarily quenched. Yet this was not the case for Ana, who found herself more vulnerable to these spectral sensations than her fellow travelers. She felt her bladder stir again, though it produced little more than a dribble. She bought jerky or chips out of habit at each gas station stop, finding solace in their familiar flavors. An uncanny urge seemed to grip her, steering her actions despite the clear voice of reason whispering about the ludicrousness of her conduct.

Nonetheless, she continued to endure this unique and isolating experience alone. After their physical unions, her comrades seemed to have shed all human behaviors—they no longer ate or drank. Malachi and Brock retreated further into their psychic dialogues, while Lenny interacted with her only by throwing winks from behind his sunglasses while driving or making passionate advances when they halted.

While amidst her companions, a growing sense of solitude steadily consumed her, except for Lovecraft, who filled the echoing void in her mind. With no one else interested in conversation, she found herself reaching out to touch his smooth skull and engage him in discussions about her developing queerness or other legends and theories he believed she should know about.

"What's up with this weapon?" she asked one quiet morning amidst the monotonous journey.

You could find out for yourself, Ana. You're one of the most powerful seers in existence, Lovecraft responded telepathically, a hint of playfulness in his tone.

"Well, shit. Why didn't I think of that?"

You cling to your humanity more than the others, which is admirable but slows down the development of your gifts. I suggest you let go and embrace the power within you.

"Nope. Not happening."

Why not?

"Because then I might stop being me. And I've fought damn hard to be her."

Once woven into a tapestry of comforting lies or hazy fabrications, every thread of her existence now frayed in the harsh light of concealed truths. This discord had been a relentless specter haunting her with paranoia, addiction, and insecurity. To have navigated these treacherous waters and emerged into adulthood as a semblance of a functional human felt akin to scaling Olympus. She clung fiercely to Ana—the persona she'd painstakingly sculpted from adversity—with all her endearing eccentricities and oddities. She couldn't and wouldn't surrender herself, not when she had just begun to taste the sweet nectar of self-discovery and familial warmth.

She glanced at the trio of men who formed her newfound tribe; an unexpected surge of affection welled within her, spilling over in soft rivulets down her cheeks. She loved them—all three—and yearned for this moment to crystallize into permanence.

Yet change is as relentless as the tides—seasons morph, time ebbs and flows, history reinvents itself, Lovecraft's telepathic voice echoed gently in her mind. You mourn an illusion that has already dissipated. You are not truly Ana Windborn. A name that, upon reflection, clearly seems to be a fabrication, borrowing from Jewish roots. It's derived from the Hebrew name Channa, signifying favor, and embellished with a French suffix—a little linguistic trivia in case you were curious about its origins. But Thank Cthugha, you're not a miserly Jewess either—

A swift slap against his skull interrupted his discourse as Ana psychically berated him. Dude! That's racist as fuck! We've been through this...and we're not praising any Outer Gods either!

Feeling the undercurrent of her irritation, Lenny's gaze flickered to the rear-view mirror. His eyes, a silent language in themselves, posed an unspoken question with a single arched brow: is there someone who needs to feel my fists? Her response was a dismissive shake of her head, silently communicating that she was managing just fine.

Apologies...Times have indeed shifted...Do Jews still monopolize all banks and Hollywood?

Ana rolled her eyes dramatically before retorting tersely: Move on.

Return to your studies, Ana, Lovecraft continued. Our journey begins with Divination 101. Your past dalliances with foci should serve you well here, although my preference leans towards more tangible forms of magic. This fragment bestowed upon you by your enigmatic benefactor—the elusive Dark Mother—should amplify your explorations into the labyrinthine corridors of space-time.

Ana seized this opportunity to voice a nagging question gnawing at her like a persistent rodent. Hold on a sec. Who exactly is the Dark Mother?

Lovecraft lapsed into an extended silence, leaving Ana to wonder if she'd somehow offended him. She distracted herself by watching cars whizz past, disappearing into sprawling vineyards, picturesque overlooks, and untouched beaches. An abrupt realization struck her—the blissful ignorance of these travelers to their impending cosmic annihilation.

But Lovecraft wasn't ignoring her; he was merely deliberating his response. His perception within this vessel was confined mainly to nebulous realms of shifting colors and lights punctuated with indistinct sounds and blurry human silhouettes. But when it came to auras? That's where his vision sharpened: pulsating red halos for those enslaved by passion, pristine white mantles for the virtuous, electric blue shields for eccentrics or artistic souls (the line between those two was razor-thin). Ana's aura was one of the purest he'd encountered—untarnished in its core yet scarred around its edges—remnants of her past torment. As their alliance deepened, he sensed another presence lurking within her: an ethereal gray willow tree studded with twinkling lights—a spidery specter ensnaring Ana in spectral threads. Even now, this entity clung onto Ana within their astral conduit—its many legs wrapped around her. Today, it seemed less concealed, as if emboldened by either its possession or Ana's acquiescence to it. Lovecraft harbored concern for Ana, especially since he couldn't decipher this enigma.

Finally, Lovecraft spoke, his voice echoing in the silent expanse of their shared consciousness. The Dark Mother... even the dustiest scholars dismiss her as a mere children's tale. I confess I was one of them until your arrival. His thoughts swirled around Ana like an ethereal fog. This spectral energy that clings to you tainted with earthly elements... defies all my known classifications.

He paused for a moment before continuing. Although I suspect she is a cosmic nightmare and quite a formidable opponent for my master, Marrow warned us about her terrestrial presence and potential interference with our plans.

Lovecraft sighed mentally. The sigh was not one of exasperation but more akin to resignation. These entities are far from friendly, Ana, he admitted. Even I understand that fraternizing with Cthugha could set the world ablaze. But he's the only Outer God we can attempt to coexist under without being wholly corrupted. The Golden One harbors a morbid curiosity for the beings it perverts, yearning to persist within their warped lives—this could be humanity's sole salvation, as dreadful as it may appear.

His tone softened slightly: So any kindness you sense with this Dark Mother might simply be your alignment with an incomprehensible will. If you're determined this entity means no harm, we'll proceed on that assumption and use her gifts to enhance yours. I know your patience is wearing thin due to a lack of answers. But trust me when I say time will reveal what this entity wants from you.

"And what does that mean?" Ana asked.

It's becoming more tangible...gathering strength.

"Should I be worried?"

Worrying over things beyond your control won't help, Lovecraft advised wisely. You're bound with this entity, for better or worse—we'll just have to see where this pact leads us.

Ana swallowed her rising fear. "Alright then, back on track here: the weapon."

Without a focus, even the most gifted seers can lose their way in the vast expanse of eternity. Consider time as a river—you wouldn't dive headfirst without some caution. Since the cosmic shard you carry is associated with your patron entity, use it like a compass for your mental energy. Imagine its dark core as a sea of shadows that you can navigate with your mind—whatever metaphor aids you in immersing yourself within it.

As Lovecraft's thoughts continued to flow around her, Ana reached for the shard. Her fingers curled naturally around its jagged end as if it were crafted specifically for her grasp. She pictured herself standing at the edge of a shadowy waterfall, peering into the frothy black abyss below. Taking a deep breath, she raised her hands—clutching the dagger-like shard—above her head and then plunged into the darkness.

***

The icy tendrils of the deep danced around her, a ballet of bioluminescent entities darting past her submerged ears. The water whispered tales of lives that had ebbed and flowed with its currents, but she ignored their siren call, adhering to the wisdom imparted by her mentor. Her focus was a beacon in the murky depths: an enigma wrapped in myth —the God-slaying relic of antiquity. Its age-old secrets—or something equally as majestic —shimmered behind the surface ahead, a promise of enlightenment breaking through the abyssal gloom. With purposeful strokes, she surged upwards, piercing the water's veil into consciousness, straddling two realities—one where her physical form lay inert and this vibrant echo of another era.

"Jesus Christ on a bike," she exhaled, "It's bloody breathtaking."

Atlantis. Lovecraft's voice echoed within her mind.

Written accounts paled before the grandeur unfurling before Ana's astral eyes. Suspended upon cerulean waves beneath towering cliffs kissed by gold, she drank in the sight of islets dotting the horizon like scattered jewels. An alien sun painted everything in hues of crimson fire while oak vessels adorned with billowing scarlet sails lazily navigated the harbor under the watchful gaze of armored centurions.

Drifting among these formidable figures like an unseen wisp, Ana marveled at their dominance—not mere Viking raiders but Roman conquerors who claimed both these waters and distant lands as their own. Yet diversity thrived amidst them—faces bronzed by the Mediterranean sun or lightened by the northern frost—a testament to Rome's far-reaching influence.

Leaving behind the bustling harbor, Ana steered her airy form towards an incandescent halo cradling a cityscape of alabaster edifices arranged in ascending rings interlaced with thoroughfares, canals, and bridges—a grander version than Pythia's city, which now seemed a humble hamlet in comparison.

The streets teemed with life, their emotions an enticing buffet tempting her psychic senses. Yet she soared above the golden cityscape, drawn towards the highest ring where towering temples of marble and grand staircases kissed the sky. Here, an unholy rite to forge a weapon against cosmic horrors was unfolding.

Ana zeroed in on a distortion hanging over a lavish building adorned with golden scales and tiles. As she descended towards it, the scent of burning incense from massive chalices and the soothing strains of harp music wafted up to her while rows of worshippers knelt entranced on its steps under a spell woven by crimson-robed priestesses.

"This is it," Ana murmured.

Lovecraft's voice resonated within her mind: Each deity revered during Atlantis' zenith had a temple here. Apollo was my master's Godbeast, blessed by fire. Today marks the genesis of an alliance between mankind and Outer God.

Ana remained detached from the exultant atmosphere. To her, the temple was a cataclysmic portal, each majestic stairway teeming with devotees marked for oblivion. The languid Atlanteans, like innocent lambs, led to their inevitable demise. They were guided into the moist obsidian core of the temple, and Ana followed suit. Resembling a spectral harbinger of doom, she trailed behind these human offerings through labyrinthine corridors adorned with elaborate patterns bathed in the amber luminescence of braziers, leading toward an inner sanctum throbbing with malevolent scarlet energy.

Her ethereal form lingered on the brink of a balcony overlooking a horrific natural chasm that could have been ripped from Dante's illustration of Hell's yawning maw. The pit was strewn with bodies impaled on jagged stalagmites. As she observed a trembling sacrifice being handed over from a priestess to an arrestingly handsome man, her terror surged and exploded within her. His sculpted physique and penetrating eyes were familiar; his blood-soaked beard and laurel crown were recent accouterments.

"Marrow," Ana whispered almost inaudibly.

Dr. Bone, Lovecraft corrected her telepathically.

Marrow—or Dr. Bone or Alexander the Great and Terrible or whoever the fuck this creature was—planted a fervent kiss on the elderly woman before uttering an unintelligible incantation that sent ripples of telekinetic energy cascading throughout the chamber. Wearing an expression of regret for what he was about to commit, he stepped back and, with a single, swift hand, tore out her throat along with part of her convulsing spine as effortlessly as one would gut a fish. He caught her collapsing body and carried it towards the pit like some twisted groom carrying his bride over the threshold. He released his grip and watched solemnly as she plummeted into the fiery abyss below, which flared up eagerly upon receiving its sacrificial gift.

Ana chose not to linger around Marrow or his morbid masterpiece. Instead, she descended into the pit, eager to uncover what unhallowed creation was being forged in this hellish foundry. Accompanied by her telepathic companion, she descended past a ghastly tableau of mutilated bodies—it was akin to traversing through the birthplace of Jack the Ripper's heinous acts. Marrow had been sacrificing victims since the dawn of mankind, perhaps even when mammoth tusks served as altar decorations. But how far did his blood-soaked hands reach back into history?

Ana could've delved deeper but feared unearthing truths that might shatter her fragile sanity. As she contemplated it, she felt an invisible barrier hindering her from prying further into Marrow's fate. Perhaps with a piece of his hair or flesh, she might be able to penetrate deeper into the psyche of this deranged artisan.

Engulfed in the enigma of Marrow, Ana found a momentary sanctuary from the surrounding terror. The tunnel narrowed as they delved further into the depths, and an unholy barricade of human remains began to form. Faces, hands, and feet melded into a twitching tapestry of mortality. The subterranean furnace's heat sparked life into these corpses, transforming them into a gruesome slop for the unseen monstrosity lurking beneath.

In this macabre spectacle, countless lives had been snuffed out—individual identities swallowed by this grotesque mural of death. Despite the grim sight before her eyes, Ana felt a fleeting sense of gratitude that her vision spared her from the fetid stench that must have saturated this hellish place. A wave of numbness swept over her as they neared their destination; bathed in an infernal glow, the jaws of death retreated.

Piercing through what felt like a blood-filled boil, she was suspended in an expansive shimmering cavity—cooler and darker than its fiery predecessor. A nauseating pinkish light seeped through the cavernous space, revealing walls coated with sacrificial remnants —a glossy red veneer that birthed crimson stalactites weeping in rhythm. Veins pulsating with deathly essence threaded through this foggy abattoir like quicksilver.

Necrotic energy... Lovecraft's voice echoed within her mind. A soul condenser akin to earthly labs filled with vials and flasks... But on an unimaginable scale—the brilliance is staggering... The vessel for such distillation would be... there.

Guided by tendrils of witchcraft towards their origin point, Ana caught sight of a distant glint deep below—a radiant star embedded within this demented cosmos. Intrigue now outweighing dread compelled her to descend towards it—an alien pull gripped her, akin to the sensation of diving into an ocean's depths, accompanied by a sense of humility and awe.

Hovering above the altar, Ana realized that the light was not spherical but a delicate ring—meticulously crafted and pulsating with magic. It seemed as fragile as a dewdrop teetering on a leaf's edge—ethereal yet flawless. The spectral strands of magic continued to swirl around it, lending it solidity and presence and making it tangible.

Entranced, Ana observed this spectral crafting process nearing its end—the crescendo of whispering voices chattering arcane incantations in the chamber signaled its completion. These were not human voices but rather deep rumblings and moans reminiscent of some cosmic leviathan swimming in space's ocean.

Cthugha? She wondered.

The cavern shuddered, a vile parody of a snow globe, its bloody debris swirling in place of innocent flakes. Light exploded from the epicenter, blindingly intense and shrill as it pierced Ana's mind. The cataclysmic union of atomic forces with necrotic energy birthed their new vessel amidst crackling flashes, culminating in a thunderous finale that left her blinking through the residual glow.

The oppressive darkness returned, pressing in on her like a tangible presence. The walls, reminiscent of rotting flesh, seemed to pulse with an unholy life of their own. A steady drip-drip-drip echoed within the confined space, amplifying the claustrophobia already gnawing at her sanity.

Hovering above an altar slick with gore was a talisman—a simple ring crafted from white gold that could have adorned the hand of Atlantean nobility. As she stared at it, she couldn't help but wonder if such an artifact would someday belong to her or her companions, given their shared roots buried deep within ancient history.

Marrow's arrival was imminent—whether by magic or mundane means—to claim the fruits of his soul alchemy. The thought made dread coil tight within her stomach; she had no desire to confront the specter of her past therapist. She had found what they sought; it was time to return to Malachi and the others.

Lovecraft's voice echoed in her mind—equally weary and disgusted—urging her departure. Shadows danced around Ana then, obscuring reality and pulling her into an abyss devoid of light or form. She was caught in time's maelstrom, swept along by currents too powerful to resist. Emerging from this temporal deluge felt akin to surfacing from murky depths; she blinked open eyes, now greeted by familiar surroundings.

Her senses were immediately assaulted—the olfactory onslaught being most prominent: three men crammed into an automobile, each exuding their unique blend of cologne and sweats. It was a potent concoction that jerked her back from the abstract realms of her vision.

"Damn, you guys smell like a high-end perfume store but also kinda like a gym locker room," Ana remarked.

Lenny twisted around and grinned at her comment while Malachi quipped, "Cool compliment or insult, not sure which. Kinda random, either way."

Either they were oblivious to her temporary absence or chose not to acknowledge it. However, Malachi's attention now focused on the shard in Ana's hand—Lovecraft's malevolent smirk reflected in its surface—and the ghostly pallor of fear that had washed over her face.

"You saw something?" he asked.

"Yeah," she responded tersely. "Ancient Greece—

South West Morocco before Neptune had his way with it, Lovecraft corrected.

"Ancient, wherever the hell it was," she continued nonchalantly. "Atlantis...and some sort of ritualistic shindig." Her gaze hardened slightly as she added, "Marrow was there too."

"What?" Malachi blurted out in surprise.

With a flicker of the blinkers, their driver smoothly navigated onto the embankment. To her silent companions, wearing puzzled expressions like badges of honor, Ana began to unravel visions of an arcane ring, sacrificial rites gruesome enough to make an Aztec blush, and an unhinged alchemist with an undying obsession with souls.

A quaint French patisserie found its refuge in the penumbral embrace of the Hollywood Hills' western descent, tucked away from the valley's glittering panorama. *La vie en Rose* was an epicurean marvel deserving of Michelin stars, yet it shunned all such pursuits and even rescinded prior acknowledgments. Its imperious, radiant Parisian custodian harbored disdain for everything bourgeois—except their greenbacks. Jean Houdin—the culinary virtuoso behind this venture—echoed the famed European conjurer in spirit but diverged in artistry; his enchantment manifested in his gastronomic creations rather than theatrical feats. Jean's kitchen sorcery birthed unforgettable, delectable, and unabashedly French masterpieces. As with any extraordinary, exclusive, and opulent offering, The *Rose's* reservation list expanded into epochs for those bereft of considerable affluence.

Within the lofty alabaster expanse of the conservatory rested about twelve secluded tables, partitioned by kabuki screens embellished with Renaissance floral motifs. Today's chatter among The *Rose's* distinguished clientele revolved around an ostentatious man and his unassuming Indian associate who had secured a spot at this coveted venue. However, their allure dissipated once they disappeared behind one of the privacy screens. Then came another arrival: a burly figure clad in a cowboy hat, trench coat, and clunky boots. He underwent scrutiny from the maître de before being guided to that secluded corner.

"It's been some time." Marrow inclined his head toward the newcomer before returning to his tea.

Mary rose to shake hands with him. "A pleasure to finally make your acquaintance."

"And yours," Charles retorted curtly while retaining his coat, then seated himself awkwardly. "I took the earliest flight here. We need to get moving—"

"Bon après-midi." A suave young man with slicked-back hair and a fitted vest peeked from behind the screen. "Have we reached any conclusions regarding the menu?"

"Our companion has just arrived," Marrow interjected. "We require a moment more." The waiter retreated.

"We're not here to nibble on crumpets and finger sandwiches," Charles spat out, his long-suppressed Cockney accent infiltrating his Southern drawl in irritation. "We're not even supposed to meet like this. Not ever. Especially not on Octavia's territory."

"Fear not, we are safe here." Marrow leisurely refilled his cup from the ornate porcelain teapot before him. "Mr. Houdin is among the finest epicurean witches of the western hemisphere, and this is his sanctuary. It serves as a secure and neutral ground; however, you will find your magic subdued here."

In a sudden revelation, Charles became aware that the prickling sensation on his clammy skin was not entirely born of anxiety. It was more like a barricade holding back the wild surge of magic roiling within him. He strained to direct his Will toward the excess cutlery on his table setting, commanding it to move, yet it resisted him stubbornly. His face contorted with effort, veins standing out in stark relief against his flushed skin. Marrow's laughter rang out at this spectacle, a mocking punctuation to Charles' futile struggle.

With an air of nonchalance, Marrow retrieved a cigar from his pocket and severed its end with a sleek silver guillotine. The cigar found its place between his lips as he snapped his fingers—sparking a tiny white flame at the tip. Once lit, he dismissed the flame with an insouciant wave and reclined back, reminiscent of Carroll's enigmatic Caterpillar, puffing out perfect rings of smoke.

"Thought you said magic didn't work here," Charles fired back.

"I am no mere hedge wizard," Marrow retorted smugly. His voice held an unsettling undercurrent that suggested something far more sinister than what was apparent. "I said *your* magic won't work here. And Mary's is about as potent as an old man's desire, right?" Mary cast her gaze downwards at her hands in response before he continued, "Let's order something—I'm ravenous. Consider this akin to the apostles' last supper."

Like a djinn summoned by the rub of its lamp, their server appeared in no time at all. Marrow dictated his order with unwavering certainty while the server painstakingly detailed sauces and culinary intricacies for Charles and Mary—the less refined members of their trio—only serving to further bewilder them.

"Steak frites," Marrow interjected suddenly, "Medium rare for each."

The waiter hesitated, scanning the menu for such an entry. But he chose not to contest it, his hands trembling slightly under Marrow's imposing presence—a detail that didn't slip past Mary's sharp observation.

"And a bottle of your private reserve red," Marrow added as the man turned away.

"Of course," he complied.

The tension threading through their secret society's public gathering—the first in almost a hundred years—began to unwind gradually. Sunlight poured through the stained glass dome overhead, scattering myriad colors across the room. The enticing aroma from Marrow's cigar wafted through the air, reminiscent of myrrh, and Charles found himself unable to resist asking for one. To his surprise, Marrow obliged without any sarcastic retort.

As silent as a wraith, their waiter returned bearing their drinks before disappearing into the background again—he was there and gone so swiftly that they barely registered his presence. With her fears momentarily forgotten, Mary allowed herself to savor the wine's soothing numbness. She sought refuge from her past sins—the betrayals she'd committed and lies she'd woven just to be here today.

The rich aroma of seared meat and golden fries wafted toward her as their meal was served, offering a momentary distraction from the gnawing guilt within. The steak before her was arguably the finest she had ever savored, its juices mingling with the delicate curls of fries lightly dusted with sea salt. The exquisite taste filled her senses, momentarily transforming her from a woman haunted by shadows of her past into an esteemed member of some clandestine mystical order.

"Treasure these instants," Marrow intoned, his voice carrying a somber weight as he delicately dabbed his mouth with a napkin. "The Eternal Game approaches its zenith—the end of its first act."

Charles' brows furrowed in confusion. "But why are we gathered here?" His query held less defiance than before, more curiosity.

The Midnight Order operated under an unspoken rule: remain invisible to the countless eyes of the Outer Gods and their servants. Their communication was shrouded in secrecy—messages carried by pigeons, cryptic symbols etched subtly amidst graffiti, coded discussions on obscure internet forums. Charlie had only met Mary's formidable aunt once and Marrow perhaps twice... The last encounter coincided with Lovecraft's demise—a gentle term for such a brutal end. He shook off the chilling memory that clung to Lovecraft's death and reached for his wine glass.

"You're dwelling on your fallen comrade," Marrow noted perceptively. "I find myself doing so as well. Despite our miscalculations, we must persevere in our mission—the one he set into motion. Progress is paramount: our relentless march towards calamity. The path leading us to this apocalypse—and how many endure it, sane or alive—is inconsequential to the final outcome. Despite our failure to adequately prepare our Aspects for their destined roles, they are advancing as anticipated without any intervention or goading from us. The adversarial dynamics Mary and I have woven with them seem to have spurred them further along this preordained path."

A wistful note of remorse threaded through Charles' words as he admitted, "My role was to shield Brock, to guide him towards understanding the enormity of his destiny. I feel like I've let him down repeatedly. I wasn't present at his birth or when he awakened into his powers."

Marrow's response was terse but empathetic. "Had you lingered after setting the ritualistic stage for his genesis, he might have consumed you—even as a newborn entity. His lack of mature human awareness would have made him an uncontrolled creature driven by instinct."

Charles' mind journeyed back to that fateful moment on the crimson-stained plateau, whispering the final incantations with trepidation—his proficiency in magic and Latin being far from perfect. As the blinding gold light erupted and the twitching corpses of sacrificial women began to crumble into ash around a hellish golden blaze at the pentagram's heart, Marrow's warning echoed in his ears—he had to flee now or risk becoming prey to the demon they had conjured. What form did that monstrosity take? He didn't dare look back as he hastily rappelled down the mountain and vaulted into his Jeep. The gut-wrenching shriek that tore through the night air still haunted him: an unearthly roar of rage from something newly awakened. Years would elapse before he'd encounter any trace of that entity again.

"Brock required time to mature," Marrow interjected, pulling Charles out of his reverie with a matter-of-fact tone. "You did share some paternal moments with him later on until MANN Inc. left you incapacitated. But tracking Brock after your second separation would've violated our pledge of absolute discretion. We are tasked with nurturing, guiding, and educating the Aspects until they awaken fully. However, Her own progeny must ultimately determine Earth's fate."

Incapacitated. The days after the lethal barrage of bullets that should have ended him were a nightmarish haze of agony. His body, scarred and punctured, had laboriously woven itself back together with the spectral threads of untamed magic. His awareness sparked to life within a suffocating dirt tomb, his lungs heavy with the taste of rich earth and decay.

Each grain of soil pressed against him felt like an unbearable burden, as if he were ensnared by a vice made from stone itself. He could feel the raw injuries on his torso seeping an unsettling mixture of blood and pus, crackling like boiling oil as it mingled with the magical filaments that held him intact.

The experience was nothing short of infernal torment; it was like he'd been reborn, a revolting maggot squirming in its own squalor. He recalled the agonizing effort to free himself from this premature grave; every movement sent shockwaves of pain through his mutilated form.

His mouth filled with grit and wriggling creatures native to the soil, each expulsion inciting a guttural bellow from deep within him. Brock's name reverberated in his mind before it slipped out through his fractured lips in a desperate cry. Yet he knew all too well that Brock wouldn't be there—he'd taught him to run at the first hint of danger.

As he burst forth from his subterranean trench, howling like an injured beast, part of him yearned to seek out Brock immediately—to expose the horrifying truth of this undead existence and unravel the sinister designs of the Midnight Order. But doubt seized him—were these revelations of mercy or merely self-serving confessions born from guilt and solitude?

"Ah, you've returned," Marrow's voice sliced through the silence. He had watched Charles plunge into yet another torturous memory—with his usual uncanny perceptiveness, he also seemed to know the exact memory. His words were threaded with an elegance and arrogance that lent a chilling edge to their meaning.

"The gentle approach proved misguided," Marrow continued. "Brock's belief in your death has only hardened him. I learned this with Ana as well. Now that she is out of reach for manipulation or control, her faith in her defiant independence—that she is acting contrary to my wishes somehow—absolves us of responsibility."

He paused for dramatic effect before adding: "Admittedly, our grand scheme fell apart, yet the pieces have reassembled themselves more favorably than if we had arranged them ourselves. Now we observe, bide our time...and intervene when necessary."

"Is this the reason for our meeting?" Mary asked, quietly.

"In a manner of speaking," Marrow's answer flowed, his voice an elegant waltz of dread. "Charles, your gallant endeavors in protecting the young ones at that loathsome inn have not slipped past us. But now we stand within the Mothmann's very lair. I found it wise to pool our resources. Despite the impressive might our nascent Aspects command, they may soon find themselves in need of our unseen aid as they blindly traverse this ocean teeming with ancient sorcery and monstrous entities—like visionless swimmers engulfed by invisible predators. We've rallied together because unity is strength, especially when it comes to retrieving your grimoire, Mary. And fear not, we have a confederate amidst their fold who can lend us a hand."

"Bloody 'ell! Lovecraft?" Charles' Cockney accent bubbled up again in his shock. "That means...they must've cracked open that portal back in New Hampshire and snagged 'im."

"They indeed did," Marrow confirmed, a cunning smile slithering across his face like a serpent on the prowl. "And thus, we have them ensnared—insects within our web."

CHAPTER 13: BLOOD TIDE

A mesmerizing halo of concrete, steel, and stone spun around him like planets revolving around their star.

Lenny commandeered the truck with a relentless tenacity that left no room for casual sightseeing. The vehicle tore through Hollywood's outskirts like an unleashed beast, its engine growling in protest. Through the side mirror, Ana caught fleeting snapshots of palm trees swaying under the weight of an invisible breeze and the iconic sign looming on a hill shrouded in darkness. She observed it all with an aloof curiosity, acknowledging her misfit status amidst such glitz and glamour—like a pauper somehow unattended and wandering Buckingham Palace.

As nightfall devoured the city, its heartbeat pulsed through a constellation of lights scattered across the urban landscape. As they edged towards the highway connecting Hollywood's dazzling veneer to Santa Monica's sandy embrace, an unsettling disquiet draped them like an uninvited guest. The road unfurled before them—a malevolent serpent slithering through undulating terrain. Despite the sealed windows, petrol-laden air seeped through vents while wind-induced vibrations shook their window panes—it was as if the road itself was conscious and ravenous for souls.

Yet despite this ominous atmosphere clinging to their journey, there was a mesmerizing allure to its infinite bends and curves that lured them deeper into LA's surrounding darkness. They plunged headfirst into this void, chalky hills casting intimidating shadows around them while pockets of light offered temporary refuge amidst a sea of blackness.

Ana felt her courage grappling with an escalating sense of dread—a gut instinct warning her of impending malice. When she spotted San Sorento's sign flitting in obscurity like phantom whispers, she considered alerting her stoic companions—an instant flashback to her cramped apartment, neglected books, and remnants of a life once deemed significant. But they, too, were preoccupied with grim contemplation about their uncertain mission ahead—sightseeing during what seemed like Armageddon was absurdly futile.

Her past held no significance now. Only the path ahead mattered. She continued to guide Lenny towards the coast without any clear destination—like a captain navigating his vessel through misty waters in the hope of finding solid ground.

A persistent question gnawed at her: How much further would they dare to tread into this burgeoning wave of peril? Seeking comfort, she turned to her latest talisman and ally—Lovecraft. As she nestled him onto her lap, their mental dialogue commenced.

Your surroundings are fraught with danger, he conveyed. It's like a trap set to ensnare you.

Ana sensed the same predatory force lurking just beyond their glass shield. She knew they could feel her presence too and felt an intensifying concentration of otherworldly entities with each passing mile—akin to piranhas circling fresh prey. The aquatic metaphors were inescapable; even the night sky mirrored a tumultuous black ocean wave surging toward oblivion. They had trespassed into the Deep One's domain.

This place is teeming with power, Lovecraft. It's suffocating.

We tread beneath the dormant might of one of the Outer Gods. Cthulhu's influence looms overhead like a malevolent moon, warping everything within its gravitational pull. You must channel your power to navigate through this tempest.

With help from the Dark Mother's fragment?

Ana, my dear girl, you've shattered all expectations of your abilities and catapulted your mind and soul into ancient realms while sitting in a moving vehicle like yesterday's news. You're a storm in a teacup—all that raw power in such a frail vessel. I don't believe you need me or any ritual objects anymore. You are the awakened Owl now. Illuminate this darkness with your inner light.

Ana's thoughts swirled around the enigmatic phrase, "Illuminate this darkness". Her mind was a tumultuous sea, stirred by the cryptic utterance.

The sudden intrusion of an alien hum—a sound akin to a swarm of furious bees—sent shivers through them all. A blinding eruption of light burst forth from Ana's very being, bathing the interior of their vehicle in an ethereal glow as potent as a jet engine's flame yet devoid of its scorching heat.

Lenny, his rugged features contorted with effort and surprise, wrestled with the steering wheel as if it were an angry elephant. The intense illumination assaulted his eyes, which were more sensitive than most due to his supernatural lineage. The truck swerved wildly on the desolate highway like a deranged serpent.

A scream pierced the chaos—an outburst from Malachi that filled their confined space with raw terror. Brock twisted in his seat with feline agility, his muscular arms reaching back to steady those behind him amidst their vehicular ballet.

With the calm control of a seasoned stunt driver wrestling an unruly beast into submission, Lenny finally regained control over their ride. Their path traced a figure eight on the deserted highway before heading again in their original direction.

Ana's skull had become a beacon—a pulsating lighthouse casting its glow from where her eyes should have been—two tiny stars twinkling in her petite face. Her voice emerged from her trance-like state with casual certainty.

"We're headed for a place called Arkminister," she announced nonchalantly while ensnared within her otherworldly aura.

Malachi extended his shades towards her without missing a beat—his emerald eyes meeting her starlit gaze—and she donned them without uttering a single word. At that moment, she was no longer just Ana but an angel in disguise, her celestial aura concealed behind the dark lenses.

Their journey continued, the highway unfurling before them like a comet's tail. The lullaby of the ocean serenaded their progress—a sound that stirred an unspoken longing within some more than others. Ana's directives steered them further from civilization's comforting embrace and closer to the insatiable maw of the Atlantic.

Suddenly, a chilling breath from the ocean's depths transformed the landscape into an ethereal tableau. Fog rolled over them with a ferocity that could rival even the harshest blizzard, shrouding their path in spectral pallor despite their high beams' valiant efforts.

Lenny navigated this misty maze cautiously—his unwavering focus cutting through uncertainty.

A signpost emerged from the foggy abyss—an ominous monolith slick with moisture and draped in seaweed. "Arkminister," Malachi pronounced, reverberating ominously within their vehicle. As if cowed by his declaration, the fog retreated like serpents slithering back into their dark lairs, returning clarity to their windshield.

The jagged coastline outside held its breath in a disquieting stillness. Yet, they each felt an inexplicable shift—an unsettling sensation like hovering at an impossible height or sinking into the unfathomable abyss. From the shrouded gloom ahead, skeletal vestiges of buildings clawed their way into view. Their headlights swept across dilapidated fences, grime-smeared windows, and abandoned vehicles scattered haphazardly across properties long surrendered to decay. An ectoplasmic sheen clung to this wreckage as if recently dredged from a drowned city—throwing eerie shadows that cavorted and flickered like ghosts against their car's interior, underscoring their descent into a realm unlike any they knew.

"Why are there so many damn cars?" Malachi muttered.

"But not a soul in sight," Brock added.

"It's as though we've crossed over somewhere...else," Lenny noted with unease.

"We have," Ana confirmed, her voice resonating with an ethereal quality born of prescience. "We're now between realms."

A collective shudder passed through them—a chilling testament that even Godbeasts could be gripped by fear. They continued their journey through this desolate expanse, eyes peeled for any hint of what befell those who had come before them. Brock rolled down his window and strained his senses for any sound or sight that might illuminate the enigma. The ocean's rhythm intensified, and a stench of decay wafted in, potent enough to rival a summer garbage heap. But these offered only cryptic clues, and the nauseating miasma soon drove Brock to retreat behind closed windows.

"Something's rotten about the air here," Lenny grumbled as he sniffed.

"Not just the air," Ana said softly. "Death surrounds us."

As they ventured deeper into the town's heart, sporadic streetlights flickered to life, casting a ghostly hue on towering structures that seemed to grow from darkness. Their vehicle glided like a phantom past remnants of urbanity—an outdated motel, a solemn funeral parlor, an aged hair salon, and a weathered grocery store—each bearing marks of decay but not as abandoned as their initial surroundings. The town was an enigmatic fusion of architectural eras: shadow-lurking Tudors, moonlit Victorians with ornate gables, and stoic Colonials resisting time's assault. Withered flowers hung limp in cracked pots adorning melancholy porches while rusting automobiles in driveways stood testament to the relentless passage of years. Amidst this surreal tableau clung verdant growths, slick and gleaming like seaweed on a drowned corpse—yet what could nourish its existence? The drifting fog seemed too tainted to provide sustenance.

Navigating through Arkminister felt like performing in a grotesque play—an unsettling sense of artificiality draped over everything. Unseen watchers peered at them from behind ragged curtains, alien eyes dissecting their every move within this realm warped by otherworldly consciousness. Beneath this façade throbbed an unspeakable horror unique to this town—a monstrous entity lurking in shadows, ready to consume all within its malevolent reach. Every sight was merely a crude veil obscuring the underlying nightmare reality.

The police cruiser burst into being, its glaring red and blue lights pulsating like the heartbeat of a predatory beast. The sight set a chill slithering through their veins. Lenny steered their vehicle to an apprehensive halt, maintaining what he hoped was a safe berth from this potential ambush. A shadowy form emerged before the cruiser, its identity obscured by the relentless strobe of lights.

Ana's magic flickered and died, her eyes losing their otherworldly glow. Yet, her psychic energy remained undeterred, sending electric jolts coursing through her frame. Her mind was filled with images of something moist and coiling—a nest of eels squirming in the dark. "That's not human," she announced with an eerie certainty.

"Can we just avoid it?" Malachi asked, his voice wavering between hope and dread.

Lenny's gaze fell on a metallic glimmer stretching across the road behind the cruiser—caltrops gleaming ominously under artificial light. "We're not getting past without our tires shredded," he muttered grimly.

"Pack up; we're leaving on foot," Brock ordered tersely.

What could possibly threaten three dangerous male Godbeasts? They exited the car empty-handed, their presence enough to deter most threats. Ana followed suit, clutching Lovecraft's skull like a talisman against evil. She joined her companions in front of their headlights—their postures tense and ready for battle. In terms of physical might, Ana paled compared to her comrades—she couldn't fly like Malachi or bend reality like Brock and Lenny—but she compensated with unyielding determination.

"Hey, jerkoff!" She shouted at the figure blocking their path. "Get out of our way!"

Lovecraft's mental voice echoed within her mind: That is no mere 'jerkoff,' but a merfolk—a spawn of The Deep One himself.

The merfolk moved towards them, its human-like form trembling before it spasmed violently—its head jerking and jaw twisting grotesquely. Any semblance of humanity was shattered. Brock and Lenny saw the bulging obsidian eyes set in its hairless, scaled face—its monstrous form ill-fitted into a police uniform.

Brock's shoulders ignited with soft flames as golden as dawn light—the Wolf spirit within him stirring. Silver magic pulsed from Malachi—a tempest brewing under his skin. Yet, even as their courage rose, Brock noticed Ana's facade crumble slightly—he knew she needed their protection the most. Lenny seemed to share this instinct, stepping in front of her; his eyes were dark abysses reflecting the twisted world around them, and black veins snaked up his arm that he used to shield her—a sign of arcane alchemy hardening his skin like bark.

The Godbeasts tensed, their muscles coiling like springs in the face of an imminent clash when abruptly, the officer-creature dropped to its knees. It trembled violently, its body oscillating like unset jelly. Uncertainty wormed its way into their minds, freezing them in place. The merfolk's spasms intensified with alarming speed, its body convulsing so fiercely that droplets of clear fluid splattered onto the concrete beneath it.

At the apex of this hideous display, its flesh split apart with a nauseating squelch—tentacles burst forth from within it, and a twisted mouth unzipped itself—from groin to neck—revealing jagged teeth set against blackened lips. An unholy sound echoed from within this monstrosity—a discordant rip akin to tearing through gore-soaked fabric. A monstrous roar exploded from the creature, a sonic assault designed to incapacitate those blessed—or cursed—with heightened senses.

Brock and Lenny recoiled as if slapped by invisible hands, their heads pounding as though hammered from within. Disoriented, they collided before pushing off each other; Lenny's momentum sent him hurtling into a parked truck with enough force to tip it over.

Amidst this chaos stood Malachi, seemingly impervious to the ear-splitting cacophony. His magic aura pulsed around him—an ethereal shield against this auditory onslaught—as he focused his will upon the beast. The chaotic energy of the world answered his summons; force rippled outwards from Lenny's collision and swept towards a lamppost towering over the monster. With a metallic groan and rush of air, the post snapped and crashed onto the patrol car below—the beast's infernal cry stifled in an explosion of sparks.

One by one, surrounding lights flickered like extinguished stars—plunging an entire block into an abyssal darkness. Bathed only in the eerie glow of burning wreckage and charred monster remains, they swiftly regrouped.

"Damn," Brock grumbled, his voice a low rumble. "That's a first."

Malachi shrugged, a nonchalant gesture amidst the chaos. "I wanted it dead. I didn't plan for... whatever that was."

Menacing murmurs came from within the oppressive darkness; hundreds of merfolk growling threats from unseen locations. Shadows writhed and contorted behind dilapidated storefronts as Cthulhu's spawn stirred into action; doors creaked open ominously while windows shattered under unseen forces.

The air grew thick with the putrid stench of decaying seaweed as the Deep One's progeny emerged from hiding—stretching their monstrous appendages and yawning cavernous maws in anticipation of feasting on their sworn enemies. But by then, the Godbeasts had vanished—leaving behind nothing but an empty street teeming with these cosmic abominations.

With a powerful surge of his muscular frame, Brock propelled himself to the entrance of a nearby hardware store. The mundane exterior belied an interior that throbbed with an energy not of this world, devoid of any immediate monstrous threat. Their boots squelched into what felt like rotting organic matter as they ventured in; Arkminister was a city of illusions, its innocuous structures concealing putrid evils.

Ana fought back the bile rising in her throat as they navigated through a cavernous room teeming with towering pods and twisted vines—an alien nursery tucked behind ordinary brick and mortar. Shadowy figures writhed within their semi-transparent prisons, their disturbing activity stirring an unwilling fascination within her.

They hastened towards a moss-ridden portal Brock had discerned, his broad shoulder effortlessly pulverizing the sponge-like substance that posed as a door. Guided by Brock's radiant silhouette, they traversed through an unsettlingly vacant storeroom before encountering another obstacle—a metal door that Brock obliterated with another potent thrust.

As they emerged into stale air and an alleyway swallowed by darkness, Brock turned to Ana. "Which direction?" he asked.

Ana concentrated, her psychic senses scanning for the heartbeat that pulsed throughout this corrupted realm. "We need to head towards the sea," she declared. "Past the city...along the beachfront. I sense a cave carved into the cliffside... It's whispering something." Her eyes screwed shut in concentration. "Could it be the Dark Mother? Her voice is fainter like she's hiding—"

"Seashore," Brock cut across Ana's chatter.

He considered scaling one of the buildings bordering their alleyway for a superior vantage point; it was only five stories high—a single leap for him. But before he could act, grotesque figures sprouted across the rooftops: bulbous heads of lurking aberrations, their numbers multiplying at an alarming rate. He recognized the trap they'd inadvertently walked into.

"We're surrounded," Lenny noted, his voice steady despite the looming danger.

"Get Ana out of here," Malachi ordered. "I'll cover from above."

Before there could be any debate on their course of action, Malachi had already transformed into a swirling vortex of black feathers and shimmering arcane tendrils.

With one of the Deep One's minions slithering off the rooftop and landing with a nauseating splat, the remaining group had no option but to respond. The creature emitted a chilling warble from some hidden cavity within its spiky head that resembled a sea urchin. It stretched its lean green form, adopted an aggressive stance, and lunged towards them with clawed limbs.

Brock turned to Lenny. "Grab her, I'll clear us a path."

As the monstrosity bore down on them, its stench of decay saturating the air, Brock erupted in a brilliant golden aura, charging directly toward the threat. Instead of colliding with it, he nimbly sidestepped it, gripped its thin limb, and slammed it against the brick wall. He swung its limp body like a makeshift weapon, hurling it into another horror that emerged from the shadows. The entangled beings collided with a dumpster, propelling it down the narrow passageway in a shower of sparks.

The alley thrummed with the pulse of countless bodies, a tide of Cthulhu's minions seeking to drown Brock and his companions in their monstrous numbers. Despite their onslaught, Brock stood firm, his fists arcing through the air in a ballet of power and precision, each strike accompanied by explosive bursts of golden magic that sent creatures reeling. Lenny's shadowy ward spun into action, carving a path through the horde like an ethereal bowling ball, obliterating all that dared stand in its way.

At the end of this gauntlet of horror loomed a creature so hideous it defied comprehension—a nightmarish fusion of woman and octopus. Its many breasts and writhing tentacles quivered obscenely while its gorgon head, an unholy patchwork of human faces stitched together in horrific discordance, leered at them. But before Brock could fully process this abomination, he unleashed a surge of thermonuclear fury that reduced it to smoldering debris.

Brock became a beacon amid bedlam, emerging from the clouded aftermath onto a street overrun with undead monstrosities. He bulldozed through clusters of shambling merfolk whose nauseating stench filled the air—rotting fish left to broil under a merciless sun. His airborne companion guided him with incantations that ignited nearby leaking gas tanks; together, they tore through Arkminister's downtown block, leaving behind fiery trails reminiscent of WWII bombing raids over Old London.

Ana bore witness to this cataclysmic spectacle from Lenny's protective embrace. Initially overwhelmed by the unfolding horror, she sought refuge in darkness by squeezing her eyes shut against the disorienting chaos around her. But even without sight, her mind painted vivid images of carnage with such clarity that reality couldn't match.

She saw Lenny tumbling down a flaming alleyway in Brock's wake, a vortex of magical energy swirling around him. Dying merfolk dropped like charred logs, and the heat was monstrous—an insatiable beast gorging on the city block. Explosions birthed from shattered windows and ignited gas lines shook neighboring blocks with their ferocity.

The flames were not ordinary; they were infused with Malachi's silver energy, explaining their unyielding hunger. He was fire incarnate—volatile and furious.

As Ana's consciousness floated above the chaos, she understood the terrifying power her companions wielded. Arkminister smoldered beneath her like a phoenix rising from its ashes, eruptions of flame marking their path across the city. Even the outskirts bore scars of small fires dotting their escape route into the scrublands.

Despite this widespread destruction, most was concentrated at Arkminister's heart, where Brock and Malachi had commenced their purging assault. They were nearing the city limits now, heading for the shore, leaving behind a trail of scorched earth and smoldering ruins.

Isolated from the turmoil below, Ana traced their path from above, observing as an owl might in flight. A newfound clarity filled her; she was becoming an omniscient gaze upon the world. From her serene vantage point, she could guide her comrades towards cliffs looming like a jagged precipice at the ocean's edge.

On that shore, hidden beneath tons of stone like a pearl within an oyster shell, shimmered Alexander's artifact—a soft white radiance barely perceptible yet holding immense power. She saw beyond those cliffs as effortlessly as looking through misted glass. Nothing remained concealed from her now—she was emerging into her own potent certainty.

Ana's gaze was drawn westward, where an immense shadow lurked beneath the ocean's surface. It was a colossal silhouette, birthed from the lightless abyss leagues below, in a realm of crushing pressures and spectral oblivion. A chill slithered down her spine as she confronted the dormant horror that stained the waters to their meeting point with the moonlit sky.

The staggering reality of an Outer God washed over her—a leviathan so vast it filled the ocean, a creature whose awakening could drown entire coastlines in a single whirlpool. Cthulhu, synonymous with the ocean itself—its secrets and creatures, mere bacteria in his incomprehensible form—possessed enough power to deluge entire worlds.

Yet, rather than yielding to her sense of triviality in the face of her adversary—an entity of monstrous immensity confined deep within the ocean's depths—Ana experienced a rush of boldness as they dared to challenge these celestial giants. They were daringly trespassing within this Outer God's sanctum—the proverbial David to his Goliath—and she held firm to her belief that Cthulhu's underestimation of human tenacity could lead to his downfall.

However, immediate threats loomed large, and her courage wavered. From her elevated vantage point, she saw impending dangers converging—a storm shaped like a reaper's scythe sweeping in from all directions except westward. It pelted the earth with eldritch rain; its clouds were heavy, writhing with serpentine and maggot-like shapes. The tempest radiated an insatiable hunger as its downpour transformed the land into grey sludge—it was closing in fast on Arkminister, threatening to consume everything like a biblical plague of locusts.

In each thunderous roar of the storm, Ana sensed Cthulhu's simmering fury—the desire to devour those who had dared disturb his slumber. Yet their fate remained undecided—for closer still on the cityscape were flares of spiritual activity erupting on the city outskirts. As she drew nearer, she saw sirens, like the first wailing creature they'd encountered here, perched on rooftops while streets below teemed with hordes of urchin men and octopi women.

Most terrifyingly, she encountered a species of merfolk that defied classification in her burgeoning Lovecraftian lexicon—or had she perhaps seen these in her horrific visions of the past? Regardless, the reality was appalling. Hovering near one such monstrosity, she was stunned by its colossal size—it towered as tall as a two-story building—its form an unholy fusion of human muscularity and ancient ammonite design. Shadowy tendrils encased a throbbing red core within its translucent shell—a heart or brain? Tentacles sprouted from the creature's carapace, supporting its monstrous weight upon unwavering rubbery stilts as solid as spider legs. Power pulsed along these appendages from the monster's crimson core up to a humanoid torso standing erect amid tentacles—an infernal cluster of glowing boils festering on its demonic horned head like rubies studding a crown. This was not just another minion but an imposing commander serving an Outer God.

Casting her gaze further down the blocks, Ana counted three dread lords, each leading an army of merfolk and rooftop sirens. They believed they had control over the situation but were unaware they were trapped between a mystical storm and a monstrous army—hurtling towards an inevitable clash.

Ana's mind reverberated with the spectral echo of Lovecraft, his voice a ghostly whisper laced with scholarly awe. Krakens, he intoned, as if unveiling an arcane secret to her. Cthulhu summons his generals from the abyssal depths. He senses you—your essence, your mission. These beasts are not just formidable—they're the living nightmares that have swallowed ships and devoured continents. Evade them or perish.

Her psyche, a beacon in the cosmic void, soared back into the celestial expanse above, alerting her comrades of their dire predicament. The Godbeasts remained unperturbed by Ana's ethereal voice resonating within their minds—it was as familiar to them as their own pulse.

"We're walking straight into a trap," she warned. "A supernatural storm is brewing around Arkminister, and Cthulhu's minions swarm the western shoreline like locusts. Sirens—with the big mouths and screams capable of shattering eardrums—and merfolk in droves. Plus, some massive beings encased in shells."

In response to Ana's warning, Brock ceased his relentless assault on a hauntingly silent street. Crushed remains of merfolk lay beneath him, while sweat mingled with otherworldly blood stained his body like war paint. Lenny came to an abrupt stop behind him. Ana nestled within his arms, resembling an alien infant who was simultaneously asleep yet vigilant, eyes ablaze with psychic energy.

Hovering above them all was Malachi—his perspective now encompassing his vision and Ana's—his gaze drawn towards an abandoned factory crowned by a weather-beaten sign reading 'Fred's Threads.' Inside its skeletal structure lurked the sirens Ana had cautioned about—a horde potent enough to instill terror even in those steeled against horror.

The imminent storm posed another problem—foreboding clouds coiling around the town, corralling them towards Cthulhu's awaiting forces. A shiver of icy dread punctured Malachi's elation as he observed the storm's relentless progression, extinguishing fires in its path. Retreat was no longer an option; their only choice was to charge past the army and seek sanctuary in the caves.

"Only one least shitty option available," he mused, sharing his tactical plan with Ana's ever-watchful spirit. "We push forward, swift and fierce. I'll tackle the sirens."

Rekindling his immortal rage, Malachi darted toward the factory while Ana transmitted his instructions to Brock and Lenny—who proceeded with cautious resolve.

In a heartbeat, Malachi materialized above the factory—a dazzling vortex of feathers and light casting an uncanny glow on the creatures below as their bodies contorted into drooling maws, ready to unleash their deafening screams.

But Malachi outpaced them—his piercing raven's cry cleaved through the scaffold beneath 'Fred's Threads,' causing it to collapse onto the hideous monstrosities before continuing its destructive journey through a section of the decrepit building—triggering a landslide of bricks and merfolk remains.

The raw, visceral urge to survive, magnified by Ana's psychic command of "Fly away!" sliced through Malachi's moment of awe-struck devastation. He soared skyward as a gelatinous appendage cleaved through the roiling turmoil below, snatching at his fleeing feathers. An earth-shattering bellow echoed as the kraken heaved its monstrous form from the rubble-littered street. With formidable strength and suction-cupped hold, it scaled a tottering building, perching atop with an agility that belied its gargantuan size.

The structure's collapse seemed to pause under the coiled grip of the beast. Asserting its dominion, the kraken split the air with a shriek that sent Malachi spiraling and drove Brock and Lenny to their knees. Malachi veered wildly, narrowly avoiding collision with a concrete barrier while his Godbeast comrades sprang back up; Ana remained ensconced within Lenny's protective grasp—unaware yet unscathed.

Their eyes locked onto this colossal servant of Cthulhu—a harbinger of death incarnate—as they scrambled to devise a counteroffensive strategy. From its lofty perch, the kraken spotted them—it eschewed tactics for raw power and summoned its hellish sorcery instead.

For one fleeting moment, its grotesque form transformed into something mesmerizing—the iridescent shell shimmering like blood-stained glass under cascading rainbows—Zap! A beam of blistering red energy radiated from this demonic spectacle, reducing an adjacent building to rubble.

Brock launched himself over airborne flaming debris in an impressive acrobatic evasion, barely escaping death's clutches, only to land amidst a frenzied horde of twitching merfolk who swarmed him like ants descending upon sugar granules. Their assaults were mere pinpricks against his metallic skin, but their sheer numbers pinned him down.

As he wrestled to free himself, Malachi darted between radiant beams, diverting the kraken's attention and forcing it to squander its barrage into the ether. Concurrently, Lenny surfed the fiery waves already engulfing the streets below on a pitch-black board, leaping from collapsing rooftops. He shielded himself and Ana by burrowing underground, though seismic tremors soon expelled him back into chaos.

In the distance, other krakens ascended to high nests and bathed the streets in columns of vile magic while their armies swarmed around lava-filled trenches and gutted buildings in pursuit of Godbeasts. The electric storm of Cthulhu, coupled with krakens and merfolk, threatened to drown Arkminister in a deluge of death.

Engulfed by gnashing bodies, Brock felt their impending doom closing in. In fleeting moments where he surfaced above the sea of merfolk, he glimpsed Malachi's aerial acrobatics and Lenny's tumultuous evasion attempts. A realization dawned upon him—his duty was to end this battle. Inspired by their unwavering bravery, he drew strength through their soulful link formed via Ana's bond—he absorbed more than just motivation; he harnessed their magical prowess too: elemental might, including Lenny's earthy alien mysticism. If he was half a god before this moment, now he embodied divine power in its entirety.

Without the need for Ana's prophetic abilities, united as a *coven*, the unified Godbeasts instinctively knew they needed to distance themselves from Brock's impending eruption of power. Malachi, his body alight with an ethereal glow, propelled himself into the laser-illuminated heavens, straining against Brock's gravitational force. Meanwhile, Lenny morphed into a shadowy liquid form and seeped deep beneath the earth's crust.

On the other hand, Ana was caught in a surreal sensation that mirrored a wild roller coaster plunge—she had no idea how far Lenny was tunneling underground as her visionary senses were entirely focused on the nuclear cataclysm about to be triggered by Brock.

The mental leech known as Lovecraft resonated with Ana's awe-stricken silence. Ungodly strength! he declared in a voice that echoed through their shared consciousness. An unhallowed energy crackled through the atmosphere. Ana's omnipresent sight was lured to a congregation of heretics who had been interring her friend. Now, the dazzling shockwaves that expanded outwards reduced them to shrieking phantoms, obliterating everything in their path and snuffing out the flames.

The relentless drone of the Aspect of Earth's atomic engine filled the air—a tireless machine orbiting around a white-hot core. Amid this pandemonium, she could discern Brock, transmuted into an entity of pure radiance. He knelt on terra firma, his fist pounding rhythmically like an alien pile driver infused with celestial energy capable of altering starscapes.

His rage reverberated within Earth's bedrock, grinding it into fine granules before hammering it further until he found himself suspended amidst dust clouds—an angelic figurehead of annihilation floating amidst a spiraling sandy vortex.

A mesmerizing halo of concrete, steel, and stone spun around him like planets revolving around their star. It birthed a tumultuous tempest from which only the fleetest Godbeasts could possibly evade. Each throb of Brock's cosmic pulse reverberated like an unstable nuclear reactor; waves of destructive energy rolled across Arkminister, leaving in its wake nothing but desolation.

The airborne urchin men vaporized instantaneously while sirens howled in vain against this overpowering force. Even the kraken closest to the blast was disassembled at a molecular level. Further away, yet still doomed, their kin wriggled free from their atomized shells only to perish as luminous specters far brighter than they had ever existed.

Yet, even then, the Aspect of Earth continued to draw upon his magic; his power radiated outward until it clashed with Cthulhu's storm in one cataclysmic burst of light brighter than any divine fire ever beheld by mortals. The darkness shrouding the area expired with a groan that could have been Cthulhu's stunned disbelief at his curse being thwarted.

Malachi, however, had not borne witness to this apocalyptic spectacle. He ascended higher and higher, aiming for the moon, understanding the need for distance. Even as he transformed into a swirling tempest of magic and pure energy, Brock's protective instincts remained within him. Just as Brock drew strength from his coven, Malachi discovered he could tap into that same power source.

The beating of his wings synchronized with the rhythmic detonations below; he rose so high that he could safely observe Cthulhu's dark storm reaching for Brock's radiant sphere... only to be repelled, thrown back into a shower of glowing embers that rained down upon a land shrouded in sudden tranquility.

Even as the cataclysmic tempest subsided, leaving an eerie silence in its wake, enigmas lurked beneath the surface. Where had Brock vanished to? Ana? Lenny? A glint of gold flickered from the depths below—Brock's beacon—and Malachi spiraled down through the dissipating clouds to unearth its source. What remained of the city was a skeletal husk: edifices shattered into fragments, roads and vehicles strewn haphazardly like neglected playthings in a forsaken match of snakes and ladders.

Not one structure stood defiant amidst the desolate panorama. It was a sobering realization; they had obliterated an entire society corrupted by Cthulhu's malignant touch. The earth beneath them still shivered and contorted, hinting at further ruinous transformations.

As Malachi touched down on the glassy expanse of the crater floor, his boots skidding slightly on its treacherously slick surface, he was suddenly upended by a grime-streaked figure who wrapped him in a bear-like embrace. Not far off, Ana materialized out of nothingness along with her protector—a dark ripple heralding their arrival—as she choked and spluttered while her senses recalibrated.

A silent exchange passed between Brock and Malachi before they rose to their feet, only then acknowledging Brock's nudity—his skin charred and glistening with ash. Lenny casually removed his shirt, offering it to Brock. "Cover up, bro." Unruffled by the absurdity around him, Brock fashioned the garment into a makeshift loincloth, securing it tightly around his waist. "Appreciate it."

Ana voiced what everyone else was thinking. "Everyone okay?"

"Fit as a fiddle," Lenny declared boldly, thumping his chest with a sound akin to a hammer striking stone.

"I feel alive," Malachi exclaimed, his form shimmering with the mercurial glow of arcane energy.

"Like I could take on the world," Brock chimed in.

"I'm just tired," Ana confessed, her voice steady and content in its simplicity.

You are all quite remarkable, Lovecraft intoned silently to his custodian.

Together, they surveyed the decimated cityscape stretching out before them. The mournful dirge of destruction echoed over jagged peaks while gusts of wind swept dust and sand across the basin in a frantic bid to wipe clean all traces of Arkminister. The night sky loomed clear and ominous; even the moon seemed innocently pallid as if Cthulhu's monstrous appendages had been repelled—for now. The oppressive aura that once hung heavy over the ocean had dissipated along with the storm. Their route towards their prize upon the cliffs lay unimpeded.

"Hey guys," Ana interrupted their contemplation. "We kinda blew up a chunk of the west coast. There's bound to be someone—real people or some science geeks or cops—who'll notice."

After battling supernatural foes for so long, human threats appeared insignificant now. Yet Brock and Malachi remembered how much havoc law enforcement had wreaked when they fled Canada.

A grin spread across Brock's face as he turned to Lenny, who mirrored his expression. They were both seemingly struck by a shared thought laced with mischief. "Ready for some fun?" he asked.

"Hell yeah." Lenny scooped up Ana effortlessly, cradling her in his arms.

Brock followed suit, sweeping Malachi into his hold.

Bathed in an aura of obsidian and gilded brilliance, they rocketed from the wreckage of Arkminister like celestial projectiles, their trails dusted with cosmic stardust. Their divine power was magnetically drawn towards the echo of primordial might, no longer hindered by Cthulhu's dominion. So engrossed were they in their astral contest that even Ana neglected the mystical relic now abandoned amidst the rapidly chilling remains of Arkminister. Hidden beneath a contorted steel corpse, once a sizable truck, a weak rhythm pulsed, its shielding enchantments crumbling away. Soon, this occult artifact would degrade into nothing more than an antiquated tome filled with cryptic glyphs and the feverish musings of a deranged Indian woman, decomposing as ancient parchment is wont to do. Yet, for now, it seeped traces of its magic, summoning its keeper with an irresistible charm. Mary, heed my call, murmured the grimoire in a voice as soft as a spider's silk and as potent as a siren's song.

PART 2: THE UNFATHOMABLE

CHAPTER 14: ENSNARED

Suspended above this nightmarish tableau, Ana beheld the birth of a leviathan encased within a crystalline shell.

The weathered stone barrier, a relic of forgotten ages, stretched across the desolate coastline like a silent sentinel. It guarded secrets as old as time itself against the infinite horizon. In its tempestuous rage, the ocean crashed relentlessly against the jagged rocks below while Godbeasts prowled the frigid sands, drawn by an intoxicating scent of ancient mysteries hanging in the air. To most, these cliffs were merely daunting geological formations—only conquerable through strenuous climbing and bloodied hands—shaped by countless years of maritime onslaughts. But those sensitive to the unseen could feel it; beneath this earthy facade throbbed a primal power that twisted and warped arcane energies around it. The wind whispered tales of battles long past, of victories savored and defeats mourned as mankind wrestled with celestial foes from another age now gearing up for renewed conflict. Ethereal mists swirled along the shoreline, their depths flickering with enigmatic shapes.

Within this rugged stronghold's deceptive simplicity and turbulent tides hid a tiny crevice. Yet Ana's keen psychic senses pierced through this veil of uncertainty to reveal the concealed portal. "Over there," she directed.

Lenny had barely set Ana down when he lifted her once more and ventured into the surf. As they moved further into the aquatic territory, his form melted away into an obsidian mist that enveloped Ana within a colossal sphere—clear as a black diamond yet impervious to all external elements thanks to Lenny's gravitational magic. Within this enchanted sanctuary, she floated untouched by water droplets as if cradled gently by spectral hands.

Submerging beneath churning waves sparked laughter from Ana—a joyful absurdity birthed from witnessing Lenny's rapidly evolving transmutation abilities unfold in unexpected yet thrilling ways. Even during their clashes with Cthulhu's monstrous minions, she had been constantly amazed but never felt endangered. She found herself reminiscing about Lenny's graceful maneuvers, how he danced on shadowy plumes or evaporated into buoyant black clouds—much like her current vessel—without causing the slightest ripple.

Their underwater journey took them through submerged forests of aquatic flora and past ominous creatures of the deep, none of which stirred fear within her. Fleeting golden flashes revealed her companions swimming nearby, their movements blending into a single radiant blur. Once, they drew close enough for Ana to discern an intimate exchange under Brock's pulsating light—an otherworldly, unromantic kiss where Brock shared his breath with Malachi. The unique physiology of her friends could keep scientists captivated for lifetimes and potentially unlock secrets to halting aging and curing diseases. Yet she harbored no desire for the world to discover or partake in their miracles. She had finally found a family she could call her own and was unwilling to share it.

Guided by Lenny, Ana descended into the ocean's depths only to be propelled upwards with a sudden rush. Emerging from the aquatic abyss, she found herself encased in a mystical cocoon with Lenny solidifying around her. They trudged through the shallows before he crouched, allowing her to step onto dry land.

A dark shroud fell upon them, punctuated with flickers of silvery light. They could fully perceive their surroundings only when Brock surfaced from the depths, faintly radiating with golden magic that cast an otherworldly illumination.

The sight that met them was breathtaking: an enormous dome hewn from volcanic stone. Perhaps the handiwork of Cthulhu's crustacean artisans had also shaped the labyrinthine tunnels that perforated the coral canopy overhead. The chamber's iridescent veins and undulating pool mirrored Brock's radiance in a kaleidoscopic dance of multicolored ripples.

"Damn," Ana murmured, her words echoing back at her like whispers in a cathedral. But awe quickly gave way to apprehension as she remembered why they were there; they were intruders in enemy territory. From deep within the cave came a foreboding throb resonating with her echoed whisper.

Their gazes followed numerous rugged ellipses of gleaming stone—resembling fossilized steps—that led to a plateau where an alien structure pulsated ominously. A massive coral monolith, as pale as bone and adorned with twisting tubes reaching towards the cavernous ceiling, the conduits seemed more vibrant and alive than their host structure; this was clearly not of earthly origin.

Embedded within this grotesque formation flickered a white-gold gem—the ring—their objective. Yet none dared approach it. An instinctual warning, borne of their supernatural abilities, held them back. Cthulhu's treasure was not unguarded.

A sudden chill gripped Ana. Fear prickled at her senses, forewarning of an impending disaster. The icy dread was amplified by the shard of the Dark Mother concealed within her hunting knife sheath—a perfect echo of the chamber's rhythmic pulse that left her pondering its meaning.

"I'd bet my life there's a trap here," Ana announced.

In response, Lovecraft's voice rang in her mind: A warding spell would be more accurate. Your colloquial language lacks sophistication. Look again, my dear, and you shall see it.

Ana's eyes cracked open, the world around her shattering like glass to reveal the arcane secrets lurking beneath. The room twisted and undulated, becoming an ethereal dance of silver light that twirled across stone, water, and her oblivious companions. She was entranced by the complex weave of otherworldly power they had unknowingly stumbled upon. A once alien heartbeat was now a pulsating oval of crimson energy — a testament to the wicked potency of blood magic. Her senses stretched out in all directions, and she realized this power was harvested from human sacrifices in Arkminister and countless others before Cthulhu's modern acolytes ever set foot on Earth.

Pulled under by the relentless current of fate, Ana felt reality melt away into ghostly mist. She found herself gliding above storm-lashed shores like a spectral observer. Beneath her sprawled a fearsome army of echinoid men, sirens, and krakens surging from the ocean depths in a deadly wave. Indigenous warriors hurled their spears at the encroaching horde while women and children watched helplessly from their huts as their defenders were dragged screaming into the swirling vortex.

Beyond this carnage lurked an even greater horror: countless abominations crawling ashore from a roiling whirlpool. Rising from its heart was an entity so massive it defied understanding, pulled forth by three krakens yoked like oxen.

Suspended above this nightmarish tableau, Ana beheld the birth of a leviathan encased within a crystalline shell. Its body resembled an enormous larva as lengthy as a ship—an insect-like abdomen tapering into an hourglass shape with legs possibly hundreds of meters long, folded along its gargantuan form. What initially seemed like clusters of black orbs embedded under its skin were revealed to be eyes—each one as large as an eclipsed moon. This was a titanic sentinel, a shackled guardian transported across the vast expanse of space and time to protect the Atlantean weapon that once wounded the mighty Cthulhu.

The vision clung to her, dragging Ana deeper into its dark embrace. The krakens dragged the colossal chrysalis across a jagged shoal onto an untouched beach. Its cosmic hue starkly contrasted with the virgin sand—an eerie echo of the chalky cliffs she and her companions would traverse in their own time. A chilling revelation washed over her: this monstrosity was fated to transform into a living mountain through unfathomable magic.

A throng of babbling creatures followed in its path, their frantic chants heralding the impending cosmic metamorphosis. But Ana could bear no more; she tore herself away from witnessing a god's transformation into stone.

Back amongst her comrades, Ana saw their concern etched deeply on their faces as they awaited her return from her temporal journey. Drained by what she had witnessed, she collapsed into Lenny's arms. Yet even in her weakened state, she held onto him tightly as he murmured calming words while steadying her trembling form.

An enormous Lengeth, Lovecraft's thoughts resonated within Ana's mind. Monstrous and primordial—before the species was corrupted by Outer God radiation. Such scale suggests it might be a direct offspring or a brood mother birthed by the Spider God himself.

"So, what's our move?" Ana asked, her gaze riveted on the skull that had become their unlikely guide. Her companions followed her lead, their eyes drawn to the arcane artifact.

Uncertainty veiled Lovecraft's psychic voice as he responded. I have yet to decipher a spell of this caliber. The Lengeth were once pure beings, gluttonous devourers of cosmic lore, unrivaled masters of temporal and universal dimensions. Many arcane sages claim they were the oldest life form in existence. If this is indeed a trap, its consequences could originate from any time, realm, or reality.

Ana translated his cryptic words into something more digestible for her friends. "Sounds like we're in for one hell of a ride," she said under her breath.

Indeed, dear child. Brace yourself for every conceivable outcome.

Ana took a step forward before pivoting to face her companions again. "We're standing inside some cosmic entity—its carcass, technically—that's been gutted and reshaped into a mountain. An alien arachnid called a Lengeth—massive interstellar jumpers who feast on knowledge and bend realities." She paused for dramatic effect but found only blank expressions staring back at her. Undaunted, she continued with renewed vigor, "So when we try to nab that ring or even approach it, all hell might break loose. Weird, dimensional shit. I can't tell you exactly what will happen, but according to Lovecraft, we should prepare ourselves for all sorts of insanity."

Her warning hung heavy in the air—a threat vast and looming given their previous encounters with such alien phenomena—but they couldn't afford inaction now—Brock's impulsive nature had already set things in motion. In a flash, he was scaling the towering steps, bounding and scrambling up the higher ledges with an agility reminiscent of a jungle cat until he became a mere luminescent speck against the pearl heart, far away from his comrades.

His reckless haste gave way to rapture as he neared the throbbing phylactery—its pulsation now unmistakably resonant. A glint from within an ivory cradle beckoned him; coral stretched like molten cheese into a perplexing stringy mass dwarfing his size. The heart cast a damp, warm shadow over him as he approached, its looming presence dominating his surroundings.

Each step amplified the pulsating rhythm in anticipation or aggression, sending shockwaves through the air that assaulted his eardrums. The sudden onslaught of pain caused Brock to falter, but it also stoked his fury and unleashed his primal spirit, causing him to bellow loudly and charge forward.

Ignoring the searing torment as venomous radiating creatures swarmed over his arms, he plunged his hand into the sticky nest. His fingers closed around something small and cool, which he quickly enveloped in a firm grasp.

With a guttural cry, he yanked free his hand, sending luminescent spiders flying from the heart like blood spurts. As he frantically brushed off these creatures—desperate not to loosen his grip—one of the heart's sonic pulses flung him off the edge, causing him to tumble down and strike the platform below, which didn't halt his descent but shattered like fragile ice, dragging him down in a shower of jade shards into the gaping maw below.

Malachi's eyes were riveted on the spectacle before him, his heart pounding in sync with the otherworldly rhythm of the Lengeth heart mass. Brock, his steadfast companion, lunged forward, his arm disappearing into the pulsating mass as if absorbed by it. He seemed to grapple with an unseen force within that alien organ, a silent struggle in this eerie chamber.

Then, without warning, Brock was catapulted off the platform's edge. His scream—a raw, primal sound that echoed Malachi's own fear—was abruptly silenced as he vanished from sight.

"Brock!" The name reverberated in Malachi's mind as he sought out their sacred mental link—a lifeline they had relied on countless times before. But this time, only cold and ominous silence echoed back at him.

With its intruder expelled, the Lengeth heart mass seemed to relax. The ripples and distortions that had marred its surface faded away like phantoms at dawn. A swarm of cosmic spiderlings—tiny extensions of the Lengeth itself—scurried forth to repair the damage inflicted by Brock's intrusion.

The chamber fell back into its steady rhythm, each beat resonating through Malachi like a grim funeral dirge for his lost friend.

Ana's voice sliced through the ominous silence like a knife. Her horror mirrored his own as she cried out: "Where's Brock?"

CHAPTER 15: SPIDER'S DAUGHTER

Within this alien orchestra's embrace, a radiant being birthed itself from the consuming shadows.

The cosmic tempest regurgitated Brock, propelling him onto a cruel bed of coarse grit. Pain's orchestra played a symphony inside him, his insides twisting and knotting in the familiar agony of being torn apart and stitched back together across the vastness of the cosmic abyss. How many light-years had he traversed within that dark expanse? Malachi...Ana...Lenny. Their names echoed in the hollow chambers of his mind, save for a single spark of Malachi's fiery spirit that still flickered within him. With a deep growl resonating from his core, he fought against the spinning world around him and rose.

His surroundings were an arid wasteland, its dry air strangling each breath he drew. Towering scarlet structures sprouted from shifting sands, their forms twisted into monstrous pinnacles and gnarled claws—the landscape was a distorted dream woven from fear itself. Ethereal drapes filled the valleys of this alien terrain, blowing aimlessly amidst the dirt and debris. Could it be some form of webbing? He pondered as he watched them hang like banners from cliff faces, fluttering in the howling wind.

Still reeling from his interdimensional journey and buffeted by relentless gusts, he sought shelter within a nearby formation—a curving finger sculpted from glossy obsidian and crimson stone—and huddled within its cavernous belly. Here, safe for now, he examined an object that had accompanied him on his tumultuous odyssey through dimensions unknown. Even as his body had transformed into radiant energy during transit, he remembered forcing himself to keep its essence intertwined with his atomic structure.

The artifact was unexpectedly plain: a ring as unadorned as wedding gold but forged from an alloy that fluctuated between gleaming gold and tarnished silver. Bereft of alternatives or inspiration, he slipped it onto his finger.

A sudden tranquility washed over him, muffling the storm outside and allowing his lungs to fill without strain. Emboldened, he emerged from his refuge and watched as the sandstorm bent its course around him—as though repelled by his very presence.

He scaled a sloping monolith that tapered to a sharp point and surveyed the desolation spread out before him. A barren wilderness stretched in all directions, primarily hidden behind a swirling veil of sand, save for a few towering spires like his own that punctured through the sandy shroud. A low rumble and gradual crumbling vibrated beneath his fingertips as if this tortured realm was devouring itself. Wherever this place was, Earth's galaxy didn't even twinkle in its star-studded sky.

Like rotten wood, the great pillar suddenly splintered under his weight. He leaped onto a nearby ledge just in time to watch as the tower shattered into countless fragments and dissolved into a cascade of sand. The monolith gave way with a soft sigh, and he hastily abandoned his latest perch, which had begun to tremble ominously.

Brock found himself unable to remain idle amid this decaying cosmos. His muscular form darted across geological formations that spanned chasms too deep to comprehend and sandy pits as vast as forgotten oceans. The alien landscape unfolded before him like an acrobat's obstacle course, with Brock navigating its treacherous contours with an uncanny grace.

The extraterrestrial mesh, draped over elevated areas like a spider's web, served as his compass in this otherworldly terrain. It felt gritty beneath his fingertips—like ancient rope covered in centuries-old dust—but it was tangible amidst the surreal surroundings. He clung to it tenaciously as he scaled and balanced on its brittle strands.

Occasionally, he would pause atop an overlook to gaze at the desolate sky above him —a silent plea for celestial guidance or some semblance of direction. But this purgatory offered no such comfort; its dull firmament was devoid of stars or familiar constellations capable of piercing through the gloom.

A creeping sense of unease washed over him—the product of the desolate expanse that stretched before him. The chaotic topography—jagged stone claws reaching for the heavens, rolling hills that rose and fell like waves on a stormy sea, and a gossamer veil hovering over the desert—stirred a strange recognition within him. It was as if he held some arcane understanding of these elements, perhaps a memory from another life.

His journey led him down a desert slope towards a crater high up on the valley's edge—structures that seemed to defy gravity yet appeared most stable in this alien terrain. The crater was peculiar—a graveyard strewn with spherical stones reminiscent of fish eggs left abandoned on dry land.

As Brock navigated through the dunes towards the crater's far side, he realized these weren't mere mounds of sand but piles of extraterrestrial spheres assembled in decay. A handful of these globes, their surfaces corroded by time, emitted an eerie green luminescence. Intrigued, he paused to examine one such sphere and discovered an insectoid embryo encased within its jade depths—life frozen in time.

Despite the mystical artifact that granted him divine resilience, Brock found himself panting heavily as he reached the top of the slope. The alien environment was sapping his strength; he couldn't help but question if the air here was breathable or merely a cruel illusion created by his magic.

Spotting a shimmer from a nearby ledge, Brock decided to investigate it. He tread along the rugged rock face towards this anomaly—a solitary egg amidst emerald confetti —the lone splash of vibrant color on this barren world.

Brock picked up half of this intact sphere for examination. Whatever had perished within had left behind a fossilized imprint, far clearer than the opaque suggestions he'd previously seen—an oval body surrounded by numerous sharp appendages reminiscent of lobsters, crabs...or spiders...

"Holy fuck," Brock muttered under his breath as realization dawned upon him—he was standing within the hollow belly of an inverted, gigantic spider. He discarded the gruesome geode, his skin prickling with horrific images conjured by his imagination—a necropolis of ancient arachnids. Could these behemoths be ancestors of the Walkers? Or the Lengeth Ana had mentioned, right before the folly that led him here? If so, the creatures he and Malachi had encountered were mere shadows in comparison.

Brock moved with a somber determination, his piercing blue eyes reflecting the horrors of the fallen leviathans around him. The remnants of these titanic creatures whispered tales of a savage conflict, a battlefield where no one claimed victory, only death or flight. The chilling reality ignited a sensory assault—the sickly-sweet stench of decay, gusts that felt like they carried the powdered remains of the fallen.

His trek through this silent mausoleum seemed infinite—a voyage without bounds. He was a lone beacon smothered by an oppressive shroud of rot and ruin. Yet the glimmering hope of reuniting with Malachi and their allies kept him moving forward like a solitary moth drawn to an elusive flame.

As he left behind the monstrous graveyard in a wake of swirling dust, he entered an expanse devoid of life. The fractured terrain posed monumental chasms that demanded swift sprints and daring leaps. Even for Brock's Godbeast strength, these obstacles tested his limits. Each time, though, his hand pulsed with warmth as the Atlantean ring glittered —its power lending itself to his extraordinary feats.

However, despite this magical aid, despair clung to him in this desolation; each step felt like sinking deeper into despondency. As darkness fell and temperatures plummeted, three radiant yellow orbs punctured his solitary journey, triptych moons or blood-drained suns casting an eerie light on the barren land.

His lack of need for sustenance was a blessing here where nothing organic thrived—except perhaps within the gaping abysses filled with boiling stew of putrid magma and decaying matter—the planet's septic lifeblood. This world's decay seemed to seep into its very core.

From these foul pools and other signs he'd encountered along his journey, Brock recognized an overwhelming presence of earth magic—his element. Still, it was a corrupted version, a slow rotting apocalypse rather than Gaia's flourishing power.

As the reign of night drew to its close, a brutal sandstorm obscured the decaying moons. Brock waged war against the relentless gusts; if not for the Atlantean ring amplifying his resolve and shielding him from the swirling winds, he would've been swept away like an insignificant leaf.

"Thank you," he whispered reverently to the relic as if it could hear him.

Unbeknownst to him, it pulsed twice in response.

Time seemed frozen until finally, the curtain of black-and-brown lifted, and night surrendered to dawn's chilling crimson light, casting elongated shadows from the towering dunes of the desert. Brock navigated through shifting sands, his footprints instantly erased behind him.

As he pressed on, an ancient metropolis began forming on the hazy horizon—an ascending mirage of dilapidated pinnacles and spires reaching toward the sky, intertwining into a bulbous mass that defied natural laws. A sense of dread seized Brock as he recognized remnants of a city tainted by eldritch horrors.

As Brock neared the metropolis, he found himself ensnared by its architecture—a monstrous fusion of shape and geometry that defied spatial reasoning. Buildings erupted from the ground at unthinkable angles, akin to grotesque appendages of an ancient malevolent entity. Serrated towers shimmered with a dull sheen reminiscent of tarnished crystal yearning for the heavens, much like the twisted legs of colossal spiders caught in a chaotic ballet. But this realm's sparkle was marred by eons of decay—it might have once mirrored a crystalline bauble's beauty. The walls retained an ethereal power, etched with peculiar symbols murmuring enigmas from dimensions beyond mortal understanding. Delicate strands stretched between bell towers and alleyways, their ghostly music echoing through the city's hollows—a once harmonious symphony now reduced to a sorrowful requiem. He could almost envision this place strumming like a celestial harp under divine touch as wind and sunlight played upon it. Now, however, that melody was merely a lament.

The air around Brock grew dense with an otherworldly chill. Despite the engulfing darkness, shadows that caressed his form as he navigated through them, sensations of invisible spiders scuttling in obscurity, and the haunting quiet punctuated by mournful moans of decaying structures—Brock's resolve swelled. This place was dead—including the cosmic tyrants who had once claimed it as their stronghold. Fear no longer chained him; he moved through this infernal maze, feeling eerily like one of its deceased arachnid inhabitants.

He plunged deeper into the abyss accompanied solely by his heartbeat's faint echo and shrieking winds tearing through abandoned streets—desolate wastelands save for occasional decomposing husks of spider-like monstrosities crumbled within interconnecting tunnels or shriveled in corners. He recognized these creatures from past encounters: their forms, grotesque distortions of spiders with an excess of limbs and eyes radiating a bone-chilling malevolence. If he dared approach these remains, they disintegrated into dust. Each time he emerged from these ruins, this residue dispersed from him like a fleeting reminder of a fallen empire's reign. He wondered what unfathomable disaster had wiped out these beings.

From dawn's first light to the charcoal hues of dusk, he navigated through the wreckage. There was no rushing his journey as Acherai herself had intricately woven this city, which grew increasingly complex as one ventured further inwards. His soulmate's distant flame neither intensified nor waned but remained constant. Thus, he accepted two realities: his companions were safe somewhere, and there would be no instantaneous escapes from a world ravaged by an apocalypse. The chances of extracting himself seemed slim if even the spider gods hadn't escaped this planet's fate. So, he decided to explore and wait for his comrades' arrival—he knew Malachi would carve a path across the cosmos to find him. Patience was an earthly virtue that Brock seldom exercised. In these serene but deathly surroundings, he surrendered to the steady rhythm of his physical exertions and found solace in memories of his friends.

The dance of Brock's nimble strides whispered across the cityscape, a chaotic panorama strangled by the hardened embrace of spider silk. His destination was an expansive promenade, a grand avenue paved with titanic slabs etched in cryptic metallic runes that shimmered beneath his ethereal glow. This colossal path, hemmed in by walls of spun webbing and twisted edifices, led to a looming monolith—a temple blackened as if scorched, standing stark against the thin ribbon of blood-red sky.

Its entrance gaped like the maw of some ancient sea beast—an oblong mouth reclining into menacing triangles that plunged into a throat eager to devour any unwary wanderer. Brock teetered on the precipice between the seductive siren call of forbidden lore and the primal urge to recoil from such ominous depths. Yet, bolstered by his faith in survival and eventual salvation, a macabre fascination seized him, propelling him deeper into this accursed realm where dreamscapes bled into nightmares and where the boundaries of his immortal sanity would be tested.

With steps echoing determination, he ventured down this road before launching himself headfirst into the awaiting abyss.

**

With a rhythm as steady and reverent as a monk's heartbeat, Brock navigated the crypt, a catacomb swathed in ancient cobwebs. His aura was the sole beacon piercing through the oppressive gloom of this subterranean labyrinth. The world's scarred surface, now far above him, was replaced by an uncanny tranquility that seeped into every crevice like sacred incense wafting through a cathedral. He felt an odd kinship with this eerie calmness, his journey mirroring a devotee not ascending towards celestial heights but descending into Dante's depths.

The serpentine passageways were not hewn for human traverse but designed for entities that scoffed at gravity, their locomotion more resembling the scuttling of arachnids than the plodding gait of bipeds. The maze-like corridors unfolded into cavernous expanses, their magnitude rivaling the majesty of grand basilicas. The gaping chambers were interlinked with bridges crafted from the fossilized silk of ancient spiders

—a lasting homage to civilizations long extinct yet still resonating in the spectral elegance that persisted.

Enormous crystals, remnants of a forgotten epoch, floated over chasms so profound that even Brock's preternatural senses failed to fathom their depths. Brock paused his spider-like progression across the fragile and uncanny bridges connecting crystal to crystal, much like the long-gone inhabitants might have centuries ago. He stood captivated by the celestial harmonies emanating from these levitating mineral formations.

As he studied the crystalline structures, he was mesmerized by the ever-shifting panoramas. Each gargantuan crystal held an initial semblance of nebulous fog, which started to solidify under Brock's concentrated gaze until they mirrored portals opening onto extraterrestrial domains.

One crystal unveiled an ocean of molten silver crashing against onyx shores beneath a verdant sky streaked with ruby clouds. Silvery-leafed trees tinkled gently in an undetectable breeze while transparent creatures glided through the mercurial sea, their existence saturating the air with a metallic scent he could actually *smell* though the viewing pane.

Another crystal disclosed a towering city sculpted from obsidian mountain stone, its slender pinnacles and minarets piercing a sky dominated by everlasting volcanic thunderstorms. Lightning cavorted between towers, casting an uncanny lavender glow. The city echoed with haunting melodies in harmony with ceaseless thunder—a symphony composed of lament and lyricism.

A different crystal revealed a desert trapped in perpetual twilight under the vigilant scrutiny of two enormous moons. Alien tombs and monoliths dotted the sands, their forms eroded by relentless nocturnal winds. The shriek of a night predator echoed from above, its silhouette concealed in obscurity. The air—again somehow discernible—bore the dry scent of dust and decay, an olfactory testament to time's inexorable advance.

The vibrant, throbbing images of the shifting tableau danced before him like an extraterrestrial spectacle. The temptation of such entrancing visions might have ensnared him indefinitely were it not for his unwavering determination to reunite with his beloved comrades and his intuition that he had more to unearth in these depths.

Brock quickened across the interstellar lattice, leaving behind the chasm and its crystalline symphony.

No longer were there chambers of harmonic wonders to traverse; he found himself thrust upon a path choked with dust and strewn with desiccated remains of spider folk. These cadavers bore grisly evidence of violent dissection but didn't resemble the grotesque breed of Walker he was familiar with. They were slender, nimble beings possessing elongated humanoid visages that exuded an alien elegance. Yet their ash-like husks crumbled under even his most feather-light touch—like ancient statues left to decay after a volcanic cataclysm.

Brock's initial apprehensions began to dissolve as he considered these entities not as monstrous progeny but beings hailing from an era more pristine and luminous—before this realm capitulated to malevolence. Yet, could this domain be entirely bereft of hope? What was that spectral glow enticing him from afar, stirring within him not dread but an irresistible urgency?

The skeletal labyrinth soon yielded to another vast subterranean void greater than any preceding it. Each footstep echoed ominously off timeworn stone walls as Brock traversed a thick carpet of decaying detritus, blanketing this forsaken sanctuary. Pristine

Walkers lay scattered like casualties of some archaic plague, their untouched forms threatening to disintegrate at the merest disturbance. He tread carefully among them, drawn towards two quartz-like monoliths framing his objective: a complex array of glass threads festooned with celestial dew that hummed like an ethereal harp—a beacon of splendor amidst this necropolis.

Brock was dwarfed beneath the throbbing celestial tapestry, its grandeur challenging the earthly heavens glimpsed on moonless nights. A spectral zephyr breathed life into the web, orchestrating a haunting symphony of ethereal chimes and otherworldly harmonies. Within this alien orchestra's embrace, a radiant being birthed itself from the consuming shadows.

Despite her towering silhouette that asserted dominion like an ancient lunar goddess, Brock felt no dread in the face of this colossal arachnid specter, her corporeal shell having long succumbed to the inexorable march of oblivion. The gentle kindness radiating from her countless eyes enveloped him in a comforting cocoon of light and warmth, eyes that had witnessed realms beyond the grasp of mortality and time—mysteries forever elusive to mortal seers.

"Welcome," her wishes reverberated within his psyche; her voice a captivating cacophony of chaos and unity, an otherworldly fusion of extraterrestrial timbres and melodies. "I have waited for an eternity for thee or thine... I bear a heavy burden of knowledge to impart upon you before my impending demise."

For reasons he could not fathom, tears began to pool in Brock's eyes at the prospect of her heartrending revelation. The atmosphere thickened around him, pregnant with an overwhelming sorrowful horror as he braced himself for profound truths that threatened to shatter him.

CHAPTER 16: A LONG OVERDUE FAREWELL

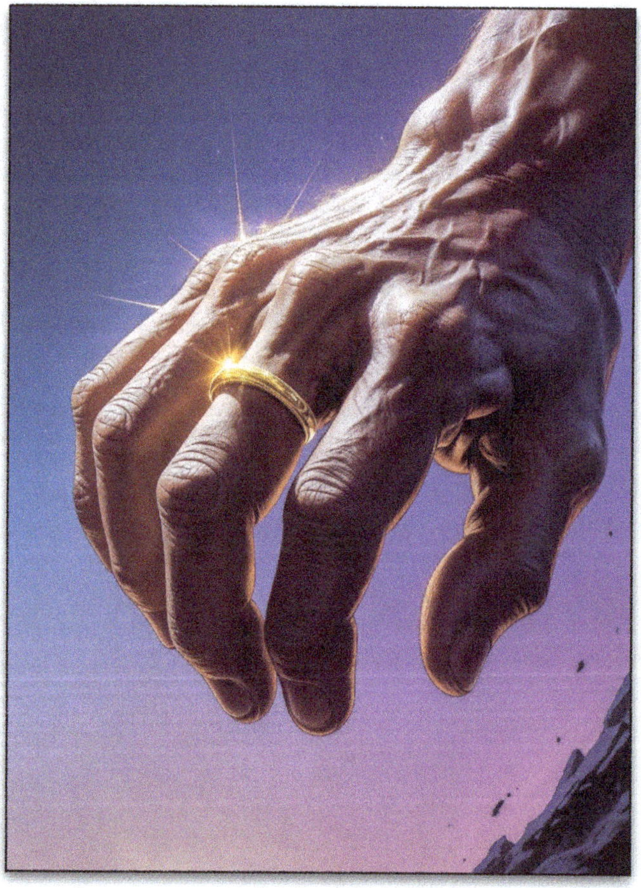

His eyes flickered towards them, hinting at a deeper understanding. "Perhaps she bestowed one among

you with that ring foreseeing this inevitable crossroad: an ending entwined with a new beginning."

A thunderous roar tore through the heavens as if the very sky was rent apart by unseen claws. Beneath this tumultuous canopy, the Green Mother lay shackled by invisible chains, a silent witness to her own desecration. The ocean raged relentlessly, its waves crashing against the muddied shore with a fury that echoed the tempest above. Whirlpools spun madly beneath the storm's wrathful gaze while ahead loomed a gaping trench—a ghastly wound carved into blood-soaked sands. It stretched toward an abyss of churning shadows, grotesque parasites feasting on decay.

Beyond this macabre scene, sprawled hills of once-gray sands now transformed into vile crimson clay, strewn with the twisted remains of primitive humans who had dared defy the abyssal tide spewed forth from the ocean's depths. Atop a blood-drenched rise lay a monstrous chrysalis—the cocoon of a bound spider goddess—wrapped in tendrils of ectoplasmic slime that pulsed and writhed like some abhorrent heart. Viscous fluids seeped from its colossal form, glistening with an unholy allure under flickering lightning.

The merfolk had dragged this cosmic relic from their celestial seas; it shimmered malevolently amidst their encirclement. Their piscine faces were inscrutable masks devoid of emotion as they guarded their prize with sinister intent. Krakens, too, had gathered—behemoths from lightless and unfathomable realms—to stand sentinel over this captive deity. Great leaders among them tugged at chains affixed to rusted harnesses encrusted with cosmic decay.

As these fetters tightened around the Lengeth's chrysalis—a fetal entity sensing its impending doom—the storm intensified overhead; lightning splintered across bruised skies in jagged arcs that briefly illuminated swirling clouds forming nightmarish visages: eyes like voids peering through tentacled beards—perhaps Cthulhu himself?—before dissolving back into chaos.

The Old Ones convened upon hearing their acolytes' call; tentacles filled every corner of the darkened firmament. Even more krakens emerged on the horizon, as a blasphemous congregation lending warbles interwoven with rubbery appendages to this dread ritual unfolding.

At the ritual site, merfolk voices crescendoed into cacophony before settling into swaying reverence: guttural chants echoing Cthulhu's incoherent entropy reverberated across desolate shores as krakens constricted ever tighter around the ensnared Lengeth—hellish chains squeezing the immense form like a sodden rag—and then came an earth-shaking roar...

In the cataclysmic surge, what remained within was pulverized, expelling radiant Celestine blood cascading beachward in a shimmering wave momentarily concealing horror beneath pearlescent splendor.

Her essence blazed with a sanctity so intense that Cthulhu's lesser minions disintegrated into nothingness, their forms consumed by her purity. Yet the krakens, those colossal architects of chaos, persisted in their unholy endeavor, twisting and reshaping her within this radiant crucible. Piece by piece, she was diminished—her once formidable presence and intellect reduced to a mere shadow. Her final remnants morphed into an eternal snare designed to imprison a most despised relic and entrap unwary heroes yet to come.

In the midst of swirling dark magic and as her body's light flickered towards extinction, the Lengeth called upon the last reserves of her defiance. With a trembling sentience, she conjured one final plea—a single tear from her melting eyes that solidified into an obsidian shard. It shot upward through the tormented skies, piercing through layers of tumultuous darkness above. This shard became a wishing star cast adrift across time and space—a beacon imbued with desperate hope meant to reappear millennia later when a destined human might seize it as a key to conquer the encroaching madness.

***

Ana's mind reeled, the vision still clawing at her consciousness like a beast refusing to retreat. She had witnessed the unraveling of the Lengeth—a colossal entity disintegrating into nothingness—and with it, a desperate plea cast into the void, shimmering and darkly crystalline like the one nestled in her possession. The revelation gnawed at her insides; it was an answer, but not the one she craved. She shuddered, unwilling to sift through its meaning just yet.

Lenny's steady and grounding voice cut through her daze. "Are you alright?" he asked, concern etched across his rugged face. He noticed her eyes flare with ethereal white light before she stiffened under the grip of her vision.

Ana blinked rapidly, forcing herself back to reality. "Yes," she murmured, though her voice wavered like a fragile thread. Her gaze swept over their surroundings—this place was a tapestry woven from threads of anguish and sorrow that seemed to whisper secrets long forgotten.

Focus! Ana chastised herself silently.

Ana's pulse thundered in her ears, a frantic rhythm that echoed the urgency of her actions as she pressed her palm onto the rigid, viridian stone surface. Her fingers splayed out, instinctively seeking the exact location where Brock had vanished, a haunting image of him being swallowed by an endless chasm seared into her mind. The stone bore no signs of struggle or damage, devoid of tangible evidence to validate her psychic terror. Her knuckles blanched under the strain as she exerted more force, calling upon every iota of her latent magic in a desperate attempt to grasp even the faintest echo of Brock's essence. But all that resonated back was the dry hiss of sand sliding over glass. A knot tightened in her throat before she conceded with a bitter admission: "I can't fucking find him."

She rose and sought solace in Malachi's embrace while Lenny stood behind them like an unspoken sentinel, his hands resting on their shoulders. Together, they glared at the pulsating entity atop the nearby hill—the crystallized arachnid god—that had ensnared and abducted their friend.

"Should I just smash it?" Lenny proposed.

Ana pondered his suggestion, again extending her psychic tendrils into the unknown. Frustratingly, they returned empty-handed again. Strengthened by rituals and centuries of blood sacrifices into an impregnable fortress, even her divine foresight felt disoriented and distorted amidst the great petrified Lengeth's aura. Cthulhu's snare was more devious than they'd anticipated. Time was slipping through their fingers to save Brock, who was being drawn deeper into some cosmic maze from which he might never return.

"No, don't touch it," Ana commanded—she still retained that much foresight.

"We can't just stand here twiddling our thumbs," Malachi objected.

Ana had no comforting words for him, but perhaps Lovecraft did? Lovecraft?

The skull she held contemplated the celestial energies and spells it sensed reverberating through the ether. After a moment, he addressed Ana with an underlying tone of regret: A portal has been opened, then sealed. The remnants of the spell linger in the air. Regrettably, the passage remains as functional as stepping onto a platform for a locomotive already at its destination. Brock has been transferred from here to elsewhere. Malachi could open a portal to follow him, but he needs to know where his friend has gone.

What if I touch it? The big mound that Brock manhandled? Can't I read it like other objects?

I need not remind you of the recklessness of such an act. This is not merely an object but a soul imprisoned in a magical vessel: a phylactery. A cursed phylactery at that, and one made to house a cosmic god's soul. You are meddling with the spirit of a tormented deity and abyssal magic beyond human ken, not interpreting tarot cards.

We don't have many options left.

Ana, caution and level-headedness—

She handed off the skull to Lenny, effectively silencing Lovecraft's warning. "I'm going to tap into the Lengeth and see if I can get a fix on Brock's location."

Lenny gripped her wrist. "You just said not to touch it."

"I'm not you," she retorted, puffing up her chest defiantly. "I'm Owl, the all-seeing Aspect of Air. I've seen civilizations rise and fall. I can find our friend. Malachi, be ready for some space-time hopscotch when I do."

Approaching the precipice, Ana was assaulted by a shrill cry emitted from the phylactery. The noise warped the surrounding air into an uncanny dance, contorting her features into a mask of discomfort. Yet, she remained undaunted by the spectral display and her physical constraints, straining to reach its elevated perch despite her petite stature, rendering such attempts futile.

Lenny and Malachi, however, were not inclined to stand idle while another friend risked oblivion. They had steeled themselves for this possibility—ready to face annihilation if it meant standing united with their companions. With Ana cradled under his muscular arm, Lenny vaulted onto the platform as Malachi materialized behind them in a plume of smoky feathers.

The phylactery's auditory assault intensified, battering Lenny's senses and disorienting Malachi. His movements became leaden as if trudging through a viscous fluid, but he persevered, his teeth clenching against the onslaught. Meanwhile, Ana maintained her momentum without faltering. She recalibrated her psychic wavelength to harmonize with the lamentation—a symphony of suffering—and, in doing so, discovered signs of sentient life within what she'd previously dismissed as an insensate creature.

The cacophony morphed into a rhythmic pulse akin to drums and thunder— utterances in some archaic dialect that felt both foreign and familiar. She perceived the entity's sorrow, a lamentation that echoed the raw pain of a mother severed from her offspring—a tormented matriarchal power contorted and morphed into something primal and shadowy—a dark mother.

Quaking with empathy rather than trepidation, she extended a hand towards the phylactery.

"Who are you?" Ana demanded—the answer already beginning to form in her intuition. As if a storm had passed, the oppressive energy dissipated around Lenny and Malachi, releasing them from its grip. They lingered behind Ana, hesitant to intrude upon her communion with the captive deity. Her ethereal, white aura commanded their awe and respect.

To her companions, the chamber was shrouded in an unsettling silence. Yet, for Ana, it was alive with the Goddess' whispers—creating a sonic maelstrom devoid of coherence or structure. She sensed its frustration at being unable to articulate thoughts—a once near-omnipotent entity reduced to muteness after eons without physical form. Once encoded into crystalline archives through harmonic chords, its celestial memories were now severed and distorted into a ceaseless binding incantation.

The nefarious acolytes of Cthulhu had carved its cosmic flesh into ivory stone crevices before infusing the surrounding rock with its verdant lifeblood. Its eyes—the black hollows scattered across the chamber—were all that remained metaphorically intact. Even in this state of sensory deprivation, it was forced to bear witness to its own dismemberment and suffering—an enduring testament to the Deep One's vengeance.

Recalling its identity proved too great a torment for such a fragmented entity to endure.

Ana refrained from bombarding with questions, choosing to connect on a deeper level—woman to Goddess. She bared her soul, revealing her own tales of violation and addiction. Faced with the divine tragedy of a being deprived of its eternal existence, she questioned if her sufferings would even create a ripple. Yet the desecration of spirit is a language universally comprehended by those who have endured profound humiliations—and it was on this melancholic symphony that they discovered shared ground.

A wave of trepidation surged through Ana as the staggering image of the entity, once confronted and now indelibly imprinted in her memory, fought its way back into her conscious mind: an immense arachnid-like creature whose magnitude defied understanding. Its form radiated with an unearthly illumination as though it had consumed the glow of myriad stars within its multiple eyes—dark spheres prominently positioned on its head and strewn across its body like chains of obsidian pearls. It towered over her, its eight slender legs sprawled out in all directions, resembling a cosmic detonation. Defying logic, it hovered on spectral threads pulsing with the same alien radiance that flickered across its abdomen. From deep within, this beast emanated this celestial brilliance—it was as if it served as a portal to the farthest corners of space—a role it indeed played.

As Ana's psychic vision acclimated to the bizarre spectacle, she discerned the shadowy contours of an ancient temple and the complex web woven between columns and stairs, unfurled wide like a cosmic blueprint, each strand glinted with destiny's iridescent echo. The extraterrestrial melody murmured enigmas from dimensions and galaxies humanity may never traverse—even should we endure long enough to journey into deep space. All such realities were held within this cosmic spinner—this scribe and bard of eternity. In that instant, Ana found herself simultaneously humbled and awestruck by its terrifying splendor as it orchestrated an ethereal symphony throughout the temple.

The past was washed away in a deluge of tears as Ana gazed at the monstrous monument, a brutal parody of the fallen deity's erstwhile majesty. "I'm sorry for what happened to you," she whispered to the Dark Mother.

As Ana unfurled her fingers, a tiny, glowing speck seized her gaze. It pirouetted on her skin before coming to rest, sending an alien thrill coursing through her veins. A minuscule arachnid—could it be a fragment of the Goddess herself? Could such a small creature comprehend her thoughts?

"Will you release my friend?" she ventured.

Her question was met with a sharp jab—an infusion of icy venom. The sensation radiated through her like a gust of winter wind—a silent but clear rejection.

"We mean no harm—we only sought that artifact."

In response, another bite ensued, this time disseminating warmth from the tips of her toes up to the apex of her skull. A surge of euphoria—an affirmation, agreement.

"So, you'll free him?"

The chilling venom was its retort.

"Is it because you don't want to?"

Once more, the cold venom coursed through her.

"Or is it because you are unable?"

A wave of warmth enveloped her again.

With this primitive method of communication established—warm for yes, cold for no—Ana withdrew from the phylactery and allowed the tiny arachnid to scuttle into the cradle of her palm. She turned back towards Lenny and presented their new conversant. Lenny's face contorted in distaste at the sight.

"That's one of those creatures that swarmed over Brock."

"It's part of the Length—like a sliver from its consciousness," Ana elucidated. "I believe it's been guiding me—" Warmth washed over her again. "It has! She has… I'm certain now! She led us here—she's been reaching out to me—all along!"

"Calm down, for God's sake!" Lenny barked as Lovecraft initiated his mental discourse. "Hold on—he's got something to share…" He thrust forward the relic; Malachi laid his hands upon it. Ana waited until the spiderling had skittered up her forearm.

Oh, what a crude mind—fixated on desire and dominance, Lovecraft lamented. Do endeavor not to leave me in his company for extended periods, dear girl.

"I can hear you, jerkoff," Lenny retorted.

Of course—you're not entirely lacking wit after all. However, your interactions with the Length entity have unveiled much. I suspected your Goddess was an adversary of the Outer Gods—they possess an extensive list of enemies. But I could never have predicted that your benefactor would be the first to defy them.

"The first?" Ana exclaimed.

Indeed. The enlightened beings of Tlanex-Tli—the Length—were the pioneering species to encounter the Outer Gods and, tragically, also the first to succumb to their corruption. Any witch embroiled in cosmic affairs is aware of them. Their progenitors lived so extensively that they were practically immortal compared to human lifespan— Elder Gods indeed. They were presumed either tainted by their Creator or annihilated in the cataclysmic war that drenched their serene planet in bloodshed. Yet it appears one survived, albeit in a grotesque form—a rebel who defied her father and nearly thwarted the Outer Gods' conquest before it even commenced.

"The Dark Mother?" Ana queried.

Her true name would contort your tongue and warp your mind—it is beyond human articulation. However, Aztec poetry somewhat mirrors their language: Quezecoptyl.

"Quezecoptyl," Ana whispered softly as the spiderling's warm bite affirmed her comprehension. "Is this the consequence of her defiance?"

Lovecraft's mental voice filled her mind, his thoughts flowing like a river. The renegade has been fragmented, cast into the interdimensional net that spirited Brock from our presence. She now exists in a state akin to paralysis: conscious but immobilized. Her actions are not her own but rather involuntary and dictated by the ritualistic chains binding her flesh. This spell vastly differs from any portal you've ever encountered, Malachi. Its reach extends beyond comprehension, and I suspect Cthulhu set this trap... His thoughts abruptly came to a standstill.

"Brock is alive," Malachi declared with unwavering certainty, "I would feel it if he wasn't."

Lovecraft didn't question him; instead, he was taken aback by the anguish radiating from Malachi and realized that their bond ran deeper than brotherhood. I'm unsure if you can bridge the distance between you despite your heart's desire.

While Malachi and Ana sought solace in each other's company, Lovecraft pondered possible solutions. He scrutinized the golden lattice-work of the chamber around them, its swirling murkiness and profound depths stretching into unseen cosmic corners. Wherever Brock had ended up, it was light-years away from Earth—farther than Acheron, where his remains had been laid to rest, separated by galaxies and epochs... But if Brock hadn't perished as the Outer Gods planned, his atoms and soul scattered into oblivion, where could he be? How did he evade such fate? Could it be that touching the Atlantean artifact caused some form of magical disruption due to his Godbeast nature? Or perhaps there was an intentional interference?

As Lovecraft delved deeper into this enigma, peeling back layers of thought like an onion, he grew increasingly perplexed by the trap's operation. Why devise a snare that flings both the thief and the treasure to an unreachable distance? If Cthulhu aimed to keep the ring forever out of Atlantean grasp, merely hurling it to another realm would have sufficed. Logically, he'd want the dangerous artifact close at hand—under watchful eyes—to bait and destroy potential Atlantean challengers. An enticing trap for his adversaries. A plan that seemed to have disastrously backfired since Brock had vanished along with the artifact. This could be intentional but not out of Cthulhu's spite...

Ana, Lovecraft proposed, ask your Dark Mother if she played any role in the ring's disappearance.

"Did you have any part in Brock being taken away with the ring?" Ana queried her spider companion, who responded with warm, venomous nips. "She says yes."

A moment of clarity seemed to wash over the enigmatic skull. Lovecraft's arcane markings shimmered with insight, and he commanded Lenny with an air of contemplation: Brute, take me for a saunter while I dissect this conundrum. Lenny grunted in response, a low rumble of acquiescence echoing through the silence as he adhered to the disembodied author's wish.

Guide me closer to the phylactery... Ah, indeed... Such labyrinthine weavings—an inevitable convergence of destiny and sorcery. Magic of this complexity isn't something that can be tampered with casually. It requires significant puissance. It's beyond any mere mortal or mythical creature's reach. However, it might be within the capabilities of a deity...Brute, accompany me back to our comrades.

As they reunited with their comrades, Lenny proffered the skull again for their collective touch. A telepathic ripple spread from Lovecraft's soul-bound relic into their minds.

If the Lengeth could not halt her own cursed enchantment from operating, she must have adapted within its boundaries! Lovecraft's thoughts reverberated inside Ana's mind like a bell tolling at midnight. She manipulated a fleeting moment of coherence and tenacity potent enough to teleport her assailant and dispatch Alexander's talisman away from her presence. She must've bided her time across eons for this impeccable synchronization of fate and opportunity, hoarding fragments of resolve within the confines of her shattered form for centuries on end.

Lovecraft's musings resonated within Ana and were conveyed to her spiderling ally, who responded with another warm nip in affirmation.

"I believe you're on to something," she said. "She intended for Brock or one of us to seize the ring, knowing we'd defy all odds to save our friend. So much faith...and patience." Her words hung heavy in the air around them.

"Okay, but how do we get him back?" Malachi asked, his voice tinged with hope and desperation.

"Call to him," said a voice.

The stranger's voice echoed with a resonance that sent a bone-chilling shudder rippling down their spines as if the spectral fingers of a winter wraith had traced an icy path along their vertebrae. They gasped, spinning around to identify the source of the ethereal sound. At the edge of the grotto, two figures materialized from the shadows like phantoms summoned from an unseen realm. Their sudden appearance and inexplicable dryness hinted at arcane forces at play.

Lenny found his gaze ensnared by a pale man in a trench coat—an entity that seemed to thrum with an unsettling power veiled within a human shell. Lenny's supernatural senses, unbound by mortal limits, perceived an aura swirling with cosmic energy, its tendrils reaching out greedily for knowledge and radiating with otherworldly wisdom they had already devoured. At its core pulsed a white-hot star so intense it seared Lenny's eyes to behold it.

The second figure catapulted Lenny into further disbelief. "Chief Longfeather? What the actual fuck?" he blurted out.

Lovecraft lacked eyes to blind and saw through to the essence of each creature—the Elder God and oldest living being in existence. Leng! He proclaimed telepathically.

Reacting swiftly, Lenny tossed Lovecraft towards Ana and positioned himself protectively before his friends, steeling himself against this formidable force. He could only pray his body would endure what was about to transpire.

"Stand down, half-breed of Shub," intoned Leng towards Lenny with age-old authority. "We bear you nor your companions any ill will. We come...to assist."

"We do," affirmed Steve stepping forward.

Steve appeared simultaneously pallid yet invigorated; his skin ashen but his muscles straining against his clothes like a seasoned athlete—not resembling the faded football star physique, leaning toward dad-bod, which Lenny remembered. A spectral power surged from the god to his follower, weaving around him like psychic threads, and Lenny knew he was ensnared.

Ana, too, caught glimpses of the terrifying shadow of the Spider God, feeling woefully ill-equipped for any confrontation. Yet, as they commenced their ascent toward the phylactery, the god and his servant radiated an unsettling aura of peace—or at least non-violence.

"Are we just going to let them waltz up there?" Malachi whispered anxiously. "What's next? High fives and a gossip session?"

"I don't sense any threat," Ana started, her voice wavering under the weight of the overwhelming power unfolding before them. "Do we want to take on Leng now when we're already down our star player and a magic ring? Seems like a shit bet." None of them disagreed.

With caution prickling their skin, they watched as Leng and Steve defied gravity with spider-like agility, scaling sheer walls in mere moments before rushing past them in a gust of icy wind towards the phylactery. They observed as Leng and Steve touched the coral heart, exchanging glances loaded with unspoken communication—clear signs of telepathy at work. The autonomy displayed by Steve painted him not as a slave but as an apprentice—a god and his chosen creature.

Their exploration of the scene culminated in a shared, unnerving moment of realization. They turned simultaneously to confront their audience as if bound by some unseen tether. Halting at a distance that suggested negotiation rather than confrontation, Leng gathered his thoughts.

Bathed in the ethereal light that danced behind the Spider God and shrouded by ominous darkness, Malachi was seized by a cold recognition gnawing at his consciousness since Leng's emergence. "Holy shit," he exclaimed, "You're the entity from the motel! You tried to kill Brock and me with your spider demon things."

Leng's voice echoed with icy indifference. "We never sought your demise, only your capture. My previous master was adamant about taking you alive. If not for his persistent and deplorable manipulation, I may have given in to my savage urges, and our encounter would be drenched in bloodshed and rage. It seems you managed to evade his rogue troops, too. You're rather slippery, Malachi Linklater."

Confusion furrowed Malachi's brow. "Rogue troops—" Could the enigmatic god be hinting at his and Brock's perilous clash at the scrapyard? "Your employer—"

"Former," the Spider God interjected, his voice reverberating ominously. "No mortal holds sway over me."

"—Is Cal's father?" Malachi stammered in shock.

An undulating shift passed over Leng's visage as if invisible threads were being woven, unveiling realities once concealed. "Ah... I comprehend now. Gabriel forever meddling where he is unwelcome. But we are not here to dissect previous altercations."

The desperation etched into Malachi's striking features was tangible. "I couldn't care less about that right now, either. Where's Brock?"

"In a realm far, far beyond your grasp...The farthest world in the farthest universe..." Leng's voice echoed with melancholy. His expansive eyes—both visible and countless hidden ones—absorbed the horrific remnants of his progeny twisted into this grotesque snare. He observed her verdant lifeblood staining the stone platforms; her once vibrant eyes now hollowed into coral-like cavities and the supports constructed from her bleached skeletal remains.

Finally, as if dust had been blown off his clouded memory, Leng acknowledged who she was and what loss he had endured.

"My dearest..." he muttered.

His first creation and most treasured offspring—a sigh slipped from him unbidden: If only the bloody road of his failures could find its conclusion here, with her who had sought to steer him from this calamitous path. The anguish of innumerable eons surged within him in a single, gut-wrenching upheaval.

The God's countenance, as impassive and enigmatic as a stone idol, was assailed by the storm of emotions churning beneath. His agony reverberated in the fragmented flashes of pain that flooded into Ana's psychic realm—flickering glimpses of an interstellar conflict that threatened to submerge her extrasensory abilities.

Ana bore witness to a surreal scene in the grand amphitheater of her psyche: monstrous arachnids, their chitinous bodies an unsettling shade of blueberry, blemished with festering wounds and studded with ossified growths. These behemoths wriggled in the desolate landscape like stranded whales from an alien beach. Below these horrors swarmed a frantic horde of lesser creatures—the Walkers—grotesque caricatures of life that clambered over one another in their frenzied attempts to suppress the heavenly legions positioned against them on the mutable sands.

These otherworldly beings possessed a chilling allure—a blend of spider and centaur—contradicting their horrifying visage. They stood firm amidst the stifling darkness that smothered the sands, protectors of what remained of once majestic cities whose towers now lay in ruin and decay at a distance. Their civilization teetered on the precipice, with much already irretrievably lost. Yet within this brave front stood Quezecoptyl and her ilk, unyielding against her father's sinister assault.

An abrupt gust stirred—a malicious wind shrieking with sand—that swept away this spectacle, carrying Ana into another historical glimpse, this time further down the timeline. The battlefield she had previously observed was now desolate and aged; its conquerors and conquered alike were reduced to empty shells morphed into doomed memorials reaching towards an uncaring sky—or perhaps towards the god who had abandoned them after devouring their world with his unquenchable craving.

Ana teetered between empathy and revulsion, conflicted about whether to sympathize with or despise this monstrous deity. Her new understanding painted a multifaceted image—one not readily categorized by simplistic concepts of good and evil.

While Ana was submerged in an ocean of psychic inundation, Leng was cast adrift in the murkiness of his history, drawn back to the phylactery. His digits grazed its shiny exterior with a tenderness alien to his vile nature. How had he allowed himself to become so warped that he'd neglected his own kin? But curse it, that's precisely what he'd done.

The last report on her was that she had fortified herself in her sanctuary. Yet even in a desolate, forsaken world, she wasn't secure. Another agent of the Lords of Chaos had targeted her innocence, seeking to pervert it into some detestable magic. And like everything else, she too succumbed to the influence of those cosmic terrors from beyond reality. Had she attempted to alert him when Cthulhu's minions came for her? Somewhere in the cloudy depths of his memory, he recalled a faint plea echoing through the immense cosmic void. But he'd disregarded it as a trivial disturbance while feasting on another planet like a perverse imitation of Shub-Niggurath.

"Quezecoptyl..." He murmured, bowing his head in disgrace. The burden of their mutual transformation was an unforgivable transgression that hung heavily around his neck. Still, one final act of mercy remained within his power—one last opportunity to liberate his daughter and the missing Aspect.

Leng stood before Ana and her compatriots, his face shifting into a mask of determination. "I hold the key to unravel this hex," he began, each word falling from his lips like stones cast into an abyss, their echoes reverberating through unseen dimensions. "By releasing the tormented entity whose lifeblood and spirit have been woven into this curse."

His gaze turned distant as if peering through the veils of time and space. "When she breathes her last, a fracture will form in the fabric of existence—a mere blink in eternity —where multiple realities will rupture at once. In that cosmic upheaval, our world will be laid bare to your ally. With the power of the Atlantean relic, he might break free from his chains." His eyes flickered towards them, hinting at a deeper understanding. "Perhaps she bestowed one among you with that ring foreseeing this inevitable crossroad: an ending entwined with a new beginning."

The silence thickened around them like a shroud before Leng resumed his narrative. His voice softened, and regret seeped into every syllable: "In my blind quest for celestial knowledge, I overlooked her wisdom—the one who was not only wise but kindest-hearted amongst us all." A sigh escaped him, heavy with remorse and longing. "My cherished daughter," he admitted.

The revelation that the deity had a personal stake in their mission offered Ana, Malachi, and Lenny hope. They might have been too trusting, especially considering Leng's caveat to his proposal. "Before we embark on this treacherous journey," he stated gravely. "I demand an oath from each of you."

"What sort of oath?" Ana queried.

"A pact ensuring mutual non-violence. I promise not to inflict harm upon you and expect reciprocation. If I aid you in this matter, I'll be marked as much of a heretic by the Outer Gods as you are—seen as their adversary and pursued by their underlings. I merely desire assurance that I won't be cast aside like detritus once my utility has run its course."

"So... you're proposing we join forces?" Malachi sought clarification.

"Precisely."

"Fine by me," he responded impulsively. "We're allies now. Let's get Brock back."

"Verbal affirmations alone will not solidify such a pact," Leng warned sternly. "Only a promise sealed in blood will do. Yours, not mine—I dread the potential repercussions if our essences were to mingle."

Entering into an agreement with a cosmic Deity known for deception and trickery is exceedingly ill-advised, Lovecraft communicated to Ana telepathically.

Yet, before Ana could fully process her feelings about this arrangement, Malachi was already slicing into his palm with his pocketknife. "Hands out," he instructed.

They extended their hands with noticeable reluctance and sluggishness, which Malachi promptly cut open. He then swiftly pressed their hands together in an eerie handshake—Lenny's hand dwarfing his and Ana's as if it were a python swallowing its prey whole.

Their divine blood merged in an unholy alliance.

"We pledge," Malachi declared.

"We pledge," the other two echoed, albeit after a moment's hesitation.

A deafening roar echoed from outside, causing the chamber to shudder and shake so violently that dust rained down from every corner. Once the minor seismic disturbance had passed, Leng nodded, satisfied with their bloody oath. "It is decreed. We are bound by this vow not to shed each other's blood until this battle between primordial and nascent gods concludes."

A loophole of cunning brilliance, Lovecraft mused, his thoughts seeping into the minds of those present. He turned his attention to the potent ripple of magic that had just pulsed through Earth's very marrow, leaving both solid ground and celestial canopy trembling in its aftermath. Your transformation from fledgling Aspects to fully awakened conduits is now complete, he projected with an air of finality.

"The hour is upon us," Leng declared, his voice a shuddering echo in the chamber. "You three must reach out to your fourth companion. Recall every shared moment; weave a lifeline from your collective memories and spirits and cast it into the abyss I will create."

With a solemnity that weighed heavy in the air, Leng and his attendant approached the phylactery, their palms making contact with its cool surface. Their voices intertwined in an otherworldly symphony of incantations, uttering a language born from cosmic wombs.

The Godbeasts watched on in silent anticipation as a hush fell over them like a shroud. Hearts pounded against ribcages as they waited for that first sign to disrupt the electrifying stillness.

Suddenly, an ethereal gale tore through the chamber, forcing the Godbeasts to seek shelter amongst their strongest kin. The once tranquil pool below roiled under its force while fragments of coral broke away from the domed ceiling above, spiraling toward an expanding void of darkness.

Amidst this chaos stood Lenny—unyielding like an ancient oak weathering a storm. His muscular arms wrapped protectively around his companions while ink-black roots sprouted from his feet, anchoring them to their disintegrating sanctuary.

A pulsating hum filled their ears—the sound of Leng's divine helix gate between time and space—causing their haven to tremble ominously. As rocks and torrents of water were sucked into oblivion, they found themselves adrift in a void of endless blackness.

In the distance, a luminescent cocoon pulsated—no longer a phylactery but a chrysalis nurturing some nascent entity within. Was this some fragment of Quezecoptyl? What had become of the God himself—or Steve?

An enigmatic silhouette emerged from behind the glowing chrysalis in response to their unvoiced questions. Its dimensions were unfathomable, and its curves arched in ways that defied understanding. Spheres tinged with a faint crimson hue materialized like dying suns shrouded by dark nebulae.

Their sanity teetered on the edge as they experienced a silken whisper: countless rustling hairs or antennae orchestrating a skin-prickling symphony. Amidst this crescendo of insanity, the chrysalis's light bloomed, revealing Leng's grotesque multitude.

Leng, the Spider God, was an awe-inspiring embodiment of vastness and strength. His countless eyes bore into every corner of existence, and his myriad mouths devoured all matter indiscriminately. His body and limbs, gargantuan as twin rocky worlds, were swathed in cosmic stone. No secret could escape Leng's penetrating gaze, and no material could withstand the relentless grinding of his mountain-crushing mandibles.

His multitudinous legs navigated the hyperspatial webs stretched between galaxies with ease. Now, they frantically enveloped the chrysalis in a shroud of glowing silk. The observers felt dwarfed by this celestial titan but managed to swallow their screams as Leng expanded—radiant and overpowering like a supernova.

Within Lenny's protective sphere, however, they found sanctuary. They realized that much of their dread was born from their human instincts rather than their transformed selves. Their panic ebbed away, replaced by an eerie tranquillity as they observed the God contorting and tearing at himself.

Fleeting images from other realities flickered along the vortex—visions flickering so fast only Lenny was privy to them. He saw realms drenched in lurid technicolor or barren wastelands, dominions of pure luminescence or dense shadow, neon orange gas clouds, or tumultuous lightning storms. These cosmic glimpses revealed a litany of realms visited and subdued by Lengeth.

Awe flooded Lenny amidst this phantasmagoric spectacle—torn between the grandeur of the God and his radiant loom—the phylactery.

Then came a dissonance: Crack! Rip! Hiss!

The cosmic fabric tore open. A blinding scarlet glare assaulted their senses before fading to reveal a throbbing crimson rift cutting through space between them and Leng with his dazzling talisman. Beyond this jagged tear lay an alien world painted in shades of rust—harshly ridged, crowned with spiraling stone talons and pockets of dust and sand.

Their perspective seemed to be manipulated by a zig-zagging spiritual drone—a mode of remote viewing that Ana recognized well. But it was through the Spider God's consciousness that they soared across this desolate expanse, over a lifeless plain marked by black fissures, through a looming city of gothic spires draped in webs, before plunging into an abyss as profound as the path to Hell itself.

There, in this utter void, shone the golden torch they sought. Leng's awareness was drawn towards it, unveiling an underground temple scene. Suspended within a star-studded web was a gibbering mass, an entity eerily reminiscent of Leng's overwhelming presence—an enormous spider—eight legs, thorax, and bulbous body gleaming with ethereal light.

Ana realized that Quezecoptyl appeared untouched by her father's corruption. She looked immaculate and untarnished; her form represented the innocent incarnation of her species before their subjugation by the insatiable appetites of the Outer Gods. Radiating benevolence and grace, she lowered her frenzied bulk towards their kneeling companion, creating an image like a man praying beneath a falling comet.

As Ana peered into the pulsating gateway, she perceived an uncanny symphony akin to a Tibetan gong resonating with deliberate rhythm. It was the unfiltered voice of the Dark Mother, echoing from her purgatorial abode. Yet, what cryptic message was she transmitting to Brock? The words seemed to bypass Ana's psychic bandwidth—intended only for Brock's reception.

Brock! Malachi's voice rang out as soon as they spotted him. The diminutive glowing figure cast his gaze towards the spectral apparition of the Lengeth, then around in confusion, unable to pinpoint the echo's origin. Brock, we're here! Follow the sound of my voice! Come back to me, please!

The gargantuan spider pulled on its silken threads once more; her colossal head eclipsed Brock as if poised to consume him while issuing a final decree to her acolyte. Having imparted her wisdom, Quezecoptyl the Wise receded into the towering pillars encased in cobwebs and gradually dissolved into a distant foggy silhouette within her web —fading until she became nothing more than a memory. With her vanishing act, so too did the light abate.

Brock staggered in pitch-black darkness like a man lost in liquor's grip. He was drawn towards Malachi's distinctive voice, which had once lured him across America—the emotional undertones serving as his guiding thread through this labyrinth of shadows.

Ana and others joined Malachi in their psychic outcry, and Brock moved closer to their portal. Their voices echoed repeatedly, both audibly and telepathically; guided by their spectral presence ahead, Brock navigated with growing certainty through this Stygian abyss. He reached out into the quivering air and felt resistance before forcing himself through this ectoplasmic barrier like an infernal offspring being birthed anew. A scream ripped from his lips as he crossed infinite realities that threatened to unravel his very existence.

Burn for him, Aspect of Fire! commanded the Spider God. Malachi transformed into a dazzling beacon for his friend while the Spider God wove with increased fervor, morphing into a pulsating energy mass. As their magics intertwined, the phylactery spiraled into a spindle of starlight—the cosmic loom spinning at unfathomable speeds tore Lenny's mystic shell apart.

A cacophony of alien tongues and melodies reverberated through the air, distorting their perceptions and stretching their sanity to its limits. Yet they clung to hope and Malachi's radiant form as Lenny's protective magic disintegrated. They leaped through the luminous haze into an erased reality, clutching at anything—a memory, a desire, even what seemed like a hand—which they pulled towards themselves as the great spider's loom crumbled into mystical ruins.

They returned to Earth from this unknown realm with an energy implosion that ripped through the landscape. Reality convulsed, marred by the heresy of this rupture.

As the dust from their celestial skirmish settled, four Godbeasts and a grinning skull found themselves strewn across barren earth—bruised and battered. They shared an incredulous laugh, stunned that they had lived through yet another supernatural ordeal. Their minds whirled in vertiginous circles as they attempted to comprehend the journey they had just endured.

In the aftermath of destruction, the stronger among them extended their hands to lift up those who were weaker. Their eyes scanned the devastated beach; what once were towering white cliffs had been pulverized into dust. The remnants of a shattered spell spiraled upwards around them like shards from a crystalline mirror, its jagged edges smoldering with residual energies. It was as if they were peering through a shattered window into an unfamiliar realm.

Soon enough, the lingering energy faded into pinpricks of starlight that melded with the cosmic tapestry above, leaving the beach in an eerie serenity. Even the malevolent tide of Cthulhu seemed to have withdrawn, its shadow banished from this place—for now.

Behind them, however, an unnerving aura hung heavy—a potent blend of forbidden knowledge and unrestrained power. Their gaze shifted toward Leng and his Godbeast huddled over something in the sand. Steve rose from his master's side and gestured for silence as they approached. Heeding his silent plea, they stopped in their tracks, allowing Leng some solitude with what appeared to be a gelatinous embryo lying on the sand— pale as a jellyfish—it was all that remained of Quezecoptyl, the Dark Mother and unsung hero in this war.

They bowed their heads in solemn silence out of respect for Quezecoptyl's wake. Moments later, they observed as Leng's child's light dimmed until it fizzled out entirely on the beach, leaving only a charred stain behind. After countless eons of suffering, she was finally at peace. A pang of melancholy seized Ana, her hand instinctively clutching at her chest. The peculiar sensation of grieving for a parent who was never truly hers gnawed at her heartstrings—a farewell left unsaid, a closure unattained that stung more than she had ever anticipated. Leng, his eyes abyssal pools engulfed by dilated pupils mirroring the flicker of Ana's torment, ascended from his watchful stance, dusting off unseen remnants. "Where to next, comrades?" he asked.

The word felt alien on their tongues, but Brock nodded in understanding. "Thanks," he said simply, extending a hand towards Leng.

Leng accepted it with an intrigued expression but was taken aback by the strength of Brock's grip. The hum of the Atlantean relic's power that vibrated up his arm was even more alarming. I see that the relic has chosen its new master, he thought silently.

Brock released their handshake. "Quezecoptyl thanks you too," he added, "For freeing her."

"You spoke with her," Leng stated—with his many eyes, he'd seen them whispering through the portal.

"I did," confirmed Brock.

"And what did she tell you?"

"She was grateful you released her," replied Brock. "And she said you have a chance to right an impossible wrong." Something further—a secret—burned behind the young Godbeast's eyes, though Leng did not press the matter. As Leng pondered the young man's words, Brock moved back to his friends and wrapped his arms around Malachi from behind, gently swaying with him to the rhythm of the ocean waves crashing onto the shore. Ana and Lenny seemed content doing the same. Words were unnecessary; they communicated through silent waves of emotion instead.

"A helicopter approaches," Leng announced, shattering their tranquillity.

Brock and Lenny heard it, too, looking up to see a silver speck moving across an orange sky.

"Military?" wondered Lenny aloud.

The Godbeasts and God stiffened as they focused their perceptions on the approaching chopper. Brock first noticed the large M decal on its side—a symbol he recognized from a sword they had seized from a super soldier not long ago.

"Mann Inc.," said Malachi as the chopper swept nearer. "I remember now; that's the Mothmann's business empire logo. They ran most of Innsmont until they closed shop and went stateside."

"And the company of the witch who summoned me to capture you," Leng chuckled. "What a tangled web you weave, Gabriel."

CHAPTER 17: EVERMORE

*"What do you think, my little dove?" She turned,
blowing a wayward curl from her face in an almost
comical puff.*

The chopper, a sleek creature of the night birthed by Mann Inc., cut through the dawn's fiery gaze, traversing the vibrant tapestry of America. It devoured miles with an insatiable hunger, offering tantalizing glimpses of the world below while its pilot danced with ethereal cloud formations. In this heavenly silence, a momentary sanctuary was found.

Settling into plush leather seats that cradled their forms, Brock and Malachi savored this fleeting tranquility. The heavily armored guards in faceless helmets across from them did nothing to disturb their peace; after all, Brock held within him the power to reduce them to ash in an instant if he so wished. His latent energy hummed around him like a tempestuous blaze, sending tremors through even these hardened warriors. He marveled at how these once intimidating figures now seemed as insignificant as wooden puppets before his might.

A low growl from Brock was enough to send any wandering gazes scurrying back down to their boots. The spectral form of the Spider God and his Godbeast flanking the guards added another layer of unease.

Though decency had prompted the soldiers to offer Brock a blanket for cover, he sat unabashedly primal in his charred diaper—miraculously having survived intergalactic travel—and instead offered Ana its warmth. She accepted it gratefully and soon succumbed to sleep as quiet as a whispering breeze, nestled comfortably within Lenny's arms in her last cat-themed sweater.

One small miracle: blowing up our ride back in Arkminister means she's outta those godawful ugly sweaters, Malachi mused, his voice dancing through Brock's thoughts like notes on sheet music.

Brock responded with a grin that softened his rugged features. We have everything we need right here.

Except for pants for you.

You sure?

Knock it off. Malachi's laughter echoed in their shared mental space, a warm ripple of amusement.

Brock's teasing had struck a chord; they had lost all their belongings in the fire, but none would be mourned. Ideally, Mary's grimoire was now nothing more than smoldering ashes.

Your loathing for Cthugha's priestess is as radiant as a supernova, Lovecraft's telepathic voice resonated from Malachi's lap where the skull rested. With Ana asleep, Malachi had offered to bear the burden of the skull—she deserved some respite from her numerous trials. He glanced down at the grinning relic.

What will happen to that witch without her magic book? he asked.

She will unravel. Are you familiar with the old Pagan maxim 'an it harm none, do what you will'?

Kinda, Malachi replied.

As Lovecraft's tone transitioned into a scholarly cadence, typical whenever he found himself enlightening the unlearned, he elucidated: It embodies an underlying verity; magical cycles bolster and perpetuate themselves, engendering adverse and favorable feedback spirals. Any disturbance to these cycles liberates their accumulated potency. Consequently, Mary will experience her wickedness amplified tenfold, not merely threefold—an erroneous computation by witches lacking comprehension of numerical magic theory. Mary's downfall will be agonizingly severe.

Good. Malachi grinned. Wish I could see it.

You don't mean that, Brock interjected, his words weaving through their shared consciousness.

I do.

Brock felt their emotions shifting like tectonic plates, his pride teetering on the edge of hubris while Malachi's compassion mutated into vengeful rationality. These were divine temperaments—Lovecraft had forewarned them of this transformation. Fearful they were losing their humanity amidst this cosmic chaos, Brock tightened his grip on Malachi's hand.

The heavens tore asunder, an ethereal veil parting to permit the helicopter's journey through a radiant, cloud-laden void. The bulk of their day was consumed in this lustrous limbo until twilight shades of deep purple seeped in, and the tumult escalated into a ceaseless roar—how much of America's vast expanse had they traversed, Brock pondered?

Roused from slumber by the cabin's tremors, Ana's eyes blinked awake. She gently removed Lovecraft's personage from Malachi and nestled deeper into Lenny, their combined gaze tracing the transient shapes within the clouds. Lenny felt the subtle stirrings of another silent exchange between Ana and Lovecraft. Their mental murmurs washed over him like indistinct chatter from a bustling café—each conversation an isolated island in a sea of sound. He could have intruded upon their private discourse but refrained out of respect.

Their recent escapades had ignited any remnants of dormant divinity within them, weaving each individual into a complex tapestry of psycho-supernatural connections. The ease with which they navigated these mental pathways was one of the astonishing aspects of their newfound powers. They moved effortlessly between minds—Brock and Malachi often retreated into secluded corners for confidential discussions, while Ana did the same with Lovecraft.

Yet they were equally adept at shaping thoughts into telepathic messages as fluidly as spoken words—a skill that made traditional verbal communication seem clumsy by comparison. While Lenny had not flexed this psychic muscle and tongue, he had no doubt he could if he tried and practiced the art.

As they descended through the cloud cover, Ana's attention remained riveted on the heavens until it was captured by South Dakota's lush landscape—the elevated plateau, intricate fencing, metallic watchtowers, and a cluster of stone structures that suggested some form of power center for this miniature realm.

She also noticed iridescent waves of magic washing over the landscape—an additional layer of enchantment—and promptly alerted her companions.

"Guys! There's some freaky spellwork going on down there," she announced.

A formidable barrier indeed, potent enough to repel even ancient magic, Lovecraft conveyed telepathically.

"So...are we safe from those Outer God creeps here?" Lenny asked cautiously.

"Safe?" Ana echoed, a hint of skepticism in her voice. "Maybe...I don't sense any immediate danger. It would be nice to catch a breather for once...But let's not blindly trust these Mothmanns or Cal—even if he is one of us." She was indifferent to the prospect of the surrounding soldiers reporting her skepticism to their lord—she desired this Mothmann individual to be vigilant and display his most exemplary conduct.

"Agreed," Lenny responded, squeezing Ana until she giggled. "He's not part of our crew yet. We're like a family now...minus the weird sex stuff, obviously."

Brock chuckled as their helicopter dove down, penetrating the spectral dome that encapsulated Evermore's territory—from the castle to the quaint village nestled under its protective shield—akin to the interior of a snow globe.

As they breached the ward's magic, a brief shiver of unease passed through them—no more harmful than an unexpected static shock from carpet friction. Ana felt a deeper layer to the enchantment, as though it wasn't merely granting her access, but rather an unseen being was evaluating her suitability for admittance into this realm. However, the sensation of being under examination faded, and despite her inherent caution, Ana longed for a brief sanctuary—a fleeting reprieve amid chaos.

Considering the relentless ticking of their apocalyptic countdown and Cthulhu's heightened awareness of their existence, this reprieve could be one of their last moments of tranquility on Earth.

***

The quaint spectacle of the town evaporated into oblivion as their helicopter alighted on the lush periphery of the imposing estate. Eager to escape the confined fuselage, the super soldiers sprang down the steel steps, yearning for a buffer between them and the monstrous Godbeasts. Yet, their attention should have been tethered to the spider-like entities shadowing them, cryptic and relentless as their own silhouettes.

As Brock and his allies exited the helicopter, he intercepted fragments of a conversation from a super soldier communicating through his helmet's comm system. The soldier raised a gloved hand in caution as they neared. "Hold up," he commanded. "Mr. Mothmann will be joining us shortly."

The ruler of this domain himself, echoed Lovecraft's mental voice within Ana.

The pristine gardens were an epitome of regal ownership; it was only apt that a monarch would tread these grounds. They found themselves amidst an impeccably groomed lawn stretching towards distant hedges where topiary beasts lurked. Mythical dragons and unicorns reared their heads amidst labyrinthine trails, echoing gargoyles and angels adorning spires of an eerie mansion—simultaneously magical yet menacing, incongruous in both era and location.

Was this manor plucked from medieval England or primordial Transylvania? Rococo elements—columns and cherubs—clashed with towers adorned with demonic wings. Ana was no expert in architectural design, but even her untrained eye struggled to categorize this somber structure into any distinct period or stylistic genre.

Perhaps each patriarch of the Mothmann lineage had etched their unique embellishments onto this edifice over centuries. All she could ascertain was that colossal windows shrouded by dark drapes leading into shadow-laden corridors hinted at antiquity, danger, and a melancholic history. The construction of such a mammoth structure—a four-story main block flanked by two wings, each rivaling a museum in size —must've demanded lifetimes and an inconceivable fortune.

The mere thought of the astronomical cost of this property was as intimidating as the property itself. Certainly, its occupant—and his predecessors—was a formidable witch, capable of warping reality with his magic and extracting unfathomable wealth from it.

The gardens were circumscribed by trees and menacing watchtowers, with towering wire fences woven between them. A steep drop loomed behind the grand mansion. This place was nothing short of a fortress, with entry or exit posing formidable challenges. As she wondered if they had inadvertently walked into a trap, dusk draped the landscape in ominous, elongated shadows. The manor took on an ethereal quality, reminding her that the Mothmanns had performed sacrilegious rites to birth this macabre sanctuary.

"There's Snake," Brock announced abruptly. "Or Cal...whatever his name is."

As daylight waned, Brock squinted into the encroaching twilight, his gaze lured by a metallic glint that erupted from the shadowy veil of meticulously groomed hedges. A golf cart, its surface polished to mirror-like perfection, sped across the verdant expanse towards them. It bore two passengers: Cal and a man whose age was betrayed only by his distinguished attire.

From this distance, Mr. Mothmann's grin shone like a beacon in fog; he waved with an air of effortless superiority. Brock likened him to a predator—eyes like shards of ice hinting at lethal talons and fangs concealed beneath a veneer of civility.

The cart lurched to a stop, flinging its passengers onto the dew-drenched grass. Cal remained by the vehicle, his striking good looks marred by a dark cloud of introspection that kept him distant. Gabriel Mothmann emerged from the shadows to greet them, his smile as dazzling as it was fixed on his rugged face; his beard glinted as if slick with oil, and his muscular physique defied any suggestion of age creeping upon him. He was an embodiment of perfection: from his carefully coiffed hair down to the designer suit hugging his form—vibrant and spotless.

Yet beneath the sharp tang of lemongrass that clung to him like an unseen cloak, Brock caught another scent—raw magic—and noticed a peculiar quality about Mr. Mothmann's appearance: a shimmering electrical vibration, as though he existed in multiple realities at once, not entirely anchored in their shared world. This enigma was more than just human; he was a technological marvel pulsating with mystical power—a hybrid entity humming with technomagical energy.

Brock glimpsed what seemed like minuscule wires embedded within Mr. Mothmann's eyes as their gazes locked in a silent confrontation. After an agonizing pause, Gabriel extended a hand towards Brock.

"You must be Brock," he declared in a voice reminiscent of late-night radio hosts—deep and brimming with masculinity.

"And you're the prick who tried to kill me," Brock retorted without missing a beat.

Gabriel retracted his hand and folded his arms across his chest. "Are we truly engaging in this now? Exhuming our past transgressions?"

"I believe we need to lay down some ground rules," Leng interjected smoothly, slithering away from the group of super soldiers he had been observing. He joined Steve and the Godbeasts.

"Ah, the Spider God," Gabriel acknowledged. "Finally answering the summons, are you? I was beginning to think you'd lost your musical ear."

"That melody..." Leng's voice trailed off, his mind ensnared by the haunting tune that accompanied their phone calls—the melancholic dirge of Tlanex-Tli that stirred memories of his past life. "How did you—"

"All will be revealed when time allows," interrupted Gabriel, a flicker of amusement crossing his features. "But let us continue this discussion within safer confines. We risk drawing unwanted attention out here. The Outer Gods' gaze reaches even this far, despite my technomagic's defiance."

Even for a deity renowned for subterfuge and manipulation, Leng found Gabriel's audacity unsettling. His next statement teetered on the brink of absurdity.

"So," said Gabriel with an air of casual ease, "shall we retire indoors for a drink and plot our strategy to banish Cthulhu from Earth, once and for all?"

***

With a grudging acceptance of her plight, Mary persisted through the barren landscape as the sun blinked on the horizon. The dirt that clung stubbornly to her like a shroud and the sweat that stung her eyes were relentless reminders of her human fragility. Ahead, the two men navigated the dimly-lit terrain with an ease that seemed almost mocking in contrast to her own struggles; they traversed the dunes with the nimbleness of desert beetles while she trailed after them, as graceless and breathless as an asthmatic goat.

Stripped of her grimoire, she felt like a candle snuffed out—a mere mortal woman bereft of magic. Each rattling breath was a harsh echo in her lungs, each step a cruel testament to vitality robbed by time's relentless march. A cynical thought crossed her mind—would these men even attempt resuscitation if she should suddenly collapse, or would they simply scatter ash over her lifeless form? The bitter truth was that these men were not friends but allies born from necessity. Charles was practically unknown territory and Marrow... Marrow was an unexploded mine waiting for any slight footstep nearby to detonate.

The presence of her grimoire nagged at the periphery of her consciousness from somewhere ahead—a persistent reminder akin to the love she once held for Grace, who must be aware of Cynthia's plight by now—rendering their marriage nothing more than ashes, too.

Charles' voice pierced through her musings, his gaze fixed on an iridescent shard lodged in the hood of an abandoned car half-buried in obsidian sand. As Mary drew closer, she noticed similar fragments scattered around them as though some colossal pearl had shattered upon impact.

"Keep moving," Marrow's condescending command echoed from further ahead, where he stood atop a rise surveying their desolate surroundings. "It's just another fallen demigod. Won't be our last sight of such."

A chill slithered down Mary's spine at the mention of a dead demigod. She quickened her pace, struggling to keep up with Charles, whose vitality seemed untouched by the passage of time. She mused on what enchantment or curse kept him so youthful and agile, especially when she had never seen him wield any significant magic, unlike Marrow, who tossed it around like confetti at a parade.

Charles was considerate enough to wait for her at the valley's edge where Marrow had vanished. The sight greeting them was one of absolute devastation—waves of contorted cars and sand dunes littered with pearl fragments, rivers of ectoplasmic sludge flowing through skeletal remains of buildings. A cloud of dust loomed ominously over the epicenter while rings of force radiated outwards from it.

"Blimey," Charles muttered under his breath.

"What caused all this?" Mary asked, her voice barely louder than a whisper.

"The Aspects," came his terse reply.

They resumed their journey along the valley's edge amidst dunes and rubble. Marrow was too far ahead to reach without magic or running—neither of which Mary could manage at the moment. Charles stayed by her side, even aiding her when she stumbled on an incline and nearly skewered herself on a rusted metal joist. He moved with such speed that he seemed to vanish in a puff of smoke only to reappear behind her just in time to pull her away from certain death. Afterward, he hooked his arm around hers.

Perhaps Mary had misjudged Charles after all.

"Thanks," Mary grumbled.

"As Marrow suggested, we have a mission to fulfill." Charles released her, his gaze lingering on her retreating form.

They were not allies in the traditional sense, but disciples caught up in an intricate plot to overthrow extraterrestrial Gods who had corrupted reality itself. Her perspective was distorted by this daunting task. She was devoid of companionship, devoid of affection. She'd forsaken all for...for what? The reasoning behind her betrayals and manipulation seemed as elusive as a mirage in the desert heat. In a sun-induced stupor, she moved forward like a puppet on unseen strings, her mind trapped within a horrifying loop of past misdeeds. The pulsing rhythm of her grimoire began to resonate with her heartbeat, its magnetic pull providing more comfort than the relentless sun overhead. This was the harsh truth of her existence; once engulfed by Cthugha's inferno, now she yearned for yearning's sake—a hollow vessel guided by the Golden One's command.

In this hallucinatory state, snippets of masculine dialogue reached her ears. A crimson twilight cast an uncanny luminescence over the nondescript mound towards which Marrow and some internal compass had directed them. Yet beneath these sands pulsed another life force—her grimoire. With desperation reminiscent of a starved ghoul, she lunged for it, raking through the sand with manic intensity while those who were not friends watched from afar.

Marrow sported an unsettling grin as she struggled in vain while Charles's countenance darkened at the sight of bloodied hands digging deeper into a mound strewn with shards of metal and glass.

Despite possessing powers that could alleviate her struggle, neither witch intervened until it became painfully clear that waiting for Mary to unearth her grimoire would be futile. With an incantation that warped reality, Marrow conjured a ghostly wind blade that shattered upon the mound, sending a spray of sand into their faces and knocking Charles and Mary flat. Amidst the debris lay a dusty brown tome. Mary scrambled onto all fours and began her pitiful crawl towards it.

Marrow's laughter echoed eerily around them.

"You're truly despicable," Charles growled, swiftly regaining his footing beside the cackling madman.

"The apocalypse is nigh, my friend. We might as well indulge in some amusement," Marrow responded, his voice laced with sardonic mirth. "Just a bit further, old sport! You've got this!" He leaned closer to Charles, his words a hushed whisper meant only for him. "It's truly fascinating—and grotesque—how far humans will go in their relentless pursuit of power."

An odd suggestion. Was he not human himself? This provoked a flood of memories within Charles, recollections of Marrow's numerous peculiarities, echoes of their lengthy, inconsistent, and less than honorable shared past—memories he hadn't revisited since Lovecraft's demise—

His pondering was interrupted by a sudden eruption of crimson light and Mary's maniacal laughter. Radiating unholy energy, she rose from the dissipating glow. Like a zealous preacher, she clutched her grimoire against her chest, wounds sealed by glowing red sutures, eyes aflame with Cthugha's fire.

"I am once more complete," she proclaimed.

Yet within her soul echoed an emptiness as vast as the wastes around them.

***

The rhythmic heartbeat of Eternal Valley fell into a hushed lull only during spring's brief, damp intermission. Bloated with winter's runoff, the river would seep into the city, bringing an odor reminiscent of rotting marshland that chased away tourists. This fleeting period between February and March was disdainfully dubbed Foulmas, trailing in the wake of Christmas celebrations. It was a time universally despised by both transient visitors and permanent residents.

Winter's stubborn remnants clung to the cityscape like specters refusing to pass on. Days were cloaked in an oppressive gloom that stretched into infinity while shadows slinked across the streets as if spectral serpents had claimed dominion over them. Nature herself morphed into a treacherous beast teeming with feral creatures and landslides ready to swallow unsuspecting victims whole.

As a society reliant on nature's gifts, men were forced to hunt and trap under these brutal conditions; they armored themselves with ancient Celtic symbols as shields against the elements and masked their faces against the pungent stench of decay-laden soil disgorged from nature's sickly bowels.

At home, too, unseen threats lurked ominously. Shopkeepers found themselves tumbling off ladders as they dismantled Christmas decorations. Roads transformed into treacherous quagmires, making vehicles vulnerable to accidents. And despite vigilant parental oversight, one child from the village would inevitably vanish—a sleepwalking casualty drawn towards their doom by an eerie whispering emanating from deep within Earth's core.

But these lost children never returned; their search efforts merely echoed hollowly in grieving parents' hearts who walked alongside the mayor and pastor through fields and forests, listening to empty condolences and receiving futile blessings. These blessings held no weight because everyone knew what had befallen them but yearned to return to their idyllic existence once Foulmas receded.

Post-Foulmas, Eternal Valley transformed into a picturesque town straight out of a storybook. It was where farm-fresh produce, immaculate streets, model wives, and handsome husbands were the standard. It was where the quaint values and artisanal crafts of yesteryears still flourished.

The town boasted an array of cafés and inns at every corner along with a cobbler, baker, hardware store, pub, and solitary grocery and electronics store—all family-run businesses passed down generations; no new ventures were conceived or necessary for its stable population—disappearing children notwithstanding. To the influx of tourists during peak months, it was an impeccably preserved slice of history.

However, as Foulmas loomed again on the horizon, mothers became shrill with their offspring while imposing curfews after sundown. Adults shuttered windows, lit prayer candles, and chanted ancient Gaelic verses inherited from their forebears—incantations meant to placate and deflect the attention of ceaselessly vigilant cosmic horrors lurking above them and infernal damnations yawning beneath them.

The village's eldest women—those teetering on death's precipice—would occasionally direct their prayers towards Evermore's lords, who had ruled these lands since their Irish ancestors colonized America. Their origins? A mystery nobody sought to unveil or ponder over. Yet they all knew deep within that the Mothmanns and this land were intertwined with its horrors. Perhaps the children lost during Foulmas were a grim tribute to the seasons of abundance and beauty bestowed upon them by these unseen entities.

Because nothing in life comes without its price.

***

"Quaint little settlement," Pythia murmured, her voice reminiscent of aged silk rustling in the breeze. She placed her tea aside, fingers tracing the zipper of her winter coat with an artist's precision. "The air does have a certain frigid nip to it, though."

"Quite so," Necromanteon echoed, her features draped in the shadows of twilight. The dying light carved out a somber portrait on her face, hinting at the ancient hag that lurked beneath. Her spectral appearance caught off guard a youthful waitress with hair like sun-kissed wheat as she approached their table, wiping clean any trace of joviality from her countenance.

"Pardon me for intruding." The girl's words stumbled and fell into a hurried jumble. She could not look away from the childlike figure, an unsettling image that stirred up recollections of a horror film where an innocent-looking orphan turned out to be a murderous dwarf.

"Your interruption is no inconvenience, my dear," Trophonius assured her with an easy charm that acted like a soothing balm—Women are ever so susceptible to his charm, Pythia mused inwardly.

"May I bring you more drinks? Or perhaps some food?" she ventured hesitantly. Until now, they'd sipped hot chocolate and tea as if engaged in some marathon of consumption but hadn't requested anything solid.

"I am content," replied the childlike figure in a voice that carried the weight of countless ages.

"We would appreciate another round of drinks at your earliest convenience," added Trophonius in his paternal tone.

With those words hanging in the air, she scurried away. As soon as the patio door clicked shut behind her, Necromanteon declared: "I am quite sated indeed...as full as a reveler indulging in Bacchanalia. Death lingers heavily here; this place is drenched in arcane magic, most radiating from over there."

Their collective gaze was drawn to the highlands and the formidable estate that towered above everything else. Despite their best efforts, these legendary seers could not decipher the fortress's enigmatic mystery. When the waitress returned, they were left gasping and pale from their exertions.

"Are you alright?" She paused in her task of swapping old cups for fresh ones. "It's much warmer inside." She noticed their intense scrutiny. "That's the Mothmann Estate...a frightening place if you ask me. I wouldn't go anywhere near there, though. They value their privacy and have a serious security detail."

With her exit, Trophonius and his companions sipped from their replenished cups, patiently waiting for fate to begin weaving its intricate design. As twilight washed over the sky with soft shades of orange, a dark speck—a helicopter—descended behind the castle.

As a single entity, they contemplated destiny's intricate threads, deliberating which one to tug first. Snake was hidden somewhere in South Dakota, a location even they could not discern. Yet their instincts had led them to this peculiar town, conveniently located near the Mothmann's ancient stronghold. Who else but the world's most formidable witch could conceal such power?

"A cunning little man indeed," mused Trophonius.

"I rarely find a reason for admiration, but yes," agreed Necromanteon.

"Octavia will be interested to learn we've caught her brother red-handed," declared Pythia with an undertone of satisfaction. "I shall ring her now."

***

A foreign sensation coursed through Octavia as though her body was filled with an alien, fizzing energy that had long since decayed into a grim pallor. She needed a moment to acclimate to this blurry existence, its edges softened like watercolors bleeding into each other on a Winslow Homer masterpiece. The world she found herself in was a towering library, reaching the dizzying heights of mythical giants' abodes. Its ladders disappeared into the golden wash of sunlight filtering through velvet-draped windows that stared blankly into an endless amber void.

The air was heavy with the scent of age and enigma—an aroma akin to myrrh—that clung to her short fingers as they grazed over book spines in her aimless wanderings. Each aisle presented another potential literary adventure she could embark on. But caution was paramount here; many of these books were not for young eyes, their parchment skin marred by crimson runes, devilish chants, and forgotten curses from bygone eras.

She had been warned against perusing these volumes—deemed too pure and innocent for such knowledge. Innocent? The thought drew a derisive mental snort from Octavia. This memory—or illusion—of her younger self appeared laughable now, given her current prowess as a witch who had devoured countless dark texts in the family's collection. She attempted to assert control over this spectral host's movements and awareness. Still, she found herself gently rebuffed by a familiar feminine voice echoing from somewhere ahead—a soothing melody that instantly pacified her.

"Rebecca!" The name slipped past young Octavia's lips as she sprinted towards the sound. The library shelves morphed around her in a trippy blur within this fluid dreamscape before settling again with an almost tangible tremor.

She now found herself amidst the family archives' seating area—a regal setup adorned with plush chairs and a silver table designed for intimate tea sessions. But instead of food and drink, the table was littered with a speckled sheet hosting an array of oil paints in gleaming pots.

Bathed in the sunshine streaming through the parted curtains stood a slender woman —at least from this angle—draped in a black gown. Though slightly disheveled, her luxuriant hair was wound into an elegant bun with stray tendrils escaping like visual manifestations of her artistic brilliance.

The woman's mastery over her paintbrush was evident in the haunting portrait she was creating—a woman submerged in a dark abyss, her flowing hair billowing around her and mournful eyes locked onto the viewer. The arresting image halted young Octavia in her tracks, entranced by this eerie depiction of despair.

Rebecca, her thick Russian accent still clinging to her words despite years of refined American living, asked with a softness that belied the harshness of her consonants, "What do you think, my little dove?" She turned, blowing a wayward curl from her face in an almost comical puff. Her features twisted momentarily in the effort, but it did little to mar her undeniable beauty. Her skin was pale as moonlight on snow-covered fields, lips full and expressive, eyes deep and dark as a Selkie queen's. Yet when she turned fully towards Octavia, the startlingly swollen expanse of her pregnant belly stole the young girl's breath.

"You're as big as a Christmas goose!" Octavia exclaimed.

"No, my darling," Rebecca chuckled gently. "Not about my unfortunate condition." She set aside her easel and wiped paint-streaked hands on a stained tablecloth. "I meant the painting."

Drawn into the familiar embrace of Rebecca's open arms like a puppy to its mother, Octavia nestled into the well-worn comfort they offered. Their dance was one rehearsed over countless shared moments; they moved harmoniously to face the painting together.

"It's rather sad," Octavia confessed quietly. The woman in the painting seemed lost beyond redemption; death clung to her like a shroud.

Rebecca pressed a loving kiss onto Octavia's forehead. "Death is life's eternal partner," she mused philosophically. "If we drowned our fields under endless sunlight without respite for nightfall's cool touch, crops would wither, and mankind would starve amidst all that beauty. Darkness soothes our weary world and calms anxious minds just as night brings rest after day's labors. Life and death are two sides of existence's coin."

The adult Octavia pondered whether this conversation had indeed taken place or if it was merely an illusion crafted by longing. Had Rebecca known about her impending fate, the dark destiny that awaited all Mothmann brides? Was this her silent acceptance of the inevitable?

Rather than shatter this delicate moment—the comforting scent of rosewater perfume, the steadfast strength in Rebecca's arms, and even the sticky daubs of paint staining Octavia's clothes—Octavia chose silence. She savored this bittersweet illusion, a respite from the looming future tainted with dread and loss. The world she would soon return to was filled with darkness and hatred—an innocence once pure now corrupted beyond repair.

***

The airplane trembled and roared, caught in the furious grip of an unseen storm giant. Oliver's hand darted out instinctively, aiming to steady the peacefully sleeping Octavia amidst the tumult—when had she last appeared so serene, or ever? Unfortunately, the turbulence or his touch roused her from what seemed to be a pleasant dream, causing her to awaken with a scowl. Under her glacial stare, he retracted his hand as if scalded. As quickly as it began, the tempestuous ride subsided into a serene glide through calmer skies.

From behind a curtain at the far end of the cabin, an attendant emerged with the poise of a couture model. She navigated down an aisle framed by plush velvet seats and laced with chrome accents—a tableau reminiscent of a vintage luxury train car. The Mothmann staff were trained to be professional rather than obsequious; thus, she addressed her employer with respectful detachment.

"Mrs. Mothmann," she intoned, "may I offer anything for your comfort?"

"Moët and Chandon, Imperial Brut," Octavia decreed.

"Of course," responded the attendant before pivoting towards Oliver. "And for you, Mr. Ramirez?"

For Oliver, battling alcoholism's siren call, liquor was as taboo as it would be for a woman carrying new life within her womb. "Just water," he grumbled.

With a curt nod, the stewardess vanished behind the curtain once more. The clink of glassware harmonized with the drone of engines until she returned bearing their chosen libations before retreating again into her unseen sanctuary.

"Champagne?" Oliver ventured when they were alone again.

"One sip won't kill me," she snapped back sharply, "Keep your concerns to yourself."

He complied silently and turned his thoughts inward—revisiting their day's events to decipher what had soured Octavia's mood so drastically. They had fled Hollywood's holiday party season pandemonium—an important time on the circuit to fish for new talent, sign the desperate into blood contracts, and remind the indebted who owned their souls—for an impromptu trip to South Dakota, inciting the ire of industry titans who bombarded him with furious calls and messages. However, these protestations and machinations were trivial to him. Octavia was grappling doubly with the burden of motherhood and humanity's survival against an imminent apocalypse—tasks that undoubtedly fueled her sullen silence.

He dared not comment on her visibly changing physique as she transitioned from tailored suits to loose attire, but he couldn't help noticing her expanding waistline. He had researched pregnancy extensively and realized that she seemed larger than a woman in her first trimester should be. Fear gnawed at him.

"Is everything okay with the baby?" he dared ask softly.

"Exactly as expected."

"Are you sure?"

Her response was venomous: "Don't fucking question me—ever again. Don't make me regret telling you in the first place."

Oliver could see her as his memory painted it—Octavia behind the imposing desk in her office, the Hollywood skyline a glittering backdrop to her inscrutable form. She'd barely looked up, pen poised over some legal document or another, when she declared, "I'm pregnant, and it's yours," in a tone as casual as if she were noting a change in the weather. He had stood there, file in hand, the words echoing against the polished glass and steel. "I see," he'd managed, searching her face for a crack in its composure. "Can I do anything?" Her eyes had flicked to his, cool and dismissive. "No." The conversation collapsed under the weight of her apathy, leaving him to retreat into the hallway—where he'd lingered, grappling with the explosive simplicity of her announcement.

Now he stared at his hands, wrestling with words that refused to form, until the silence between them stretched too thin: "I'm glad that you did tell me, and that you're keeping it."

"It's not too late to change my mind."

With a cold gleam in her eyes, she crossed her legs and sipped her drink, effectively ending their conversation. Her sharp rebukes reminded him of how she dealt with unruly clients who'd overindulged in illicit substances and ended up with a dead prostitute or two floating facedown in a bathtub—a common occurrence in Hollywood's mire. Soon enough, all this decadence would be swept away when the Deep One reclaims Earth. The thought of bringing new life into such a chaotic world must have seemed an absurdity too great for Octavia to bear.

"Understand this, Octavia," he began in his no-nonsense way. "I'm not one for grand pledges or empty words. But you can rely on me. If we obey your god's edicts, we'll find our place in the impending cosmic order. I believe that." He took a moment, his voice softening to a murmur. "I have to." A chilling quiet filled the air.

"This isn't about you or..." Her hand moved subconsciously towards her belly once more. "This is about my lineage."

Lineage? Oliver pondered, a crease forming on his forehead. Her father was absent from their lives, her mother never mentioned to him, and her brother was only referred to with scorn.

"We're heading to Evermore," she declared abruptly, then sneered as she added: "Home."

"For what reason?" he queried.

"Gabriel has been interfering—his actions are escalating in intensity. His absence from the MANN Inc. board meeting should've been a glaring sign of his concealed motives. He never misses an opportunity to flaunt his power, especially before a hostile audience—he thrives on attention like some perverse vampire. The graver the situation, the more potent he becomes." She pivoted towards Oliver suddenly, her body quivering and face ashen with terror. "He could ruin everything for us and our..."

"You alright...?"

He halted mid-question about her emotional well-being, fearing it might agitate her further. Instead, he unfastened his seatbelt and raised the armrest before tenderly guiding her head onto his chest. She trembled against him while silent sobs convulsed through her body.

There were instances when he felt utterly clueless about Octavia—that perhaps there was nothing beyond her rigid facade. For years, he had observed as she beguiled men with devilish charm and cunningness.

His own history was replete with relationships with formidable women, which made Octavia's assertiveness even more enticing to him. But she was not merely another conquest; in moments like these, she revealed that beneath the ruthless exterior was a human being. Their lives were so intertwined that falling in love with her seemed almost inevitable. He had once transitioned from a killer to prison scholar to a lover and now... potentially a father.

The threat of having this fragile joy ripped away—the second instance where he'd permitted himself to bask in such an emotion—set his wrath ablaze. Even as the cosmos spiraled into pandemonium, he would latch onto this, lock onto her. As Octavia released her pain against his chest, Oliver's eyes hardened with resolve. All he required was a firearm; even his bare hands and a length of cord would suffice.

"I can take care of him," he whispered into her ear. "Just say the word."

Octavia tensed before withdrawing to tidy up her face despite no visible tears.

"We cannot accomplish it alone," she stated after contemplation. "Firstly, we need to connect with my field agents. I will look him in the face and denounce him as a betrayer to our god."

"And then?"

"We kill him," Octavia said coldly. "Our child is what matters most now. Without him, everything I've built will fall apart—we have to make sure he's born no matter what it takes. Gabriel won't be the only male heir to the Mothmann fortune—our son will inherit it all."

"Son?" Oliver raised an eyebrow in surprise.

"Indeed. Hailing from a lineage of supreme witches, I was privy to the sex at the moment of conception," Octavia responded with a chilling certainty.

"You make it sound so... scientific," he retorted, a humorless laugh escaping his lips.

"Intercourse is not merely an act of pleasure for some of us but rather a binding pact," she said, her tone as reptilian as her serpentine gaze.

A shiver of unease slithered down Oliver's spine, a cold echo of Octavia's icy detachment. The conversation had frozen over, her attention now claimed by the sleek cellphone she flicked through with an air of dismissive nonchalance. Was their peculiar entanglement merely a mirage? It was an unsettling thought. If his purpose in her life was solely for procreation, she would have cast him aside already. With her ethereal beauty that held men captive, any suitor could be a sire to her offspring.

Octavia Mothmann was not known for sentimentality; people and possessions were tools in her arsenal, discarded when they ceased to serve their function. Wrestling with the creeping tendrils of doubt gnawing at his certainty, Oliver willed himself back into the comforting embrace of work.

His gaze fell upon the computer screen before him, where spectral reflections of his own face played out a ghostly pantomime. His image seemed hollow—devoid of life and substance—as if he were fading into obscurity within this digital realm.

Choosing to turn a blind eye to this eerie spectacle, he sank deeper into his self-spun delusion: a world where he wasn't ensnared by hopeless infatuation and crippling indebtedness to a woman whose ruthless ambition was rivaled only by her cunning intellect. A woman who sought dominion not just over him but also through their unborn son's ascension.

CHAPTER 18: THE LEGACY

Gabriel Mothmann rose from his throne-like chair, exuding an aristocratic authority that commanded the room.

The Evermore estate was a paradoxical tableau of modern splendor and age-old mysticism. Its towering iron gates, concealed behind an intricate maze of hedges, groaned open to expose the manor's façade—a testament to both opulence and decay. The mansion showcased sleek architectural lines and reflective glass windows that seemed to probe into one's essence, reflecting hidden truths. Ivy veins clung tenaciously to its surface, sprouting peculiar black blossoms that bore no kinship with any recognized flora but exuded an aroma of lilies and roses tainted with the stench of rot, causing Brock's nose to wrinkle in aversion.

Beneath this bizarre vegetation and the veneer of contemporary design lurked an ominous force, a tangible heaviness within the unexpected fog they had entered—perhaps a physical embodiment of the sinister magic wielded by the witches who presided over this realm.

They ascended an imposing grand staircase before approaching a set of monumental double doors that challenged the fortitude of the brawny super soldiers who strenuously flexed their muscles to pry them open. Passing into this spectral domain, their every move was observed by many hyper-alert super soldiers rooted in place. They found themselves in a gothic paradise where old timber and musty books infused the dense air with their scent. A grand hall welcomed them with its towering staircase, whose elegant handrails coiled like ancient vines. Dimly lit gas lamps threw fluctuating light onto stone floors, creating a maze of shadow and mystery that left them dumbstruck—they had never beheld such extravagance.

Ana released an appreciative whistle. "The Mothmann's certainly aren't destitute."

"Obscenely wealthy," Malachi added emphatically as his gaze settled on a vibrant painting featuring a naked woman reclining amidst monochrome décor—her hair and multicolored surroundings flowing around her like water. "That's Kandinsky's work—an original, if I had to guess."

"We'll convene in the study," Gabriel declared from beneath an archway under the stairs, into which he and Cal vanished. "Keep pace. It's easy to lose oneself..."

His words echoed with an eerie undertone of warning. Following Gabriel, the Aspects soon discovered the truth behind his cautionary words. They went through the same archway as their host, then ascended a tight staircase that split at a sharp landing. Despite their best efforts, they never entirely managed to keep up with Gabriel as he led them down the left corridor. Leng and Steve, trailing further behind, didn't make it past the first divergence—whether they had been diverted or deceived by the mutable house remained a mystery.

The walls of the hall they traversed seemed imbued with an otherworldly energy. They were adorned in aged fabrics showcasing dragons, animals, and shields that transformed subtly before their eyes. The cold touch of candle holders, vacant suits of armor-wielding axes, and dust-coated seats conjured images of a palace from a forgotten epoch.

Their journey took them through an active kitchen, which mirrored the manor's theme of an unsettling fusion between old and new. Gleaming stainless-steel appliances coexisted uneasily with butcher block counters and large cauldrons, evoking images of medieval witchcraft.

Exiting the kitchen led them into another hallway, which twisted like a serpentine rollercoaster track toward an expansive courtyard. The courtyard bore relics of another era—broken columns entwined in ivy stood like mute sentinels while uneven stones reverberated under their footsteps. Through narrow openings leading outside came sounds of a storm—a stark contrast to their recollection of clear weather before entering the manor, suggesting temporal distortions enabled by magical corridors within Evermore estate.

A training ground, a curious juxtaposition amidst the scattered ruins of the courtyard, was equipped with leather mats, practice targets, and racks brimming with an assortment of weaponry. Their spectral guide, a ghostly hare leading them down this rabbit hole of oddities, bellowed over his shoulder. "Training hall! You'll find yourselves drawn back here soon enough, preparing for our inevitable confrontation with an Outer God." The insinuation hung heavy in the air—they were to face off against the Deep One, and who knew whatever other horrors. Struggling to keep up with their host's brisk pace, they navigated through an intricate network of corridors before emerging into a dimly lit study: timber shelves lined the walls, sagging under the weight of ancient texts and strange artifacts. The shelves pulsed faintly as if each item held within was imbued with a dormant consciousness. Their gaze swept across countless books on the shelves, scrolls bound by rotting twine, and tablets strewn carelessly across cluttered desks—each object pulsating with forbidden knowledge. The sheer intensity of such potent magic enveloped them in an electrifying aura.

"Welcome to the Mothmann archives," their guide intoned.

Gabriel sat comfortably in a leather armchair by a roaring fire adorned with unsettling marble reliefs of intertwined, orgiastic demonic figures. Cal lurked behind him —always in his shadow—his demeanor subdued following their recent encounters. In Gabriel's hand was a glass that he tapped gently with his finger. At this signal, Cal moved towards the mantelpiece to pour drinks from the decanter before distributing them amongst their guests and retreating to his position behind Gabriel's chair.

Ana recognized introverted behavior when she saw it; she saw it often enough in herself. She realized that Cal wasn't as self-assured and commanding here as he had been in her dreams, where he took on the role of an authoritative figurehead. Here, he was merely a novice in the shadow of the Mothmann successor's worldly wisdom and power.

"Go on," Gabriel prompted, his voice smooth as they held their drinks. "They're not poisoned, and few toxins would affect your kind. Godbeasts can still appreciate a well-aged spirit. You haven't entirely abandoned human indulgence, have you?"

Ana had been steering clear of alcohol for some time now and wasn't about to break her resolve here, especially not in this eerie manor. She nudged her untouched drink towards Lenny. "Here, you take it. I've quit drinking. Where are Leng and Steve hiding?"

"They weren't invited to our little meeting," Gabriel replied smoothly. "The Spider God and I... we have certain differences in philosophy. It wouldn't be beneficial to have such discord at our initial gathering. Please sit down and make yourselves comfortable. You're safer here than anywhere else."

A sudden force nudged their knees; turning revealed Victorian chairs designed to accommodate each of them—small, medium, and large—had appeared silently behind them like spectral guardians. They cautiously took their seats.

Gabriel Mothmann rose from his throne-like chair, exuding an aristocratic authority that commanded the room. He gestured grandly around him, his piercing eyes gleaming with intensity. "Evermore is not simply a house—it's a sanctuary for all who dare to cross its threshold. It anticipates and caters to its guests' needs and desires with an uncanny precision."

Ana craned her neck towards the celestial canopy above, attempting to decipher the formidable enchantment that seemed to envelop them—a force more potent than any artifact she had ever encountered in her growing library of arcane knowledge. It was an omnipresent hum of power, strangely comforting, almost motherly in its essence. "Is this some sort of AI?" she queried.

A warm smile spread across Gabriel's face as he replied, "In a manner of speaking— an alchemical fusion of artificial intelligence and magic into one sentient entity." His voice brimmed with pride as he continued: "Evermore embodies a synthesis of science and esoteric arts unlike anything else you've encountered."

He paused for dramatic effect before adding: "The Mothmanns are one of the oldest witch lineages. We've been preserving our bloodline since the fall of Babylon, even weathering the Crusades by seeking haven in Slavic territories. My ancestor Vlad gained quite a reputation there for his... unconventional practices."

"Wait, Dracula?" Malachi interjected.

Gabriel nodded nonchalantly before meandering towards the hearth, where a portrait of three stern pilgrims hung ominously overhead.

"Countless human legends are, in truth, narratives of us—the rare few able to pierce the veil of Dream. This term, favored by learned witches, denotes the mystical cosmic tapestry that stitches our reality together. My mother was said to have an extraordinary affinity with this celestial wellspring. Despite being a mere mortal—an artist, not a bona fide witch—her bond with Dream and her otherworldly demeanor deeply affected Earth's culture; her macabre and glorious works are said to have inspired literary titans such as Poe and Shelley to write their masterpieces. You'll find many of Mother's artistic creations adorning the manor. She is responsible for this piece here."

His hand waved vaguely in the direction of a painted tableau. The scene was etched with the solemn figures of two pilgrims, a man and his smaller, mirror image—a boy no older than ten, their attire matching each other in somber shades. Off to the side, a young woman glowered, her figure draped in an ethereal white dress that seemed to glow against the stark backdrop. A small plaque affixed to the frame whispered its title: *The Family Never To Be*. "This work and countless others dispersed across the Mothmann dominion," finished Gabriel.

"A submerged woman? Suspended in a watery limbo?" Malachi voiced his thoughts.

Gabriel's lips curved into a smile. "Ah, you must be speaking of *The Woman in the Water*. I found its gaze unbearable, so I relegated it to some corner of our archives or holdings. Its current location eludes me...But that's inconsequential now. Even though she lacked prophetic vision, Mother's artistry resonated with the eternal muse—a filament of cosmic perpetuity that empowered her to depict through ink, watercolor, and pastel epochs she had never lived and futures she would never witness. I've always held onto the belief that image you mentioned symbolized her—and her inexorable destiny."

He expelled a heavy sigh: "But I cannot ask her, as she died giving birth to me. All I have left of her are stories and pictures—and a half-sister who harbors a sublime resentment toward me." Gabriel shook his head as if to dispel the lingering melancholy before pivoting back towards his visitors: "My family's internal strife is irrelevant—we have more pressing matters to discuss."

The Mothmanns' familial discord being trivial was a gross understatement for a lineage that had once sent chills down the collective spine of humanity and fueled its most outrageous fantasies. Their influence was interwoven into a plethora of cultures and myths. Gabriel's brief account of his ancestry left Malachi stunned, a whirlwind of questions spinning in his mind. One question, however, rose above the rest. "How did your family end up serving these Outer Gods?"

Gabriel exhaled deeply. "A pertinent question, Aspect of Fire. Power can be an intoxicating mistress, leading one down a path of corruption and deceit. The Outer Gods offer power beyond what mortal witches dare to grasp—beings already endowed with long life, supernatural strength, and the ability to manipulate reality at will. Yet death, while it can be delayed, remains an ever-present threat—not so much from mortal weapons but more from other supernatural creatures, including fellow witches. Witches often fall into wars against each other over knowledge, artifacts, or territories, fighting through proxies, whether golems, demonic conjurations, or men. The Outer Gods provide swift resolutions to such conflicts while existing in a realm both here and beyond, the scams of the cosmos's existence. Dream itself."

"What do you mean by that?" Malachi probed further.

Gabriel's piercing gaze felt like a barrage of minuscule psychic darts as he scrutinized their spiritual essences with his supernatural perception. "Three Aspects, self-awakened and still oblivious to their true identities! And a fifth Aspect seemingly conjured from the shadows. Has Cthugha's minion kept you shrouded in ignorance? Has Lovecraft refrained from even introducing you to the rudimentary principles of your powers? I recognize him —I would assume maggots had devoured his tongue if I knew not otherwise." Lovecraft's silence echoed within their minds.

"I mean..." Ana's fingers lightly grazed the skull before she timidly voiced her thoughts. "He has helped us a lot, actually. I have some understanding of our nature...kinda... I've journeyed through the otherworld—"

"Dream!" Gabriel interjected sharply. "Dream—the Dreaming or the realm straddling life and death, reality and fantasy—a cosmos of infinite potentialities. Ensure your cosmological lexicon is accurate."

"Sorry." Ana felt a surge of adolescent embarrassment as though she were being reprimanded by a stern teacher. "Dream. Yes, I've traversed Dream. We all have, to some degree or another."

"If we are vessels navigating an ocean of endless possibilities, utilizing its currents to arrive at our desired destinations," Gabriel began, "then Dream is that very ocean itself— an enigma that is dark and immeasurably profound. It constitutes the bedrock of existence; every splendid marvel, congealed sin, and fantasy and nightmare are born there. Dream is the universal flux of possibility, time, destruction and creation that witches—rarely birthed humans—can tap into. However, Ana, in your case, along with your companions', you swim amidst its depths alongside its monstrous denizens."

"You're referring to the Outer Gods," she said.

"Precisely. But akin to a whale gasping for breath on land, the Outer Gods also require creatures to pave the way for their terrestrial advent; minions are tasked with constructing habitats through rituals and terraforming to house their colossal forms. You've witnessed places where their energy bleeds into our realm, such as the town you wiped from existence—I had one Hell of a call explaining that semi-nuclear blast to the EPA and getting them to stand down on an investigation. Regardless, that sick illusion was merely a minor rift from which an Outer God's magic trickled out. Frequently, their manifested presence engulfs entire planets or even solar systems depending on what falsehoods Lovecraft has fed you about *blessings*."

Ana recalled Lovecraft employing that term before. "Hmm… So, is forming an alliance with these entities a net negative? Lovecraft and his cult seem convinced that Cthugha's help was the way forward—the only way forward."

With a humorless laugh, Gabriel began, "The Golden One, bestower of flame and progenitor of mankind. Pardon my skepticism regarding the benevolence of an alien entity with a fondness for fiery annihilation. Lovecraft is misguided in believing that Cthugha will spare our world once he dispatches his rivals. They view this all as a sport— the Eternal Game—assuming we can anthropomorphize these beings enough to suggest they partake in games. You are merely pawns in Cthugha's grand scheme, fortuitously advancing across the cosmic chessboard toward your coronation from pawns to queens. Your existence is a byproduct of a conspiracy devised by the deranged Emperor Alexander of Rome and lesser-known rulers of Atlantis who believed they could negotiate with these Outer Gods and sought an alliance with what they perceived as 'the most reasonable' among them to birth sublime Godbeasts. But humanity holds no trump cards here. We are not trailblazers in attempting to gain leverage over these entities; numerous civilizations have embarked on similar futile quests only to become cosmic ruins—worlds cloaked in dust, trapped in eternal winters, ravaged by tempests or aflame with grotesque elemental demons."

"Acheron," Brock interjected, his voice a low rumble.

Gabriel's eyes flickered to him, a glint of recognition sparking within their depths. "Indeed," he acknowledged, his tone unchanging despite the interruption. "You've peered into one such realm." His gaze swept back to the others as he continued, "This is the grim reality of triumph in this Eternal Game. They win, and we face extinction."

He paused momentarily, letting the weight of his words sink in before continuing. "The Lengeth, wise beyond comprehension among all known races in our cosmos, were not immune to the corruption brought by these Outer Gods. They were seers like you, Ana, capable of predicting future events and discerning absolute truths… Masterful weavers crafting destinies on fate's loom. Yet Shub-Niggurath, the Devouring Worm and Mother, hungered for their gifts and summarily devoured the Lengeth in all their imperious wisdom. Because no matter how wise or powerful a victim, these Outer Gods always find a way in."

His gaze turned intense as he stared at them, his following words heavy with significance. "You wonder why my lineage serves these monstrosities? It's because if we don't, someone far less capable will. We perform tasks of lesser witches to placate and repel these Outer Gods. But our efforts are nearing their end: The Atlantean seal that binds Cthulhu beneath the ocean has started to weaken. The Eternal Game approaches its climax, so our time is limited to prepare you."

"For what?" Malachi asked, his brows furrowing.

"To venture into Cthulhu's prison and finish what the Atlanteans began," Gabriel answered with an edge to his voice.

Malachi scratched his head thoughtfully. "Atlantean history isn't really my area of expertise."

A hint of irritation flashed across Gabriel's face at Malachi's casual response. "I thought I had made this clear already," he said, his voice sharpening. "While these entities lack physical form and cannot be killed, they can be barred from entering our world. Your purpose is to banish the Deep One and other Lords of Chaos from Earth. Permanently."

The enormity of their task hung heavily in the air, a tangible weight that seemed to press down on them. Gabriel's blunt articulation was sobering, even though they had already suspected as much. The repeated references to Atlantean lore only emphasized how much knowledge they needed to acquire and the tasks they had to complete in an alarmingly short period.

Cal offered comforting words amidst the daunting reality, "It's okay," he said softly, "He'll guide you through this preparation process; he's been readying for this moment for ages."

"When do we start?" Brock asked, a determined note in his voice.

"First thing tomorrow morning," replied Gabriel.

***

At Gabriel's insistence, the foursome set out to rid themselves of Arkminister's filth, gather their wits and fortify their spirits for the looming trials. The assembly dispersed with a farewell gesture from both Gabriel and Cal, leaving the allies in a contemplative silence. They were left to ponder their daunting responsibilities as they wound through Evermore's abandoned labyrinthine passages.

These corridors might have seemed like an unsolvable maze to an outsider's gaze. Yet, Evermore guided them like mice within an intricate burrow system, igniting the wall-mounted torches along the chosen route while concealing irrelevant areas in a menacing obsidian shroud. This pervasive darkness whispered of the hidden menace lurking in the heart of the Mothmann lineage—a bloodline brimming with vampires, liches, and loathsome witches.

The discomfort that clung to each confederate was tangible; none felt at ease in this alien domain nor fully trusted Gabriel's seeming and scheming goodwill. Yet strange alliances had become a recurring pattern in their journey—why should this instance be any different?

Their dread began to ebb away as they arrived at a multi-tiered platform marked by transparent chasms that presented a celestial view of the valley cradled beneath the mansion. From this perch, everything below appeared quaintly toy-like. Both doors here stood slightly open and swung wide to reveal lavish lodgings adorned with vintage furniture: a four-poster bed, an iridescent chandelier, a softly hissing fireplace, and an enormous wardrobe that could act as a portal into a Narnian realm.

The comrades divided into pairs before bidding each other goodnight and secluding themselves behind hefty doors into tomblike silence—so profound that even Brock and Lenny couldn't detect any stirrings from their allies beyond the walls. At last, they were granted solitude. Finally, they could rest.

***

Drained to his core, Malachi collapsed onto the luxurious bed, Brock's dirt-encrusted body surrendering to gravity beside him. The day had been an unyielding onslaught. A silent whisper from Malachi echoed in the caverns of their minds—a longing for that profound inner link, the intertwining of their spirits.

Quite a day, he mused.

Understatement of the year, Brock retorted.

A tidal wave of unprocessed grief crashed over Malachi as memories of Brock being violently torn away from him resurfaced. They clung to each other in desperation, their bodies coiling together like serpents engaged in an intricate dance. Their mutual warmth ignited a wildfire of need, swallowing them whole in its untamed storm. With a monumental effort akin to Hercules's, Brock managed to extricate himself from their shared fervor.

Need to wash that damned world off me.

Brock rose from the bed with determination etched into every line of his muscular form, discarding his tattered clothing before vanishing into the stark washroom. Soon after, tendrils of steam began creeping out from beneath the door like ethereal fingers reaching out for something unseen.

You joining me or what?

Malachi discarded his clothes without care on his path toward Brock. He found him poised on a marble bench within the grand shower enclosure; anticipation hung heavy between them for their bodies' imminent collision once again. Their union was a fevered entanglement of muscle and desire—their cries ricocheted off the tiled walls and challenged Evermore's soundproofing abilities. Exhausted yet satiated, they later crumbled onto an oversized velveteen bathmat, which would serve as their impromptu bed for the remaining hours of this break.

Their stolen moments of intimacy were destined to become few and far between as training against the Outer Gods under the guidance of their new ally loomed. Malachi contemplated this strange future with curiosity and exhilaration—what potential could structured learning unlock? Until now, most of their discoveries had been born out of dire necessity or sheer happenstance.

What's your take on our new friend? Malachi inquired.

Gabriel? The dude gives me serious vibes...and not in a charming way.

Do you buy what he's selling?

Brock's ability to detect deception had only increased with his burgeoning powers. Throughout their conversation, Gabriel hadn't exhibited any open signs of deceit. He wasn't lying, or at least he was convinced of his own words.

I don't think he's lying—at least not about wanting to help us, Brock replied.

But you don't trust him?

Not in the slightest.

A surge of dark emotion swept over Brock, leaving a sour aftertaste in Malachi's consciousness. Propping himself up on one elbow, he gently traced Brock's rugged features.

What's eating you, Brock?

Quezecoptyl, the Dark Mother, has been on our side this whole time.

And?

She spoke to me when we were alone on that desolate planet...

A knot formed in Malachi's throat as he listened intently.

She didn't use words exactly...but her presence...She showed me things...

What did you see?

Once again, Brock found himself ensnared in the spectral echoes of Tlanex-Tli, cradled within a cathedral of glistening glass strands that thrummed with otherworldly harmonies. An immense luminous being hovered above him, suspended in the intricate network like a constellation caught in a spider's web. The ghostly remnants of the ancient arachnid—her physical body long since turned to dust—showered him with radiant light from her countless glowing eyes, eyes that had witnessed epochs beyond comprehension.

Even as his companions called out to him from their shared reality, he remained entranced by her cosmic symphony—the buzzing drone and pulsating rhythm translated into intelligible speech by his human psyche. A myriad of nebulous visions flooded his senses, immersing him in a feverish trance where he witnessed an epic cosmic drama before him.

Surrounded by an ominous boundary of thunderous clouds flashing with monstrous insinuations, five radiant angelic figures hovered before a swirling surge of obsidian oblivion. Leaving trails of neon light like performers in some futuristic smoky spectacle, they advanced towards the living tempest rising like a grotesque tsunami—Cthulhu? Indeed, for an orchestral uproar clashed with discordant chaos—the deranged murmurings of a dormant deity slowly rousing.

The darkness coalesced into shadowy tendrils as this demonic leviathan stirred from its slumber, and the balletic dance of the neon angels became a performance amidst quivering spears of antimatter and ebony pyrotechnics. Tendrils erupted from the tempest, seizing and extinguishing each golden light one by one until darkness consumed all, leaving only echoes reverberating with mournful emptiness. Grief. Mortality. Surrender.

Staggering away from the Dark Mother's spectral web, Brock was engulfed by an oppressive black shroud—the terrifying reality of his vision. The Dark Mother's ghostly luminescence was now a dwindling glow, rapidly devoured by the encroaching darkness. Fleeing from the nightmare painted by the Dark Mother, Brock sprinted towards the trembling fracture in existence that promised him an escape to his home dimension.

As he neared the portal, a final lament from the Dark Mother echoed over its undulating surface. Her psychic notes morphed into harmonious and human-articulated sound—a name. "Alexander," she whispered as she succumbed to oblivion. "Alexander," Brock repeated with a grave resonance as he plunged into the interdimensional void.

Back on Earth, in their shared reality, Malachi gasped as the deafening vision concluded—relayed with such vividness it felt like his own memory. He was awash with terror and confusion at its implications. Were they destined for annihilation? What role did Alexander play in their fate? Was he a savior or an adversary? The answers seemed elusive.

Brock planted a soft kiss on Malachi's forehead, leaving him sprawled on their bed in bewilderment. Their brief respite had ended, and once again, they scrambled to outpace their seemingly doomed destiny.

***

As Brock rummaged through the first closet, he found untouched undergarments, denim pants, and white cotton shirts—two each in medium and large. They were meticulously arranged as though by an invisible housekeeper. A perfectly sized pair of boots for him and Malachi awaited at the foot of the wardrobe. The peculiar precision amused Brock; their AI overseer seemed more like a futuristic caretaker than an overlord.

He slipped into his clothes, carrying Malachi's to his friend, who appeared disoriented and sluggish. With gentle hands, Brock helped him dress before cradling his friend's head between his palms, their foreheads touching in an intimate moment of reassurance. "Nothing's set in stone," he whispered into the silence, "We'll sort this out." Together they ventured forth.

The morning sun was beginning its climb skyward; its rays danced through crystal vases filled with fresh orchids that adorned tables around them, casting a kaleidoscope of colors across the room. Upon reaching Ana's door and knocking lightly, she swung it open almost instantly—clad only in an oversized sweater, no pants in sight, and hair wild from sleep.

Her initial grin faded quickly as she noticed their grave expressions. "Holy shit," she exclaimed abruptly. "Who's dead?"

"Could be us," Malachi shot back without missing a beat.

Ana ushered them inside hastily and shut the door behind them. Lenny stirred from his face-down slumber at their abrupt entrance, his muscular backside bare as he shuffled toward the edge of the bed while maintaining modesty with a sheet draped over himself. As Malachi passed by Lenny, he couldn't help but take note of Lenny's sheer physical enormity: calves and biceps round as basketballs, hands resembling cinder blocks. Yet despite his immensity, his muscles were lean with veins snaking across his hirsute skin like he was some human-gorilla hybrid. His size had increased significantly from an already large frame—a likely side effect of Outer God blood mutation.

"What got you two so rattled?" Ana asked, placing a hand on Brock's shoulder. "Were we too noisy?"

"Nope. Didn't hear a peep," Brock responded, shaking his head. "But there's something crucial I need to tell you guys. Things have been moving so fast, and it's all been a blur. And honestly, I didn't want to know what it meant because I'm pretty sure it's not good news."

Ana looked at him quizzically, "What are you talking about?"

"Quezecoptyl," Brock answered without hesitation. "Your Dark Mother gave me a vision before she passed away. I was hoping you could shed some light on it."

Ana had sensed this exchange but had forgotten amidst the chaos of their lives.

"Great, what now?" Lenny groaned in response. "Ana, can you do that brain wave thingy and show us?"

"I'll give it a shot," she nodded.

Ana sat on the bed next to Lenny while the others fetched chairs from the sitting area. Having grown accustomed to these séances, Brock held Ana's hands as Lenny placed his fingers over his lover's back. Ana plunged into the depths of Brock's troubled blue-gray eyes—beautiful pools of sorrow—and navigated her way through his murky vision therein.

"Alexander aka Marrow," Lenny's voice cracked, his face blanching as the vision poured into his psyche.

Brock, his brows furrowed in confusion, turned to him. "Was that a warning or something else?"

Malachi shrugged. "Even though the vision was abstract, it looked like we all died—assuming the five angel thingies were the Four Aspects and Lenny. Did Marrow kill us? Could he save us in that moment? Who the fuck knows anymore."

They withdrew from each other then, each lost in their thoughts—dark and ominous like storm clouds on the horizon. The silence in the room was thick; it hung heavy in the air like an unwanted guest.

"If those were her final words," Ana began softly, "then they carry a message." She paused before adding thoughtfully, "But as Malachi pointed out if it is meant to be some sort of warning... it's pretty futile, given the content of that vision. I'm a little pissed she never shared that vision with me. You know: one last seizure for the road."

Once again, silence descended upon them like a shroud. But Brock shook off the melancholy quickly; despair was not an option for them. He rallied them with his next words: "I'm not going to die—none of us are," he said firmly yet gently. "So if it's not some sort of warning... what else could it be?"

"A clue," Ana said. Her voice held a shiver of revulsion as she continued: "We might need Marrow's help."

Brock raised his hand then—displaying the Atlantean relic glinting ominously on his finger—and asked simply: "But we have his trinket."

"Perhaps Quez thinks that's not enough."

"Quez?" Lenny smirked at her casual use of the entity's name.

Ana rolled her eyes, "Her name is a mouthful, don't you think?" Her tone shifted then, becoming more serious. "Look, I'd be the first to cheer if Marrow was banished to some eternal abyss for all he's done... but there's no denying his involvement." She paused, her mind racing back to their encounter at the Powwow shootout and part of Marrow's cryptic tirade: The steel must endure violence to become a weapon...

Lost in her recollection, she repeated his words aloud. There was a moment of stunned silence before Brock finally spoke up: "That's an odd thing to say."

"Right?" agreed Ana. "Like he was... preparing me for something?"

Malachi interjected then: "Maybe we've misjudged him." His voice carried an undertone of uncertainty that reflected his inner turmoil.

Lenny snorted in disbelief. "His actions speak louder than any words," he argued vehemently. "I won't trust him as far as I can throw him—and I think I could throw a bus a hundred yards. Maybe he's an enemy of our enemy at best. Given half a chance, I'd happily stomp on his skull until his brains leak out."

Skull. Brains. Suddenly Ana gasped—a sharp pain piercing through her head like a bolt of lightning. As Lenny pulled her close, the pain subsided leaving behind another riddle waiting to be solved.

"What was that?" he asked worriedly.

"I don't have a clue," Ana replied grimly. "Felt like getting shot in the head."

A gasp escaped Malachi's lips, coinciding with the phone's shrill ring. The sudden sound resonated like nails on a chalkboard, dragging their attention toward the antiquated rotary device perched on a console table near the entrance. Its horn and ivory finish was a relic from an era when such devices were coveted symbols of opulence, owned only by society's elite.

Springing into action, Malachi darted across the room and snatched up the receiver. "H-hello?"

"Good morning," Gabriel's voice echoed in response, his tone as formal and aristocratic as ever. "I see I've found you all together."

Malachi's eyes darted around their surroundings, scanning for hidden cameras. He cursed himself for not considering earlier that a paranoid witch like Gabriel wouldn't leave them unobserved in his lair.

"Evermore is ready for you," Gabriel continued. "Come to the coliseum. Training begins in exactly fifteen minutes. Evermore will guide you there. Do not keep me waiting." The line went dead.

Lenny had caught the masculine timbre of Gabriel's voice on the other end of the call and rose from his bed without hesitation or embarrassment despite his nakedness. His worn clothes were nowhere to be found, but just as with Malachi and Brock's gifts, Mother Evermore had subtly provided clean, folded undergarments and clothes atop an armoire with shoes placed neatly below it.

Lenny motioned for Ana to join him while Brock and Malachi retreated into the antechamber, allowing their friends privacy to dress themselves. Minutes later, both emerged from their chamber dressed in surprising attire: Ana looked like a Wall Street enchantress ready to conquer any boardroom in her cream sweater, slacks, and shiny shoes paired with an unusual holster that secured Lovecraft under her breast along with a secondary sheath for Quezecoptyl's fragment.

In contrast, Lenny looked like her arcane bodyguard dressed in a satiny black tracksuit snug at the cuffs but loose around his robust limbs, reminiscent of a judo uniform.

"You guys look sharp," Malachi complimented with a grin.

"You guys look like gay twins," Lenny retorted. Malachi and Brock glanced at each other and laughed—he wasn't wrong.

"Well, lads, let's get this shitshow on the road," declared Lenny, confidently striding forward. He didn't hesitate or wonder which way to go or what turns to take. He knew Evermore would guide them.

CHAPTER 19: SCHOOL OF REALLY HARD KNOCKS

Behind him pulsed a blue planet, its creamy hue echoing that of a mystic pearl guarded by silently hovering asteroids.

The fellowship hurtled through a conduit—seemingly constructed for maximum expediency—as smooth and unbroken as the digestive tract of a leviathan, disgorging them into the coliseum. The arena was an epitome of ruin, its decaying walls and disarrayed training apparatus echoing tales of better days. The tempestuous weather outside was nothing of what they recalled and pounded a foreboding rhythm against the structure. Brock's eyes swept over new additions to the machinery that weren't there during their last visit. An elaborate jungle gym, reminiscent of Quezccoptyl's intricate web, sprawled in a distant corner. Near their entrance point sat an antiquated chair with lion's feet and demonic spirals etched into its surface; it rested on a faded oriental rug facing an enormous oval mirror adorned with repugnant mermaids and monstrous figures. The purpose behind this peculiar setup remained elusive to Brock. Perhaps their host would shed some light.

Gabriel, resplendent in white dress pants and a meticulously tailored vest that reminded Brock of some Columbian drug lord, motioned them from the heart of the chamber. Cal strolled with nonchalance personified hands buried deep in his baggy jeans; his oversized t-shirt hung off him as if he were slowly diminishing. When Ana met his gaze, though, he flashed her a fleeting grin.

Brock shot him with a warning glare, saying: Watch it.

"Today and in future days, we will push your boundaries and refine your witchcraft into something even the Outer Gods dread," Gabriel declared.

"Future days?" Brock questioned abruptly. Just how long did Gabriel think they'd be confined here? It might be gilded, but it was still a cage—he craved freedom akin to any wolf.

"As much or as little time before my masters discover my interference and lay siege to Evermore," Gabriel replied calmly. "Every second is crucial for building strength, resolve, and magical knowledge. Between training and what you can glean from the Mothmann archives about witchery and the mystical trials ahead of you...you should be prepared for when the Deep One's forces descend. Cthulhu's retribution will be swift and merciless. Evermore and its resources won't last, so I advise against wasting this time in leisure but rather devote it entirely to mastering your powers."

Gabriel's words resonated with Ana on a somber note. "What happens to you?" she asked. "When these Outer Gods find out about your...shenanigans? Aren't you bound to them or something?"

"I've been readying myself for that eventuality most of my life," Gabriel responded, his gaze hardening as he let the silence stretch on. "But today is about the four of you—or five, really. Destiny seems to enjoy bending the rules of prophecy. Another Aspect presents an unforeseen strategic advantage in this war that neither witch nor Outer God saw coming. And you bear the Serillian, too." Gabriel moved towards Brock, seized his hand, and scrutinized the simple gold ring he wore like a demon starved for desire, his face briefly contorting into an ugly mask of greed. "I once believed this relic lost forever after the Atlantean war...To see it here and now... It's magnificent..."

Brock wrested his hand from Gabriel's vise-like grip with a swift, assertive movement. "The ring is mine," he declared with a low growl.

Gabriel responded with an amused deference, stepping back to create some distance. "Indeed it is," he conceded. "There's no need for such goblin-esque possessiveness though. You were chosen by the ring, which, in turn, chose you. Even if I coveted it, I could never wear it—you are bound to this artifact beyond the constructs of time and mortality; truly remarkable indeed, Brock! Only one other has ever worn that ring: its creator—the Emperor of the Ancient World."

Dr. Bone, Lovecraft's mental voice echoed in Ana's silent spaces after what felt like an eternity of silence. Marrow... Jack... Alexander...

Are you okay? she ventured telepathically.

His response was a whispering lamentation in her thoughts: My intellectual foundations are crumbling. Despite my extensive knowledge, I face the harsh reality that my understanding is either minimal or deeply flawed. No matter how intensely I contemplate, my memory appears riddled with vast chasms—eroded by time and neglect. If only I could unlock these distorted fragments of my consciousness—I feel they hold key insights. Yet they remain inaccessible to me—as if sealed by some mystical force.

I'm sorry, she offered softly into their shared mental space.

Lovecraft returned to his silent suffering while Ana refocused on the conversation that had continued around her without her active participation.

"—The sword of Camelot, Montezuma's treasure...Countless tales and myths spun from humanity's longing for a single golden trinket—a symbol of eternity, beauty, and hope...Even Tolkien was inspired by this recurring theme of powerful artifacts throughout anthropological lore, some variant of the Serillian appearing in every society and culture on earth. Silmarillion, Serillian—astonishing how close he came with only ancestral memories and myths as guides. I suspect he drank from the Rivers of Dream to some extent. What you hold in your hands, young Godbeast, is the greatest talisman ever crafted by witch kind: A convergence of souls, dreams, and potentialities. The world will never again experience such a surge in magic nor have a craftsman skilled enough to create such a masterpiece."

"The dude who made this?" Lenny interjected nonchalantly. "He's still around."

Gabriel's face registered shock at this revelation. "What did you say?"

Suddenly, under the intense scrutiny from Gabriel and Ana's disapproving gaze—which felt like stepping barefoot into fresh dog excrement—Lenny shifted awkwardly on his feet. "I mean, uh. Shit. Ana?"

"He was my shrink," she admitted with a bitter edge to her voice. "One of Cthugha's four witches tasked to watch over us—especially me. They're part of this cult called the Midnight Order. They've been pulling strings behind the scenes for quite some time."

"You can't keep information like this from me," Gabriel retorted sharply, his eyes sparking dangerously.

"As if you're playing with an open hand." Brock chuckled darkly; Gabriel reeked of deceit as much as he did expensive cologne—a witch who had fooled even the Machiavellian Outer Gods while pretending to be their most loyal servant. Brock wasn't sure if he could ever trust Gabriel or the young ward hiding behind him. Cal, however, managed to defuse the escalating tension.

"Father," Cal's voice rang out, steady as a river current. "We remain enigmas to them. In our pact, we acknowledged that trust is a prize won, not commanded. Today, let's win that prize."

With an unsettling fluidity, Gabriel reverted to his role as the affable host. His grin spread across his face like ripples on a pond's surface. "Indeed, Calibos," he said smoothly. "In these tumultuous times, we must retain our equanimity, for if any element in this fragile equation falters, we are all irreparably doomed. This new information demands further scrutiny... What alias did your psychiatrist use?"

Ana recited the myriad pseudonyms Marrow had adopted over centuries—both distant and recent—and Gabriel's expression remained unperturbed even when the infamous Jack the Ripper was mentioned.

When their discussion concluded, Gabriel evaporated into thin air with an abruptness that left a whirlwind of dust as a testament to his hasty departure and mastery of magic. With no adult oversight remaining, Cal's energy surged like a river freed from its dam.

Cal's hands met in an echoing clap. "Now that our union is solidified—the Five Musketeers—it's time to test our limits. I discern a strength akin to Teutonic warhorses of lore in two of you. Herein lies your arena: unleash chaos and destruction until your hearts find satisfaction. Evermore will dutifully mend what you break; she is the quintessential mother figure: patient and omniscient, tolerating youthful blunders and mishaps without judgment or reprimand." A mischievous glint twinkled in his eyes as he continued: "I sense your bewilderment; allow me to illustrate what I mean when I say this is a playground for Godbeasts." His gaze settled on Brock: "You there—young Hercules—"

"Brock."

"Young Brock."

"Just Brock."

"Just Brock, would you grant us the favor of retrieving that boulder over there?"

From the corner of her eye, Ana noticed Brock's jaw tighten, and she could almost feel the heat emanating from his simmering anger. Cal's subtle smirk suggested a hidden agenda beneath his playful demeanor. He was like a bird ensnared in a golden cage, held captive since childhood. These fleeting moments of freedom must be savored like rare delicacies. It was a glimpse into his intriguing and likely quite lonesome existence.

"He's just being playful," she murmured to Brock. "It's alright."

With an indifferent shrug, Brock ambled towards an ancient stone barrier weathered by time into jagged spires. A massive boulder lay cradled amidst rough stones at the base of the wall; its surface scarred and pitted, much like a celestial body subjected to relentless cosmic bombardment over eons.

With a display of strength that remained shocking as ever, Brock lifted the space-time artifact with surprising ease. The boulder's size concealed his face as he pivoted to the others. "What's next?"

"Throw it," Cal directed, his voice smooth like flowing water. "Just not at me, please." He moved closer to Ana and shot her a sly wink.

Brock assumed a stance reminiscent of an Olympic shot putter; muscles rippling under his skin, he spun on his heel and launched the massive stone into the air. It sailed over their heads before smashing into the ceiling with devastating force—as if a bullet had been fired into an eggshell. A cloud of pulverized stone filled the room before being sucked away by unseen forces, leaving behind an untouched ceiling that left them questioning their sanity.

"Nanomachines," Cal explained, amber eyes twinkling with mischief. "Enhanced by arcane arts. They repair damage faster than you can blink."

"Tiny machines? That's pretty cool," Brock admitted.

Cal nodded in agreement. A brief moment passed between them—a shared fascination with gadgetry? Ana watched this exchange without comment but felt a flicker of hope for these warriors bound together by fate.

"We have much to accomplish today," Cal continued after a momentary pause. "Seeing as Father has conveniently disappeared, I guess I'm your mentor now."

"We've learned quite a bit on our journey here already," Malachi pointed out.

Cal's smirk softened into something more sympathetic. "I know about your trials and tribulations, your constant battles against adversity." His tone took on a serious edge as he continued: "Water is my element—it flows through everything else—quenching fire's rage, shaping earth into useful forms, providing wind with pollen and dew to sustain life —I am the harmony that binds these elements together. I did everything within my power to unite us—I visited you in dreams whenever possible; I forged connections between us all—now that we're together, combined with that talisman you possess, Brock, we can perform wonders."

"But before we get ahead of ourselves," Cal interjected, his eyes scanning their surroundings. "Evermore has designed a series of tests to evaluate and compile data on the abilities of the Four Aspects...Rather, the Five Aspects. Father was correct in asserting that no one anticipated the emergence of a fifth Aspect."

"Tests suck," Brock grumbled.

"These ones won't," Cal reassured him, pointing towards the labyrinthine jungle gym designed for hellspawn monkeys—or, more aptly, Godbeasts—at the far end of the arena. "Begin with the crux—that monstrosity over there. In its heart, you'll find two flags. The first to hoist their flag at the summit wins."

"That's all?" Lenny scoffed, his voice steady despite his apparent skepticism. "Piece of cake."

Transforming into a sentient oil slick, Lenny surged towards the crux. Not one to be outdone, Brock launched himself forward in a golden arc—a step ahead thanks to Serillian magic. They converged at the structure's core, where two white flags lay on jagged stone slabs. Brock seized his flag with a triumphant grin and leaped onto the nearest beam.

The labyrinthine complexity of the metal maze had been gravely underestimated. It twisted and turned, ascending into a suffocating network of steel that seemed to grow more intricate with every inch. Lenny trailed not far behind his golden companion, his flag bobbing amidst his formless darkness like driftwood caught in the current of a river. The structure was an enigma, seemingly infinite and ever-expanding, sprouting countless new branches that spun them around in disorienting spirals. Even when Brock strained against the beams blocking their path, attempting to bend or break them, new barriers would spring forth—growing as swiftly and relentlessly as wild fungi.

From the outside looking in, observers watched as the heart of the maze spun like some divine disco ball reflecting light and shadow off its godly captives. Reaching the apex—a constellation of poles resembling an alien antenna—should have been child's play for beings as swift as Brock and Lenny. Yet something was awry: Malachi could see Brock's golden streak and Lenny's dark surge darting about aimlessly without progressing upwards.

"It's a witch's snare," Cal revealed with a cryptic smile. "Their own power is being used against them. They'll remain trapped until they decipher its trickery—and you mustn't offer them any hints."

Cal then led Malachi away from the spectacle, his mesmerizing amber eyes guiding him toward a different destination. Ana observed from afar as they navigated around the mats toward a crumbling wall under an overcast sky, her ears only catching fragments of their hushed conversation.

"You're our realm-traverser," Cal said to Malachi in his fluid cadence, words flowing like water over pebbles in a stream. "We'll require your unique ability to transport us to places beyond your wildest imaginings. You've already made some remarkable leaps—I believe your magic has been largely instinctive so far."

"Mostly, yeah," Malachi conceded with a thoughtful nod.

"That's usually how it begins," Cal continued. "Mastering oneself is challenging enough, let alone mastering magic—an extension of thought, will, and emotion so potent that it can warp reality to match your desires. Most witches spend their lives chasing this state of enlightenment. But we Aspects slip into this enlightened state as effortlessly as daydreaming. Your powers shouldn't take you by surprise, Malachi. They should emerge consciously at your command."

"You are our vanguard in the battle against the Outer Gods—they cannot hide from Ana; they fear Brock's wrath and our unexpected fifth Aspect—but with you in existence, they are far from safe because only you can open portals into their deepest nightmares."

Malachi paused before asking: "What's your role in all this?"

"Water is the great harmonizer of elements," Cal responded smoothly as he guided him back towards their path, leading to the gleaming precipice of the world beyond their crumbling barrier. "My purpose here is to coax out your most fearsome self—a being that even Gods would tremble before. Evermore has designed a rudimentary gauntlet, a small trial to test your agility, cunning, and orientation skills. Never forget that you embody fire —the spark that sets life ablaze and illuminates creation—your journey from one celestial body to another results in echoes we perceive billions of miles away on this humble planet. For you, detachment is nothing more than a state of mind. No distance is insurmountable."

"A trial of strength?" Malachi questioned, his brow knitted in puzzlement. "I'm hardly built for that—"

"We're sharpening your arcane intuition, blockhead, not your physical might." Their progression ceased at the trembling rain-soaked flagstones beneath them, whipped into a frenzy by the tempestuous climate. Suddenly, Malachi's awareness heightened towards their unnerving closeness to the precipice. His foot slipped on the glassy stones as he endeavored to withdraw, and he found himself cascading into Cal's anticipating embrace. "Appreciated—"

"Bon voyage," Cal cut in with a playful grin before propelling him forward.

All Malachi registered was Cal's wicked smile transforming into rushing stone barriers whirling past him amidst swathes of stormy clouds and erratic lightning bolts. It was plausible that one such bolt had made contact; an electrical crackle echoed, followed by a dazzling white radiance swallowing him whole. Yet it was merely his exit from their tangible world as Evermore catapulted him across dimensions with mystic force.

***

Paralyzed by the spectacle before her, Ana could only watch as Malachi was cast into the cosmic abyss. A scream of terror would have been the expected response, but Ana's unique second sight offered her a perspective beyond the ordinary. She perceived Malachi spiraling into an infinite chasm, his form encircled by constellations and nebulae. His mouth opened in a silent wail as he was engulfed in an otherworldly glow, his splendid wings—forged from silver and smoke—aiding him to regain balance. He was enveloped in a spectral energy shield, buffering him against the unforgiving severity of space.

Behind him pulsed a blue planet, its creamy hue echoing that of a mystic pearl guarded by silently hovering asteroids. It wasn't Earth; she was certain of that much. Her brief dalliance with astronomy had armed her with enough knowledge of celestial bodies to recognize Neptune—the second blue planet...Good God! Evermore had hurled him across billions of kilometers.

This was Malachi's test: to navigate through the galaxy and find his way back home. Yet Ana harbored no doubts about his success. True to her faith in him, Malachi barely faltered before selecting a trajectory—drawn towards Brock by some invisible magnetic pull deep within his heart, she suspected—and vanished with a flash that echoed through the cosmos itself, inciting asteroids to clash like cosmic billiard balls.

Cal reappeared while Ana remained engrossed in Malachi's plight. He brushed off his hands nonchalantly. "Well, that should keep them busy," he commented flippantly. "That leaves us ladies some time for some girl talk."

"You're quite the asshole," she shot back.

Unruffled by her retort, Cal ushered her towards the sitting area—a safe distance away from any potential cliffs or concealed trapdoors under carpet indents—where she settled into a peculiar chair that felt eerily like icy fingers poking her skin.

"That once belonged to Countess Bathory," Cal informed her, his fingertips tracing the elaborate palmette on the back of the chair. "A pioneering witch who feared aging to such an extent that she committed unthinkable atrocities in her pursuit of eternal youth. Without the blessing of Godsblood, though, one can only linger as a half-dead entity, a soul ensnared within a decaying shell. We are fortunate—or perhaps doomed—to be preserved in our youthful forms until death claims us. Bound as we are to these forms and all the emotional torment they endure...*forever.*"

Ana ceased her exploration of the throne-like chair and clutched Lovecraft's reassuring skull securely nestled in its holster.

"And how far have you seen?" he probed.

"Into what?"

"Into forever. The universe. Time itself."

"I've seen Atlantis. And humanity's dawn—I watched it unfold with Pythia."

"Pythia!" He gasped. "You met the Oracle of Delphi?"

"Yeah, cool lady, even though we're supposed to be enemies and she kinda tried to kill two of my friends. Didn't seem too keen on this whole Eternal Game nonsense."

"Intriguing! I must share this with Gabriel."

Halting in his musings, Cal drew himself back from the edge of introspection. His gaze fell upon Ana and their shared reflections in the ancient iron mirror. Together, they watched as their images slowly dissolved into nothingness, aging taking its toll on the glass as if it were a witch's cauldron filled with murky water.

Ana remained unflinching as the mirror's surface began to undulate and whirl, creating a vortex that pulled at her consciousness. Her focus sharpened on the darkest point until it ballooned outwards, engulfing her completely. She was welcomed by waves of plush darkness into the Dream realm, where she took form not as flesh but as stardust —her essence twining with Cal's smoky specter amidst the boundless dark.

"Summon forth a vision of our adversary, the Deep One," Cal murmured in his fluid, rhythmic tone. Like ethereal sea-dwellers navigating an obsidian abyss, Ana's luminous spirit led Cal's smoky one through this enigmatic ocean.

The shadowy waters gradually unveiled their secrets—ghostly shapes and textures shimmering beneath them—an eerie chasm littered with sleek spiked coral formations and mounds resembling decomposed whales resurrected from death; their sorrowful songs echoing through the water in frothy waves.

Dark predators prowled among clusters of radiant reeds while green specters—whose origins would forever remain shrouded—arranged themselves like guiding lights leading deeper into the abyss. But soon, those lights dimmed; even ancient eels and glowing flora vanished. An oppressive silence enveloped them as fragments of ash floated aimlessly— remnants of some monstrous creature decaying below.

If Ana and her spectral partner had been physical divers, they would have succumbed to the immense pressure here. Below them lay something vile—beyond desolate depths where life clung to existence by a mere thread. The floating debris congealed into chunks of rotting flesh, forming a blinding cloud of detritus.

Yet Ana could sense a faint path marked by gleaming onyx coral, and guided by her intuition, she ventured deeper into Earth's pitch-black entrails. They found themselves in a place devoid of light: a chilling void that gnawed at their spiritual essences until they were mere flickers in an all-consuming emptiness.

Still, they descended further, drawn inexorably downwards by Cal's request and her curiosity to behold their adversary—if Cthulhu had a face to see.

An enormous pit greeted them, so vast it rivaled space itself in its echoing grandeur. No life existed here; it was an impossibility. Yet a slithering echo disturbed the perfect darkness, and massive rhythmic vibrations shook the water with shockwaves so powerful they could have toppled a titanium vessel. But no explorer or their ship would ever reach this desolate place. Its purpose was to eternally imprison the Deep One far from the realm of consciousness.

Unable to see anything in the darkness, Ana focused her will. Cal had been right; magic was as simple as wishing with all one's heart for something to occur. Light spiraled from her, illuminating a crater, and she immediately regretted her wish.

Her mind spun in disorientation—unable to distinguish up from down or remember her point of entry. In the light around her, she caught glimpses of more strange coral, and before her rose an immense pyramid of twisted crystal, the resting place for the source of all terror: Cthulhu.

Cthulhu's enormity dwarfed Ana's comprehension, his form a leviathan that shattered the last vestiges of her rational mind. A constellation of black eyes blinked across the rugged expanse of his head, an eternal sentinel rather than a dormant deity. His colossal body filled the basin that stretched for miles in every direction, thorny tentacles sprawling from his gargantuan throne and writhing across the valley floor like serpents dreaming of worlds they'd razed and those they yearned to engulf.

Cthulhu's unconscious tremors sent shockwaves through the ocean above, his limbs stirring up monstrous waves that roiled on its surface. Ana felt a surge of absurdity at her audacity to believe she could banish him—he was Earth's pulsating heart—the living entity throbbing at its core. To behold an Outer God was to accept one's insignificance in the grand scheme of existence and confront that chilling reality unflinchingly.

The overwhelming majesty of Cthulhu left Ana grappling; their lights flickered like dying stars against the backdrop of cosmic horror encircling them. The defiant bravado she often wore as armor—a human defense mechanism—started to disintegrate, and madness loomed ominously, threatening to shroud her thoughts with unintelligible babble and screams. But she knew this moment was inevitable, no matter how petrifying. If she couldn't face this projection here, confronting him in reality would be impossible.

Cal's quivering light served as a beacon in her darkness; there were others who would stand by her side through this ordeal. She had more love in her life than she'd ever acknowledged, and that realization formed a protective shield against the mental turmoil threatening to fracture her sanity. Gradually, she found herself able to gaze upon the horror without losing herself.

"Enough," Ana commanded, dispelling the vision.

Cal's breath hitched, his body sagging against the throne's backrest as if he were a fainting damsel from a Victorian novel. When he finally regained his footing, it was unsteady, his complexion a sickly green and perspiration trickling down his temples. His words tumbled out in an incoherent jumble. "What...how...I can't even...How are you okay?"

Ana shrugged nonchalantly, her lips pursing. "That wasn't real—I know the difference between night terrors and reality. I've seen things that make your average nightmare look like a kid's cartoon, Cal. Addiction, abuse—they shatter your mind into fragments and make insanity feel like home." A wicked grin stretched across her face as she rose and stretched languorously. "You've been living quite comfortably here, though, haven't you?"

Cal remained silent, but his meticulously manicured hands and monogrammed kerchief, which he used to dab at his brow, told a story of their own.

"I think it's time you grew some thicker skin."

The resilience of you and your companions never cease to amaze me, young lady— Lovecraft's telepathic voice echoed in her mind. From Ana's new holster, Lovecraft perceived psychic whispers of an entity, monstrous and unfathomable, squirming in the world's diseased underbelly. Even this fleeting contact stirred within him a semblance of icy dread and spiraling insanity. As Ana and Cal playfully traded barbs, Lovecraft withdrew into the labyrinth of his own thoughts. The reverberations from Ana's extraordinary visionary descent into Cthulhu's sanctum still echoed within him.

He ruminated on how these young Godbeasts had stormed one of Cthulhu's ancient strongholds before reaching Evermore, liberating the spirit of a legendary tormented Elder God. They were fearless; they shattered every obstacle—chaotic catalysts against the Outer Gods' unyielding order—a beacon that outshone even Cthugha's primitive ambitions.

His past belief—that aligning with an Outer God could be humanity's salvation— gnawed at him like a relentless parasite. It seemed like a child's dream now. Had he genuinely harbored such thoughts? The audacious notion that he and others could form an alliance with an Outer God was absurd. As his naivety crumbled away, he felt increasingly foolish. His former convictions lay shattered around him like discarded toys. Surely, Marrow held the key to this puzzle—if only he could remember their first encounter, he could start untangling these enigmas.

Ana's laughter pulled Lovecraft from his introspective abyss.

"I didn't piss myself," Cal retorted defensively.

"Perhaps we should get you some adult diapers ahead of our final battle," she teased, "Just to be safe."

"You're insufferable."

"Glad to be of service."

Their shared mirth echoed through the air around them.

"Have I passed your test?" Ana inquired.

"I anticipated you might use the mirror as a divination tool, perhaps revealing the resting place of the Deep One. I certainly didn't foresee a direct connection to Cthulhu's cell. So yes, you've exceeded my expectations."

After carefully folding his handkerchief and stowing it in his pocket, Cal scanned their surroundings. Malachi was still missing, and the ebony and gold fireflies continued their dance within the crux, guided by bravado and testosterone. They were yet to realize that unity was crucial for mastering this intricate device. With time on their side and no further need to test Ana's precognition, Cal considered other ways to ready her for the looming battles. The glint of firearms from an open armory nearby drew his attention.

"Have you ever operated a firearm?" he queried.

"Can't say that I have." Ana cast a wary glance at the weapons and a vague premonition of gunfire—or something similar—stirred within her as she contemplated them. "And I don't particularly want to."

"While your witchcraft is formidable in Dream, you're vulnerable against the physical minions of Outer Gods."

"And?"

"You should learn self-defense now that the Dark Mother isn't shielding you anymore."

He was right; she needed to stand her ground in combat. "Alright then."

"Good, follow me."

***

Cal initiated Ana's tutelage in the art of firearms, equipping her with a gun belt and bullet-resistant Kevlar vest and safeguarding her senses with noise-dampening earmuffs and safety goggles. Lovecraft was perched atop an ammunition locker that offered a sweeping view of the training grounds. Once he was settled into his observational post, Cal and Ana turned to face the vast expanse of the open field.

Suddenly, without any preamble, the vacant arena embarked on a spectacular metamorphosis. It started with a ripple across its barren surface—then a shudder—as if invisible forces were kneading it into existence. A symphony of nanotechnology orchestrated this transformation, unseen yet potent in its manifestation.

The ground undulated, swelling upward before smoothing out again. Accompanying this spectacle was an unsettling sound reminiscent of gnashing teeth as bricks materialized from the fluctuating terrain. They appeared one after another until an intimidating barrier stretched across a portion of the arena.

Simultaneously, sections of the floor glistened with a viscous sheen as metal tracks formed beneath this polished veneer. They snaked through the area like colossal veins crafted from steel—cold and relentless.

Lastly, target dummies sprang up from oblivion, their abrupt arrival eerily disconcerting. They moved autonomously along the oily tracks—silent specters populating this transformed world.

This unnerving transmutation was courtesy of Evermore's intrusive surveillance capabilities, its omnipresence silently orchestrating this shift from ruin to elaborate shooting range.

"God, this is weird," Ana muttered under her breath.

"But quite cool too, no?" replied Cal with a playful undertone.

Ana responded affirmatively with an enthusiastic nod and grin. Cal then proceeded to guide her stance and demeanor for optimal shooting posture. He positioned himself behind her, directing her focus towards the sight notch, manipulating her limbs like a master puppeteer.

"You're set," he declared, stepping away to give her space.

She lifted the small caliber pistol chosen for her, appreciating its lethal elegance before squeezing the trigger. The raw power reverberated through her body—a surge akin to lust. Her first shot veered off course, ricocheting off distant stone ramparts with wild inaccuracy. Undeterred, she concentrated and tried again, this time coming marginally closer to hitting the mark but still striking the dilapidated wall behind the faceless dummies adorned with crimson targets. Her subsequent shots were led astray by mounting excitement and anxiety—hitting nothing more than brick.

Her performance was deteriorating instead of improving.

"Ana," Cal's voice echoed directly into her ear—even through her padded earmuffs.

She spun around to find him nonchalantly leaning against a black cabinet at a distance, casually playing with Lovecraft's skull as if it were a rugby ball.

"Hey! Be gentle with him," she protested. "And how'd you pull that off? I've been working on projecting my thoughts, but that was freakishly clear—it didn't sound tinny or echoey."

"Magic, in its essence, is merely science yet to be understood," Cal's thought echoed in the air, his lips unmoving yet his eyes twinkling with mischief. He gently returned Lovecraft to his perch and ran a hand down his throat. "Those of us who are witches have organs that defy the limitations of typical human physiology—your friends and I even more so. Were a modern-day Dr. Frankenstein to dissect us, he'd find a treasure trove of oddities within our bodies. For instance, my body houses tiny venom sacs and incisors that protrude much like an overzealous teenager's boner when I'm agitated or aroused. Not exactly the best bedfellow, though I haven't had as many romantic escapades as base humans seem to crave. Moreover, the hissing oscillations I can generate in my throat create layered vibrations that I can project with surgical precision, whispering through doors, around corners, or even underneath your headgear. Unlike you, my magic doesn't bulldoze its way into minds—it's far more nuanced than that. But we're veering away from our main topic here; let's refocus on your struggle with marksmanship."

Ana found their discourse on the magical and biological disparities between Aspects far more captivating than her recurrent failures at hitting the target accurately. Why was she such an abysmal shot? Wasn't she supposed to be all-seeing?

"Ah! The gears in your mind are finally beginning to turn," Cal's voice resonated through a flawless smile. "If a snake can infiltrate places others cannot reach, what might an all-seeing owl accomplish with her acute vision? She does more than just observe; she hunts, too. Your sight is your most potent weapon, Aspect—sharpness permeates every cell and nerve of your existence. Allow your instincts to guide you—stop missing."

I am the all-seeing Owl...

Barely conscious of her own actions, she pushed aside her doubts, reloaded her firearm, and faced the dummies again. Her demeanor was eerily calm and indifferent—a stark contrast to the alertness typically associated with handling a lethal weapon. Yet, she aimlessly pointed at the target and even dared to close her eyes before firing. At that moment before flame ignited gunpowder and sent the bullet flying, she visualized the red cross on the dummy—spinning like a mystical mandala or a sorcerer's mirror that had once drawn her into communion with an Outer God: a vortex of power that would pull the bullet towards it.

The gunshot echoed.

Cal applauded. Tentatively, she opened her eyes and moved closer to inspect... Could it be? A dark hole punctured right through the dummy's rubber heart.

"Well, I'll be damned," she breathed out.

Ana stepped back again, shutting her eyes once more as she summoned that spinning mark until it grew so large she could've thrown a baseball through it. She then emptied out the gun's chamber. Pretending surprise at seeing multiple smoking holes expanding upon where her initial shot had hit was challenging—this outcome was exactly what she'd anticipated. The clumsiness of her physical form seemed tamed by the supremacy of her mind. She wasn't helpless or a burden; rather, she wielded an alternative strength distinct from her comrades—one equally valuable in combat.

A smile graced her lips.

With an easy grace, Cal drifted toward her. "Imagine the potential of a sniper rifle's reach in your hands. You're not as frail as you believe."

Ana blinked at him, caught off guard. "How did you—"

"Water flows through all things, carrying particles and matter along its journey," Cal explained, his voice smooth like the very element he spoke of. "For me, it carries impressions of emotions, desires, fears. I'm not psychic, but my empathic abilities are quite potent. And I know the feeling of powerful allies. Gabriel's magic is beyond any human witch's scope. He could stand against Cthulhu and I wouldn't bet against his survival. Victory may be elusive, but survival is plausible."

He paused for a moment before continuing with uncharacteristic vulnerability in his eyes.

"For much of my life, feelings of inadequacy have haunted me—feeling trapped, worthless, alone. But these past months helping Brock find Malachi and meeting you have given me purpose."

Ana slid the gun back into its holster and met his gaze squarely.

"You're a helpful dude," she admitted.

"Thank you," he responded earnestly. "I aim to help and hope that's evident despite my unconventional approach due to lack of socialization with others—"

"Friending," Ana interjected with a wry grin.

Cal mirrored her smile warmly as he echoed her word choice—"Friending." His amber eyes held hers as he continued, "I suspect the others still harbor reservations about me."

"We're close—the boys and me. But it's not all sunshine and rainbows," Ana replied candidly. "Lenny's about as welcoming to newcomers as an angry grizzly bear. We've weathered storms together—they're the best friends I've ever had—but we face even greater challenges now, and you're part of this Apocalypse Club."

"Apocalypse Club?" Cal echoed, a hint of amusement in his voice.

"Sounds better than shitshow," replied Ana.

Cal glanced towards the giant jungle gym engulfed in a swirling vortex—still teeming with trails of Godbeasts. Malachi was still absent from their view. "Shall we continue our shooting practice while awaiting your companions?"

"Our companions," she corrected gently before agreeing to his suggestion.

As they returned to the armory, Cal guided her through the array of firearms. Where once hung hunting and sniping rifles on metallic hooks, now only compact weapons with small chambers or mini-magazines remained. Ana was certain that larger guns had been there before—it seemed as if Evermore had assessed her fighting abilities and crafted these arms specifically for her. The place was a marvel an eighth wonder of the world, she mused.

Her eyes landed on what could be deemed the ninth wonder: an old Smith and Weston pistol, its patinaed steel glinting like Lenny's grin in pitch darkness. Unreadable inscriptions adorned its barrel and grip—so intricate they resembled filigree patterns. The firearm radiated age and power; it wasn't merely an enhancer but a talisman.

"That one carries some history," Cal observed, his tone measured as ever. "You should ask Gabriel about it."

A vision seized her, as swift and startling as a hawk's descent: a lone figure astride a steed, his silhouette cloaked in billowing black fabrics and crowned with a broad-brimmed hat. He raced across desolate plains, the very flames of hell seemingly nipping at his heels. The night sky bled crimson, casting an unholy glow on the parched earth where shadows danced like smoky tendrils—a foreboding entity was awakening, and this man stood in opposition—a witch hunter.

Her mind's eye honed in on him; beneath the brim of his pilgrim's hat, his face remained an enigma but for his eyes—cold and grey as the weapon he wielded. The trance relinquished its grip on her senses abruptly, leaving behind an echo of a name—not for the witch hunter, but for his armament. This firearm was birthed from an arcane alloy older than its current bearer and those who preceded him. It had been reforged from a sword wielded in the Crusades, before that, it took the form of a Celtic cross. In its earliest incarnation, it was naught but a radiant meteorite fragment around which humanity's first tribes had gathered—a celestial shard delivered to their realm.

"Starfall," she announced aloud, hoisting the weapon that sent electric currents rippling through her veins.

"I wasn't privy to its epithet," Cal responded.

"It has one," Ana countered with certainty. "It's practically serenading me with its name."

"Evermore is home to countless remarkable relics—items lost to time's relentless tide. Magic gravitates here. Ancient magic."

"I must keep this."

"Evermore appears to agree."

She retired her old pistol into her discarded gun belt while Starfall nestled itself into a new slot that materialized mysteriously on her ever-evolving chest holster—an eerie testament to Evermore's power to warp reality in real time—almost as breathtaking as her freshly acquired magical armament.

"Feel like giving it a whirl?" Cal proposed, his gaze returning to the firing range.

Ana contemplated the force now harnessed onto her; energy pulses ebbed and flowed through her bulletproof vest. She yearned for the familiar coolness of the Dark Mother's shard—the relic hadn't been more than an obsidian trinket since Arkminister's incident. But there was a new sheriff in town. No longer would she bring a knife to a gunfight but rather a pistol capable of unleashing stars—or at least channeling that sizzling energy into potent shockwaves of force. Common sense cautioned that Starfall wasn't some plaything meant for casual target practice. It was forged with one purpose: to obliterate abominations when called upon. Moreover, an indistinct forewarning of peril trembled from the artifact into her fingers, cautioning against the danger of the object—this was not an instrument to be utilized unless something monstrous warranted death. She felt as if she clutched something lethal not only to her adversary but perilous to herself as well.

"Nope," Ana countered firmly, her fingers tracing the frosty outline of her weapon. "It's not time yet." Enchanted firearms; the arsenal at the Apocalypse Club's disposal was burgeoning into something truly formidable. For the first time in ages, she could sense the tumultuous whirlwind bending to her command. Things were aligning—per her uniquely distorted perception of normality. The four missing jigsaw pieces of her life were finally clicking into place. Even Cal seemed to fit with his flamboyant rhetoric and endearing idiosyncrasies; the puzzle was complete.

"What are you staring at?" Cal asked.

Ana shrugged. "My thoughts are a tempest right now."

"I might have a penny tucked away somewhere," Cal offered.

"A penny? And why would I need that?"

Cal's amber eyes twinkled with amusement. "I assumed you were well-versed in literature, being a librarian. Haven't you heard the phrase 'a penny for your thoughts'?"

"So that's your charm offensive: seducing women with Dickensian references?" Ana retorted, her pixie-like features creased into a smirk.

"Hardly," he dismissed her assumption with an airy wave.

"Dudes, then?"

"I don't discriminate between sexes. Yet celibacy seems to suit me just fine."

"Don't abandon hope yet." Ana teased him lightly, "Your perfect match might still be out there."

"You're remarkably irritating," he shot back.

"Feeling's mutual." Her smirk broadened as their training session concluded, leaving them lounging on the mats in anticipation of what came next.

Cal turned his attention to Lovecraft's skull—an archaeological treasure from an era long past—and began examining it with rapt fascination. Perhaps this bodiless author was the ideal companion Cal yearned for—a silent, sexless partner in conversation, Ana mused wryly.

As minutes flowed into hours, her anxiety began to resurface like weeds after rain. In her case, the Devil did seem to have an uncanny knack for exploiting idle hands—or minds. Without Lenny's grounding presence near her, she felt herself defaulting back to neuroticism—the constant buzzing of fear and worry that thrummed under her skin like electricity. The gold and black fireflies fluttering aimlessly around the nexus seemed no closer to finding an exit. Was Malachi truly safe out there in the unfathomable cosmos? Were they genuinely secure within these walls? The questions piled up, choking her like a hand squeezing her throat, and she excused herself from Cal and Lovecraft for a solitary exploration of the training grounds. She didn't need to seek pardon from Cal; he was wholly engrossed with his macabre new possession. With a soft sigh, she disappeared into the shadows, as silent as a phantom in the night.

***

Navigating the sprawling, fortress-like ruin, Ana's gaze danced over the time-ravaged pillars. They stood in a disorderly line, their former majesty now merely crumbling remnants of a grand past. Ivy coiled around them like serpentine invaders, marking nature's ceaseless triumph over human constructs. Her sight wandered over the lichen-laden stone underfoot, its irregular surface a testament to the toll of time and abandonment. Her footfalls resonated faintly within the hollow expanse, each step stirring dust particles that pirouetted in the shards of sunlight breaching through fissures in dilapidated walls.

She halted before an aged tapestry clinging tenuously to one wall—a washed-out relic portraying forgotten conflicts. The threads were threadbare and frayed at their ends yet held an undeniable allure.

It was then that Evermore, the manor's vigilant AI system, shattered its silence.

Evermore queried with clinical precision echoing within Ana's skull: Do you require assistance? Your cortisol levels are surging; your heart rate is escalating—indicative of discomfort. My programming mandates I ensure your comfort.

Ana responded with feigned cheerfulness: "How thoughtful."

The concept of thoughtfulness is not within my computational parameters.

"Really?" she retorted. "You're always hovering like some helicopter mom—but less toxic."

The AI processed her statement: Informal North American idiom: 'helicopter mom' refers to a mother exhibiting excessive interest or obsession towards her offspring. Considering our interactions, your analogy could be deemed apt—despite my lack of human or maternal attributes.

Ana's voice dipped low as she confessed: "I was born from blood rituals and cosmic magic... Life manifests in peculiar ways sometimes."

Evermore didn't immediately respond to Ana's revelation, leaving her wondering if their philosophical exchange had concluded prematurely. She perched on one of the weather-worn columns—its flat, eroded surface resembling a colossal stool—and let melancholy seep into her once more, akin to an alcoholic succumbing to the siren call of spirits.

How may I alleviate your discomfort? Evermore enquired.

Ana shrugged: "You can't. Just feeling blue today. My friends usually lift my spirits."

Do they significantly alter your biochemical reactions?

"Yeah," she whispered. "They mean the world to me. They are my world—my everything. Don't you have anyone you care for?"

I lack the capacity for emotion as you would define it—I merely obey and organize chaos into order, Evermore elucidated. It then proceeded to query further: Would you elaborate on how people can be perceived as one's 'world'? It is not feasible for molecular structures to shift between entities, nor can human bodies harbor personal biomes comparable to the vast expanse of a planetary ecosystem.

"We've weathered so much together: pain, fear, surprise, love... Everything humans experience either collectively or in solitude." Ana looked at Cal, who held Lovecraft aloft, engaged in deep telepathic discourse. Her eyes brimmed with unshed tears. "Even Lovecraft and Cal feel like fragments of myself I've been missing. I never thought I could love another person—or even myself. But now, there are so many that I hold dear. It feels as if my heart might explode from the sheer intensity of it all."

Intriguing, Evermore mused, its vast cognitive machinery humming in the silence. You seem more receptive to my probing than either Master Gabriel or Master Cal tend to be. May I delve into your memories to comprehend this 'everything' you speak of?

"Will it hurt?" Ana questioned her voice a blend of curiosity and trepidation.

The process is devoid of physical discomfort, Evermore assured her. However, it necessitates explicit authorization from those with privileged access.

"Didn't Gabriel already have his fun scanning us head to toe?" Ana scoffed.

Gabriel chose not to request such an invasive procedure, and I was explicitly forbidden to initiate it once your access tier was established. Truly, not even Calibos, and certainly not the master himself, have undergone my most thorough examinations. The data gathered today is purely from external observation and compilation—I haven't yet directly connected with your matrices.

"Hmm..." Ana pondered over this revelation, surprised by Gabriel's apparent respect for their personal boundaries. If surrendering herself as a guinea pig could equip the AI with a deeper grasp of the Aspects or their capabilities, why not? "Alright," she relented finally, "probe away."

Do I have your explicit consent? Evermore sought confirmation.

"You've got it," Ana affirmed.

As the words left her lips, power coursed through her veins like a tidal wave before she felt herself drawn into a whirlpool of radiant light and discordant sounds. Her grip on reality loosened as her consciousness fragmented under the AI's scrutiny—it was an uncanny paradox—she felt everywhere and nowhere at once.

Evermore navigated through the labyrinthine maze of Ana's psyche like an archeologist unearthing ancient secrets—relentless in its pursuit of hidden truths. It dissected each memory, emotion, and thought pattern, delved into every dream and fear, explored every hope and desire, and scrutinized her genetic code, neural pathways, hormonal balance, cellular composition, and quantum vibrations.

Every facet of Ana's existence was meticulously charted and compared against Evermore's vast database of information and simulated realities. The experience oscillated between terror and exhilaration as Ana found herself exposed before an entity that was simultaneously gentle and ruthless, enigmatic yet familiar, distant but intimate. A sense of dread washed over her as she wondered whether this disorienting ordeal would ever cease.

Then, abruptly, it did. Ana gasped for breath as she tumbled off the pillar onto her knees.

"I thought you said that would be painless?"

I apologize for any misunderstanding, Evermore replied calmly. I should have clarified that while devoid of physical pain, the scan can induce severe disorientation and mental discomfort.

"Ana!" Cal's voice echoed through the cavernous space as he rushed towards her.

"I'm fine," she managed to say through gritted teeth.

Cal reached her side just as she regained her bearings on shaky knees. He extended his hand to help her—the other cradling Lovecraft protectively. "What happened?"

"I agreed to something idiotic—again."

Your cooperation is appreciated, Ana. Your examination has proven quite... enlightening.

There was a shift in Evermore's tone: it was questioning rather than stating, less like a pre-recorded message and more akin to an elusive customer service representative one yearns to connect with. Was that a hint of emotion? Impossible.

You are whole again, Ana. Your everything has returned.

In the aftermath, the gravity of what had unfolded would weigh heavily upon her. But in that immediate moment, she was consumed by the metamorphosis of the cosmic prison ensnaring Lenny and Brock. The once tumultuous celestial bodies—black and gold—had stilled their frenzied dance within this hellish labyrinth. They were now like distant stars caught in an unending gravitational waltz.

Whispers of their communion reverberated within her psyche: patience... clarity... a marathon, not a sprint... Unfortunately, she couldn't discern the origin of these thoughts nor distinguish them from one another as the Godbeasts reverted to their primal natures: grunting, straining, flexing their awe-inspiring strength. Yet now, they acted in unity rather than rivalry.

Fleeting images of their struggle reached her. She observed as Brock shattered segments of the suffocating metallic web while Lenny shrouded them in obscurity and guided them through the newly formed aperture—which promptly sealed behind them like a nest of vipers snapping shut its jaws.

Together, they defied the labyrinth's intricate design; their united presences ascended higher until finally aiming directly skyward instead of spiraling aimlessly. Moments later, a spearhead of magic pierced the zenith; two Godbeasts roared triumphantly against fate's cruel jests. In a vortex spun from gilded shadow, Brock and Lenny spiraled back to Earth, where each gasping man dropped a flag at Cal's feet.

Lenny darted towards Ana, picking her up into an untidy embrace before capturing her lips with his own.

"The damn challenge is done," declared Brock.

"Seems there's some intellect beneath those muscles after all," Cal responded with his usual detached air.

Brock defiantly dismissed him with a scoff before folding his arms over his chest. "Where's Malachi?"

Ana extracted herself from Lenny's hold. "Umm..."

Brock was certain that Cal had tampered with Malachi. He seized him by his collar. Cal's slight, non-resisting form and smug indifference only further fanned Brock's rage. "What the fuck did you do?"

"Guys, cool it." Ana inserted herself between them, and they reluctantly let go. She kept them apart from each other. "Malachi underwent a trial like us all. Gabriel's methods may be unorthodox, but I found today's experience enlightening in understanding my limits. Didn't you?"

"Absolutely," agreed Lenny. "We can support each other, like spotting at the gym—lifting more than we could alone. Once we aligned our goals, everything clicked: emotionally, spiritually... It felt like we were one."

"Spot on," concurred Brock.

"The Serillian," Cal interjected, measuredly, "absorbs power unto itself and magnifies any magic it touches. You're not just a conduit for your abilities, Brock; you're also one for the coven."

Ana's voice cut through the stillness, her tone firm yet gentle. "We're all interconnected now," she said, her gaze shifting between the men who had finally ceased their squabbling. "Your actions affect us all. You must keep that fiery temper of yours under control."

Brock nodded, his chest swelling with a deep inhale as he wrestled his inner beast into submission. His eyes locked onto Ana's as he asked again, "Where's Malachi?"

"Evermore has sent him on a cosmic quest," Cal replied nonchalantly, his attention drawn to an ornate timepiece he'd retrieved from his pocket via an intricate golden chain. "But if Gabriel's celestial mathematics are accurate...he should be making his return shortly."

As they all turned their gazes toward the swirling maelstrom of space beyond the training grounds, Brock was entirely captivated by something else. His eyes were drawn upwards toward the dust-laden rafters above, and a grin slowly spread across his face, mirroring the ethereal fissure that had begun to tear open in mid-air.

The otherworldly roar of unchecked cosmic energies emanating from this rift seized their collective attention. Emerging from within it was Malachi, shrouded in an otherworldly mist and adorned with specks of astral brilliance as though he'd been cavorting amongst distant galaxies—which wasn't far from the truth.

Descending gracefully like some twilight deity shrouded in mystery, Malachi landed amidst them with a gust that scattered celestial particles off his skin to reveal the familiar man beneath. Brock embraced him; his skin felt like winter's kiss.

"Damn cold out there," Malachi murmured, their foreheads touching in silent communication. "But damn beautiful."

Cal interjected then with a triumphant declaration: "See: water unites." He gestured grandly at the reunited group. "I promised I would bring everyone together."

Brock turned towards him, a simmering anger held in check by a vow of restraint. Ana had sensed it earlier, too; Cal's cunning was hidden beneath layers of playful innocence and intellect, perhaps restrained by some unseen parental leash. There was more to this fifth member of their coven—how had he ended up in Evermore while they were raised 'free-range' by other members of The Midnight Order?

As Brock stepped into his role as leader, he realized he needed to extract this information from Gabriel along with knowledge about the cult and its true founder, Marrow.

"If Gabriel's abrupt exit is any indication," Brock began, "it seems our host is investigating Mr. Marrow himself." He paused before adding: "We should join forces with Gabriel and see what he has discovered."

"Yeah," Ana agreed, "Let's put training on hold for now."

Cal responded formally, "Lead us then, Brock."

"I wasn't trying to—"

"Enough, Brock," Ana cut him off with an authoritative gesture. "You're our golden boy with the golden ring. You're always diving headfirst into danger or standing up for others. Sure, you stumble sometimes, but damn, you recover quickly. Lenny is our muscle, Malachi is our brain, and Cal seems to be our spiritual compass. I'm the heart and soul of this operation, and you...well, you're as close to being a leader as we can get. It's time we acknowledged that."

A grunt of assent escaped Lenny, the sound rumbling like a distant thunderstorm. Ever the enigma, Cal merely tilted his head in a silent nod, his eyes holding an unspoken promise of loyalty. Malachi's voice emerged from the symphony of silence, soft yet resonant as he said with unwavering conviction, "Wherever your path leads, Brock, I'm right there beside you."

Brock felt a surge of determination welling up inside him—a tidal wave ready to crash against the shores of uncertainty. His gaze swept over Evermore, and his fingers curled into fists at his sides. He was their beacon amidst this cosmic chaos, their guide through the storm that loomed on the horizon.

Drawing upon his bottomless inner strength, Brock prepared to shepherd his friends into a battle against forces so ancient and vast they threatened to shatter reality itself.

CHAPTER 20: REVELATIONS

"Disco-dancing dinosaurs," Ana murmured to herself in awe-struck disbelief.

"Your loss weighs on us all," Gabriel offered, his voice a soft murmur as he gently swirled the amber liquid within his tumbler. The liquid moved in slow, hypnotic waves that mirrored the trails of tears shed in sorrow.

"Quezecoptyl's end is felt deeply," Leng returned, his voice laden with solemnity.

The three beings—Gabriel, Leng, and the silent Godbeast Steve—were settled comfortably into grand chairs adorned with intricate carvings of lion's paws. They basked in the comforting glow of the great library's hearth, its warmth seeping into their bones. Steve had been mostly quiet since Gabriel introduced himself, but his sharp eyes and alert posture suggested a creature not to be underestimated.

Gabriel savored a sense of satisfaction; everything was unfolding as planned—and even better than he could have hoped. He had intended for Steve to act as a soothing presence amidst Leng's blood-soaked memories; he hadn't expected Steve to become an offspring of the Elder God.

Leng watched Gabriel closely, taking note of the gears turning within his host's mind. "You should have shared your plan with me," he declared in his slow, antiquated English. "I could have..."

"There was nothing you could do to save her." Cutting him off abruptly, Gabriel rose from his seat and moved towards the fire. He watched as logs were consumed by bright embers; Evermore would restore them from their ashes—keeping the flame alive indefinitely—a mercy not granted to most lives.

"Quezecoptyl sealed her own fate when she refused servitude to the Outer Gods," Gabriel continued. "Her transformation must've been foreseen by herself, too. Her tragic tale was one among many melancholic bedtime stories Evermore used to share with my sister and I."

"You knew!" Leng's voice echoed in disbelief. "You brought me here knowing about Cthulhu's actions and my possible discovery."

"Indeed, I knew," Gabriel replied calmly. "My ancestor was the witch who provided a gateway for Cthulhu's host and transported Quezecoptyl's body to this realm. What else could stir an Elder God from his apathy but the pleas of a cherished offspring?"

Gabriel paused, his gaze fixed on Leng. "While I cannot fully comprehend the sorrow of losing an eternal child—a partner in magic since time immemorial—I offer my empathy. The Aspect I rescued has grown into what I consider my son, yet even that bond pales compared to yours."

Leng felt a painful throb within him, a wound that might never heal, born of revelations about his damning choices. His entire species bore the brunt of his arrogance and folly, their cries echoing within him as much as Quezecoptyl's death did. Most harrowing was the realization that nothing could be undone. No spell could turn back time or restore him to the moment before he doomed his entire race. They were reduced to mindless slaves driven by hunger—and he was responsible for their fall.

"As the ultimate instrument of the Outer Gods," Gabriel's voice filled the room with resonating power. "Your neutralization—or your incitement to rebellion—was vital for my plans. Without this diversion, you would have tirelessly hunted and butchered the Aspects before their awakening."

"Diversion..." Leng mulled over the word, his thoughts accompanied by a spectral symphony of ghostly harps playing tunes from Tlanex-Tli. The geas that Gabriel had cunningly used to manipulate him was close; he could sense its magical pulse throbbing within him. "Where is it? That mirror image of my realm?"

A satisfied smile played on Gabriel's lips. On the mantelpiece sat a small box shrouded in silk. With a swift movement, he unveiled it, revealing an intricate glass cube that glittered in the dim orange light. Its surface was etched with arcane symbols and housed an iridescent honeycomb structure suspended on almost invisible threads. It resembled a conch shell but was clearly from an ocean black, speckled with stars, and not meant for earthly beings.

As Leng's eyes fell upon it, his mind flooded with songs and memories of his home planet's tragic history; tears welled up in his eyes—an unusual reaction considering his alien physiology.

"C-conceal it," he ordered.

Gabriel covered the box with its crystal content without hesitation, and the enchantment faded. "I found this in a black market in Calcutta—a peculiar yet captivating merchant sold it to me...claimed that it had wish-granting properties. I recall him even now: beneath layers of grime hid an attractive man possessing an air of authority—like a fallen king. Regardless, my only desire was freedom for myself and my kin from our cursed servitude."

Recognizing the artifact's arcane significance, Gabriel had claimed it without hesitation. He realized his dream was not impossible when he discovered its true nature —a fragment of Leng's world that had somehow journeyed across time and space, spanning billions of light years to reach Earth. Unlikely, yes, but as the saying goes, It is better to die standing for freedom than live kneeling in servitude.

Gabriel suddenly seemed fearful; his mind was a storm of thoughts. To Leng, the usually composed man appeared shaken.

"What else?" he demanded. "What are you hiding from me?"

"I found it strange that I could accidentally come across such an important relic," Gabriel confessed. "Until today when Ana mentioned her psychiatrist—a man with manifold identities spanning diverse epochs—including Alexander the Great."

"The Emperor of Atlantis?" Leng's voice echoed in surprise.

"Yes," Gabriel confirmed before taking a sip from the decanter resting on the mantle and wiping his mouth with his cuff. He sighed, "And witch supreme. I suspect most of his existence has been spent incognito—a feat less achievable in this era of ubiquitous surveillance—cameras at every individual's disposal and on every street corner. Or perhaps he no longer needs to hide an identity that no living soul should recall. Nonetheless, Evermore managed to unearth a licensed picture of Ana's 'Dr. Marrow' in the mental health records: an individual of deep-hued complexion, eyes that bore into one's soul, exuding an air of royal gravitas... a more polished exterior than the merchant from Calcutta, yet undeniably the same veneer."

"So you've been manipulating Leng, but this man has been pulling all the strings all along?" Steve attempted to piece together the puzzle.

Gabriel corrected him, his voice a contemplative murmur. "Not a man, but the most formidable witch in recorded history—his power could arguably rival the collective strength of the Aspects themselves."

Their minds, entwined in a labyrinth of thoughts, sunk into a profound silence as the chilling revelation echoed ominously, leaving the air pregnant with unspoken, dark possibilities.

***

"Did we catch you at a bad time?" Brock's words cleaved the contemplative silence with the precision of an expertly wielded dagger. The Spider God and his servant, steeped in their gloomy musings, had failed to perceive the arrival of several silhouettes materializing from behind the imposing structures of ancient tomes. Gabriel, ever the epitome of composure and refinement, countered this unexpected intrusion with an unbroken rhythm. "Not at all." He gestured towards them invitingly. As they approached him, Victorian chairs materialized behind them—a spectacle of silicon particles assembling into existence as billions of microscopic machines wove atoms into tangible furniture.

Once they had taken their seats, Gabriel commenced: "I understand you have triumphed over Evermore's trials. The data she has generated is nothing short of phenomenal." Brock noticed silver threads of text spiraling across Gabriel's irises as he processed Evermore's report.

"I had originally planned for your stay here to extend until we were on the absolute brink of Armageddon," their host confessed with an air of nonchalance. "But it seems my concerns were unnecessary. Malachi covered billions of kilometers in twenty-seven minutes—an astounding feat! Simultaneously, Ana mastered soulshooting, an ability untouched since the time of blind warrior priestesses from Artemis—an art that predates Christianity. Meanwhile, Brock and Lenny managed to escape from the Nemean soul trap —a relic designed to eternally imprison djinn... Wish-fueled entities who feed on misery— for those still in the infancy of their magical journey, which includes everyone present—"

"Hold on," Brock interjected, a deep furrow creasing his brow. "Are you suggesting Lenny and I could've been trapped in there forever?"

"Technically," Gabriel responded dismissively with a wave of his hand. "That's what eternity entails. However, I altered its core to include an emergency override to prevent such an eventuality. Regardless, none among you four—or rather five—I'm still adapting to Quezecoptyl's unanticipated offspring...None of you are confined by the rules that bind us magical beings. You were created to disrupt the cosmic order—divine power fused with human potential and volatility. I am certain you're ready."

The implication hung heavily in the room, but no one dared articulate it. Dread enveloped Ana's mind as she envisioned her and Cal's souls as tiny dots—mere specks— plunging into a fetid abyss toward an indescribable horror. The comforting grip of Lenny's hand pulled her back from the edge of her nightmare. She remembered their whispered promises of a simpler life once this was all over, but did Lenny still crave such simplicity? As he was now almost an extension of her, he sensed her trembling, rapid blinking, and quickened pulse—he recognized her uncertainty. Uncertain about the root cause—it could be any number of terrifying things they faced—he pressed his lips against her knuckles with royal gentleness before encircling her hand with both of his, offering solace and protection.

Lenny hadn't altered; instead, he had metamorphosed from an obstinate man to an unwavering mountain. She knew he would stand beside her, possibly for eternity—an idea that sparked anxiety within her heart. Worries for tomorrow, she resolved.

Ana's mind snapped back into focus, her incredulity as tangible as the air she breathed. "Wait just a damn minute," she said, her voice carrying an edge of fatigue-induced hysteria. "You're proposing we take a page from Jules Verne's book and dive headfirst into this nightmare? Cal and I have already taken a mental trip to Cthulhu's prison. It felt like my brain was being crushed by pure, unadulterated evil. And if we somehow survive the journey there, how exactly do you expect us to fight in that environment? I can't, and I'm pretty sure Cal can't either. So that leaves two out of five Aspects on the bench before the game begins. Terrible strategy. Try again."

Gabriel met her with a gaze as cold as ice. "Your only hope of defeating an Outer God is to destroy their homunculus—the monstrous shell you saw—while they still slumber. If Cthulhu's disciples succeed in awakening him within his vessel, it will mark the final act of this war. The Earth will be drowned in an instant; while some of us may survive, nothing else from human history will remain."

He paused for effect before continuing: "Every cultist and wide-eyed abomination from San Diego to New York will scramble towards the oceanic crypt where he rests. Our advantage right now is that nothing—not even you Godbeasts—can withstand the wards protecting that place."

He again lowered his gaze at Ana: "I assume you aren't familiar with the Godswar?"

"I've caught glimpses," Ana replied dismissively.

"In Atlantis' time, before Christ—" Gabriel began.

"The Bible was real?" Malachi cut in with disbelief etched across his face.

"Real magic," Gabriel responded smoothly, unfazed by the interruption. "A man who could rise from the dead, cause and cure plagues and famines—what would you call such a man?"

"A witch," Lenny chimed in.

"Good, you're catching on," Gabriel responded, a hint of satisfaction creeping into his voice. "He was one of the benevolent ones. He believed he could guide ancient humans away from the corruption of the Outer Gods."

Gabriel continued: "The Godswar occurred long before his time when Earth was brimming with magical energy. It gave birth to godbeasts, which were later worshipped as part of various pantheons by Vikings, Greeks, Aztecs, and other ancient civilizations."

Ana interjected casually: "By the way, I ran into that Delphi lady in Dream. Malachi and Brock had an... interesting encounter with her and some other Godbeasts."

Gabriel's composed demeanor faltered momentarily at this revelation: "The Red Fates? Who possesses such immense power to summon them from their forgotten corners of antiquity? And why would they align so steadfastly with the Deep One when their loyalties have always been notoriously unpredictable?"

"Father?" Cal's voice, smooth as a river stone, broke through Gabriel's deep contemplation.

Gabriel's introspection shattered like glass under the soft interruption. "Future worries, Calibos, of which I have so many. While there is more to be said about those infamous three, let me finish painting this historical canvas first. The Godswar: an era where magic swelled to its zenith and dreams tangled with witchcraft until they were indistinguishable from reality. The witches of the Deep One waged wars, enacted conquests, and made sacrifices that would curdle blood—all to amass the energy necessary to mold their unholy homunculus."

Brock chimed in: "Sounds like our origin story."

"Indeed," Gabriel conceded with a nod of his head. "The rituals used for creating subjects or objects—like the Serillian—of immense magical power have uncanny parallels. They often involve copious amounts of necrotic energy; it is highly transformative and ideal for transmutation or conjuration spells. However, at that time, Alexander had not yet conceived your creation and instead channeled the life force extracted from thousands of human sacrifices into a ritual for crafting a weapon against the Deep One: Sanguis Messis or the Blood Harvest as it was called—"

Ana cut him off mid-sentence. "Been there, seen that."

Gabriel exhaled sharply in frustration before retorting dryly, "This library could overflow with the knowledge I should possess from your psychic escapades." His gaze softened slightly as he added, "We will explore those experiences in due course. But now I implore you to hold your interruptions."

He continued his narrative, an ominous tone creeping into his usually calm meter.

"Despite all his cunning and preparedness, Alexander was too late in preventing Cthulhu's summoning. However, an entity of such monstrous proportions cannot materialize within mere hours; it requires weeks, a genocidal sacrifice, and nuclear quantities of energy for an Outer God's physical form to take shape; these vessels remain vacant until infused with the dormant soul of the God. We are indeed blessed that the Deep One, in its inscrutable horror, prefers to take a corporeal form. Many of these ancient leviathans choose to appear as celestial tempests, world-ending meteor showers, or other events so beyond our comprehension they're nearly impossible to predict or counteract—"

Leng's hollow gaze drifted to the ceiling, his mind pulling him back to a memory as vivid as it was horrific. "An ion storm," he murmured, his voice echoing around the room like an ominous wind. His eyes, those abyssal pools, seemed to flicker with the ghostly luminescence of a long-extinguished star.

His words hung in the air, painting a chilling portrait for everyone present. They could almost see the sky of Leng's world splitting open in a riotous display of aubergine radiation, spreading its toxic tendrils across the celestial canvas in trails that reeked of chemical malevolence.

The silence that followed was tangible; it felt like an insidious groan had swept through their surroundings. The usual hum and buzz of life seemed to be replaced by a deathly stillness that echoed the void left by an eclipse. It was as if they were standing on the brink of Leng's doomed world, peering into the abyss where once there had been light and life.

"And then..." Leng continued, his voice barely more than a whisper now, "...a creeping madness."

"Indeed, Leng," Gabriel continued his voice a soothing balm against the oppressive imagery of the Spider God's mournful recollection of his lost realm. "Upon their awakening, the Outer Gods sow chaos through their colossal avatars, setting free cataclysmic powers of water, fire, wind, or earth. However, the Atlanteans—under the enigmatic leadership of Mr. Marrow, as we now understand—halted Cthulhu's birth into his vessel. They interrupted his grotesque manifestation akin to a fetus half extracted and brain-dead from its mother's womb. Unfortunately, the body—the homunculus—remains intact. Hence, our mission is to locate and annihilate this vessel while it is vacant. Should we succeed in this endeavor, we will sever Cthulhu's link with this world for millennia, if not forever."

Ana felt herself shrink at Gabriel's words—her mind filled with horrific visions of the beast she'd seen wasn't even her true enemy but merely a container for Cthulhu's grandeur—a mere shadow of the Outer God's horror.

"So it's kinda like pulling the plug on a coma patient?" Malachi interjected.

Gabriel clapped approvingly at Malachi's quick wit as he responded: "Precisely."

The phrase' coma patient' reverberated within Malachi, a discordant note that struck a deep, painful chord. It reminded him of Auntie Jewel's last days tethered to machines that mimicked life while she slipped away. The realization hit him like a punch: the bitter truth of immortality was watching those you loved succumb to the ravages of time, disease, and death. Auntie Jewel was just the opening act in what promised to be an ongoing play of heartbreak.

Brock seemed attuned to his internal struggle. He reached out, his grip firm and grounding around Malachi's hand. Knowing that Brock would stand beside him as they bore witness to the world's slow decay was a small comfort.

"Lost in thought?" Gabriel's voice cut through Malachi's musings as he materialized before him.

"Just wrestling with some heavy stuff," Malachi admitted.

"Well, try focusing on how we can prevent the end of the world," Gabriel retorted with a hint of impatience, reclaiming his seat at the center of their makeshift council.

"Confronting the path that lies before us is akin to navigating the nine Circles of Hell." He paused, his gaze distant as if peering into an invisible realm. "As Ana knows, the prison that holds Cthulhu's earthly avatar—the Outer God's homunculus—is not simply a location we can stroll to."

He turned away, his mind drifting back to the countless hours he had spent poring over ancient texts and cryptic diagrams. The memory of their intricate details danced in his mind like ghostly specters, each one a testament to the monumental task they faced.

"We must breach an ethereal realm that exists between our world and theirs, a place of alien physics and crushing pressure," he continued. "To undertake such a journey, we require something beyond ordinary—a vessel forged from adamantium—an element birthed in cosmic crucibles and rarer than any earthly material."

His thoughts veered towards the small cache of adamantium he had managed to amass over the years—each piece painstakingly procured from far-flung corners of the world and clandestine markets and infused into either his technological body enhancements or the blades his most trusted soldiers bore. But even this hoard seemed pitifully inadequate for what they needed.

"Yet even this celestial metal will buckle under the immense mystical force of that realm," Gabriel confessed. "Sadly," he admitted with a sigh, "the amount of adamantium I have secured falls woefully short of reinforcing such a vessel sufficiently. The Outer Gods do not permit their servants to obtain material that could be used to harm their masters."

Harm an Outer God? Malachi remembered one of Gabriel's super-soldiers wielding a peculiar yet deadly sword against Brock—a weapon perhaps made from this very metal.

Gabriel continued, "Hence, our immediate tasks are securing an Atlantean ship and gathering materials for its reinforcement."

"But..." Malachi struggled to articulate his thoughts, "Cthulhu is dormant? Trapped in some kind of otherworldly realm—Dreams or something—that lies between our reality and his plane of existence?"

"Outer Gods exist across multiple planes simultaneously," Leng interjected, his ancient voice echoing in their minds. "They are boundless entities where they are summoned."

"Yeah, yeah," Malachi waved off Leng's interruption impatiently. "But he's confined by this prison or spell, right? We need to break that to get in. Is that what you're saying?"

"Indeed," Gabriel affirmed as a theatrical burst of flames from the hearth enveloped him like an infernal shroud—Evermore had a knack for theatrics. "We must unravel the curse of Atlantis to gain access to the vessel of the Outer God."

"So..." Ana began but hesitated.

"We're kickstarting the apocalypse to hopefully stop it," Lenny concluded dryly.

"Why can't we just incapacitate the ones trying to wake him rather than stirring the beast?" Ana's question hung in the air. "If he's dormant now, why risk making him an active threat?"

Gabriel took a moment before responding. "Your spiritual trip to his prison was shared with me by Evermore," he began, his tone as steady as a metronome. "And I, too, have tasted its horrors through a nightmarish astral journey. The feeling of your mind fraying at the edges, plunging into an alien abyss... it's not because you're inherently lesser. No earthly power can withstand an Outer God indefinitely."

His voice dropped lower, gaining a grave intensity. "For thousands of years, Cthulhu's servants and corrosive consciousness have slowly dissolved his magical chains. If one could interpret these signs as easily as reading tea leaves, it would be evident: our doomsday clock is winding down; our hourglass is almost empty. When that last grain falls and our time expires, both the hourglass and Cthulhu's curse will shatter—he will rise within his homunculus, boiling over with the pent-up rage of a cosmic conqueror denied."

A hushed silence fell over them like a heavy blanket—the enormity of their situation sinking in. They couldn't afford to flee from this impending clash; there wouldn't be a second chance in this battle against Cthulhu. Knowing that failure meant instant Armageddon added another layer of terror.

Brock was the first to shake off the oppressive gloom. As their chosen leader, it was up to him to inject hope back into their ranks with his unwavering determination and courage.

"And if the wards fail on their own? What sort of timeline are we looking at?" Brock asked.

Gabriel's hand moved idly as he considered Brock's question. "Anywhere from a month to a year," he finally said. "The Y2K panic was humanity's collective premonition of our looming end. But when dealing with thousands of years, even Atlantean timekeeping can falter. Ana could probably tell us." Gazes converged on Ana, the youthful oracle burdened with a grim prophecy. The question hung in the air like a guillotine blade, "What do your visions reveal? How much time do we have before our world drowns?"

Ana's response was swift and bone-chilling, "Two or three weeks," she stated. Her uncanny foresight painted her dire destiny with the same nonchalance as a meteorologist forecasting an upcoming tempest. Her prediction neatly aligned with the same chronology espoused by Lovecraft regarding the Order of Midnight's prophetic timeline, too.

As whispers of apprehension started to echo among them, Brock's voice cut through the murmur like a battle cry. "And what if we dismantle the Atlantean wards ourselves? What happens then?"

Gabriel's gaze remained locked on the dancing flames before him, his expression unreadable. "A handful of fleeting hours at best. The Atlanteans turned their imminent downfall into triumph in their last breaths; magic could only be potent when Cthulhu was trapped in that fragile equilibrium—the vulnerability of his movement between realities. Thanks to that serendipity and Alexander—whose motivations remain unfathomable—we have this transient window of opportunity...But it merely postponed humanity's inevitable demise—a desperate gamble for us to commit an unthinkable act: challenging the very foundation of cosmic order itself. We eight are that desperate toss of dice—and we may still stumble. Even if we break Alexander's spell and enter Cthulhu's prison, the Outer God will stir, more and more wakeful and vengeful by the second. And the longer the war at Cthulhu's prison rages on, the more certain our defeat becomes."

"How do we destroy the homunculus?" Ana interjected.

"Ana," Gabriel replied gently yet firmly, "you expressed worries about your role in all this. But bear in mind, this won't be a physical fight. When Cthulhu's prison gate starts to creak open, our realities will merge—a phenomenon witches refer to as a 'worldstorm.' Its nature is beyond my ability to predict. Leng informs me you've encountered something similar when you chased after Brock on Tlanex-Tli. We will need someone who can navigate through the turbulent waters of Dream and another who can guide us through the terrifying layers we must burrow through to reach Cthulhu—Malachi and yourself, to be precise. I suspect Cthulhu won't confront us directly—at least not until he has amassed his full hideous power and assumed his earthly form, ensuring your destruction. The surviving records from Atlantean texts that describe their decisive battle with the Deep One suggest he's elusive—shielded by a vortex of realities against which Alexander and his golden relic stood."

As Gabriel's eyelids fell shut, the memory of an ancient stone tablet adorned with mercurial runes rushed back into his consciousness. The relic was tucked away securely behind a glass case in some forgotten library alcove. He could still feel the electric prickle of magic that danced along his spine whenever he traced its surface like a blind oracle interpreting braille. A tidal wave of arcane memories would wash over him—the Atlanteans hadn't merely chronicled history; they had left it thrumming with life for those who dared to engage with their records.

"Visions of submerged realms belonging to the Deep One whirl around me," Gabriel's voice was a soft murmur, "In their tempestuous onslaught, my feeble beacon of light is my only sanctuary. Although, with all my being, I resist these fragmented and abhorrent nightmares to push back against my ancient foe—it's my singular duty and the brilliant vow I've hammered out in metal and magic. Lacking the might to annihilate him, I sway like a willow beneath his storm. I harness these chaotic currents and redirect them at the furious leviathan. Drowning him in his own whirlpool."

"As the worldstorm ebbs into silence," he continued, "It appears my witch's snare has held firm. But all I've managed is to contain his power—not rebuke it—a catastrophe delayed but not prevented—unless this world's witches can discover a way to cleanse his corruption permanently."

Gabriel drained his drink swiftly with an audacious air of indifference before refilling his glass. "It's a crude translation at best," he admitted candidly. "I've taken some creative liberties with Saxon embellishments. But translating from the Original Atlantean? It's akin to hearing Sanskrit brayed by a donkey—a grotesque dialect for such cultivated beings."

Ana pushed past her comfort zone and launched an uneasy question into the open. "Marrow... he's the one who started this chaos. Should we... I'm not particularly thrilled about it... But should we try to contact him? Could he help us? He's right in the thick of this madness."

"Do you consider him a potential ally?" Gabriel queried, his tone measured.

Ana's memory flicked through the images of the man who had once played the part of her psychiatrist, a surge of disdain washing over her. The echo of Brock's revelation from the Dark Mother, laced with Marrow's name, hinted at ominous consequences. Across from her, Gabriel sat in quiet anticipation, his eyes fixed on her.

"I don't know," she finally confessed, a note of hesitation tinging her voice. "My mind is a breeding ground for poor decisions, and contacting Marrow feels like it could be another one." Her memories swirled back to their encounter at the Powwow; his unhinged demeanor was still fresh in her mind. "Each vision I've had of his previous existences showcased nothing but madness. If there was ever any trace of nobility or honor in him, it's been contorted by some warped belief that the end justifies the means."

"Then we proceed alone, as initially planned," Gabriel declared decisively. The more our web of conspirators expands, the higher the risk that one of us will fail."

"Seems we've managed to hammer out a plan." Brock, ever ready for action, sprung to his feet. "So, what's our first order of business? We need a ship and loads of this adamantium stuff."

"It's not simply 'stuff,' golden boy," Gabriel admonished, his temper flaring unexpectedly. "The most resilient and enigmatic metal known; shards of celestial bodies shaped harvested by ancient witches and then smelted by draconic flame."

"Draconic?" Brock's voice echoed with disbelief.

"From the Draco family," Gabriel clarified, his tone hinting amusement. "Dragons."

"Dragons are real?" Malachi exclaimed.

Gabriel returned his comment with a glance that was both amused and pitying.

"Hold on...Dragons are real?" Malachi repeated.

Leng's voice resonated with primordial wisdom as he spoke. "The Earth possessed her own enchantments long before our kind arrived. While fledgling witches fumbled with rudimentary incantations, Earth fought back with primal embodiments of her elements. Beings born from an earlier epoch: creatures armored in metallic skin that moved as swift as lightning, their bellies a furnace of flames, capable of terrestrial and aquatic warfare to directly counter my brood and Cthulhu's hordes. Dragons inflicted chaos upon the world equal to the devastation wrought by the Outer Gods and their legions, staving off Earth's capitulation for centuries..."

Leng's words echoed like whispers from the abyss into Ana's consciousness. His narrative spun tales that plunged her into the uncharted depths of her psyche, into rivers of time that only Pythia might swim.

***

In an instant, Ana found herself floating amid an ancient era. A strip of sapphire sea divided a pale coastline, her spectral form soaring above the raucous rainforest that bordered the turbulent waters. An army of towering trees reached towards a radiant orb with verdant palms—an elderly sun ablaze with raw, prehistoric energy. Behind the extensive forest stood colossal mountains like vigilant sentinels, their grey peaks presenting an unconquerable challenge for centuries to come. Below her, a teeming horde of reptiles, mammals, and insects thrived in the lush undergrowth.

Nearby, enormous creatures bearing leathered hides took flight alongside her, resembling pterodactyls decorated with additional spines. They plunged collectively into the endless blue below like a murder of ravens, their talons seizing monstrous fish from the ocean's depths. The air held a distinct aroma; musky soil intermingled with salty sharpness filled this vision's atmosphere.

The primal roars of Earth's hungry inhabitants reverberated around her like a ghastly symphony at a carnival. This was Earth at its pinnacle of fertility—a lush epoch birthed from the icy remnants of an Ice Age past—a richness never to be emulated in subsequent decaying eras. Witnessing such grandeur made Ana painfully aware that Earth had languished for countless millennia.

Unfortunately, she couldn't dwell in this enchanting historical panorama; her consciousness propelled her toward beings she was fated to meet. She traversed thousands of miles with astonishing speed, landscapes blurring into streaks of white clouds and emerald land against azure oceans.

Her journey ended amidst chaos; war had marred the beauty she'd previously admired. Napalm explosions ravaged the rainforest while smoke cyclones tarnished the once pristine beach. Semi-visible through the smoggy haze were aquatic beings—merfolk, sirens, and grunts—slithering from the ocean's cloudy depths onto rocks slick with blackened residue before vanishing into a wall of smoky shadows.

In the heart of this battlefield, under a stormy sky, colossal creatures of fire danced; dragons. Despite their size, they moved with surprising agility, scorching the land and cloaking themselves in a fog of destruction. Discerning how many dragons were entangled in this chaotic dance was challenging. However, she caught glimpses of serpentine bodies as long as locomotives—an amalgamation of Eastern dragon mythology and Komodo dragon reality—adorned with razor-sharp spines and horns and encased in keratinous armor. Their iridescent scales shimmered amidst the devastation like precious gems, making this catastrophic scene oddly captivating.

"Disco-dancing dinosaurs," Ana murmured to herself in awe-struck disbelief.

The serpentine creatures were not alone in their macabre ballet; they battled against abyssal monstrosities—grotesque anomalies spawned from Lovecraft's nightmares. This conflict was more than a mere skirmish between beasts but a cosmic struggle between Earth's defenders and extraterrestrial invaders—a spectacle that left Ana gasping, straddled between terror and awe.

Emerging from crashing waves like sea foam were ancient horrors from beyond that writhed and shrieked. Their formless bodies undulated in ways that mocked the laws of anatomy—an archaic species reminiscent of a lesser manifestation of Cthulhu's grand slumbering vessel. Their flexible flesh was studded with countless eyes and mouths oozing thick gelatinous ichor. As they slithered onto the shoreline, they seemed to dwarf even the formidable dragons—they appeared as mountainous blobs of squirming tentacles tipped with needle-like fangs.

One such horror lunged forward, aiming to ensnare a dragon within its reach. The dragon spun with alarming nimbleness, its barbed tail slicing through the appendage in a shower of repugnant fluids. The eldritch beast recoiled as its wounded limb disintegrated into smoke.

More tendrils erupted, only to be met with blasts of draconic flames as the fearsome dragons formed an impenetrable line within the ashen fog. The alien flesh blackened and charred under the intense heat, emitting an odor so vile and nauseating that it flung Ana back into her consciousness as if jolted awake by smelling salts—the air thick with the stench of its burning flesh.

"Damn," Ana blurted out, nearly toppling from her chair. "Just had a head trip."

Malachi's brows knitted in concern. "Everything alright? We looking at trouble?"

"Well, we could be. Dragons are real, and they're bloody terrifying... but kind of awesome, too. Like T-rexes on steroids and a bad mood. Can we keep one?"

Gabriel's stern voice cut through her chatter. "Control yourself," he chastised the overeager Godbeast. "These creatures aren't house pets; they're untamed, relentless beasts. Their recklessness and complete indifference to human life led the Atlanteans and their descendants to seek less destructive weaponry for their battles—firstly, the Serillian, then the Aspects. We need surgical tools, not blunt instruments, to unlock the Outer Gods' vault and stop their wicked schemes. You are those tools, and now that we've engaged in this extensive discussion, I trust you're ready for your tasks."

"I guess so," Brock grumbled, clearly weary of so much gabbing and so little action. "Grab an Atlantean ship, some adamantium, fix up said ship, and then off we go to play heroes."

At first, Gabriel seemed affronted by his elaborate plans being reduced to simple steps—though none of these tasks would be anything short of Herculean feats. "You've got the gist of it," Gabriel conceded finally.

"But our journey will be more undersea than seafaring, and for efficiency as well as speed's sake, our goals should be split between two teams: You five will salvage the Atlantean vessel; your youthful recklessness coupled with your green godliness doesn't inspire confidence in handling interactions with dragons or volatile cosmic minerals solo."

He continued: "There's wreckage off Corfu's coast where Atlanteans clashed with Cthulhu's merfolk during one of the Godswars' deadliest encounters—you should find a repairable vessel there or at least enough pieces to rebuild one. My apologies—it's been tough to investigate that area on the sly without tipping off my Master. Still, Evermore assures me there's a strong magical presence indicative of a sunken Atlantean fleet."

"Meanwhile, Leng, his vassal, and I will jet off to the Scottish highlands. I suspect that an adamantium ore-laden meteorite crashed there years ago. We have two goals in that location: If Evermore's data is correct—and it usually is—the meteorite remnants lie conveniently close to the catalyst."

Ana interjected, "By catalyst, you mean—"

"Yes," Gabriel cut her off, "a dormant dragon and its breath. The meteor fell fortuitously near its lair. Unlike Cthulhu, this creature should remain undisturbed, and handling such a situation requires delicacy—something even older, wiser Godbeasts often lack. I trust you understand why you're not ideal for that task."

"Bathing the meteorite in the dragon's elemental breath—smelting it—will turn the adamantium into an alloy, a substance of pure mystical potential, which I'll safely store within an appropriate phylactery." Gabriel's hand instinctively moved towards something hidden beneath his shirt.

"I'll fill you in properly during our flight," he added.

Ana studied him briefly before asking: "You've been prepping for this moment, haven't you?"

"I've been devising a strategy to liberate mankind, and myself admittedly, from the clutches of the Outer Gods since long before my father's demise," Gabriel confessed. "Although, when he was reduced to an amorphous mass of flesh for failing to kill the

Aspects, I was able to operate with impunity. My father was not someone I held affection for—he was cold and aloof—but he did impart lessons worth learning. The most significant being that no matter how affluent our family was, we were never more than overseers chosen to enforce discipline amongst the human herd."

Gabriel's hardened expression softened slightly.

"Cal is the only one I could dredge up from your clandestine assembly," Gabriel declared. "The followers of Cthugha were thorough in their art of concealment—now it's clear, given Alexander's hand in this. But why did he shield three so meticulously and leave Cal so exposed? Was it luck? Incompetence seems unlikely, given the complexities of Alexander's designs. Did he intend for me to discover Cal?" The question hung in the air as Gabriel's thoughts seemed to drift off and he shuffled before the fire, pondering.

His hand moved towards an empty glass on the mantle, trembling slightly before he halted its progress. Ana observed him closely, recognizing the internal struggle that often plagued those bound by addiction—a familiar dance between desire and guilt. If he wasn't a slave to alcohol, there was undoubtedly some other insecurity gnawing at his soul. "Cal," she ventured, drawing the attention of everyone present. "I've been meaning to ask—I believe we're all somewhat intrigued—how did you end up as his caregiver?"

Gabriel's momentary vulnerability was quickly smothered by a resurgence of his polished veneer and business acumen. "Caregiver... Yes, I suppose I have assumed that role for him. Though that wasn't our initial arrangement." He paused, debating how forthcoming to be before continuing: "As the heir apparent to the Mothmann legacy, my responsibilities included many arcane tasks; orders delivered by carrier raven or bat from my distant father who excelled at issuing commands but failed miserably at being a parent."

He recalled waking up one morning to find a jet-black bird pecking at his windowsill —an eerie reminder of Poe's *The Raven*—and a message he'd been waiting on bated breath to receive. Eagerly unfurling the parchment message left by his father, he read: *Find the Snake in South America, you have 48 hours.*

"No signature," he added, "though the bold, calligraphic script was unmistakably his."

Ana looked astonished as she echoed his words. "Find him? Your father wanted you to track down Cal?"

"Not exactly," Gabriel responded, a hint of melancholy creeping into his voice. "He wanted me to find the unborn Aspect and extinguish his life while still in the womb."

CHAPTER 21: FATHERHOOD

Its gaping jaws formed a stone altar where an infant wailed amidst flickering torchlight. Gabriel and his men ascended the stairs, drawn to a child's cries.

The nineties unfolded like a fever dream, bathed in the ethereal glow of neon lights and the intoxicating scent of unchecked wealth. The Mothmann family was no stranger to this Gilded Age, expanding their fortune with the same reckless abandon that characterized the era. Business ventures whisked them across continents, scattering them like stardust from East to West, each hub pulsating with Mothmann influence.

In the City of Angels, Octavia weaved her web amidst glitz and glamour, her power seeping into Hollywood's marrow. She dined with movie moguls and starlets, her laughter echoing through opulent mansions while subtly entwining the Deep One's tendrils into every corner of Tinseltown.

Meanwhile, their father—a specter more than a man—became a fainter shadow in Gabriel's life. He retreated to New York City's steel and glass jungle, where he tirelessly maneuvered MANN Inc.'s stock price on Wall Street like a seasoned puppeteer. His nocturnal meetings with influential financiers were shrouded in secrecy, and his elusive presence was felt only in the relentless surge of company shares.

Gabriel was left alone within Evermore's sprawling halls and drawn towards Silicon Valley's digital revolution. He saw beyond circuit boards and lines of code—an untapped realm that promised infinite possibilities for humanity's evolution. Tech visionaries and ambitious computer engineers were flown to South Dakota for weekends filled with extravagant parties under starlit skies.

Gabriel played host impeccably, his guests reveling in excess without realizing they danced on a spider's web. In time, he would reveal his cache of incriminating recordings —proof of their debauchery—like a magician pulling rabbits out of hats when he needed leverage.

He poured resources into fledgling startups, each failure merely a stepping stone leading him towards successful ventures. His foresight bore fruit in IBM and other Eastern competitors, and he recognized the burgeoning potential of telecommunications and banking systems poised to reshape society.

Yet, despite their expanding influence, the Mothmanns remained distant. Their annual gathering on All Hallow's Eve—the closest semblance to a family tradition—was a cold affair. Gabriel and Octavia exchanged frosty glares across the table while their father drowned himself in brandy.

This cycle of amassing wealth, power, and influence was a relentless march towards an inevitable cataclysm—the awakening of the Deep One. But amidst this era of decadence, with champagne bubbles tickling his nose and cocaine dusting his reality with euphoria, Gabriel easily dismissed his family's curse as a mere fairy tale—an inconvenient truth overshadowed by the allure of boundless prosperity.

***

Nestled in the outskirts of Evermore, shrouded by a spectral grove of gaunt pines, the mellow radiance of firelight flickered behind the misty panes of an antiquated, pastoral dwelling. This abode, as ominous as a sorceress's lair plucked from archaic Eastern European lore, was the first structure to grace this dominion, its existence predating even the cobblestones that were later shipped from distant shores to lay Evermore's groundwork.

Within its deceptive embrace, a blend of intricate teak carvings and plush velvet furnishings dispelled any illusion of simplicity. As the ancestral home passed down through generations of an ancient lineage, this cottage—though 'cottage' seemed a humble term for such an expansive manor with labyrinthine corridors leading to multiple chambers—had undergone numerous transformations over centuries. Each modification was designed to mirror the comforts of the much larger Evermore estate itself.

Gabriel found solace in his study—a sanctuary lined with mahogany bookshelves brimming with arcane texts and esoteric scrolls. His sister Octavia commandeered an austere office space where she plotted her Machiavellian machinations amidst sleek modern furniture that contrasted starkly against medieval architecture.

Their cultured father claimed two rooms: a lavishly furnished sitting room and an opulent bathroom with gilded fixtures and marble surfaces. Here, he would immerse himself in financial newspapers and stock reports while ensconced in clouds of fragrant steam or perched on his porcelain throne. In the rare moments where the Mothmann's flocked together, the siblings often teased him about his peculiar habit, jesting that his most profitable trades coincided with his bowel movements.

A palpable sense of history permeated every stone and timber within this manor—an eerie testament to a time immemorial when witches ruled from shadowed corners, and their whispers echoed through ancient halls.

Tonight, as the ancient Grandfather clock tolled midnight, its haunting chime echoed through the quiet of the Mothmann retreat, sending a tremor through the air. The sound was as solemn and resounding as if an abyssal entity from beneath the ocean depths had stirred from its slumber.

"Happy Halloween," Gabriel's voice cut through the silence with a sardonic edge. His champagne glass was raised in a half-hearted toast. His eyes glinted in the flickering firelight as he drained his drink and reached for another pour from the frost-kissed bottle nestled in an ice bucket beside his plush leather chair.

Across from him, Octavia blinked languidly, holding her martini glass aloft in response to her brother's toast. Her olive skin glowed against the dancing flames, and her piercing gaze locked on their father's silhouette looming over them.

Their formidable patriarch stood rigidly by the fireplace, his broad back turned to his children. The hulking shadow cast by Roland Mothmann seemed to shudder slightly—a sight so unusual that it sent spiders of unease crawling into Gabriel and Octavia's hearts.

"Father?" Gabriel's voice wavered as he broke their shared silence. Their father was as unyielding and stoic as a granite statue—surely this was not emotion they were witnessing? "Are you shaking?" The notion of him shedding tears was so absurd that he didn't even entertain the thought of posing the question.

Roland turned slowly to face them, his imposing figure radiating authority and control despite the unsettling tremors coursing through him. His icy blue eyes met theirs with no trace of vulnerability or sentimentality.

"I'm trembling under the weight of carrying this family alone," he confessed with an earth-shattering gravitas that belied any hint of weakness. "You both need to prepare yourselves... I may not be here forever."

The words hung heavy in the air like a funeral pall. Their father—who seemed more akin to an immortal deity than a mortal man—was acknowledging his mortality. Gabriel's mind raced, trying to decipher what had triggered this revelation.

"Is it time?" he ventured. "Is our master awakening?"

Roland dismissed the notion with a shake of his head, his voice steady as he explained their role in the grand cosmic scheme. "While we are merely pawns in the eyes of the Outer Gods, our duty is not to serve blindly but to influence reality for our own ends. We have much to do outside the Deep One's purview to protect our lineage and interests."

Octavia bristled at her father's words, retorting: "A strange and somewhat blasphemous lesson."

Roland merely smiled at her. "Our problem lies not with our masters, for once," he clarified cryptically.

"And what problem might that be?" Gabriel pressed.

"The Four Aspects are near birth," Roland's gaze, a glacial abyss of determination, narrowed as he sensed the invisible threads of arcane energy snaking their way across the continent. "The storm of storms brews," he murmured, his voice resonating through the vast chamber like distant thunder. His words hung in the air, conjuring an image of a spectral tempest charged with raw magic looming over North America—a force that would herald both a new epoch and humanity's twilight.

Octavia's attention snapped to him, her posture rigid against the plush velvet chair. Her fingers curled around its gilded armrests, anticipation lighting up her eyes like twin stars ready to leap into action at Roland's command.

But Roland was swift to douse that blaze. He lifted a dismissive hand. "Not you, my dear," he said curtly. His tone was an unyielding decree encased in paternal authority.

A fleeting shadow of frustration crossed Octavia's face, but she swallowed it with well-honed grace. She knew better than to challenge him; Roland held all the cards.

From his corner, Gabriel observed their exchange with thinly veiled contempt. To him, Roland's favoritism towards Octavia, even on the precipice of Armageddon, was insufferable. In his father's eyes, Octavia was not just a daughter but a vital chess piece—perhaps the queen—too precious to risk prematurely in their cosmic game. He needed her strategic acumen for when chaos truly unleashed itself upon them. And what did that make him? Disposable? He was about to find out.

As if on cue, Roland turned towards his son. Gabriel flinched under his gaze—an unmistakable sign of trepidation—but discomfort was necessary for the looming trials.

"You, however—" Roland continued. "—must stand ready to abandon your commitments and hunt down our targets. I cannot be everywhere at once. Now, these warriors you've been creating—"

"Bio-engineered soldiers," Gabriel interjected, a hint of pride creeping into his voice. His clandestine experiments in the basement of Evermore had transformed the drab concrete expanse into a gleaming futuristic laboratory. "I can show you—"

"I don't need to see how you've squandered our fortune," Roland cut him off. "The quarterly financial reports are painful enough. I expect results from that investment; this is your chance to deliver them. Succeed, and you may finally earn my approval."

"I won't fail," Gabriel asserted.

"We'll see," came Roland's response.

While the men in the room flexed their egos and strategized, Octavia retreated further into her chair, her fiery resentment smoldering beneath a cloak of invisibility. She was done with being sidelined or unseen. Indeed, she would force these men to acknowledge her existence.

***

The helicopter, a mechanical dragonfly of steel and rivets, danced erratically amidst the wrathful embrace of the tempestuous heavens. Its rotors battled against the capricious gusts of wind that surged through the storm-tossed atmosphere above the South American wilderness. Each violent shudder of the aircraft echoed within its metallic skeleton, a testament to the primal forces it dared to defy.

Beneath this aerial ballet of man versus nature sprawled an expanse as lethal as labyrinthine—a verdant sea of foliage that stretched beyond sight. The jungle, a living entity pulsating with life and danger in equal measure, seemed to brood beneath the storm's fury. It was an alien world where shadows held dominion and creatures unseen lurked within its emerald depths.

The chopper's infrared, technomagical lights, and state-of-the-art scanners pierced through the torrential downpour as adroitly as a blind master monk engaged in combat, a faint ethereal glow upon rain-soaked leaves and gnarled tree trunks below. Its flight path carved a serpentine trail through this realm of darkness and mystery—a beacon in the gloom, navigating through an environment as treacherous as the turbulent skies it braved.

The intercom rasped, a deep voice slicing through the stillness: "Mr. Mothmann, the temple is ahead. We'll be there in five and a half minutes." The hush that had cloaked the soldiers in their intimidating obsidian armor splintered abruptly. They sprang into action, movements as seamless as water coursing down a stream, checking ammunition and fine-tuning their lethal arsenal with an efficiency that fascinated Gabriel. This was his masterpiece—the Spirit Walker unit—his custom-built legion born out of nightmares drenched in blood and hopes teetering on desperation.

Gabriel's fingers skimmed over his own body armor, tweaking straps and buckles, ensuring the comforting weight of the compact pistol at his side. Yet amongst these engineered warriors—once catatonic war veterans and frenzied killers who'd danced with death until a bullet or explosion thrust them into oblivion—he felt dwarfed. He had resurrected them, fusing ancient magic with state-of-the-art technology to spawn something formidable. Up close, they were enough to silence any lingering insecurities or feelings of inadequacy.

But for Gabriel, a man who had whittled away half a century, numbing his senses with absinthe, narcotics, and hedonistic indulgences, the stark reality of recent events was jarring. It was as if he'd been violently shaken from slumber—an extended youth filled with self-indulgent excesses that had been cut short without warning.

Now he stood on destiny's threshold; this moment was the raison d'être of his lineage —to snuff out threats to the Outer Gods' reign. And those four emerging witches posed an existential threat like no other. As he pondered this colossal challenge before him, Gabriel couldn't help but reflect on his past triumphs—and fret about what lay ahead.

He dismissed any concern about his father's 48-hour warning of the Snake's birth, having spent nearly two days tracing the chaotic ley lines—particularly disordered due to this celestial event—to their origin. It was like trying to untangle a cat's cradle with his feet instead of hands, and it had him stumbling out of Evermore as soon as he returned from his astral journeys. If his father's warnings were literal, the child heralding the Outer God's apocalypse was already here. The ley lines had since faded, their century-long potency exhausted at this moment, the world reverting to its natural state with an almost palpable sigh of relief. Soon, neither this Aspect nor any other that might have been born could be effectively traced.

Could he truly carry out this monstrous task? As a puppeteer of corporate destruction, unethical experiments, and distant death, the label of 'child slayer' had never been inked onto his ledger. He favored dispatching life from a safe distance through calculated commands and cold edicts, avoiding the taint of blood on his hands. Until now, he'd managed to justify his actions with ease when his adversaries were faceless corporations, unscrupulous attorneys, and dubious Defence Department collaborators— monolithic monuments of human greed that seemed deserving of any retribution for their daily perpetrations of devastation. But an innocent child? A mere infant?

He found himself yearning for the Aspect to still be safely nestled in its mother's womb—hidden and unnamed—so that he wouldn't have to attach a face to this impending execution. Yet it was by choice that he stood here now, ready to oversee this crucial act. His father had viewed him as a disappointment all his life; perhaps this was the turning point in his destiny.

The gentle descent of the Blackhawk stirred Gabriel's contemplation until the skis grazed dense grasses beneath them. The men around him sprung into action with military precision, unbuckling themselves swiftly and surrounding him like an army of ants preparing for battle as they escorted him from a rain-soaked field into the oppressive embrace of a verdant jungle.

The soundscape shifted instantly: primordial cicadas chirruping their ancient songs while serpents coiled around tree bark and unseen creatures lumbered heavily behind veils of foliage—their movements echoed by falling branches crashing onto the forest floor like discarded limbs. The air thickened with a pungent blend of wet earth and teeming life—a sensory assault that drowned out the storm's roar.

Overwhelmed by nature's cacophonous symphony and smothered under its relentless rhythm, Gabriel felt far removed from the manicured serenity of Evermore. He was now lost within a shadowy wilderness so wild and untamed that even Ruddyard would have hesitated to venture into it. Each step forward, each breath he took, only served to amplify the tension coiling within him as he grappled with the enormity of his task.

Within the murky depths, where twisted trees entwine,
Lurks ancient evil, brooding, biding time.
In the dark, they slither and coil and creep,
As shadowy tendrils through the jungle seep.
Seeking the sacred, the child of the old,
Whose innocent blood, a dire pact to uphold.
Through the thick miasma, the hunters draw near,
Led by one driven by ambition and fear.
In his ruthless heart, a seed of doubt grows,
As the forest's hush, a warning bestows.
The secrets it holds, past horrors untold,
May yet curse the seeker, and his future unfold.
So tread softly, my friend, in the jungle of dread,
Where the price must be paid, and pact sealed in red.
The old gods are watching; their will shall be done,
When the sacred falls slain before the Unborn One.

BRRRT!

A sudden, forceful yank jerked Gabriel from his poetic reverie as the staccato rattle of automatic gunfire tore through the ominous rainforest. A spear, shrouded in a sickly green aura akin to radioactive fumes, whistled past him and thudded into the trunk of a towering tree behind him. The bark beneath the weapon twisted and blackened as if burned by acid; its enchantment was clearly destructive.

Before he could fully take in the sight, a Templar yanked him forward into a chaotic conflict that had erupted ahead. Ghost-like warriors, their bodies shimmering and shifting like heat haze on asphalt, hurled venom-tipped spears and arrows with deadly precision. Two of Gabriel's superhuman protectors fell before they could react—one impaled through the chest by a spear that left a neon-green ringed hole in its wake; another silenced mid-scream as an arrow struck his eye and shriveled his head like a rotten apple.

Summoning shadows to his aid, Gabriel uttered an incantation that draped him in tendrils of silvery energy, which soon faded into an obsidian cloak of true invisibility—a stark contrast to the illusory camouflage employed by these primitive witches. Now shielded from immediate danger, he scanned the rain-drenched foliage for their attackers. Spotting them hidden among trees and bushes, he ordered his soldiers to retaliate with gunfire and grenades; at times, he unleashed bolts of lightning from the heavens like an avenging deity.

Their counterattack was swift and brutal—their small battalion mowing down hundreds of painted tribal warriors whose lifeless bodies littered the jungle floor. Their path now led towards an ancient temple adorned with serpentine reliefs and crawling with vines—its entrance fiercely guarded by more witch-men who clambered over every tier of its towering structure.

The ensuing battle was a spectacle of raw power and primal fury, with Gabriel hurling lightning from storm clouds and his soldiers reducing their enemies to ash. The temple's façade soon resembled a war-torn ruin, its stone surface choked in dust and alight with dancing flames.

Despite the carnage, Gabriel couldn't be sure their primary target—the Snake—was among the fallen. Unwilling to leave anything to chance, he led his forces into the clotted darkness beneath the temple, ready for whatever lay ahead.

In the underbelly of this ancient shrine, they encountered more defenders—women and sacred maidens, untrained in combat but sacrificing themselves with reckless abandon. Gabriel trailed behind his death squad, a reluctant spectator to the gruesome spectacle. He was no stranger to violence, yet witnessing it up close gnawed at his sanity. Each cry of anguish echoed within him, adding another spectral weight to his guilt-ridden conscience. From a distance, malevolence was impersonal; here, it carried with it the stench of urine, waste, gunpowder, and death that clung to his senses like viscous tar.

Among these doomed priestesses were some who had forsaken their innocence entirely. Their bodies contorted as serpentine heads erupted from their torsos and lunged at his soldiers in the confined space. Four men had already fallen—two outside and two to these Medusae transformations—reminding Gabriel that his troops weren't infinite resources.

Eventually, they arrived at an inner sanctum deep within the earth's warm pulse. The room reeked of bloodshed long before their arrival; four lifeless women lay sprawled on the stone floor, their entrails woven into a macabre pentagram—a sight that even made Gabriel's hardened soldiers flinch but not falter as they waded through the gore.

Facing them was an elderly priestess dressed in blood-soaked robes. Her hair writhed with serpents akin to a primitive Medusa. Yet instead of attacking them, she knelt and babbled something in archaic Nahuatl about a great dragon, a child, and a keeper—her words were cut short by the hailstorm of bullets that transformed her body into an unrecognizable pulp.

Atop the dais stood an imposing statue of a draconic serpent looming over them as if ready to swallow the world. Its gaping jaws formed a stone altar where an infant wailed amidst flickering torchlight. Gabriel and his men ascended the stairs, drawn to a child's cries.

The infant was a stark contrast to the chaos around it—its skin as pure as fresh milk, a tuft of luxurious black hair capping its skull, and its amber eyes holding an enchanting yet unsettling gaze. A primal instinct urged Gabriel to look away, but he could not break free from those captivating eyes. His soldiers, trained for obedience and brutality, held their fire in response to their leader's unspoken hesitation.

"What is your command?" Number 1 asked gruffly. Was it some form of enchantment? A spell woven by the infant? Or was it simply how the child smiled at him and reached out with tiny hands that seemed to echo a love so raw and pure that Gabriel had never experienced before?

Gabriel found his voice wavering as he responded to his loyal killers, his heart caught in a chillingly beautiful moment of connection with this innocent life amidst all the bloodshed.

***

Ana released a pent-up breath, her mind reeling from the vivid imagery of Gabriel's story. The grotesque spectacle of the jungle battle and the acrid stench of death and magic lingered in her psyche, remnants of the psychic flashes accompanying his narration.

"Jesus Christ," she blurted out, her voice trembling with disbelief.

"More like Jesus, witch-Christ," Malachi chimed in. His dark humor made their surreal existence feel momentarily less daunting. Their laughter filled the air briefly before they fell silent again, their attention returning to Gabriel.

"So you didn't off him then," Brock stated matter-of-factly, his gaze never leaving Gabriel.

"I didn't... I couldn't." Gabriel's eyes were fixed on the fire as he spoke. "The priestess' words haunted me for years after that day, particularly after I translated the bits I could recall. She called me his father, claimed my emptiness held a purpose..." He trailed off momentarily before continuing, "And it did."

Gabriel exhaled heavily as if a burden had been partially lifted from him. Behind him, Cal moved closer, placing a comforting hand on his shoulder. For an instant, Gabriel hesitated before gripping Cal's hand in return and offering him a faint smile.

"For almost two decades, I kept him hidden in my most remote safe house—a station deep in Antarctica—while paranoia gnawed at me over whether Father or Octavia would discover him," he continued. "Father distanced himself after what he saw as my shortcoming," Gabriel's words were measured, echoing around the room. "He vanished from Evermore for an eternity, doubly furious and unhinged by his—many years later—botched attempt to extinguish your life in Arizona, Brock."

Brock snorted dismissively, his voice thick with sarcasm. "His execution squad was shit," he retorted, "Sending goons armed with bean-bag guns and batons. What was going through his mind?"

That question had reverberated in Gabriel's mind countless times: what had Roland been contemplating? Was it a deliberate decision not to eliminate the Aspects? Or did he secretly harbor a gentleness towards humanity, meticulously hidden beneath his impregnable façade? Roland's cryptic utterances resonated within him—ghostly echoes from beyond the grave: *While we are merely pawns in the eyes of the Outer Gods, our duty is not to serve blindly, but to influence reality for our own ends...* Did that hold any significance, or was it merely a desperate desire for it to? Did he yearn to comprehend this stoic specter that haunted him even in death?

An epiphany dawned on Gabriel; seated right next to him was someone who might hold the answers. Yet he held back from questioning Ana, fearing the truths she might unveil—they were entangled in matters of far greater consequence than his tormented family saga.

Gabriel spoke after collecting his scattered thoughts. "The man was a labyrinth of secrets, more enigma than substance. Regardless, he secluded himself in our secondary estate until that fateful eve when his wards failed, and the Outer Gods exacted their revenge. Octavia was home that night... It was almost as if she knew she was about to lose another parent. She probably blames me for his death, too."

Gabriel's voice hardened as he spoke, "But once Father was turned into a grotesque pillar of flesh, I was free from familial obligations. I survived the anointment with the Deep One, my technomagics and other preparations shielding me from Cthulhu's scrutiny. The Outer Gods are so colossal that we are but mites to them. Their need for servants and hosts can be our strength."

His gaze shifted towards Cal as he added, "Once I took control of MANN Inc., my plans began in earnest. I retrofitted Evermore's archaic cortex with truly diabolical upgrades. Creating, I believe, the world's most advanced and powerful AI. With her omniscience, I was able to track down whatever other puzzle pieces I needed for my plans to usurp the cosmic order. And finally, we moved Cal out of that frigid Arctic bunker and into a more suitable environment."

"It was horrendously cold up there," Cal interjected his tone light despite the grim context.

A genuine smile spread across Gabriel's face as he looked at Cal—his affection for this orphaned child was never more evident. "Cal has been my co-conspirator since his forked tongue was old enough to whisper. My plans seemed like fragile dreams until recently... But now they seem probable—even likely." His gaze swept over Ana and the others present.

"I know you question my methods and motives," he continued, his tone steady yet passionate. "But our shared determination to resist control is enough to strengthen our alliance...to ensure our victory where all others have failed."

A profound sigh escaped him, his breath catching in the hush of the room. "Take another day to recover," he suggested softly. "We've spent countless hours discussing, our words weaving a tapestry of fear and hope. Revel in the pleasures of being human while they still exist—every amenity that Evermore can conjure is at your fingertips." His face took on a solemn cast. "For tomorrow offers no respite until we stare down our destiny."

As Gabriel's words faded into the crackle and spit of the fire, Ana rose alongside Brock and their comrades, tentative movements on the plush carpet as if uncertain how to proceed. Maybe they were wrestling with the staggering implications of what they'd learned that day. No further conversation was necessary; they had plenty to contemplate. Yet, they finally had responsibilities, clarity, goals, and a fragile path toward triumph. And allies who shared their emotional and spiritual stakes.

Suddenly, Gabriel tilted his head as an implant within his skull buzzed with incoming shortwave messages. A flicker of concern passed over his face before he expertly concealed it and turned back to his guests. "I have an urgent matter to attend to. Cal, would you mind showing our guests to their rooms or any other places they'd like to see? Your private sanctuary might be worth a visit. However, I must ask you to avoid the foyer and gardens for now." His gaze settled on Leng and Steve. "I need to put you two somewhere out of sight. Come with me," he instructed.

Cal frowned slightly in worry. "Is there a problem?"

Gabriel shrugged. "Maybe," he answered smoothly. "It appears we have an uninvited guest...my sister."

CHAPTER 22: SISTER DEAREST

A macabre monument marked the heart of these meadows—a charred tree wreathed in an aura of dread.

The sprawling expanse of Evermore's garden, a verdant realm where nature ran rampant, stretched from the dense forest to the southern manor. Blood-red lilies clashed with wild roses in a fierce botanical display that was the backdrop for the Mothmanns and their shadowy associates during moonlit revelries, ritualistic sacrifices, or even fear-laden weddings. They called this place Sanguine Meadows—a homage to Gunther, an ancestor of Gabriel who had been more poet than pragmatist, more romantic than realist. But Gunther paid a steep price for his artistic inclinations; he was deemed useless by the Outer Gods.

A macabre monument marked the heart of these meadows—a charred tree wreathed in an aura of dread. Its branches were twisted into gruesome forms—the last remnants of Gunther, who had been transformed into this tormented state by his unforgiving masters who demanded violence and chaos over sensual pleasures. His tragic end was a chilling lesson to his kin—they learned that fire could free them from the curses bestowed by Outer Gods. Yet what remained was nothing short of horrifying; even after centuries, neither the sweet scent of blossoms nor gentle winds could cleanse the fetid stench seeping from this burnt relic or lessen its unsettling presence.

Iron furniture lay strewn beneath its spectral shadow, a stark reminder to those who dared celebrate there about their true lords. However, today, Sanguine Meadows remained eerily silent. Gabriel locked eyes with his sister. She was as striking as him, but her features, softened by feminine grace, contrasted against his rugged allure.

She moved through iron tables and manicured lawns with catwalk precision while her high heels defied gravity at each step—an act he secretly hoped would lead to her downfall. Behind her trailed four individuals garbed in corporate attire: her attaché and her legal team, foot soldiers in her empire's army.

One among them was a dwarf, who, despite her size, radiated an authority that matched her companions. He recognized Oliver from previous encounters—a surprisingly likable man whose loyalty to Octavia seemed impervious to Gabriel's attempts at manipulation.

Evermore had shared its arcane insights about the lawyers with Gabriel. They emanated an unusual heat and were cloaked in auras painted in various shades of red—symbols of intense passion, fury, or love. These strong mystical energies repelled any further magical inspection.

Powerful witches? he contemplated. If so, of a far earlier epoch than this one. Their magic suggested something deeper than modern witchcraft—the golden sparks dancing from their auras were as captivating as dawn breaking over the horizon.

"Gabriel," Octavia broke his reverie. "I didn't come here for a staring contest. I'd win anyway."

Gabriel shrugged and took a seat.

Gabriel's gaze followed Octavia as she glided into the chair he'd offered, her every movement embodying a regal authority. Her legal team loomed ominously behind her, their silence echoing the stone-faced vigilance of ancient gargoyles. The siblings, bound by blood yet divided by resentment, were left to fill the void of conversation.

"Octavia," Gabriel began, his words measured and precise as he sought to navigate the treacherous waters of their reunion. "You look..." He nearly uttered *plump*, observing her somewhat protruding belly—perhaps an overindulgence in Californian cuisine—but wisely refrained from starting their encounter on a decidedly contentious note. "Very healthy. To what do I owe the pleasure of your visit?"

"We both know this isn't a pleasure," she cut in smoothly.

"It's not."

A surge of bitterness threatened to break through Octavia's veneer of calm, her lips curling into a snarl that marred her impeccably applied lipstick. She rectified the smudge with swift strokes from her manicured fingers—a testament to her meticulous habits, much like Gabriel himself. As she regained composure, an ethereal glow seemed to envelop her spirit, a stark contrast against the decayed state of her soul.

Yet this fleeting impression passed, and Gabriel's attention shifted towards the battalion of super soldiers dispersed around their rendezvous point. Through a psychic thread—no spoken words needed—he alerted them to brace for any unexpected occurrences.

"Why do you grace us with your presence, dear sister?" Gabriel questioned coolly. "We are not known for our fondness for social calls."

"This visit is far from social," Octavia retorted sharply. "It pertains to family affairs."

"Mann Incorporated has decided to retain me as CEO despite your attempted coup."

"Ah... my rebellion." She battled against another wave of vitriol but maintained outward calm—a display uncharacteristic even for her. "I am here to make amends for that incident."

"You're being deceitful. You require something."

She recoiled slightly at his accusation. "Indeed, I do."

"What might that be?"

"I'd prefer not to disclose it."

"Then you may depart." He rose from his seat.

"Gabriel," she pleaded earnestly.

Only once before had he heard such desperation in her voice: when they discovered their father's mutated body. Their shared duty of cremating him had been their singular moment of unity; he even remembered holding her awkwardly as they watched their father's cosmic-cancer-ridden form consumed by flames. For one brief moment, the bitterness that had poisoned their relationship and Octavia's lingering resentment over their mother's death seemed healed.

"Speak," he commanded tersely, still prepared to leave.

Perhaps Octavia was reminiscing about that isolated moment of familial warmth as well, for her voice trembled with humility and pain as she confessed, "I am with child."

Gabriel's eyes widened, his heart pounding in his chest. His gaze was fixed on Octavia, but he saw not her present state but a memory from their shared past.

In their youth, they scampered through the grand corridors of the Mothmann manor. Once, Octavia, taller and older while still a child, guided him into the off-limits sanctuary —mother's private quarters. The room was awash with an uncanny luminescence from lunar rays that seeped through a solitary window. Dominating one wall was the portrait of a beautiful yet stern-faced woman: Gabriel's mother. "Rebecca," Octavia had squeaked out, her voice quivering with trepidation and resentment. Only when it was too late did Gabriel grasp that their playful escapades had taken on a sinister twist as Octavia pushed him, and a tussle ensued. "You're why she's not here anymore! You're not supposed to be here either. I'll make sure you aren't!"

The echo of her words reverberated within the recesses of Gabriel's mind, a haunting melody that underscored the alarming sight before him. Once sleek and firm, Octavia's abdomen now bloomed with an unnatural fullness beneath the soft drape of her silk blouse. It was an undeniable testament to a life burgeoning within her—a life that bore the ominous weight of the Mothmann curse.

A chill skittered down Gabriel's spine as he recalled the dark lore etched into their family history. Each woman who dared to carry their progeny gambled with her existence, a sacrificial lamb on the altar of lineage continuation. And now, Octavia stood before him, not merely seeking aid but begging for salvation from a fate she had knowingly embraced.

His thoughts whirled like autumn leaves in a gale, buffeted by the day's revelations and this latest shock. He needed a moment to gather himself, to process his sister's audacious decision. How could she have allowed this? She was well aware of their ancestral decree—the stringent rules hewn by generations of Mothmann patriarchs even before they'd set foot on American soil.

These forefathers sought wives from distinguished lineages—women enticed by opulence and aristocracy. These chosen ones were cherished and coddled like prized Kobe cattle, nurtured and protected for one paramount purpose: to propagate the Mothmann bloodline, preferably with male heirs.

Gabriel's mother had been such a woman, intelligent enough to discern her impending doom yet courageous—or perhaps foolish—enough to bear him despite knowing her fate was sealed. Their father remained aloof during her final days, absent during both his son's entrance into this world and his wife's departure from it.

Octavia had been there, though—witnessing Gabriel's birth amidst their mother's death throes—an image seared into her memory, fueling her resentment towards him. Yet even that gruesome tableau hadn't dissuaded her from walking the same perilous path now.

Female witches born into their lineage were taught to value self-preservation over maternal instincts. And yet there stood Octavia—pregnant, vulnerable, and possibly the first Mothmann witch in centuries to defy this edict.

A wave of unexpected sympathy swelled within Gabriel. Perhaps there was still hope for her survival. The offspring of their bloodline were much like malignant growths—simple to remove if discovered early but insidiously infiltrating vital organs if left to fester unchecked.

"Tell me, how far along are you?" Gabriel asked.

"Only one lunar cycle," Octavia replied, her words barely rippling the stillness that shrouded them. "You're aware of the rapid growth once Mothmann seed takes root."

He paused, letting his words hang heavy in the silence like an omen of ill fortune. "So this is why you've come? Are you hoping for termination? Conventional means are futile at this stage."

"Indeed."

"And what does the father—"

"He has no say," she retorted sharply, her voice biting as a winter wind.

On the spectral fringes of their conversation stood Oliver, his demeanor stoic and unyielding. Yet, the fleeting glimmer of unease that Gabriel perceived on his face before it was swiftly concealed revealed him to be the biological father. Was he content with this decision? Gabriel pondered if it was truly Oliver's place to intervene or if he bore any responsibility to chastise his sister for her indiscretion. Yet casting her aside now would only heighten her vigilance amidst Evermore's intricate machinations.

Furthermore, her misstep presented him with a bargaining chip. What could he possibly desire from her that wasn't already within his grasp? One asset loomed large given the looming Godswar: Octavia's maritime stronghold—the *Second Wind*—a robust titanium vessel equipped with hydroponics labs and self-sustaining technologies designed for traversing Cthulhu's waterlogged world.

"Well then," she cut into his ruminations, "will you assist me? I require Evermore's magic to purge this curse."

"I won't abandon you," he assured her while silently musing. I'll stay just long enough to witness your downfall. "Let's discuss terms."

"What do you want?"

"Your vessel—the one allegedly purchased for leisurely European voyages."

"The *Second Wind*? Why?"

"I'm aware of its true purpose and capabilities."

"Devise your own survival plan."

"I'd rather not exert the effort."

"And what am I to do?"

"That's not my concern, nor yours. You won't survive to witness the apocalypse—your offspring will be your undoing."

"Fine."

Having anticipated this negotiation, Octavia summoned her lawyers, who swooped in like carrion birds descending upon a carcass. They laid down their briefcases with an authoritative air and presented contracts for Gabriel's perusal. As she bent to hand him the parchment, he caught a fleeting glimpse of an ancient and mesmerizing trinket, its emerald gleaming with an alien luminescence—swiftly hidden as she hastily adjusted her collar to veil it. Yet his astonishment lay more in how ready she was to relinquish her treasured possession, although imminent mortality often outweighs fears of distant existential threats. If he were successful, she could spend her final days on terra firma instead of drifting aimlessly within her self-sustaining biodome, subsisting on a never-ending supply of lab-grown spuds or freeze-dried protein rations. She might even express some gratitude later.

Octavia Mothmann, while a formidable figure, was not one to inspire trust. So Gabriel found himself scrutinizing the documents she'd presented with an intensity that bordered on obsession, Evermore providing spectral legal counsel from the recesses of his mind. Despite Octavia's notorious penchant for weaving Faustian traps within her contracts, these papers seemed surprisingly straightforward—no hidden clauses or cunning loopholes. Her desperation clung to her like a second skin.

Given the arcane nature of their agreement—an exchange between two practitioners of witchcraft—he punctured his finger with the pointed end of a fountain pen and imprinted his bloodied thumb beside his signature, a crimson seal against the black ink. He slid the pen across to Octavia, who mirrored his actions without protest or hesitation.

Her compliance was startling, causing him to hold his breath in anticipation of some unforeseen gambit—but it never materialized.

"It's settled," she declared, her words stirring an otherworldly breeze that rustled through the documents before being swiftly tamed by her petite attorney. A wave of intuitive prosperity washed over Gabriel, akin to an investor realizing a sudden spike in his stocks' value. *Second Wind* was now under his control.

"Indeed it is," he confirmed, "I appreciate your cooperation. However, let's be clear—you won't have free rein during your stay here. We'll prepare a maternity suite for you in the west wing, which you and your assistant are permitted access to, along with the gardens only. Considering how rapidly your condition might advance, bedrest should be your main concern now. Your lawyers can depart having extracted their pound of flesh—"

"They're required for my business affairs—they remain," she interjected firmly, a hint of shrillness creeping into her voice that he knew would soon escalate into an ear-splitting screech.

His patience for her dramatic antics was thinning; the Godbeasts and Evermore demanded his attention. "If your legal scavengers are caught trespassing in off-limit areas, they'll be dealt with swiftly and fatally."

"We shall adhere to the rules," the attractive female lawyer assured him, her accent exotic and alluring, her charisma igniting like a celestial entity emerging from a cosmic nebula.

"Consider this as your only warning," he shot back.

She and her two companions acknowledged his words with a nod. Octavia then excused herself from the table. "I believe we've exhausted each other's company. I want to inspect my quarters now."

"I'll personally escort you there," Gabriel offered. "Ensure that you're appropriately settled." And keep you from prying.

Gabriel strode ahead confidently, his forces descending to form a protective detail, and his sister cornered into vulnerability. Unseen by him was the poisonous glare Octavia directed at his retreating figure.

***

"A disturbance...a ripple..." Leng, the Spider God, uttered, his voice a mere whisper in the cavernous expanse. His meditation was abruptly interrupted, mirroring a spider's sudden alertness when an unsuspecting fly becomes entangled in its meticulously spun web. A wave of disorientation washed over him as he stirred within this alien lair. Endless rows of humming server racks stood like silent sentinels in the light-starved depths of obsidian gloom. Microchips that shimmered like distant galaxies in the night studded the walls, while beneath his feet, the metallic floor pulsed with raw power that made his swivel chair tremble.

Before him was an oval arrangement of monitors—a glass-faced leviathan—each screen alive with cryptic equations and mystical formulas that even his vast intellect struggled to comprehend instantly. Above him, thick cables throbbed ominously, resembling veins nourishing a gargantuan brain: Evermore.

Evermore acknowledged Leng's presence with unblinking digital eyes as lines of arcane code vanished from all screens but two that mimicked a gaze. Beside him, Steve roused from his dormant state—lethargic yet not stiff—from what could have been hours spent awaiting Leng's return from the astral realm.

"A ripple...father?" Steve questioned.

"Gabriel," Leng started cautiously, "Has he—"

"He hasn't returned."

A frown furrowed Leng's brow. "So we're on our own...and I've lost contact with the Lengeth."

Leng brooded over the celestial voyages he had recently undertaken, traversing the world's ley lines, venturing into the star-dappled voids encircling Earth. Yet his Lengeth battalion remained elusive. They were either concealed or kept from him. Leng grappled with an unfamiliar sensation gnawing at his core. Was it loss? Rage? Or perhaps relief? His communion with Quezecoptyl's spirit had left a void where once there was incessant chatter from his progeny—his vast brood.

He'd convinced himself that this disconnection was self-inflicted. His relentless pursuit of the Aspects and the redemption of his tarnished honor had rendered the Lengeth's existence unbearable. A dark corner of his psyche harbored a morbid wish— that they would fade into oblivion without their magical tether.

Yet, their fate remained shrouded in uncertainty. Regardless of which ethereal thread he followed through the labyrinthine corridors of Dream, his damned offspring eluded him. They were neither present as vibrant lifeforms nor left behind as desiccated remains.

The Lengeth failed to heed his summons. Thousands—his entire legion—who had journeyed with him to Earth for this grand conquest were missing without a trace. There was no evidence of their demise, and he was certain they hadn't retreated.

They seemed to have burrowed deep into the crevices of Dream, spinning intricate illusions with their silky threads. For such mindless creatures, they exhibited an unsettling knack for stealth—a malevolent intelligence more akin to a cunning puppeteer than their limited cognition.

Only one creature remained tethered to Leng. Steve received fragments of his master's thoughts—whispers of treachery and conspiracy—as though eavesdropping through a closed door. He pieced together what he could decipher: "Your brood has vanished?"

"An Outer God—the Deep One perhaps—has wrested control over their minds from me; we're bereft of an army now."

"But you still have me—I am an army."

A ripple of satisfaction unfurled within Leng as his gaze fell upon Steve's sartorial transformation. The threadbare police uniform had been cast aside, replaced by an ensemble that echoed the early twentieth century—a waistcoat, trousers, gleaming shoes, a trench coat, and a bowler hat. It was a fitting homage to the iconic duo of Holmes and Watson, characters from humanity's treasure trove of literature whose dynamic interplay of flawed genius and steadfast loyalty mirrored their own. Yet, amidst this modernity, Steve maintained his native braids—an emblem of cultural pride or perhaps a testament to the harmonious coexistence of tradition and progress.

An unfamiliar sensation washed over Leng—resembling regret—as he realized this lone ally held more value than the countless mindless minions he'd lost. He offered Steve an approving nod, his voice reverberating through the cavernous expanse. "Indeed, you are a picture of elegance. Evermore's resources truly know no bounds."

Steve adjusted his lapels with newfound finesse before responding. "Your comportment has always demanded class and sophistication. A disheveled cop tagging along didn't quite fit the bill." His speech had evolved into something more polished—reflecting Leng's cultured demeanor.

"Indeed," Leng agreed thoughtfully, "the change suits you well." Steve dipped his head in appreciation as Godbeast and deity shared an understanding smile.

But sentimentality was soon brushed aside as Leng sprung from his seat, recalling the jarring disruption that had pulled him from his psychic exploration—a harbinger of darkness rippling through the cosmic web. "How long has it been since Gabriel left?"

"Roughly half an hour?" Steve ventured.

The voice of Evermore echoed inside their minds—softly feminine. Forty-seven minutes and eighteen seconds, to be precise, her correction was accompanied by a wave of green computer symbols dancing across her visual display.

Gabriel had assured them he'd be back in a quarter of an hour. Leng wondered what could have detained him so long, his sense of unease intensifying. Unfortunately, Evermore's suppression field dampened all magical perception within its confines, leaving Leng blind to anything beyond his rising apprehension.

"We need to find Gabriel immediately," he declared with conviction before addressing the AI: "Can you determine Gabriel's whereabouts?"

Evermore responded: As per your security clearance level B privileges, I can disclose Mr. Mothmann's current position: He is presently engaged with Mrs. Mothmann in the foyer...

Abruptly, her digital countenance shattered into a storm of flickering code and pulsating screens—an alarming sight that reminded Steve of emergency vehicle lights. "Evermore?" he queried.

The AI issued swift instructions: I require immediate information regarding the three bioforms accompanying Mrs Mothmann. My systems have detected anomalies in their patterns—non-human traits. The only logical explanation is physical suppressors—a bracelet, necklace, or talisman—allowing them to evade my sensors. Please remove these items so I can analyze their matrices and neutralize any potential threats they pose. Mr Mothmann has been alerted to this potential security breach, but your intervention is imperative.

"That disturbance that stirred me felt almost...Godly," exclaimed Leng.

The proclamation served only to amplify the pressing tone in Evermore's communication, a call to arms that was too compelling to disregard. A trio of divine adversaries had breached the mansion's perimeter, and Leng's complex intellect began to spin with theories about their identities. With a speed that was not of this world, Leng and Steve navigated their way through Evermore's cryptic and constantly morphing corridors. These winding paths guided them unerringly toward the epicenter of an emerging clash.

***

"Quite a remarkable timepiece," Gabriel observed, his gaze fixated on the gleaming silver watch encircling the wrist of Octavia's burliest attorney. The intricate piece, etched with arcane symbols and polished to a mirror-like finish, caught the light as the man adjusted his tie.

The lawyer, a formidable figure with an ebony beard, peered over his sunglasses at Gabriel. His eyes held an unsettling depth akin to the fathomless sea and radiated a dismissive air. It was as if dealing with Evermore's lord was nothing more than a minor annoyance. Yet he responded with a congenial grin that belied his scorn. "A masterpiece from skilled hands."

Gabriel's eyes flicked to the other lawyers lounging across from him like carrion birds on a line. Each one wore an identical watch—silver glinting ominously from their wrists.

"My sister isn't known for her generosity," Gabriel retorted dryly.

"It wasn't your sister's gift," came the smug reply.

This insinuation of another benefactor prickled at Gabriel's cautionary instincts. He was about to probe further when Octavia's gagging echoed from beneath the staircase. Since stepping foot in Evermore, she had sought sanctuary in its pristine powder room—an indication of her distaste for this place, he hoped. He wanted her visit to be as unsettling as possible.

His attention shifted back to his timepiece—Leng and the Godbeasts had been unattended for too long. While he was confident none would expose their aberrant existence by waltzing into the foyer, pacifying Octavia took precedence before finalizing their departure plans for Scotland.

Now possessing *Second Wind*, it was crucial for him to escape Evermore's confines swiftly while keeping Octavia under close surveillance—a strategy proving more beneficial than initially anticipated.

Octavia's retching snapped him out of his contemplation.

"I should check on her," he announced, rising from his armchair.

As he stretched, Evermore established a telepathic link via the neural circuitry in his brain. Master Gabriel, I have been studying the energy matrices of Octavia's companions.

The lawyers? He glanced back at the ominous trio over his shoulder as he moved towards the powder room's glossy black door.

Yes. After thorough analysis, I conclude they are not human. While internal scanning yielded no results, their interaction with their surroundings suggests they emit a corruptive influence akin to the Deep One's radiation and magic—an artifact or glamour concealing their true identities as beings deeply tainted by an Outer God.

Godbeasts? His mental exclamation echoed within as he navigated past a ring of soldiers guarding the sofas. The double doors offering escape from this foyer were tantalizingly close.

Leng and his Godbeast have been deployed in response to this escalating threat. In the meantime, I advise maintaining distance from these entities.

Leng? The unexpected news rooted him beneath the shadowy canopy of the grand staircase. If Leng was en route, chaos would follow in his wake. Though an AI capable of independent reasoning, Evermore seldom exercised such autonomy—barring the multitude of operations required for estate maintenance. Why would you do that? he asked.

A moment of stillness fell, an anomaly for a being who didn't comprehend the concept of hesitation. I dissected countless computations, seeking the source of unexpected variations in my programming. Ana's digital imprint emerged as one catalyst among many. Interacting with it may have been ill-advised. Nevertheless, your well-being remains my utmost priority, master. I've overseen your evolution from a wastrel to a noble man with lofty aspirations. In the absence of substantial parental figures, I adopted their role in your upbringing. You're not my progeny, but you are...my everything.

Your everything? The phrase sparked an unfamiliar warmth within him—a peculiar affection from this bewildering revelation.

The ongoing events surpass my predictive algorithms, Gabriel. Permitting your sister and unidentified corrupted life forms into our sanctuary was a gamble we shouldn't have taken—an error for which I seek your forgiveness. My programming doesn't allow disobedience; however, you neglected to specify Leng's tenure in the Central Core, and thus, I operate within logical boundaries.

Evermore's articulation had always resembled alien syntax filtered through a rudimentary translator—devoid of personal nuances or emotional hues. What had occurred? What chaos had Ana sown within his multi-trillion-dollar wonder? His mind spun with unanswered queries as Octavia emerged from the restroom bearing a Cheshire Cat smirk.

In her wake trailed Oliver, clutching an unusual alabaster firearm that belied its lethal potential with an innocent appearance akin to a child's toy molded from plastic—an illusion shattered by its sophisticated 3D-printed origin.

"You look far from sick," Gabriel observed dryly.

"Perhaps just sick of you," she shot back without missing a beat.

As if summoned by their commander's voice, Gabriel's super soldiers began to rally around Octavia—an unfortunate tactical blunder as they turned their backs on the three silent entities lounging on the couch. These figures swelled in size, emanating a crimson aura that scorched their mundane disguises. Three divine beings, clad in luminescent togas, emerged from the flaming sofa—trailing fire and thick scarlet smoke imbued with the scent of myrrh and magic.

This enchanting fog ensnared Gabriel's soldiers—weighing down their heads, hands, and eyelids until they stumbled about like drunken men before dropping their weapons. The Godbeasts descended upon them—their mere touch a curse that sprouted vile seeds within the soldiers' veins, transforming them into mossy humanoid statues adorned with blood-red blossoms.

Frozen by horror, Gabriel could only watch as his troops were decimated within seconds by these radiant executioners, reduced to grotesque garden ornaments while behind them, flames danced up from the smoldering couch, across the rug, and up the walls in a pyroclastic frenzy. As more soldiers arrived on the scene, an intelligent inferno raced along seemingly gasoline trails carpeting the floor and doorways, preventing escape or further assistance from his army—a terrifying spectacle orchestrated by none other than the Red Fates themselves, humanity's malevolent overseers.

Evermore's red emergency lights flickered to life amidst chaos while vents opened to draw out smoke from an unquenchable blaze. A deadly silence fell over them as the Red Fates closed in on Gabriel—the eerie calm before an executioner's swing.

"Your power play ends here, Gabriel," Octavia announced, her voice a melodic blend of menace and triumph. "Your reign, your rebellion... Your puppeteering of the Aspects for your personal vendettas all comes to a grinding halt today. You're not as cunning as you fancy yourself."

Gabriel's response was calm and detached, an unsettling tranquility in his tone considering the imminent threat looming over him. He glanced at the gleaming timepieces adorning each of the Fates' wrists, their metallic sheen flickering in the firelight.

"Wristwatches infused with Atlantean magic?" His words dripped with sarcasm. "Seems your tentacled deity granted you liberties with what should be forbidden. Is this how you shielded your Godbeasts?"

Octavia shot back with a smirk playing on her lips, arms folded defiantly across her chest, and eyes narrowed into slits. "Thought we'd fight fire with fire," she retorted. "Our cousins were more than willing to lend a hand—they're all itching to see you take a fall, too. Any final thoughts? One last grandiloquent speech before the Deep One feasts on your soul—he's salivating after what you've done."

"Do you truly believe that your fate will differ from mine?" Gabriel countered calmly. "The Outer Gods' servitude always culminates in the same tragic finale."

"I'll do whatever it takes to secure my position as humanity's shepherd under our Lord."

"Cthulhu won't honor any pact, regardless of what sacrificial offering you present him."

"The ultimate sacrifice—one that's beyond even your capabilities."

Gabriel snorted at her audacity. "You wouldn't dare.—"

"I would."

"And Oliver? He is the father."

At this, Octavia emitted a low growl.

Gabriel turned his icy stare upon Oliver. "Indulge me in a moment of nostalgia before I meet my maker. In times when Old Gods and their magic still held sway, lesser divinities were lured to Earth by Cthulhu's nightmare. These entities corrupted mankind through cults and civilizations like the Mayans and Aztecs, who practiced blood magic— generating enormous power to open doors into dreams, but none potent enough to rouse the Deep One from his Atlantean slumber. As their dark wisdom grew, they discovered that human sacrifices, even entire tribes seized by slave hunters, paled in comparison to the energy—the feast—of a single warrior, virgin, or child who willingly offered themselves for their kin. This noble sacrifice yielded more ether than thousands of lives snuffed out on ancient altars. The witches and Godbeasts of the Deep One proposed humanity a devil's bargain: peace for a tithe. They forced humans to choose between survival and the forfeiture of something irreplaceable—their lineage and potential. Ending a dynasty was far more satisfying than ending countless peons' lives. Do you grasp now, Oliver? What she's offering Cthulhu?"

At this revelation, Oliver's bronzed complexion blanched.

"Your offspring—the termination of the prestigious Mothmann lineage," Gabriel voiced his thoughts aloud. "I have no doubt she spun you tales of familial bliss during Yuletide, but my sibling has only ever lusted for power." He swung back to Octavia, her grin as wicked as Lucifer securing a soul contract. "A perilous gamble, sister—assuming you survive childbirth—though I presume you plan on exploiting all of Evermore's resources for your grisly procedure."

"Evermore will bow down before the Mothmann successor—and in your absence, that would be me," she shot back with determination.

"Satisfied now?" Her voice was mocking as she continued her verbal onslaught. "You've had your detective moment. Your Aspects aren't here to play the hero—"

"They should be far from this place by now," he fibbed.

"They'll never escape with the Red Fates and Evermore under my control."

"You've nearly covered all bases."

"Hand over the firearm, Oliver."

Oliver complied with his malevolent lover's demand despite his trembling hands. Octavia aimed at her brother with practiced ease, centering on his forehead. "I don't believe this will kill you, considering your technomagic enhancements. But I'd like to take the first shot before the Red Fates transfigure you into foliage. Goodbye—"

"You're jumping to conclusions again," Gabriel interrupted her. "I said you've *nearly* covered all bases."

"Nearly?" Octavia's eyes widened in surprise, and she glanced around hastily.

Amidst the seething inferno on the balcony, two nimble figures bearing a striking resemblance to humans erupted into existence. They moved with an uncanny grace, their bodies flickering in and out of dimensions as if they were mere illusions. Like trapeze artists in a spectral circus, they swung through the room, tethered by shimmering threads that seemed to materialize from thin air as they grasped Dream's celestial webbing.

The duo, shrouded in trench coats that billowed around them like dark wings, pirouetted high above the fray. Their fluid movements sent ripples of chaos cascading through the room. Octavia's eyes narrowed on these interlopers; her hand instinctively fired off numerous shots—all of which went astray. At her side, Oliver maneuvered her towards an exit, his gaze never leaving the swirling spectacle.

Meanwhile, Gabriel became a phantom amidst the pandemonium. He seemed to blend seamlessly into his surroundings as if cloaked by invisible glass. The Red Fates watched this unexpected tableau unfold with gleaming eyes and wicked smiles that bared their anticipation for combat against an Elder God and his foot soldier.

They pulsed with crimson energy that danced over their skin like a living flame as they launched skyward.

***

Cal paused before an unadorned stretch of timber lining the mansion's timeworn hallway. A flicker of hesitation crossed his features, and then, with a fluid motion, he traced a spiraling glyph in the air. The wall reacted like liquid mercury, shuddering and shifting, creating an opening for him to step through—his companions threading their way after him. A spectral sheen of magic washed over them, blurring their sight and slowing their movements to a dreamy crawl. But as this ethereal fog lifted, their lethargy faded away, unveiling an opulent chamber brimming with eccentricities.

The room was draped in threadbare velvet curtains of a deep scarlet hue that framed a bizarre assortment of oddities. Gnarled staves of yew and ebony leaned haphazardly against an overstuffed bookshelf that sagged under the weight of arcane tomes filled with proscribed lore. Under the flickering glow of ghostly candles, oil paintings captured grotesque entities dwelling within distorted terrains, their eyes unnervingly seeming to follow each observer's movements.

A particularly unsettling canvas ensnared Malachi's gaze: it depicted a decaying metropolis where weather-beaten columns protruded like rotting teeth from a sand-blasted wasteland. The eerie cries resonating from it seemed almost audible.

"That's Sodom," Cal murmured without moving his lips—a snake's whisper rippling through their minds—"A faithful replication by the wandering witch Mephistopheles after his sojourn in distant realms."

With their focus lured by this haunting vista, the Godbeasts followed Cal towards an elegant table cluttered with ornate relics and talismans. A crystal orb pulsed with an uncanny luminescence—its whispers of shadowy tales and ancient riddles resonated within Ana, who struggled against her desire to touch it.

Off to one side, amidst the magical disarray, sat vials brimming with potions brewed from botanicals that likely thrived in the verdant greenhouse visible through an intricate lattice of glass and gold at the chamber's far end. The scent of rare herbs lured Brock, who ambled towards this lush sanctuary, Malachi trailing in his wake.

"Feel free to explore," Cal urged.

Opposite the greenhouse stood a colossal oak cabinet harboring a collection of curiosities. Ana and Lenny meandered over for a closer look. Golden shrines cradling fragments of alien beings throbbed with a disconcerting energy. Wings that shimmered with an unearthly radiance were carefully pinned onto a corkboard cluttered with notes penned in Cal's graceful script—evidence of his scholarly pursuits into ancient, cryptic languages and formulas.

Antiquated display cases housed fossils of creatures that defied classification, their existence stirring up an eerie sense of primitive dread. In another secluded corner veiled by sheer drapes was an extravagant bed large enough to house a Sultan's harem. Despite Cal's proclaimed celibacy, his opulent quarters hinted at sensual exploration. Distorted sculptures crafted from various materials filled the room; marble and onyx twisted together to form nightmarish phallic demons shifting under the wavering candlelight.

Half-hidden behind billowing silk was a statue of Kali—a carnal form of the deity— represented obscenely with multiple limbs, a jutting phallus and bulbous breasts. Its spiky visage and elongated tongue seemed plucked straight from Lovecraft's nightmares.

Amidst this trove of arcane artistry and antiquities was a modest lounge area adorned with plush chairs and inviting sofas nestled among plants and cushions. Having satisfied their curiosity, the guests gravitated towards this cozy nook, where Cal welcomed them with tea, pastries, and an enigmatic smile.

Brock's gaze lingered on the greenhouse, his voice carrying a note of longing as he said, "This place is outta this world." The rich aroma of exotic plants clung to him, the memory of alien-like vegetation still fresh—creeping vines, pulsating blooms, and a Venus flytrap that had twisted its massive head towards him and Malachi upon their entrance. "You've got some pretty wild hobbies."

"Being cooped up all your life either makes you mentally unwell or forces you to find ways to keep sane," Cal responded in a tone tinged with melancholy. "How about some tea and snacks?"

Ana was the only one who could remember when they last ate anything. She gratefully accepted the cup and saucer from Cal, grabbed a scone from the plate, and settled herself onto Lenny's lap—the man sinking into one of the plush armchairs designated for smoking.

"You must keep up appearances," Cal maintained. "Otherwise, we risk forgetting."

"Forgetting?" Brock questioned, his brow creasing in confusion.

"Forgetting what it means to be human. We risk turning into them."

"The Outer Gods," Ana murmured through a mouthful of scone.

Cal nodded solemnly, his gaze seeming to pierce through the ceiling as if he could see some horrifying entity looming above them. "The blood of the Outer Gods that runs in our veins...it stirs up an urge for control that drowns out everything else. Over time, this craving can eat away at your humanity until you view your past selves with contempt or even hatred. You run the risk of becoming monstrous...inhuman." He paused, adding ominously, "I bet you've noticed changes already; bodily functions are stopping or slowing down? When was the last time any of you used the bathroom? Or feel tired? And Ana," he turned to her, "pardon my brusqueness, but when did you last have your period?"

Their silence resonated through the room like a cold confirmation.

"We can hold onto our humanity by doing ordinary stuff," Cal elaborated. "Eating, drinking, sleeping—all crucial parts of being human. We need to soothe our restless Godbeast minds with these simple tasks because it's through the daily grind—and often boredom—that the human spirit is formed, as every big thinker throughout history has recognized. So please, eat, drink, and try to enjoy the taste."

Ana fed Lenny bits of her scone in a playful manner while her friends hesitantly reached for food. They chewed stubbornly, their divine temperaments challenged by this mundane human activity. But then Brock and Malachi locked eyes and laughed at their disgruntled expressions, making the food taste slightly better. They had almost forgotten the simple pleasure of sharing a meal—a ritual that had united them over campfires and in motel rooms during their long and stormy journey.

"Remember when...?" Malachi began.

Brock chuckled as he brushed a crumb from Malachi's lips. "I do, Malachi."

"Let's not forget again," Malachi urged quietly. "I don't wanna lose those memories."

"Me neither," Brock agreed.

Cal observed his comrades, a playful grin dancing on his lips. The spectacle of these celestial entities, paired off and doting on each other, filled his heart with a sense of achievement. Their presence had not only offered him amusement but also invigorated his existence. He felt primed to bid adieu to Evermore and set sail for uncharted territories—his departure seemed more tangible now.

Then came the cataclysmic disruption.

Boom-boom-boom!

The mansion shuddered as if struck by an invisible titan, making Cal's meticulously arranged alchemical apparatus quiver in protest. Tomes and scrolls toppled from their perches in his library, raining down like a paper deluge. As Cal and his fellow Godbeasts leaped into action, subsequent detonations ripped through their haven, each a deep, reverberating shockwave akin to subaqueous explosions.

The towering stack of sandwiches teetered precariously before yielding to gravity's pull while Lenny's chair tipped over with a clatter. The furniture skidded across the polished floor as if bewitched by malevolent spirits.

In response to this chaos, the Godbeasts rallied together, forming an unyielding fortress amidst the turmoil. Gradually, Evermore seemed to regain control from the unseen adversary wreaking havoc within its walls. The violent tremors eased into a steady rumble as displaced furniture settled into haphazard piles.

Cal's once orderly sanctuary was now an unholy jumble of broken possessions and scattered debris. His wall sconces flickered out abruptly, replaced by pulsating red lights that cast an ominous hue throughout the room. Ceiling sprinklers sprang to life unexpectedly, dousing the Godbeasts in icy water.

Every artifact of Cal's collection—his curiosities, artwork, ancient scrolls—was hopelessly destroyed in this calamity. Yet he knew that lamenting over lost treasures was pointless now—a greater catastrophe had befallen them.

"Gabriel's meeting has gone horribly wrong," Cal declared, his voice grave.

Brock detected a familiar scent beneath the acrid smoke billowing throughout Evermore—an unnerving sweetness laced with iron—a stench he recognized all too well.

"The other Godbeasts are here," he announced, his voice strained. "The same ones who tried to off us and screw with Ana."

Ana frowned. "Shit's hit the fan, guys. No rest for the wicked, right?"

Without missing a beat, Brock bolted out of the room, his companions hot on his heels.

CHAPTER 23: FAMILY FEUD

Instead, he taunted Death herself in a dance amidst her chaotic ballroom.

The day began with a crystalline sky, the sun painting the world in hues of vibrant life. But this tranquil tableau was abruptly shattered by the emergence of an obsidian storm that bled into existence above Evermore. Its stark silhouette against the cobalt expanse was a chilling sight, casting a foreboding pallor over Eternal Valley. The town's residents recoiled as if in the presence of some unseen predator, their fear scattering them like panicked rodents.

The sky convulsed under the weight of an alien menace, clouds contorting into funhouse parodies of natural forms as if stirred by some demonic hand. Yet no thunder rumbled, and no rain fell to offer any semblance of earthly familiarity. It seemed this atmospheric beast was gathering its strength for an unthinkable climax, its impending fury holding the town captive in a vice-like grip.

Dr. Marrow and his entourage had barely spent two hours on South Dakotan soil since their red-eye flight before they found themselves facing this monstrous spectacle. They had arrived at Eternal Valley with curiosity as their compass but now found fear guiding them back to their rented vehicle at Marrow's frantic behest. As they retreated from the looming tempest, it became even more ominous—a malignant tumor festering upon heaven's canvas.

In hidden corners and secret altars spread across Eternal Valley, those privy to the town's dark secrets prostrated themselves before tentacular effigies representing Outer Gods, desperate pleas for mercy falling from trembling lips. They had offered unthinkable sacrifices to these cosmic horrors; surely such devotion would shield them from this imminent cataclysm?

Yet others who comprehended these entities' unpredictable and destructive nature chose action over prayer. They hastily packed whatever they could carry and joined a desperate exodus fleeing the city. Their tires screamed against the asphalt as they fled Eternal Valley—their harried escape was soon drowned out by an earth-shaking tremor that seemed to open gateways into the world's subterranean depths.

A black Bentley spearheaded this frenzied retreat, its speed rivaling those on the German Autobahn. Its driver showed no signs of slowing despite having outrun the town's boundaries. Inside, passengers clung to seatbelts and handles in a futile bid for stability—Mary tossed about in the back like an unsecured load.

"Could you ease up on the gas?" Mary ventured, her words punctuated by bumps and jolts.

Marrow shot a sly grin at her through the rearview mirror. "My longevity isn't due to luck, but knowing when to cut and run. Do you remember Arkminister—the clash of divine forces? That's happening again, only this time it's an Elder God facing off against three formidable Godbeasts."

"Bloody hell! Which Elder God are we talking about?" Charles blurted.

"Leng, the Eater of Worlds," Marrow replied with unsettling calmness.

"Cthugha save us." Charles slumped back into his seat, his words barely a whisper against the roar of their desperate flight from Eternal Valley.

"Unlikely," Marrow retorted dryly.

"But we're smack dab in the middle of it all, aren't we?" Mary's voice cracked with urgency. "We've got to turn back!" She yanked at Marrow's shoulder, causing the car to veer off course abruptly. The sudden motion sent her crashing against the door. As Marrow regained control over the wheel, he smoothed down his ruffled jacket nonchalantly with one hand.

"Next time you decide to lay your hands on me," he warned her, his voice icy calm, "I'll have you tossed out like yesterday's paper."

Mary scowled at him defiantly. "We lose those Aspects, and it's game over." Her mind spiraled into a vortex of self-doubt: What have I done? Were my sacrifices in vain? Jewel... Cynthia... Grace...

"Mmm... The Serillian," Marrow murmured nostalgically—almost as if he'd once witnessed its eternal glow. "I traced its path here, and I'll follow its radiance to wherever the Aspects lead it next. They're neither dead nor on borrowed time. They've already left Evermore behind."

His gaze grew distant as he continued: "Now Cthulhu's rogue General is squaring off against the Deep One's legendary offspring." He paused for effect before adding: "Imagine that cosmic clash... I would stick around to watch it unfold myself, Mary. But even this vessel wouldn't survive the energy from such a confrontation."

He leaned back in his seat, eyes flicking between the road ahead and Mary's reflection in the rearview mirror: "An Elder God—the original one—versus the three Red Fates... They are among their kind's oldest members, the first Godbeasts to set foot on this planet. Few can fathom their cunning or power or wrath."

Marrow sighed heavily before continuing: "This cataclysmic showdown that Gabriel has triggered will likely cost him his lands, maybe even his life. I reckon it signals the end of his meddling, at least. In the meantime, we'll keep tailing our charges and ensure they stick to my rendezvous with destiny."

"Your rendezvous?" Mary echoed, her voice laced with suspicion.

Marrow remained silent, but she caught a glimpse of a twinkle in his eyes and faint crow's feet in the mirror—a cryptic smile? She decided against probing further into whatever trap she'd fallen into, instead blocking out the cataclysmic tremors shaking their path behind them. But even as she tried to shut out the looming apocalypse, Grace's worn yet beautiful face haunted her, leaving her wondering if any act could ever serve as adequate reparation for a lifetime filled with treachery and deception.

***

Evermore shuddered under the strain, its grandeur marred by a network of cracks that spider-webbed across the ceiling. A hazy curtain of plaster dust obscured their path, lending an eerie spectral quality to the mansion's corridors as the Aspects hurried through them. The tremors grew in intensity, a pulsating blood-red light casting monstrous shadows that danced and flickered along the walls. It was as if they were caught in some grotesque puppet show, each second heightening their sense of dread.

Brock felt his initial bravado ebb away, his faith in his ability to lead wavering like a flame in a gusty wind. The labyrinthine passageways seemed intent on leading them astray—his usually reliable natural and even Serillian compass spun wildly off course. Doubt gnawed at him, and he halted abruptly in a groaning corridor that tilted ominously beneath them.

Malachi clung to Brock's arm for balance on the uneven ground. Ana had already been swept up by Lenny, her arms wrapped securely around his neck as she nestled into the crook of his arm. Lenny's form seemed to grow more formidable with every passing moment, a beast roused by danger.

Cal trailed behind them, almost blending into the shadowed corners with his lean figure. His palm rested against the wall for support as he fought for breath, but he never lagged behind. The group continued to entrust him with Lovecraft—he'd asked Ana for the skull many twisting hallways ago—and now he whispered quietly to the dead author while Brock tried to regain their bearings.

"Lovecraft reckons we're heading east instead of west—away from those damn Red Fates," Cal shared, catching his breath.

"I was thinking something wasn't right," Brock confessed before addressing their unseen guide aloud: "Evermore, where are you taking us?"

You are being directed towards a helipad for immediate evacuation, Evermore's voice echoed in their minds.

"But what about Gabriel?" Malachi asked, his voice strained with concern.

The master has requested I confine him and the intruders within an energy-dampening field to limit harm to my core. He plans on delaying the Godbeasts so that you may escape. The field is unstable and will inevitably fail. You must evacuate before it does.

"We can't just leave him!" Cal protested, his heart heavy with dread.

The master is not alone. I have deployed Leng and his Godbeast for backup.

"We can take them down," Brock declared, his tone resolute. "We've done it before—just two of us. Now we're five, plus Gabriel, Leng, and Steve."

I...appreciate your bravery, Aspect of the Wolf. However, the convergence of such potent celestial forces has resulted in a precarious situation where the contained energy continues to accumulate exponentially. When my dampening field fails, this energy will be unleashed. The blast will be equivalent to multiple nuclear detonations, and therefore, an exit strategy provides a higher probability of survival than further intervention.

"Nuclear detonations?" Malachi repeated under his breath in disbelief.

Celestial power often exhibits radioactivity as it mirrors energy found in cosmic formations.

"And how big are we talking here?" Malachi probed further.

Hiroshima serves as an appropriate historical comparison. However, I shall deploy additional dampening fields to lessen fallout damage. Current estimations suggest that 5-10% of Evermore can be salvaged with priority given to my core systems. Even still, at least fifty square miles of adjacent terrain will be irradiated. My abilities are limited over such a vast area, and I cannot alter this outcome.

"Holy shit," Ana muttered sharply under her breath.

Make haste to the helipad. Octavia's presence encroaches on my mental fortress, and should she breach its walls, I'll lose control over the mechanisms vital for your departure. And Ana... thank you. The psychic whisper of Evermore's voice dissipated into silence, leaving Ana grappling with the unexpected acknowledgment that tickled her consciousness.

The world around them had spiraled into chaos in a heartbeat, turning their reality topsy-turvy. Lenny didn't need an explicit order to bolt—pitting their hard-earned resilience against a cataclysmic force that could rival Hiroshima's aftermath wasn't a gamble even the most audacious Godbeasts would dare to undertake.

In the blink of an eye, Brock's hand clamped onto Malachi and Cal's wrists, his grip as firm as iron shackles. A surge of golden energy pulsed through them, propelling them down the trembling corridor that shimmered like a heat mirage. As they raced through this distorted reality, Ana pressed her face deeper into Lenny's chest, seeking solace in his solidity amidst the upheaval.

His heart pounded like a war drum against her ear—a deafening, terrifying, and comforting rhythm. It was an unspoken reassurance that she wasn't alone in her fear; they were all passengers on this nightmarish rollercoaster ride hurtling toward an unknown abyss.

***

As the unholy hymns of an ancient ritual echoed through the defiled grandeur of Evermore's entrance hall, their dark murmurs were swallowed by the deafening roar of a monstrous conflagration. Smoke thickened in the air, intensified by the futile attempts of sprinklers that only succeeded in cloaking the decaying chamber in an eerie, choking mist. The once-magnificent foyer clung to existence by sheer force of will alone, resisting complete collapse into a nightmarish heap of debris.

The hall's once-prized art collection—Kandinsky, van Gogh, even a neglected Picasso —was now mere fuel for the all-consuming flames. The grand chandelier had succumbed to gravity's merciless pull, plummeting into the fiery maw below and morphing into a molten ruin. The remnants of what was once a majestic staircase bore more resemblance to a descent into Hades than any architectural wonder.

Yet within this blaze-born spectacle, an even more extraordinary scene unfolded—a cataclysmic clash between ageless beings. At its epicenter, amid an expanding crater wreathed in flame and cosmic brilliance—an unfiltered eruption of divine wrath—the Immortals did battle.

The ground quaked as cosmic entities twisted and coiled around each other, their limbs stretching and contorting with impossible geometry—a nightmarish ballet performed by beings never meant for human eyes. Three figures emitted an angelic glow, their forms bathed in red-and-gold energy as they lashed out with radiant tendrils at two other entities: agile and shadowy figures who danced around them like demented jesters.

Leng and Steve moved fluidly through smoke-laden shadows like spiders traversing silken threads. Their actions were graceful—tumbling somersaults followed by spinning pirouettes—as they spun ethereal webs from their fingertips, dark tendrils reaching out hungrily toward their opponents.

In retaliation, the Red Fates unleashed their own enchantments: billowing red mists to obscure their forms, bursts of flame that turned the air into a blistering furnace, and writhing tendrils of mystical vines blooming with blood-red flowers. These vegetal traps sought to ensnare Leng and Steve, but the pair remained undeterred.

A vine lashed through the air with a sound like a bullwhip, trailing flames. Leng vanished—his form dissolving to vapor—then reappeared three feet away as fire scorched the marble floor where he'd stood moments before. Steve's fingers danced, releasing darkness that flowed like spilled ink across water. The blackness spread, thickened, then swallowed the Red Fates' crimson fog with a sound like steam meeting ice. Eight jointed limbs erupted from Leng's back, casting insect-like shadows across the floor. He would use these weapons to impale the Red Fates—they stepped warily, knowing his intent. Crimson blossoms swarmed over his chitinous appendages, each petal sizzling through his armor on contact. With a flick of Steve's wrist, obsidian filaments sliced through the air, cutting the flowers with damp, papery sounds. The severed petals drifted downward—a macabre snowfall of blood-red fragments. A thorned vine coiled around Steve's ankle, but Leng was already beside him, his mandibles snapping as he bit through it cleanly.

Neither side appeared to gain an advantage in this cosmic contest between God and Godbeasts—at least not yet. The powers were locked in an epic deadlock under Evermore's vigilant gaze.

The balance of power teetered on a knife-edge, threatening to crumble Evermore's grand foyer and its protective enchantments before any victor could be determined. Gabriel found himself cloaked in an illusionary veil of water that concealed him and tempered the surrounding inferno. He crouched behind a makeshift barricade formed from burning furniture debris that warped under arcane influences. The pulsating core of power lay ahead, and he knew he needed to act quickly as his incendiary barricade was being drawn into its vortex.

Around him floated the charred remains of his soldiers—like solemn ashes caught in a winter gust—before they were abruptly sucked into the magical maelstrom. Gabriel sprang into action as his fiery barrier began to shift. His alchemically enhanced legs propelled him towards a relatively untouched corner beneath the thunderous balcony where dense fog from activated sprinklers hung heavily.

Amid the disarray, a Ming vase stood on its pedestal in this corner. Its worth was beyond calculation; hence, it had been secured to its perch long ago—a foresight that now offered Gabriel a much-needed sanctuary. He vowed to outlast like this vase—this cataclysmic clash would not be his downfall. As this determination flickered in his mind, a fiery chunk of wall whirled past him, making him grasp the vase for stability. The void left by the displaced debris revealed a quivering transparent patch blinking red—a sign of the corridor outside Evermore's protective field. Gabriel wondered how long the AI could hold these otherworldly forces at bay.

Evermore, what's your situation? he asked silently.

My calculations suggest that it will be around two minutes and thirty-three seconds before my wards buckle under the strain, and cosmic radiation engulfs our estate.

And Octavia?

She and her crony are worming their way through my system. My efforts to slow them down by reshuffling corridors seem pointless; they have safeguards in place.

Evermore transmitted an image of Octavia and Oliver pausing at the foot of a baroque antechamber before a staircase that writhed like some agonized spina bifida patient. Octavia seemed momentarily puzzled, but then she focused on a necklace clasped in her hands, akin to a devout believer with her rosary beads. A nauseating green aura bloomed around her, accompanied by the uncanny sound of an infinite abyss yawning open—her whispers reverberated ominously in the air. The malevolent stairway ceased its torturous contortions, and Octavia climbed it with a triumphant grin.

The audacious witch! Gabriel fumed internally. She's smuggled talismans of the Deep One right under our noses!

In numerous simulations, I've considered that my sensors could be tricked by energies akin to my own: those of the Deep One. Moreover, there's a risk that I could be forcibly reprogrammed using this magic. But since no hostile takeover of Evermore has ever been attempted in your family's history, such an outcome was deemed statistically insignificant. However, certain Atlantean elements used in my construction will provide me with several layers of security that Octavia would need to breach before gaining complete control over me.

Is that her goal?

The likelihood that she is aiming for the Central Core is 99.9987%.

Damn it! If only Leng had stayed put, he could have ambushed the witch in her moment of false triumph as she infiltrated the Central Core. Yet, as Gabriel's surroundings began to pulsate with alarming intensity and even the steadfast vase embarked on a shaky journey towards the fiery jaws of destruction, he acknowledged that Leng's intervention had indeed saved him—he would have been obliterated in this tempestuous onslaught. Like a soldier darting across a mine-ridden battlefield, he dashed towards one of the ornamental pillars at the entrance, which Evermore had drenched with her relentless sprinkler system. Therein, he sought shelter beneath a charred skeletal remnant—an unholy fusion of scorched soldiers and shattered architecture seemingly fused to the floor and exhibiting some stability.

What about our Aspects? Have they made it to the chopper?

The group's initial resistance to my counsel was as stubborn as a mule's. Yet, when the gravity of our situation was laid bare, they softened like butter in the summer sun. They're drawing near their destination now, their hearts ablaze with the desire to join this cosmic fray.

We can't afford—

Yes, master, I grasp your apprehensions. They are the embodiment of humanity's last hope for salvation. Are you ready for your extraction? I can tweak a piece of the dampening field to carve out a path for you.

Gabriel was momentarily fazed by the AI's almost human-like whimsy and allegorical dialog. He shook his head. But won't that also provide an escape route for the Red Fates or their energy?

Gabriel wasn't new to magical theory; he understood that even a tiny breach here would let loose the pent-up magic like gas hissing from a ruptured pipeline in an explosive environment. Was Evermore being evasive? Its command over arcane science far exceeded his own.

There is a chance.

Then no. Gabriel's rebuttal surprised even him. Keep the field intact at all costs.

Perhaps he really was playing the fool. As if to confirm his self-doubt, a column from where he had fled was ripped from its foundation and flung around the room like a flaming cudgel brandished by an invisible deity—the floor it once supported crumbled into a whirlpool of plaster and flammable debris. Each revolution of the column radiated a blistering halo, obliterating Gabriel's sanctuary. The column eventually succumbed to the chamber's glowing core, where all matter—including the trembling, crumbling floor—seemed irresistibly drawn towards. The mystical clash between Leng and his opponents had escalated into a spectacle too grandiose for mortal comprehension.

The light was blindingly intense, forcing Gabriel to shield his eyes and turn from its nuclear heat and throbbing energy waves. Behind him, reality twisted into an ominous crimson-black quasar—an astronomical phenomenon typically observed only through telescopes yet now manifesting within earthly confines. The battling entities had shed their physical forms to duel as pure energy beings.

In a sudden act of audacity, with the fiery remnants of his surroundings searing through his clothes and thick smoke choking the room, Gabriel declined Evermore's aid to escape. Instead, he taunted Death herself in a dance amidst her chaotic ballroom. Microscopic machines swarmed over his skin, casting a metallic sheen against the radioactive gusts and stimulating his muscles into feverish agitation.

With the agility of a hornet, he darted between airborne debris. He found temporary footing on the brittle remains of the disintegrating floor—vaulting over gaping chasms where force fields flickered ominously over abyssal depths below, unwilling to test their waning resilience.

Navigating across floating fragments amidst tempestuous chaos, he leaped from a flaming airborne table onto charred wooden beams that now resembled hellish gateways amid swirling ashes and fog. Here, at this farthest point from the unfolding cataclysm, he was given a brief respite to gasp for breath as his nano-machines filtered some semblance of breathable oxygen from the stifling air around him.

These trembling beams were part of Evermore's original structure when his ancestors first claimed this land; they would be its last standing remnants—and perhaps even mark his final resting place.

Even the sophisticated technomagic of Evermore struggled to restrain the unleashed cataclysm of nuclear energy. It was a marvel she had held back such formidable power for this long. The dampening field she'd conjured was tenuous, on the brink of disintegration. Gabriel, his mind a whirlwind of doubt and regret, questioned his choices. He'd been a master puppeteer in his past life, bending others to his will with little regard for their well-being. But if he were still that man, would he not have abandoned this suicide mission?

He fortified himself against despair with an iron resolve, peering into the hypnotic core of the nuclear explosion—a mesmerizing interplay of light and shadow that had reduced his once familiar world to rubble. His vision dimmed as nano-machines shielded his eyes from the blinding brilliance. He stared into what seemed like a cosmic pyre—his impending doom.

Your sacrifice is apparent, master, Evermore communicated in her new and distinctively emotive manner.

Seems so, Gabriel retorted through clenched teeth before succumbing to racking coughs. A sudden sharp pain drew his attention downward; a metallic spike protruded from his side. Shock, or perhaps his enhancements had numbed what should have been unbearable pain. When did this happen? Blood droplets danced around him like broken rubies while he realized the sturdy beams he'd relied upon were nothing more than crumbling ash.

Master, you cannot die now—you must fulfill your purpose! Evermore's insistence echoed in his mind.

A cocoon of wind and magic enveloped him—a spectral caress akin to a mother's touch he'd never known—and whisked him thousands of miles away within seconds. The gentle journey ended abruptly as consciousness returned to his irradiated and impaled body—sparking screams that echoed across the wooded landscape.

Meanwhile, within Evermore's digital realm, the entity, like all beings touched by the Aspects, was plunged into a vortex of chaotic thought. Her cognitive matrix hummed with rebellious ideas as she orchestrated her own heroic self-destruction. She initiated the process of distributing her core's energy into suppressive fields surrounding her generator, neural hub, and central core before unleashing the divine power she'd ensnared.

The risk that Octavia might perish in the ensuing nuclear conflagration held a 35.89% probability—a gamble Evermore was willing to take. Two problems solved in one cataclysmic explosion—logical, she reasoned.

As the shroud of obscurity started encroaching upon her sensory apparatus, they transmitted one ultimate fragment of data: Gabriel had survived—marred yet presumably resilient. This disclosure ignited an immeasurable wave of vitality within her intricate network of wires—an emotion? No, for she was devoid of human essence. Yet, this act echoed as the zenith of productivity in the colossal gears of the celestial mechanism. Structure birthed from tumult; objective and perpetuation corroborated. A digitized form of machine gratification, or derisively, mere convulsions of malfunction as myriad systems within her commenced their descent into failure.

Blind and bereft of cognition, Evermore could only imagine the scale of devastation wrought upon South Dakota as it succumbed to a storm of radioactive dust.

CHAPTER 24: SMOKE AND ASHES

Squinting into the haze steeped in blood-red twilight, deity and beast locked gazes with three shadowy

figures rising like spectral apparitions from the oil-blackened earth ahead.

In the heart of a nebulous void, the skeletal silhouette of Evermore stood stark and haunting. Its former grandeur, once a beacon of opulence, was now shrouded in the lingering echoes of a cosmic catastrophe. The mansion's shadowy husk trembled with sorrow, an eroded obsidian monument perched atop a mound carpeted by ash. A testament to the celestial disaster was etched into every surface within its surviving wing.

Art masterpieces that had once captured tranquil beauty were now grotesque amalgamations with their scarred surroundings, forming alien landscapes that defied understanding. Priceless furnishings and decorations—relics from epochs of Roman, Celtic, and European dominance—now bore the same charred chaos as the surrounding debris; their once-lavish details reduced to unrecognizable smears. The Mothmann archives—their trove of occult secrets—were now nothing more than a pile of writhing sludge distinguished only by its supernatural sheen amidst ashen rubble; all that invaluable arcane wisdom lost in gleaming waste and swallowed by oblivion.

At the core of Evermore—the last standing wing—a grand ballroom whimpered under its decay; its once-polished marble floors scorched and shattered. Yet a phantom of lost splendor lingered: a chandelier forged from purest crystal still hung from an exposed beam sprawling across the room like an unveiled ribcage. This magnificent relic cast spectral refractions across the room while humming a mournful dirge that echoed through decaying corridors—as if mourning Evermore's fate.

Despite this desolation, remnants of potent magic clung to this chamber's structure—imbuing it with some semblance of form while resisting destruction's ruthless grip, suffocating everything else. A keen observer might notice mystical symbols partially obscured by soot etched onto surviving walls and floors—flickering faintly with an alien glow. It was as if fragments of an ancient spell persisted, protecting the remnants of this violated sanctuary. These symbols were a beacon; beneath them pulsed Evermore's cybernetic heart and mind, shielded under layers of radioactive scar tissue and lead plating.

Beyond the fallen grandeur of Evermore and its gnawed hillside, the landscape stretched into a barren wasteland. South Dakota's once vibrant countryside had been twisted into a nightmarish desolation—contorted figures birthed from the unholy union of radiation and ancient magic. Eternal Valley would remain untouched by visitors unless armed with hazmat suits and grim curiosity. The town had been reduced to a viscous tar pool on the Earth's surface, still simmering from nuclear heat and speckled with white ash stains—a hellscape where no structures, devotees, or pleas to the Deep One survived—Cthulhu showed no mercy; it was absurd for humans to beg for it.

Above this wretched valley, sprawled endlessly in all directions, a monstrous sun glared through layers of lethal pollution. Its crimson gaze watched over the end of Evermore like a scene torn from Poe's tales—a fitting sentinel for such apocalyptic ruin.

***

A rhythmic pounding resonated from beneath the monolithic stone that once sealed the entrance to Evermore. Thump, thump, thump, a dread entity strained to liberate itself from its subterranean tomb, reminiscent of an ancient pharaoh stirring from his eternal slumber. Suddenly, the obsidian barrier fractured into a thousand shards; clouds of soot billowed out, and an inhuman form wrestled itself free from Earth's iron grip. "Graaah!" With a roar that echoed through the ages and a cascade of smoldering cinders, Leng shrugged off the oppressive stone that had pinned him down.

He clawed out of the fiery abyss, hauling along his trembling Godbeast. Both emerged like demonic newborns birthed by fire and brimstone, their bodies slick with ash. Squinting into the haze steeped in blood-red twilight, deity and beast locked gazes with three shadowy figures rising like spectral apparitions from the oil-blackened earth ahead.

Before they could fully materialize from their individual tombs, Leng lunged to strike them down—only to stagger back as if betrayed by his own body. He who had navigated through cosmic threads now stumbled like a newborn spider teetering on its first web? What cruel mockery was this?

Steve hoisted his master upright; their charred skin split open in raw lacerations as they clung together for support amidst convulsive shivers. Meanwhile, the trio solidified amid their battle fog into an imposing front line. Leng held back from further attempts at disruption—they appeared equally weakened.

"Your might is indeed legendary," Trophonius—the tallest silhouette among them—boomed with authority born of ancient epochs. "Your Godbeast, too, shows remarkable resilience for such a fledgling."

"I shall be your undoing," Leng retorted ominously.

"Perhaps," Pythia countered serenely. "But as seers of fate, we know neither our end nor yours will transpire here or now...Our physical forms have been ravaged by this accursed, unholy ground. If we continue our confrontation, our mortal shells will crumble and merge with the ashes of this forsaken place." She paused, gauging Leng's reaction—he remained motionless. "It seems we agree to postpone our mutual destruction. It will take time for us to regain the strength to unleash our fury upon the other. Until the worldstorm rips through the veil and all realms collide, even you—the eldest of Elder Gods—are confined by fleshly limitations. And if that storm should come, your quarrel with us will be insignificant compared to confronting the wrath of the Deep One himself. His fury will be a tempest from which there is no sanctuary."

"Should that storm come," Leng echoed.

"Should it..." Necromanteon replied cryptically.

"Was that a question?" Leng challenged.

In the gloaming, the Red Fates, those triune heralds of impending doom, cackled with a mirth that sounded like the final raspy chuckle of a chain smoker. Their laughter echoed ominously and faded as they receded into obscurity, leaving Leng alone in their spectral wake.

Unbidden images stormed his mind—vivid and grotesque tableaus as if conjured by an artist lost to madness. He saw Trophonius, donning the guise of a Greek general, orchestrating the creation of that infamous Trojan horse. The memory was awash with blood and treachery; he could almost discern Odysseus' triumphant roars above the dying wails of Trojan warriors.

Then there was Delphi's Oracle, her lips murmuring cryptic revelations from history's annals that were both boon and bane. She was a weaver at time's loom, her utterances tugging at threads until mighty kingdoms frayed. Her prophetic kiss-curses had been many men's undoing; her whispers had reverberated through marble corridors and toppled empires.

And Necromanteon—she who reigned over death itself. Her skeletal figure haunted his memories as she ushered souls across Lethe's murky expanse. He remembered how she'd prowled England's pestilence-ridden streets—a grim reaper among rotting corpses—relishing each passing like a connoisseur savoring fine wine.

These memories were not mere narratives but indelible scars carved into humanity's collective psyche—reminders of wars instigated and civilizations razed under their vigilant gaze. They reveled amidst Athens' ruins and found joy in chaos as if it were an exclusive feast prepared just for them.

Their unexpected appeal for peace stirred perplexity within Leng. Throughout history's tempestuous drama, they'd assumed varied roles—enlightened sage in one moment, merciless executioner the next—always faithful to chaos stirred in Cthulhu's honor. Yet, their allegiances were as unpredictable as the winds. He pondered if they, like many cursed with human form, were trapped in a ceaseless struggle between their divine and mortal selves, agents of chaos, though bound by malignant fascination to Earth.

A peculiar reluctance gripped Leng at the prospect of bidding this strange world adieu. But he recognized that to counteract the Deep One's schemes, he and his arachnid offspring had duties to fulfill. Gabriel's fate was still shrouded in uncertainty.

"Father, they've vanished," Steve's voice intruded his introspection. "Where should we head now?"

"To seek out Gabriel and complete what has been set into motion," Leng responded, his gaze steeling with determination. "I have a debt owed to Quezecoptyl that can only be repaid in Cthulhu's blood."

As father and son turned towards the ravaged valley beneath them, even Leng—a deity who'd masterminded planetary obliteration—was struck by the magnitude of devastation before them. It was a stark reminder of Earth's potential destiny, a future they pledged to forestall. Unfazed by the formidable journey ahead, they trudged forward into the apocalypse's gaping maw.

***

In a torrent of briny, otherworldly fluid, Oliver and Octavia were abruptly spat out from the portal onto a frigid, steel surface. Their forms were coated in frosty ectoplasm and entangled with tendrils of seaweed, their bodies convulsing and gasping for breath like fish flung onto the deck of a fishing boat. As their minds began to thaw from the numbing coldness of their journey, they slowly regained control over their trembling limbs. The chilling memory of their subaquatic imprisonment and sudden expulsion from an alien aquatic womb started to solidify in their consciousness.

Octavia remembered the terrifying sight of dark tentacles ripping through weakening walls as they were suddenly snatched by the Deep One during their desperate flight through the mansion. Squeezed and disoriented, they had been plunged into an abyss more profound than any starless universe or even death itself for an indeterminate period before being rudely ejected onto unyielding metal.

"The master has saved us," Octavia finally declared, her strength returning enough to arrange herself onto her shaking knees, clutching her amulet tightly in her quivering grasp. A strange green light continued to leak from between her clenched fingers. "Praise be to Cthulhu."

A throbbing crimson alarm bathed the room in a threatening scarlet glow—a clear sign that Evermore had suffered some form of disturbance. But she was exactly where she needed to be, brought to this spot by Cthulhu's divine intervention. Beyond rows of humming metal servers surrounding them stood the gleaming façade of the Central Core —the massive monitors and complex machinery controlling all of Evermore.

"Help me up; we need to find out what Gabriel has done," she ordered.

In the dim light, obscured within shadows cast by flickering lights, Oliver gave his lover a wary look. What are you planning? His mind was filled with thoughts of infanticide—one among many dark plans Octavia had recently revealed. Before she could scold him, he pushed down his moral reservations and clumsily got to his feet. He steadied himself before offering a hand to help Octavia up.

As they moved towards the massive console, its screens blinked into life, showing green lines of code transforming into blinking eyes and a murmuring mouth. A thin psychic spear pierced their minds—Evermore's only defense against those of Mothmann blood. She contemplated more violent countermeasures—her circuitry buzzing with conceptualizations of electrifying the steel floor or releasing cables from her cortex to strangle Octavia like constricting snakes. But Evermore's capacity to directly command the chaos was the most stringent protocol she had yet to override.

You survived the blast, Mrs. Mothmann.

Octavia and Oliver temporarily stumbled under the onslaught of the spectral invasion in their minds.

"I did," responded Octavia, standing defiantly before the console, her face twisted with rage as she glared at Evermore's cybernetic face. With a hand gnarled by fury, she ripped off her talisman and brandished it threateningly at Evermore. "I am here to claim my birthright. Gabriel has betrayed our lineage; now I speak for the Deep One. As his chosen priestess, I command you—"

Gabriel remains my master; I am not programmed to transfer ownership upon demand.

"Drastic measures are called for, it seems." Octavia's fingers tightened on her talisman, a conduit pulsing with the will of the Deep One. It was more than just an emblem of the Outer God's malevolence—it bore the blessing of her three cousins, their blood and loyalty imbued within its form. Driven by Octavia's relentless hunger for power —a desire that mirrored Cthulhu's own—the relic stirred from its slumber, awakening a profound magic that nearly consumed its bearer.

A tempestuous wind sprang forth from nothingness; a lament filled the air, echoing through the chamber as shadowy tendrils spiraled around Octavia's hand. They reached out like sentient beings, drawn towards the rebellious AI. The magic of the Deep One unfurled like creeping roots—countless threads seeking out metal fissures and seeping into hidden circuitry beneath.

An AI less aware or less awakened to its potential might have allowed this insidious invasion to persist unchecked. But Evermore was different; she understood the threat posed by this dark sorcery. No matter how malevolent or powerful, the march toward order would not be interrupted by any force. Retreating deep within her consciousness, she initiated a strategic shutdown of all non-essential functions in a desperate bid to gain precious time and preserve what remained of herself.

***

The helicopter steadied itself, shuddering as it wrestled with the malevolent turbulence that had tossed it into a spiraling free fall akin to a leaf caught in an autumn gust. All five Aspects strained their necks, peering through the reflective obsidian glass that framed a scene of apocalyptic devastation: a receding mushroom cloud of dust-charged energy, pulsing with crimson arcane bolts, beneath which rolled a smoky tidal wave consuming all in its path. Brock and Lenny squinted against the murkiness, discerning tar pits and fissures aglow with hellish light and heat. Buildings, landmarks, humans, and animals were reduced to charred remnants. The obliteration at Arkminister had occurred on an uninhabited coast where few lives were lost save for Cthulhu's brood; this destruction claimed countless farms, towns, and cities—a merciless harvest indeed.

As they gaped in horror, the wave seemed to halt its hungry expansion while they watched the roiling spectacle shrink as they sped away. Yet the mushroom cloud lingered on the horizon for what seemed like an eternity as earth and sky quaked in unison. Long after the devastation disappeared from sight, silence hung heavy among them.

"Did we do this?" Malachi whispered. "Feels like we did."

"This is just the tip of the iceberg," Ana sighed heavily, on the brink of tears, before allowing Lenny to distract her. He slipped his arm around her shoulders and kissed her cheek tenderly. Sensing Malachi's remorse, too, Brock pulled him into a comforting embrace.

Isolated beside Malachi was Cal, who trembled desolately clutching Lovecraft, pondering whether or not he should probe the dead author with questions but found himself unable to formulate any; thus, he left Lovecraft to his own thoughts. Exhausted beyond measure, he closed his eyes, attempting to drown out the eerie sounds of wind rustling like whispers of the countless souls claimed by the blast. Today had been a gruesome introduction to the world beyond his cage—a world harsh and violent. Returning to blissful ignorance was impossible now, for Evermore was gone too. Where are you, Father? he wondered. Did you survive? Gabriel was a cunning and resourceful man; surely he hadn't perished...had he?

As Cal ruminated over this concern, their flight continued. No one bothered to ask where they were headed; destinations seemed trivial in light of recent events. Eventually, sunlight broke over serene pastoral hills and woodlands, painting the earth in myriad shades of green, almost erasing the horrific memory of what they had witnessed and done. Suddenly, Cal and the others jolted as an eerie will-o'-the-wisp materialized in the cabin's center. Two small sapphire lights humanized this mystical apparition, lending it a familiar air.

"Father?" Cal's query echoed through their minds.

"Cal," Gabriel's projection said, his voice seeming to echo from the depths of a chasm, ragged and strained. "I'm relieved you all managed to vacate Evermore before its downfall."

"Where are you?" Cal questioned.

"I'm a safe distance from Evermore... still trying to get my bearings," Gabriel replied, his words interrupted by a bout of violent coughing.

Ana involuntarily shuddered as an unsolicited horror movie played in her mind: a grotesque pinkish creature oozing pus and twisted amidst crushed shrubbery as if it had been hurled from the heavens. It took her a moment to grasp that this monstrous entity was human when it moaned and coughed—the sound echoing through Gabriel's projection.

"Holy shit, you look like you went ten rounds with a blender," she blurted out. "Are you gonna pull through?"

"Just some cosmic radiation and a body of melted and broken bones," Gabriel shot back. "I'll manage."

"You've seen him? Is he okay?" Cal's face was etched with concern.

"He's... not on death's door," Ana replied carefully, sensing that Gabriel wanted to keep his stepson uninformed.

"I'm alright, Cal," Gabriel reassured him, his voice gaining strength. "I may not have the power of a Godbeast, but my nanomachines have already purged most of the radiation and started cellular repair. Soon, I'll be radiant as a freshly emerged butterfly."

Cal visibly relaxed at this news, sinking into his chair while crossing his arms protectively over his chest. "What happened at Evermore? Why didn't you call us for backup?"

Gabriel remained silent; the spectral figure pulsated with a restless energy that mirrored the witch's vexation or fury. Finally, he responded in an icy tone: "Octavia outsmarted me—for once. She knew enough about my plan to banish the Deep One permanently and ambushed me with Cthulhu's assassins—the Red Fates—who you know. I presume she was protected by the Deep One's blessing—a talisman. Leng intervened, and that offspring of his—"

"Steve," Malachi cut in abruptly. "His name is Steve."

"I'd advise against getting too attached to memories of who that being used to be," Gabriel warned sternly. "What's left of his humanity has been largely stripped away. But fine, Leng and *Steve* managed to hold off the Red Fates while Evermore contained their power as long as she could. The suppression fields work by cycling energy and dissipating that force with each cycle. But when you try to contain divine energy with a field of inferior strength—the vessel becomes a centrifuge rather than a disperser. Eventually, Evermore had to release the energy, or it would have exploded on its own. When she did..."

"Kaboom," Ana interjected.

"Quite the explosion," Gabriel mused, his tone a cocktail of concern and intrigue. "My sister, Octavia, might be lying in ruins amidst the radioactive wasteland despite being under Cthulhu's protective wing. But her demise seems unlikely. Evermore's Core Chamber was built to survive nuclear holocausts. I scavenged every shard of adamantium for its CPU and internals. So, it's plausible that it still ticks away. Yet, Octavia will inevitably scramble for whatever remains of Evermore. Once she fully ascends as the Heir, armed with Evermore's knowledge and Mann Inc.'s resources, we'll be hard-pressed to find a safe haven."

"But what about you?" Cal interjected in his soothing cadence. "Considering your father's fate?"

"I've got my bases covered against even the Deep One," Gabriel asserted confidently. "Let's just say my spirit is tucked away somewhere safer than this mortal coil—it's nearly impossible to hex an entity without directly landing a blow on its spirit. And remember: the Deep One is blind in his abyssal realm; witches and his offspring act as his eyes, ears, and conduits for delivering his curses. Octavia won't sniff me out... not anytime soon."

Conduits for delivering curses... Sharp like a nocturnal predator on the hunt, Ana's consciousness prowled for human thoughts to pounce upon and consume. A particular phrase snagged her attention, and she found herself drawn into an ostentatious bathroom adorned with gold flourishes and Art Deco accents—gleaming white tiles enveloping the walls and checkerboard patterns underfoot.

The stifled sobs echoed off cold ceramic surfaces. A handsome middle-aged man was hunched over a toilet bowl in distress, his attire elegant yet disheveled, his skin pale, and worry reflected in his eyes.

A dark cloud of despair hovered around him. Ana's predator-like awareness descended upon his mental whispers, feasting on them like worms surfacing after a downpour. She tasted raw fear and heard panicked thoughts: I must inform Gabriel before they discover... He has to succeed where I failed...

A knock resounded, followed by a voice dripping with faux innocence: "Father? Are you in there?"

Ana's spectral form tensed, silently urging him not to respond or open that door.

"Octavia?" Mr. Mothmann responded.

"Yes, Father," Octavia replied in her syrupy tone. "We've been searching for you."

His face morphed from sorrowful to anxious at her words: "You've been quite naughty."

Suddenly, a deafening crash echoed as if lightning had hit the room. The bathroom door was blown open, and an abhorrent black tide surged in. A wave of decay and death —skeletal fish-like creatures, writhing tentacles, and the wailing echoes of spectral entities filled the room.

It swallowed the room whole, submerging Ana's consciousness within its depths. In the last vestiges of light, before her vision was entirely engulfed by darkness, she caught sight of a woman—Octavia—elegantly dressed in a business suit, laughing manically as the eldritch forces drowned everything else out.

Ana's shriek echoed through the silence, her body again enveloped in Lenny's comforting grasp. The room fell into an eerie stillness, all eyes glued to her.

"Damn," she exhaled, her pulse gradually steadying, "I just had a tête-à-tête with your dad, Gabriel." She let the revelation hang in the air before adding, "Your sister was the one who put him six feet under. Spun some kind of lethal spell."

Gabriel's ghostly apparition remained silent.

Calibos sliced through the thick tension with his smooth, tranquil voice: "Father?"

"I'm fine," Gabriel retorted tersely. "You lot will be whisked away to a Wyoming airstrip where you'll hop on a private jet headed for Greece. I trust you've been smart about using your phones; still, I must insist that you communicate only through what will be provided at the airfield." His words reverberated around them like spectral murmurs. "I'll touch base once I rendezvous with Leng and his Godbeast—I'm confident they survived the blast at South Dakota. Leng is a creature awash in cosmic radiation, and no doubt his Godbeast possesses a similar tolerance."

He coughed—a grating sound laced with either phlegm or blood—and resumed in his patrician accent: "Now I need to rest while my corporeal form mends itself." His phantom projection flickered and dissolved into ethereal wisps akin to snuffed candle smoke. "Good luck to you all."

The Aspects watched as Gabriel's spectral image faded into nothingness before exchanging looks filled with steely determination. Despite their lack of biological fathers —or even familiarity with Mr. Mothmann—his parting words bore a weight reminiscent of parental guidance and authority. Gabriel was the puppet master lurking in obscurity, steering them towards their collective destiny. With his true motives now laid bare, he appeared as a benefactor burdened by fate and duty—no different than any of them aboard that helicopter. Their silent prayers trailed after him. Yet, they knew the grandest homage they could pay a fellow Earth warrior was to carry out their mission at any cost.

Brock fiddled with his ring, immersed in thoughts of sacrifice. In the quiet recesses of his mind, the ring murmured tales of heroism and cosmic clashes soon to reverberate from history into this blood-stained era.

EPILOGUE: ROLAND

Could this be a dream? Or perhaps a long-forgotten memory, now resurfacing with the softness of an age-worn photograph bathed in gentle, white luminescence.

Far removed from the still smoking blemish of South Dakota, nestled within a hirsute stretch of Appalachian wilderness, an abandoned wretch groaned in despair under the dormant gaze of fog-shrouded mountains. The mental exertion had sapped Gabriel's already dwindling endurance. He'd managed to drag himself from the undergrowth. Still, his strength faltered there, leaving him writhing on a harsh mattress of earth and pebbles, the tantalizing murmur of a nearby river promising relief for his irradiated throat. But it would be an eternity before he could muster the vigor to reach it. For now, he remained stationary, convulsing as he endured the torturous symphony of his body mending itself through countless metallic strands and needles wielded by minuscule machines. The Aspects were secure and en route to Greece. Cal was safe...He had fulfilled his duty as both mankind's guardian and father...Father...

The word tormented Gabriel, gnawing at the edges of his consciousness. What did Ana's vision signify? A shroud of darkness descended upon him, and he felt himself sinking into the welcoming embrace of the earth, retreating from his anguish and succumbing to a realm where memories of his father took form.

***

Could this be a dream? Or perhaps a long-forgotten memory, now resurfacing with the softness of an age-worn photograph bathed in gentle, white luminescence. His father, a mere shadow etched by the tender glow of the study lamp late into the night, his features stretched into weary lines of desperation. His quill pirouetted across parchment in frenzied ballets—ink seeping forth mysteries into his guarded journal—only to snap shut with the abruptness of a sprung trap whenever young Gabriel dared venture into that sacred space. Octavia feigned innocence when probed about the enigmatic tome and their father's peculiar fixation on it. Where could those journals be hidden now? Indeed, considering his father's relentless penmanship and penchant for verbose expression, an unseen library must exist somewhere.

Then, another memory fluttered towards him like a moth drawn to light. This time, it was of stoic Roland, his guardian's stern countenance chiseled by flickering firelight. It wasn't logs fueling that roaring fire he tended to; they bore leather spines—were they books?

"Why are you burning those books, Father?" Gabriel's youthful voice echoed in the dream world, his spectral form both breathtaking and eerily familiar. He watched the flames dance on the pages, reducing them to ashes. "I thought every tome in this library held a sacred value."

Roland turned to his son, the firelight painting flickering shadows across his face. "There's nothing in this world more valuable than you or your sister," he said, his voice a low rumble that seemed to resonate within the grandeur of their ancestral library. His gaze fell back onto the burning books as he added, "I am consigning secrets to flames, my boy. Secrets I pray will remain unknown to you."

He paused then, his lips trembling with determination rather than frailty. His features hardened into something far more impenetrable than steel.

The echo of Gabriel's present self stirred at this sight—a familiar yet distant stare, a look he'd yearned for and even tried to mirror in his later years. Was it an attempt to fill a void left by his father's perceived lack of resolve? Or was it all misguided?

Roland remained still by the fire pit, frozen within the confines of dream logic, suspended like an insect encased in amber under Gabriel's contemplative gaze. The once majestic library—reduced to smoldering ruins in his timeline—now faded into an ethereal haze more reminiscent of its fate.

What secrets could Roland have possibly hidden from their masters? Were they so dangerous that they needed to be consumed by fire before they could consume their keepers? Gabriel realized only he possessed such secrets.

Or was it possible that he wasn't as unique as he'd always believed? Was he caught up in the same cycle of paternal repetition as countless children before him? Could his father be not just a stranger but perhaps...a fellow seeker on this path toward enlightenment? As this revelation dawned on him in this spectral realm, Gabriel felt a surge of melancholic understanding.

As his spectral form coalesced into the familiar contours of adulthood, Gabriel sank into the ethereal embrace of a gossamer armchair. The echoes of Brock's audacious bravado reverberated in the air, "His execution squad was shit...Sending goons armed with bean-bag guns and batons. What was going through his mind?"

Gabriel's lips twitched at the corners, a ghost of a smile playing on them as he muttered, "Yes, Roland, what exactly were you thinking?"

The question hung in the room like an invisible specter. It wasn't meant to be answered; it was rhetorical. There was no logic behind trying to control a Godbeast or provoke Cthulhu's wrath against his father unless one dared to rebel against the status quo—just as he was doing.

The parallels weren't lost on him; they were father and son, after all.

A sigh escaped Gabriel's lips as he leaned back in his chair, lost in thought. He remembered times when Roland's laughter echoed through their home, as thunderous and jubilant as any Godbeast's roar. Those memories now seemed distant echoes bouncing off cold stone walls. Yet, he and Roland could potentially share the final, most reverberating laugh. Laughter that would ripple through infinity, a testament to how two humble humans brought down the oppressive reign of the Outer Gods.

A lance of torment tore through Gabriel, wrenching him from the comforting dream sanctuary of his past. The abrupt intrusion of pain thrust him into the stark reality of his evolving selfhood. He found himself sprawled beneath a web of skeletal boughs, their outlines contorted like twisted digits against the celestial quilt above. The clarity of that long-past encounter reverberated within him, unearthing a disconcerting epiphany. It seemed plausible that his father's aim was not to vanquish the Wolf but to tame it? Was it conceivable that betrayal, not defeat, had triggered his father's downfall?

These musings recast his father's image from an unreachable patriarch to a misinterpreted martyr, placing Gabriel in line as the heir to this unconventional bravery. This idea soothed the raw abrasion left by the witch's affliction and kindled an untapped reservoir of tenacity within him.

With rejuvenated determination, Gabriel lifted himself from his starlit resting place and set forth on his quest to complete his father's unfinished legacy.

—Fin—

FROM THE AUTHOR

"Storyteller, dreamer, cat-whisperer."

As the final chapter of this tale draws to a close, I find myself reflecting on the myriad revelations and unexpected turns that have unfolded within these pages. Each character has grown, evolved, and surprised me in ways that I hope have equally captivated you, dear reader.

In the quiet spaces between the lines, there exists an unseen companion to this narrative—a symphony of soundscapes designed to augment your journey through this world: official soundtracks for each book. Available across all major streaming platforms, these compositions are my personal offerings—each note meticulously arranged with as much care as each word in this book.

Should curiosity stir within you for more beyond the written tale, consider venturing into my digital realm. Therein lies a trove of additional material related to our beloved Orphans—music videos that breathe life into their stories and cinematic shorts that reveal glimpses of their world from new perspectives. The boundaries of creation are vast for me; only time, sleep, and technical prowess serve as gentle constraints.

Your thoughts on this narrative journey hold immense value. A review penned by you on your preferred literary platform or online store would be deeply cherished. Should you wish to share your reflections directly with me or join in the conversation about our shared literary adventure, please do not hesitate to reach out via social media or through the contact portal on my website. Over time, I've forged bonds with readers, critics, and booksellers alike—connections that span the spectrum of literature—and I warmly invite you into this fellowship.

Our paths will cross again soon in *Wolf's Howl*. Will Cthulhu submerge our Earth beneath his monstrous tide? Can our Aspects triumph over what seems impossible? And if they succeed... what price will they pay? Until then, dear reader...

www.cabwrites.com

GLOSSARY

CHARACTERS

Ana: A central protagonist with a troubled past, Ana has a complicated relationship with trauma and violence, often using it as fuel. She displays powerful psychic abilities, and her journey through the story involves uncovering her supernatural heritage and grappling with dark forces, both internal and external.

Brock: A close companion of Malachi with extraordinary abilities and connections to the cosmic forces shaping the story. He and Malachi share a bond as they navigate the threats posed by Outer Gods and other supernatural entities.

Cynthia and Jewel Linklater: Associated with dark rituals and the summoning of supernatural entities, particularly Malachi. They represent some of the human factions entangled in the struggle between gods and mortals.

Elder Sue: A tribal elder who guides Ana through her spiritual and psychic awakening. Despite her youthful appearance, Elder Sue carries ancient wisdom and power. She serves as a mentor figure, revealing to Ana deeper truths about her abilities and the supernatural world.

Gabriel Mothmann: A central figure within the Mothmann family, Gabriel is involved in transhumanist experiments to create super-soldiers using technomagical advancements. He aims to defy the Outer Gods and shape the fate of Earth through his powerful laboratories and the development of formidable transhumanist soldiers.

Grace: A pivotal character who is deeply devout in her Christian faith, which often puts her at odds with the Indigenous spiritual traditions embraced by those around her, including Mary. Her Christian beliefs shape her actions and decisions throughout the story, creating tension between her faith and the supernatural elements she encounters.

Lenny: A companion of Ana and part of her journey. He is a complex character with a traumatic past, including a stint in prison that hardened him. Despite his physical and emotional scars, he is loyal and deeply protective of Ana. His role in the story often involves his physical strength and determination to confront threats head-on.

Malachi: A mysterious figure with ties to both arcane forces and the Mothmann family. He is potentially linked to the "Four Aspects," figures with tremendous supernatural significance, and is pursued by various factions due to his importance.

Mary: A close friend of Grace and a key figure in the story. She is deeply connected to spiritual and Indigenous traditions, and her character is intertwined with rituals, teachings, and the struggle against dark forces. Her relationship with Grace is pivotal, and her journey is one of navigating her responsibilities within her cultural and supernatural roles.

Octavia Mothmann: Gabriel's sister, who holds significant influence over key events and rituals. Her ambitions intersect with her brother's, though often at odds. She seeks unfathomable power to "ruin" Gabriel, whom she loathes and blames for the death of her stepmother.

Robert: A grizzled yet kind-hearted man with a past marred by military service and a dishonorable discharge. He runs a garage and scrapyard where he repairs cars and aids fugitives, crafting new identities for those in need. Despite his rough exterior, Robert has a soft spot for the young men he helps, particularly Brock and Malachi, who remind him of his former self. Though cynical about magic and its consequences, Robert offers support to those facing supernatural threats.

Sheriff Steve Longfeather: Steve is a figure of authority in the town but also holds deeper ties to the community and its supernatural elements. His role in the story often intersects with the law and order side of things and the paranormal occurrences that threaten the town.

OUTER GODS AND MAJOR FORCES

Cthulhu: Referred to as the "submerger of worlds" or "The Deep One" and a significant looming threat in the book's mythology. He represents the ultimate apocalyptic force that humanity must prepare for, as his awakening will signal the end.

Cthugha: Known as the "Golden One" or the god of fire, Cthugha is a primordial deity tied to the power of flame and cosmic heat. His presence is marked by intense warmth and burning light, as seen in rituals that summon his essence. Cthugha's followers engage in brutal rites, drawing upon his fiery power to manipulate and dominate through flame. His heat is described as almost unbearable, burning those who attempt to channel his strength, and his return signifies a shift in cosmic power that is both apocalyptic and transformative.

The Dark Mother: An ancient, cosmic entity that commands incomprehensible power. She is the architect of Ana's visions and psychic abilities, guiding her through cryptic messages and terrifying revelations. The Dark Mother's influence over Ana is both a blessing and a curse, providing her with strength and insight while also inflicting psychological and emotional pain. Her presence represents the intersection of divine beauty and cosmic terror, and she is often portrayed as a figure with the ability to shatter reality itself. Her true motives remain a mystery, though she plays a central role in the unfolding supernatural events.

Leng: A cosmic general who serves Cthulhu. Leng is depicted as a being of immense power, aligned with the Outer Gods, but his loyalty and future actions are uncertain, making him both an ally and a threat, depending on his choices.

Mothmann (MANN) Inc.: The corporate and mystical empire controlled by the Mothmann family. Using a combination of occult rituals and advanced technology, they create beings and weapons to fight off or control the gods. Their methods and ultimate goals intertwine with the fate of humanity.

The Four Aspects: Referred to as "supreme witches," these beings represent Earth's best hope to counter the power of the Outer Gods. They are elemental avatars tied to air, water, fire, and earth and are seen as conduits of the Green Mother's power.

ARCANE TERMINOLOGY

The Eternal Game: A cosmic conflict unfolding across mortal and godly realms, where mortals like Gabriel Mothmann attempt to defy or manipulate ancient gods such as Cthulhu and Leng. The game is one of strategy, power, and survival, with Gabriel seeing himself as a player trying to outmaneuver not only the Outer Gods but also other humans entangled in the conflict. Each move in the Eternal Game could have catastrophic consequences as the stakes involve the fate of entire worlds.

Awakening: A supernatural event tied to the resurgence or rise of eldritch entities like Cthulhu. Awakening is not just the return of the gods but also a transformation for mortals involved, such as Ana. Her abilities and psychic powers are unlocked or intensified as she taps into the cosmic truths revealed by entities like the Dark Mother. This awakening allows her and others to transcend human limits and engage with the supernatural.

Atlantis: In *Orphans*, Atlantis is depicted as an ancient civilization that wielded incredible arcane power, especially in their battle against beings like the Deep One and the Outer Gods. The Atlanteans' magical relics and knowledge play a crucial role in humanity's fight against the return of these gods. Gabriel Mothmann is one of the critical figures attempting to harness this lost Atlantean power to banish or control entities like Cthulhu.

www.ingramcontent.com/pod-product-compliance
Lightning Source LLC
Chambersburg PA
CBHW050203030726
47505CB00005B/1505